PIECES OF FOREVER

For Skyler; my reason for everything.

"I'll love you forever
I'll like you for always
As long as I'm living, my baby you'll be"
— Robert Munsch

The best time to love with your whole heart is always now,
in this moment, because no breath beyond the current is promised.
— Fawn Weaver

One

"No one ever told me that grief felt so like fear." - C.S. Lewis

This was wrong. Everything was wrong. The sun beating down on our backs; not a cloud in the sky. Sunny days were for picnics, trips to the lake, barbeques and going to the fair. All the things I would never get to do with Tyler again. Sunny days weren't meant for burying husbands. It should be storming; wind and rain, thunder and lightning, because that's how I felt as I watched him being lowered into the ground.

The pain ripped through my insides and poured out of my eyes, running down my cheeks. Still the sun continued to shine like it was any other beautiful summer day in Abilene, Texas. I could barely breathe as I said goodbye to the boy I'd loved since I was a child, for the last time. He was gone, and I was left here without him, barely able to stand, fighting for every breath and hating that each one I took proved I could live without him.

When we said 'til death do us part,' death wasn't supposed to come so soon. Barely a year. That's how long I got to be his wife. It wasn't nearly enough time. I was supposed to have forever with him, at the very least fifty or sixty years. I choked back sobs as the grief tore through me. I grieved for all the mornings I would wake up alone, without the comfort of his arms, the family we wouldn't have, the life we wouldn't build together. I grieved for the loss of the only person who truly knew me – all of me, the good and especially the bad – and chose to love me anyway. I grieved for the part of myself that died the instant I got that phone call.

His life wasn't the only one that ended four days ago. I may as well have been standing next to him when that car struck his body, because I didn't know how I was supposed to go on without him. Every breath and beat of my heart hurt. I couldn't sleep without dreaming of him and waking up calling out for him. I couldn't even eat without ending up hunched over the toilet or trash, because the ache, the pain, the loss, was too much.

He was the best part of me. He was sensible when I was irrational; responsible when I was impulsive. He was the calm to my storm, but now it just raged inside of me like a category five hurricane ripping me apart from the inside out and destroying everything good, leaving behind nothing but utter devastation. My heart wasn't just broken, it was shattered. Dead on impact. That's what they told me. In the blink of an eye I went from being Mrs. Tyler Tate, to being a widow. Only twenty years old and I was a widow.

A sob tore from my lips when the coffin was all the way in the ground. Mama and Daddy stood on either side of me. I clung to them with what little strength I had left. If it weren't for them, I would have collapsed to the ground, or thrown myself in the hole with Ty, but they held me while I fell apart.

When it was done, so many people came up to hug me and offer condolences. It was a procession of teary eyed *I'm so sorry* and *hang in there* and *let me know if there's anything I can do.* There wasn't. Nothing anyone did would bring him back to me, and that's the only thing I wanted, the only thing that could make life okay again, but I didn't tell them that. I just forced a smile, which I'm sure was more of a grimace, and thanked them.

I lost it all over again when Ty's mom embraced me. Ellie had been like a second mother to me for as long as I could remember, even before I fell in love with her son. My body shook in her arms. She squeezed me tightly and her own cries were muffled against my hair.

When we finally pulled apart, I looked over at Beth, Ty's little sister, and the anguish on her face cut through my insides like a blade. I didn't know how my body could withstand so much pain – hers,

Ellie's, my own. I felt it all. She was just seventeen and had adored her big brother. She was the kid sister I'd always wanted, and it had been made official when her last name became mine. I wrapped my arms around her, and it was my turn to hold her up while she broke apart in my arms.

Ellie and Beth rode with us to the reception. Almost everyone who knew Tyler was there, even friends from high school we hadn't seen since graduation. Most of them had been at the service, but now they all wanted to talk; to have their chance to ask how I was holding up, and then reminisce about the good times we all had.

We got into our fair share of trouble back then. Well I got into trouble and Ty was always right there beside me, shaking his head and making sure I never went too far. He'd been looking after me since the very first time I decided I had to prove I was just as fearless and capable as any boy. Then, I was just the bratty girl down the street who liked to tag along with him and his friends.

I tried to smile as they shared their favorite memories; I even forced myself to laugh at a few of the stories, but it came out more hysterical than I intended. I saw the pity in their eyes. I just couldn't do it. I didn't want to remember the good days when there would never be another one with Ty. My strangled laughter quickly turned to choked back sobs and I excused myself from the group of our former classmates, and went to look for a place where I could have a moment alone to pull myself together.

I stopped in front of the table displaying pictures from Tyler's life. I looked at the toddler with big, bright blue eyes and a mess of blonde curls. I looked at the little boy with those same eyes, holding his very first football, and then the young man wearing a jersey with the number 84 on it, the same number he wore all through junior high and high school. I saw me in my sapphire blue dress, leaning back against his chest with his arms wrapped around my waist, standing outside the limo we'd rented for prom. He looked so handsome in that tux, almost as handsome as he had on our wedding day. I couldn't let myself think

3

about that day even as the picture of us in the church stared back at me right along with rest of them.

I moved away from the table of memories I didn't want to face. I walked over to the food spread and grabbed a plate, but before I could make it through the line, my stomach revolted. The heartbreak was too much. My stomach was in so many knots, the thought of eating made me nauseous. I put the plate back and downed a cup of water instead, and went to find a bathroom.

"Come on Liv, pull it together," I sighed, leaning over the sink and looking at my pale complexion in the mirror. My hair was slipping out of the twist I'd pinned it in this morning. I pulled it the rest of the way out and let the soft waves fall over my shoulders, but it didn't help. Usually my hair was a golden brown, but it seemed duller and flatter today, and my green eyes looked greyer, or maybe it was that the world seemed dimmer now. The dark circles and red splotches didn't help any. I splashed some cool water over my face, and my eyes locked on the gold band dangling from a chain around my neck.

Our families hadn't understood why I didn't want him buried wearing it. To me it just didn't make sense. My husband wasn't in that box. He was in Heaven and he was in my heart. That's where I wanted the ring, hanging over my heart. I squeezed it in my hand and then tucked it back into my dress, feeling the cool metal on my skin. I grabbed a paper towel and patted my face dry, then took a deep breath and pushed my way back through the door.

I wished Mel was here, but she was in Brazil with her parents for another four days. They were visiting her mom's family on their ranch. No cell phones. The only way I could get in touch with her was email. I'd tried to make myself send one several times over the past few days, asking her to call me, that it was an emergency. I even almost hit send once, but I just couldn't do it. I knew she'd be so mad at me, but it just felt like telling my best friend, having her hop on a plane and rush back here, would make it too real, like maybe if there was one person who didn't know, I could still wake up in the morning and realize it had all been an awful nightmare. I knew that was crazy, wishful thinking, that

4

this was a nightmare I wouldn't be waking up from, but still I couldn't bring myself to send that damn email, so I had to do this without her.

I stood there, looking around the room at all the people that Ty's life had touched, old teammates, coaches. The man who had been like a father to Ty since Ty's own dad abandoned him. He'd given him a job at his auto repair ship in high school that turned into Ty's passion. Mick and the rest of the guys from the garage he worked at in Lubbock were here too. His cousins, neighbors, most of the congregation from our home church; they were all here to mourn the loss of the greatest man I'd ever known, and I couldn't bear to face them. It seemed that I wasn't the only one who wanted to bail out early; I watched a retreating figure make his way out the doors. There was something familiar about him, even from the back, but I couldn't place who it was. I only wished I could escape with him.

After one of the longest days of my life, I found myself back at Ellie's, curled up in Tyler's old room, drowning in more memories of him. Mama and Daddy were staying with Aunt Jeannie and Uncle John since they'd flown in from Jefferson, but I wanted to be with Ellie and Beth. I wanted to be here even though it hurt so deeply to be in the house and room he grew up in. Everywhere I looked there were posters of his favorite band in high school, a few old pictures of the two of us, his childhood trophies and everything he hadn't taken with him when we left town. Ellie hadn't changed a thing. It was only a small preview of the agony I would face when I went back home to Lubbock.

Like every other night this week, the exhaustion swept over me not long after my head hit the pillow and the dreams started as soon as sleep claimed me. In them Tyler was alive and still with me. For that short time I was able to escape my new reality; I was still whole and my world was still right.

In the morning, when I felt myself waking, I tried like hell to cling to the dream. I wanted to stay in that place with him, but I was unable to hang on. When I opened my eyes he was gone and my pillowcase was damp from the tears that leaked out. I looked over at the clock on the nightstand and it was almost noon, yet I felt anything but rested. All

I'd wanted to do for the past four days was sleep. Sleep was my only comfort and my body wanted to let it take me away.

I forced myself out of bed and downstairs. Ellie and her sister, Ty's Aunt Karen, were in the kitchen and Beth was in the living room with her younger cousins. Ellie offered to cook me up some breakfast, but I declined. I knew she was worried and wanted to fuss over me just like Mama would, but she stayed quiet. I just grabbed a banana from the counter and let her brew me some tea. There were people in and out of the house all day long, bringing food and cakes that we set out for all the visitors.

The next day was the same. I slept in, barely managed to eat anything and forced myself to visit with the people who stopped by, all the while just wishing the nightmare would end and I would wake up in bed next to my husband. The worst nightmares are always the ones that are real.

On the third day after the funeral, I needed to get back to Lubbock. I still had to sort out our apartment. The apartment I hadn't been back to since I walked out the door the morning my happily ever after turned into a tragedy. The apartment I wouldn't be able to afford on my own for much longer. Our savings didn't have much. He made good money as a mechanic working on bikes and classic cars, but he supported the both of us so I wouldn't have to get a job, and could focus on school and soccer. Scholarships paid for schooling, but he took care of everything else. I didn't know what I would do now, but I knew I had to find somewhere else to live. I didn't want to stay there anyway, it would only feel empty. It wasn't home without him. Home. That word had lost all meaning for me.

"Are you sure you don't want to take a semester off and come back with us, baby girl?" Mama asked, not for the first time, or even the second. "I don't like the idea of you being all alone up there. You could come to Jefferson and–"

"And what Mama? Sit around everyday wallowing?" We'd had this argument every day. She wanted me to go with her and Daddy, and I knew she meant well, but that wasn't what I needed.

"Or you could stay here in Abilene. Your aunt has an extra room, or I'm sure Ellie would love to have you here. You'd be close to people who care about you, and I wouldn't worry so much."

"Mama I can't do that. I have to go back to Lubbock. The season will be starting soon," I reminded her.

"Are you sure you want to go back to the team right now? It will still be there next year. I'm sure your coach would understand," she tried to persuade me.

"If I took a year off, it could be the end of my career. The Dash will be watching me this season. If I walk away now I might not get another chance with them." Coach had told me that the Houston scouts were keeping an eye on me and were even supposed to come watch me play this season.

"Surely they'll still want you in another year. Making that team shouldn't be your priority right now. Taking care of yourself should." She didn't understand.

"That's exactly what I'm doing Mama. Ty sacrificed so much for me to chase that dream. He packed up his life here and followed me to Lubbock. He worked hard so that I could go to school and play for the Red Raiders because that was my best shot at getting noticed by one of the pro clubs. If I just give that up now, then everything he did was for nothing. He shared that dream with me and it's all I have left of him." I saw when she gave in; a look of resignation came over her. She didn't like it but she accepted it.

I hugged everyone goodbye outside of Ellie's and then tossed my bag in the trunk of my silver Honda and made the two and a half hour drive north. The miles ticked by, bringing me closer to my school, the apartment that wouldn't be mine for much longer and my future, whatever that looked like now. I had never been so afraid in my life.

Two

3 Weeks Later . . .

"Ya feelin' okay Liv?" Melodie Ross was more than just my teammate. She had been my best friend since we were roomed together in the dorms freshman year. That was just two years ago, and in that time she'd become my family too. I'd been right about how mad she was at me for not contacting her right away, but mostly she felt guilty that she hadn't been here for me, no matter how much I tried to reassure her that it wasn't her fault. She'd been trying to make up for it since, being attentive and taking care of me. "You don't look so hot."

I didn't feel so hot. The whole team was out for brunch before practices started in two days. I'd felt better this morning than I had in a while. My appetite was still erratic, but I'd actually been hungry when we got to the restaurant. Now that the waitress was placing plates down on the table, I started to feel queasy. "Yeah, my stomach is still just a little weak, from all the stress I think," I told her and she nodded, understanding.

I got my stack of butter pecan pancakes with a side of bacon and started in on it, taking a few small bites to see how it would go down. I'd been eating so light, I didn't want to overdo it now. I was feeling a little warm, and wishing it wasn't so stuffy in the restaurant, but I thought I was going to be okay. Half-way through my meal though, my stomach rolled and I had to jump up from my seat. Mel started to follow, but I gestured for her to stay, and then rushed to the bathroom. I barely made it in time to lose the meager contents of my stomach into the toilet.

I groaned, thinking this was the worst possible time to come down with a stomach bug as I rinsed my mouth and face. I knew anxiety and depression could weaken the immune system, and that I should probably go see a doctor. I couldn't afford to be sick when practices started.

Once I was confident my stomach was settled enough to go back out there, I opened the door and came face to face with our team athletic trainer, Casey Hunt. He was standing outside the ladies' room like he was waiting for someone.

"You alright, Tate?" he asked in that mild Yankee accent, just strong enough to give away that he wasn't a Texas boy. I didn't know exactly where he was from, Ohio, or maybe Iowa, somewhere around there. He'd come to the team last season and could only be about twenty-five. He stood a good six inches over my five-foot-eight, looking down at me with concern etched in his features. That was the only way people looked at me lately.

"Yeah, I've just been feeling a little under the weather lately, with everything," I said uncomfortably, not wanting to make a big deal of it. His brown eyes shone with sympathy. He brushed his hand through his dark hair, making it stand up just a little where it was slightly longer on top. The sides were cropped close to his head and matched the neatly trimmed scruff on his face. I had to look away, whether it was because I couldn't stand the pity or because I had once thought he was incredibly attractive, and couldn't bear those thoughts now. There was no denying he was more than just handsome. Mama would've called him a looker and Mel liked to say he was lickable. Almost every girl on the team had a crush on him, except for me. I'd never wanted anyone but Ty, so I'd never had a problem appreciating a good looking male specimen without it bothering me, because it didn't mean anything. Now it felt like a betrayal. How could I even be looking at another guy, let alone finding him attractive, when my husband had only been dead for a month?

Oh God, he's been gone a month.

It didn't feel like it had been that long, and at the same time it felt like it had been forever since he'd pressed that kiss to my sleepy head before going on his early morning run. Tears welled in my eyes and I stared at the floor so Casey wouldn't see them.

"Olivia," he said softly, and something about the tenderness of his voice forced me to look up and meet his gaze. "Are you sure you want to be here?"

"I'll be fine. I just haven't had much of an appetite, and I'm a little exhausted."

"I don't just mean here this morning, I mean the team. Are you sure you're ready to come back? Nobody would blame you if you weren't up for this season."

If one more person said that to me I was going to punch them in the face. "I'm not sitting out the season. I'll be fine," I insisted a little harshly and then brushed past him to get back to the table. I felt a little bad for being rude when he was only trying to be kind, but I was so tired of . . . everything. My stomach grumbled when I got back to my seat, but it wasn't as bad. Still I didn't want to push it and end up with my face back in the toilet.

"It's a little stuffy in here and I think I might be coming down with a bug. I'm gonna move outside," I told Mel. She and a few of the other girls grabbed their plates and followed me to one of the outdoor tables. The fresh air almost instantly made me feel better.

Conversation was light. I don't think anyone knew how to act around me, and I didn't know what to say either. Mostly we just talked about the upcoming season and which teams we expected to be the toughest to face. Last year we'd lost in the final division championship match, but two of our girls had been out with injuries, including Mel who was our goalkeeper.

"As long as we don't lose anyone this season, with Mel in the goal and you n' Hailey playin' forward we should be able to take it this year," Amy commented. Hopefully she was right. Hailey was new to the team this year and played the same position I did. Once she got into rhythm with the team she would be a great striker and definitely help us make it all the way.

I finished about half of my meal and let Mel clean the rest of my plate. I swear that girl could out eat any guy, and she still had a figure they all drooled over. She was just shy of six foot and looked like a model. Her caramel complexion and black hair gave her an exotic appearance. Her mom was from Brazil and her dad was a Texan down to the core, and a former Linebacker for the Cowboys. She had her mama's beauty and her daddy's big personality.

That combined with my attitude and quick temper, and we were trouble together, especially out on the field. She was my partner in crime and Ty was my anchor, at least that's how things were before, but everything was different now.

"You promise me you're really doing alright, Liv?" Mel asked quietly as if catching the change in my thoughts. The other girls were still discussing the upcoming season, but Mel didn't miss anything.

"I'm as okay as I can be," I told her. Her eyes softened and took on a pained look of her own.

"You know I love you right? You don't have to keep it in for me. I'm here, whatever you need, even if it's just someone to sit with you." I did know that. She was wild and sometimes came off as a little bit superficial, but that wasn't really her. She was passionate and kind and she cared about people deeply. She just didn't always show the world that. She'd been used so many times. People wanted to get close to her because of her father and what they thought being her friend could do for them, or they just saw her as another pretty face. It was a shame, because she had so much to offer.

"I know Mel. I love you too, and I wouldn't be able to make it through this without you. I don't even know how to say thank you for everything you've done for me." When being alone in the apartment was too much, she sat with me as I cried and stayed with me until I pulled myself together. And when being there period was too much, she got me out of there. She'd also spent the last two days helping me fit the contents of my apartment into boxes. She'd offered for me to move in with her, but I just couldn't stand the thought of living and sharing space with anyone who wasn't Ty right now. I'd found a small apartment in a complex not too far from campus, and most of my things were already there.

"You're my best friend, my sister, and when you're hurting, I'm hurting. You don't need to thank me, it's what we do." I didn't say anything, couldn't without getting choked up. She didn't need me to though. She knew what it meant to me.

After brunch, I had to finish packing and get the last few things moved into the new apartment. I hugged the girls goodbye and promised coach I would get some rest before practice on Monday. On my way out of the restaurant I caught Casey glancing at me worriedly, but then his features smoothed over and his expression became unreadable. Our eyes lingered on each other until Jamie, my least favorite teammate, approached him and he turned his attention to her. I walked over to my car, and tried to mentally prepare myself to say my final goodbyes to the place Ty and I had spent the last year living out our happily ever after.

I sighed and tried not to cry when I walked into the apartment. It was almost empty, and only mine for another few hours. Mick and another of Ty's buddies from work had helped me and Mel move almost everything over to the new place yesterday. All that was left was the stuff I'd been putting off. I wanted to be alone as I sorted through the last of Ty's things. I didn't want anyone here to witness the moment. Every little thing held a memory, and packing them up, deciding what to keep and what to get rid of was excruciatingly difficult.

I picked up the last remaining item and inhaled the scent that lingered on the soft fabric. It was the shirt he'd worn the night before he died. I hadn't been able to bring myself to wash it and stick it in the donate pile like I had a lot of his clothes. I'd slept with it every night since coming back. The smell was almost gone though, only faint traces of his body wash and the smell that was uniquely him remained. I folded it up and placed it in the last box of his belongings I was saving. That was everything.

I carried the boxes down to my car and loaded them up, then climbed the flight of steps up to the apartment for the last time. I stood inside the empty space and looked around, remembering the day we moved in.

"It's really ours?" I was having a hard time believing we had a place of our own. Heck, I was still having a hard time believing we were finally married. I'd been Olivia Tate for two weeks now and I didn't know if I'd ever get used to the feeling of pure bliss I'd been experiencing since we both said "I do."

"Yeah Livvie, it's really ours." He took my hand in his and pressed a kiss to my forehead. I couldn't stop the grin that took over my face. I'd been doing that a lot lately, smiling. Everything was perfect, or at least it felt perfect to me. After my first year of college, living in the dorms and trying to balance homework, practices and Ty, we were finally together. This was our place and I loved it.

It was a lot bigger than the tiny, crappy apartment he'd been living in before the wedding. He'd rented it because it was so cheap and he wanted to save up for our honeymoon, and be able to get us a nice place once we were actually married. I loved him so much it felt like my heart would burst any minute. I thanked God that this amazing, strong, selfless man loved me, and I would thank God for him every day for the rest of my life.

I couldn't stop the bubble of excitement that rose and I let out a squeal as I looked around some more at our new apartment, our new home. It was a two bedroom with an open floor plan. The living room and bedrooms had new carpet, and beautiful flooring ran through the kitchen and the hallway to the bedrooms. The kitchen was huge, well at least compared to what I was used to, and had all fairly modern appliances that I couldn't wait to use.

Ty was staring at the living room area and I knew he was trying to figure out where he wanted to put his giant flat screen. Guys. Here I

13

was thinking about all the dinners I would be cooking for him and he was thinking about all the sports he would be watching and video games he would be playing. I just rolled my eyes, but I knew what would get his attention.

"Hey babe, can we go check out the master bedroom?" I snuggled into his side.

"We've already looked at it. Don't you think we should start bringing boxes in?" he asked.

I just grinned up at him. "But babe, I really want to look at it again. I'm not sure that we really gave it enough of our attention before. I think there's more to see in there." I raised my eyebrows suggestively and I saw the light bulb click on in his head.

"Oh . . . but, there's no bed in there yet," he said slowly.

"Is that a problem for you?" I smirked and bit my lip.

"No ma'am, it is not." He flashed a wicked grin and before I knew it, he was throwing me over his shoulder and carrying me off to the bedroom like a caveman. I laughed. My caveman.

It hurt so much. In the year that we'd lived here we'd filled this place with so much love and laughter. Inside of these walls we'd planned our future, shared our dreams and fears. We'd argued and struggled, but we always worked it out together. It was all gone now. The apartment was as empty and hollow as I felt.

"God, I promised back then that I would thank you every day. I thought I'd have a lifetime of love and memories to thank you for. I didn't know that you would be taking him home so soon, and it hurts so much that our time together was cut too short, but thank you for bringing him to me and for every single moment that I got with him."

I pulled the door closed behind me and said goodbye to that place. I dropped the keys off with the landlord and after dropping off the boxes for donation, drove to my new home, not that any place would feel like home again without Ty.

Three

Grief is in two parts. The first is loss.
The second is the remaking of life." – Anne Roiphe

I had three boxes balanced precariously in my arms while I fumbled with my keys, trying to get the door to the apartment complex open. Once inside, I started up the stairs. The building was three stories, mine was on the third floor and I have this thing with elevators, where I really don't like them. I got stuck in one when I was ten. The power was out and after forty seven minutes of being trapped alone, in the dark, I refused to use one unless I absolutely had to.

This was my third trip from my car up to the apartment, and I didn't want to make another, which is why I was carrying more boxes than I should have been. I made it to the top of the stairwell, and again was stuck with the dilemma of trying to get the door open without dropping everything. Just as I was reaching out for the door handle, it swung open and into the boxes. The one on top crashed to the ground, but I was knocked backwards with the other two still in my arms. I let out a startled cry and thought for sure I was going to topple down the stairs and break my neck.

"Oh shit," I heard a deep male voice swear just before a pair of strong hands grasped my arms and steadied me. I lowered the boxes that were blocking my face, which I had surprisingly not dropped, to see who the hands and voice belonged to.

Casey?

What the heck was he doing here? He seemed just as surprised to see me.

"I'm so sorry Tate. Are you alright?" His hands were still on my arms. He seemed to realize that at the same time I did and dropped them.

15

"Yeah," I breathed out as my heart rate finally returned to normal. "I think I may have had a minor heart attack when I thought I was going fall to my death, but I'm fine now."

"At least your heart is probably in perfect condition," he joked. If only it were true. I tried to smile, but wasn't able to force it. His face dropped as he caught on to the mistake in what he'd said. "I uh . . . I just meant, that you're an athlete and . . . I'm sorry. Again. Let me just grab this for you." He bent down to retrieve the box that had fallen and I started to follow him out of the stairwell and then remembered I was still curious why he was here.

"So what are you doing here?" *Please say visiting someone.* I didn't like the idea of living in the same building as Casey. I just wanted to be someplace where nobody knew me, where nobody felt sorry for me. I didn't want to be bumping into him in the hallway and stairwell. I didn't want him to feel obligated to be neighborly or check up on me.

"I live here, and I'm guessing you're the new neighbor in three-oh-four?"

So much for just visiting. "Uh, yeah. Three-oh-four, that's me," I confirmed as he stopped in front of my door and then pried the keys from my hand. Once the door was opened he followed me inside.

"Where would you like this?" he asked.

"You can just set it beside the counter," I told him, doing the same with my two boxes. We both stood there awkwardly for a minute before he broke the silence.

"Well I better get going."

"Okay. I'd offer you something to drink, but the fridge is a little on the empty side." Mama would call it poor manners, but I just hadn't been grocery shopping yet.

"That's alright. I was on my way out when I assaulted you with the door, anyway."

"I appreciate you helping me with me my stuff," I thanked him.

"Well it was the least I could do after almost taking you out. If you need anything else, I'm at the end of the hall in three-oh-seven." He informed me and then moved toward the door. He pulled it open and then turned to say something over his shoulder. "See you at practice on Monday, Tate."

"See ya."

Once he was gone I sighed and plopped down on couch. The apartment was small, very small, but I preferred to think of it as quaint. It had an open floor plan like the last one, but here the kitchen and living room area would have fit into just the living room of the old one. There was only one bedroom and bathroom, but really that's all I needed. I was luck to have even found a place this nice that I could afford.

I had just enough left in the account to pay my cell phone bill, insurance and hopefully put gas in the car, groceries in the cupboard, and have a tiny, not very padded, cushion for emergencies. After that I was screwed. I had two options. Go to my parents, I knew they'd help me out, they'd already offered, or find a job. I really hoped I wouldn't have to go to my parents. Monday after practice I would stop by the financial aid office and see if the work study program had any openings that would work around my class and team schedules.

I ran a hand through my hair and sank further into the cushions. I closed my eyes and let out a deep breath, trying to relieve some of the stress. Sometime between worrying about my financial situation and trying to find the motivation to get up and unpack the remaining few boxes, I drifted off to sleep.

A few hours later, I was woken up by a banging noise. I looked at the clock and realized I must have slept for about three hours. Even though the sun was still high in the sky, it was already evening. My stomach rumbled and I was reminded that I had nothing to eat here. Guess that meant I was ordering take-out. I yawned just as a knock sounded at the door. I realized the banging noise that woke me was someone knocking on my door.

When I dragged myself up off the couch, my muscles were cramped from the position I'd fallen asleep in. I stretched my arms while I took the few steps to answer the door. I couldn't hold back another yawn as I pulled it open and saw Casey standing in the hallway

17

with a foil wrapped plate in his hand. Whatever it was smelled amazing. I was actually starving, which surprised me.

"Oh, did I wake you up?" His expression was apologetic.

"I was just taking a short nap, or it was supposed to be a short nap. I've been sleeping a lot lately," I confessed. "So no worries, I needed to get up anyway."

"When I was here earlier you mentioned your fridge was empty and your cupboards looked about the same. I had a little extra when I made dinner tonight so I thought I'd bring it over." He held the plate out to me. It was still warm. "It's just some salmon, rice and vegetables. Nothing fancy." I couldn't help but smile, because it was a lot fancier than whatever I would've ordered.

"Thanks. It smells great, but you really didn't have to."

"Well technically it's my job to make sure you girls stay healthy, and I figured if I didn't, you'd probably get takeout," he presumed correctly. I smiled and then realized he was still standing in the doorway. That's twice today; Mama would swat me upside the back of my head for my manners.

"Umm, do you want to come in?" I stepped back to clear the doorway. He hesitated. I got the feeling there was something he wanted to say or ask me, but he decided against it.

"That's alright. I'll let you eat. Have a good night, Tate." He turned and walked back toward his apartment.

"Goodnight Casey." Before I could close my door, I heard him call out.

"Hey Tate?"

"Yeah?" I asked hesitantly and took a step out in to the hallway. He was halfway between our places and facing me with a nervous look on his face. He tipped his head down and rubbed one hand over the back of his neck briefly before he looked up at me again and dropped his arm to his side.

"I know you're going through a tough time, that's probably not even a good enough word for it. I can't even imagine . . . I just, what I'm trying to say is, don't push yourself too hard at practice right away.

18

Take it easy and make sure you're healthy." I didn't say anything. I just nodded subtly, but it was enough to satisfy him and he turned and disappeared inside his apartment. Was it really so obvious that I wasn't doing well?

I walked back inside my own apartment, set the plate on the counter and went straight to my bedroom. I stood in front of the full length mirror on my closet door, and took a long look. I'd lost a bit of weight, but it wasn't drastic. My cheeks were absent of color and I had dark circles under my eyes, which looked hollow and lifeless; a reflection of how I felt inside. I didn't look healthy, that was for sure. I looked like a girl who'd lost everything. That wasn't something any amount of rest would change.

Sorry Casey.

I flipped off the light in my room and went to eat my dinner even though all I wanted was to curl up and make it all go away for a few hours. I had to try though. The team was the only thing left for me.

The food was delicious and I didn't end up heaving over the toilet bowl. I actually felt better after eating. I wasn't quite so tired and decided to tackle the last several boxes. One was a smaller box of pictures; I wasn't ready to go there yet so I placed it on the top shelf in my closet. I didn't want any of them out. I didn't need help remembering. The memories were all there inside me, wrapped around my heart like a vice. I knew that someday I'd reach a point where seeing them wouldn't bring me so much pain and I'd pull them out again. It just wasn't today, and it probably wouldn't be tomorrow either.

The next two boxes I opened were full of Ty's books and magazines on all things automobile related. Most featured vintage cars or motorcycles, two things he was passionate about. I didn't have much use for them, but I'd gotten rid of so much of his stuff, I couldn't bring myself to let these go too. Maybe I'd figure out what to do with them when I figured out what to do with his bike. In the mean time it was sitting in Mel's parents' garage, and I stacked the books and magazines

19

on the bottom shelf of the entertainment center, the same place Ty had kept them before.

Lying across the last couple boxes was the garment bag with Ty's tux from our wedding. I reached down for it and folded it over my arms. I carried it to my bedroom, hugging it tightly to my chest. He'd looked so beautiful that day. When I told him that, he cringed and said guys didn't look beautiful, but there wasn't any other word for it. Handsome wasn't strong enough, and sure he was sexy and gorgeous, but none of those felt right either. Beautiful was the only word I felt captured it.

The image of him standing at the end of the aisle, in the tux that was cut to fit his broad shoulders and the hard planes of his lean body perfectly, still made my heart flutter. With his blonde hair falling in waves around his face, down to his shoulders, I'd wanted to run my fingers through the golden locks. He'd offered to cut it for the wedding, but I hadn't wanted him to. I preferred the rough edge it gave his looks, but he had shaved off his short beard and I remember thinking that I couldn't wait to feel the smooth skin.

What really got me though, and left my knees weak, was the way he'd looked at me as I made my way down the aisle. I could still see his eyes shining with so much love, and the smile that lit up his whole face. If my daddy hadn't been holding on to me, my knees would've buckled then. Either that or I would have run the rest of the way and launched myself at him, tackling him in front of God, our pastor and all our friends and family.

I looked down at the bag in my arms and noticed the wet spots on it. Another drop fell, then another. I squeezed my eyes shut to try and cut off the slow trickle of tears. That was the best day of my life, but so was every day that followed, until the worst day of my life. I was so blessed to have been loved by him, to have married him and had a whole year of best days of my life with him. Selfishly it wasn't enough though. I wanted more of them. I hung the bag in the back of my closet and tried to accept what I couldn't have.

I opened the next boxes and started pulling out model cars that Ty had put together over the years. I got him his first one for his tenth birthday. That was before I started chasing after him with cartoon hearts in my eyes. Back then he was just the obnoxious boy down the street who picked on me and wouldn't let me play with him and his friends.

Ellie made him invite me to his birthday party and Mama made me pick out a present and go. He later admitted to me that it was his favorite gift, so I continued to buy them for him every occasion after. He put so much time and work into completing each one. That's where his love of old cars started, and the reason he began hanging around Mr. Benson's garage, soaking up every bit of knowledge he could until finally Mr. Benson gave him that job in high school. Looking at the model cars you could see how his skill improved over the years, from the first ones he ever put together to the one he finished just months before the accident. I found a few shelves throughout the apartment to place my favorites, including that very first one, and the rest joined the box of pictures up in the closet.

Only one box remained and it held the few pieces of Ty's clothing I kept. His old football team shirts, his favorite hoodie, a jersey from his favorite Cowboys player, t-shirts from concerts we went to and a few others I couldn't let go of. I tucked them into the bottom drawer of my dresser.

There were a few smaller things in the box as well, like his watch, a couple baseball caps he always wore, and the leather braided wristband I bought for him on our honeymoon in Mexico. I set those things on top of the dresser, and then decided it was too much like when he would leave them lying around, so I shoved them in another empty drawer and left the bedroom.

That was it; everything was unpacked and had a place, but none of it felt right. I settled down on the couch and flipped the TV on and tried to get lost in some ridiculous sitcom. Under other circumstances it probably would have been something I would've enjoyed watching, but tonight I just wanted to get out of my own head and nothing was helping. I gave up and turned it off. The only place I found comfort and escape anymore was in my sleep, so I slipped into one of Ty's t-shirts and climbed into bed, hoping that tomorrow I would wake up and it would hurt just a little bit less. It was the only hope I had left.

"God, please let it hurt less tomorrow. Please don't let me hurt forever."

I reached over on the nightstand where Ty's iPhone was sitting, screen cracked from where it struck the pavement, but surprisingly everything still worked. I turned on his favorite playlist and let myself drown in the music.

Four

"New Beginnings are often disguised as painful endings."
— *Lao Tzu*

"Damn it," I muttered under my breath when Erica got the ball away from me for the third time since we'd started running drills. Any other day I would've been able to dribble right around her and take the ball to the goal but I was off my game today. I was slow, and I kept having dizzy spells. Overall I was playing like crap, but nobody was saying anything about it. I didn't know whether I was more pissed that I was playing so awful, or that Coach wasn't yelling at me for it. Everyone was being so damn encouraging. If I were any other player Coach would've pulled me off to the side and told me to get it together, even if it was only the first practice of the season.

My frustration grew and I continued to miss shot after shot and have the ball taken away from me. When we switched drills, I could barely even keep up with the other girls and I was the fastest one on the team, or at least I used to be. I hadn't run in a few weeks but I shouldn't be this out of shape. I felt like I was going to drop right there on the field. I almost did out of relief when Coach called for a five-minute water break.

He walked over to Casey and our assistant coach, Walsh. They started discussing something and I'd have bet money it was me. It was confirmed as soon as Casey's eyes darted to where I was standing and then quickly back when he saw I was watching them. I downed a couple large gulps of water and then prepared to get back out there when Coach resumed practice, but before I could, I heard my name. Casey was calling me over.

"What is it?" I was pretty sure I already knew.

"You're sitting out the rest of practice," he informed me bluntly.

23

"Like hell I am," I responded, turning to walk back out on the field.

"Tate," he warned. I turned back around to face him. He had an intense scowl on his face and I knew he wasn't dropping it. "Coach's orders. You're done today."

"Why? Have you not been watching? Obviously I need to practice," I said dryly.

"Yeah I have been watching, so has Coach Davis and Coach Walsh, and what we see is a girl who's pushing herself too hard. You're obviously not well and until you are, your ass is on the bench." He made it clear there would be no more arguing the matter. I turned and stormed off.

"Where the hell are you going Tate?" he hollered after me.

"To get some *rest, s*ince you guys think it's so damn important for me to get more of it." I knew it wasn't the mature response. They were concerned and they obviously had reason to be, but I didn't care. I was angry. Mostly at myself.

I yanked my duffle bag up and walked away. I didn't turn back even when Coach yelled for me. He'd already benched me, probably for the next few practices, so what else was he going to do?

I was half way back to my car when I remembered I still had to deal with my financial situation. I groaned. After this unpleasant start to my day, it wasn't something I was looking forward to. However, I dropped my bag off in my trunk and peeled off my cleats and shin guards, trading them for the flip flops in my back seat. I locked my car and turned around to get it over with. Hopefully it would solve my financial problems which would relieve some of the stress weighing on me and making me play like shit.

The financial aid office was on the opposite side of campus and the whole walk over I was going back and forth, battling my anger and frustration. Casey and Coach were just doing their jobs. I still felt a little light headed and maybe I shouldn't have been out there, but Casey was really beginning to annoy me, thinking he knew what was best for me and telling me what to do.

He does. It's his job, my subconscious reminded me, but I told it to shut up. I didn't care that it was his job. Up until a few days ago my interaction with Casey was limited to physicals and establishing nutrition and fitness plans. He was never around when I was in the fitness center. Now it seemed like every time I turned around he was in my face.

I pushed through the doors into the financial aid office. There were three ladies behind the counter, and they were all occupied. I took my spot at the end of the line. There were two people ahead of me and thankfully it wasn't long before I was standing at the counter in front of a woman in her forties with curly red hair.

"What can I help ya with darlin'?" She had a friendly smile and I hoped she could actually help me.

"I want to find about the work study program, if there are any openings," I explained.

"Okay, the person you want to talk to is Maggie. That's her office right back there." She pointed toward a door in the corner of the room. "You can have a seat in one of those chairs and I'll let her know you're here. She ain't with anyone at the moment so she should be able to see ya right away."

No sooner had I taken a seat in one of the leather chairs outside of the office, than the door swung open and a tall, slim woman with blonde hair and stylish glasses stepped out. She appeared pretty young, maybe early thirties.

"You're interested in the work study program?"

"Yes I am."

She gestured for me to follow her inside the office. She shut the door behind us and then took a seat behind her desk. I slid into the chair facing her. She punched a few keys on her keyboard and then looked back up at me.

"What is your name and student I.D. number?" I gave her the information and she typed away. She wrinkled her brow and hit a few more keys, and then her eyes met mine again. "Have you filled out the FAFSA?"

"No, I haven't."

"Unfortunately all of our work study positions are assigned based on financial need. If you haven't filed a FAFSA, then I can't place you in a job."

"Oh. Okay." I didn't know what to do now. I could go around town, but the chances of finding something that would work around my class and team schedules were minimal.

"You should have filed at the beginning of the year, but it's not too late to fill one out."

At the beginning of the year I didn't think I would be sitting here in this situation. "I know, it's just that, um, my financial situation has changed recently. I didn't think I would need to file before, but I can do it now? How long does it take?" Hopefully it was a quick process.

"Go online to this site." She wrote something on the back of one of her cards. "You can file online, it's pretty simple. It usually takes a few weeks to be processed though." That would be pushing it. I'd have to be placed in a job immediately or I'd be in trouble. "Unfortunately as far as job placement, most of the positions will be filled by then. They go pretty fast, but you can always check back and we might have something." She didn't sound hopeful.

"If it's your tuition you're worried about, you can fill out paperwork for an extension or payment plan if you have extenuating circumstances. You said your situation recently changed, you may qualify. Do you mind if I ask what changed?" I shifted in my seat uncomfortably. It wasn't that I wanted it to be some secret, but the look of pity and awkwardness after I told her was inevitable and I just wanted to save us both from it, but there really wasn't a way to avoid it without coming off as rude.

"I'm not worried about my tuition. I have scholarships that cover that, but my husband paid for all of my other expenses and, er, he passed away last month." How many times had I been through this, explaining that my husband was dead? Our families and friends, the landlord, the bank and so on. It didn't get any easier, and her reaction was exactly what I'd known it would be.

26

Shock; that wasn't what she was expecting me to say. Disbelief; I was so young. Finally, sadness and pity. I could practically hear her thinking, *"Poor dear."* It wasn't her fault. What else could she feel? How else should you look at someone who'd experienced such a loss? That didn't mean I could bear to see it. I dropped my eyes to some pamphlets and fliers she had displayed on her desk, and didn't wait for her to say anything before I continued, "So I need a job that will work around my schedule since I also play for the soccer team here."

"I'm so sorry. I truly wish I was able to help you. If you get that FAFSA done, I'll do whatever I can to make sure you get placed if you haven't found another solution before then. Most of the restaurants near campus regularly hire students. You might check into that as well, you may find someone willing to work around your scheduling needs."

I thanked her for the advice and took the website information she wrote down and promised to get it filled out. She informed me that even if there weren't any work study positions available, I could be awarded grants that I could use for any of my expenses; the scholarships wouldn't impact that.

I avoided passing by the field on the way back to my car. They would be just about to wrap up for the day and I didn't want to run into anyone, especially Coach or Casey. I knew I couldn't escape Casey for long though, it wasn't like he didn't know where I lived.

It was Mel who confronted me first, though. I was parked outside my building, grabbing my duffel from the trunk when a familiar red Audi whipped into the parking lot. Melodie pulled up beside me and got out of her car.

"Hey," I sighed and slammed the trunk shut.

"Hey yourself." I didn't bother to invite her up. I knew she'd follow anyway. She didn't even give me crap about taking the stairs, just climbed up them right behind me.

"What was up at practice today? Casey and Coach seemed pretty pissed when you took off." I tossed my bag down inside the front door and Mel made herself at home on the couch.

"You saw how I was playing today." I plopped down next to her.

"Yeah, but it was the first day back after the shitty month that you've had. You need to take it easy and get healthy before you can expect to be back at your usual level. You didn't look well out there today. You're only gonna hurt yourself tryin' to play when you're sick."

"That's basically what Coach and Casey had to say as well, I just didn't want to listen to it. I know you guys are right, but I have to play, Mel. I *need* to be ready for this season. I can't blow it." Every year that I got older would make it less likely for a pro team to want me. I was young right now and the next few years would be the prime of my career which is why I needed Houston to see me at my best or they would lose interest in me. It was a lot harder to get a try-out with them if they didn't scout you.

"The only way you're going to blow it Liv, is by pushing yourself too hard. Being careless, not listening to what your body is telling you will get you hurt and could end your chances just like that. You know that. You have to take care of yourself, and you can't blame Coach, or Casey, or anyone else for making sure that you do."

"It's my body and I know what I can handle." It came out sharper than I intended, but I couldn't stop myself. "I need you to be my friend, not my mother. I've already got her calling me twice a day worrying over me. Can you please just support me?"

"I am your friend, and I'm here for you no matter what. I understand why you want to stay on the team and I'm behind you on that, but not like this Liv." She stood. "I love you. Please think about what you're doing. Go to the doctor, take a few days off and come back to practice when you're actually ready to be there."

"Love you too, Mel. I'll see you tomorrow at practice." I could see her frustration, but she didn't argue with me any further. She just looked at the floor shaking her head and then left.

I wanted to shake my head too, at the way the entire day had turned out. I was still mad and frustrated about practice. I was stressed about finding a job and worried that the stress would continue to affect my game, which only made me stress more. It was all piling up and I

28

needed to clear my head and work off some of the pressure building inside me. Since I was still in my practice clothes, I threw on my running shoes, grabbed my mp3 player and walked over to the main building with the fitness center I hadn't really gotten to check out yet.

I immediately went to the row of treadmills and started one up. I was almost a mile into my run when someone came up beside me and reached over to shut off my machine.

"Hey!" I tore out my headphones, but before I could chew out whoever it was, he grabbed my arm and yanked me off the treadmill and started dragging me out of the fitness center. "What the hell are you doing Casey?"

"Stopping you from doing something stupid." He didn't let go of my arm and continued to pull me along like a disobedient child.

"You're going to end my season before it even starts," I snapped, trying to tug free from his grasp, but he didn't let go. He stopped abruptly and I almost crashed into him. He turned around to face me. There were only inches between us as we glared at each other.

"You're the one who's going to do that. I'm actually trying to help you, but you're making it really damn hard, Olivia." He narrowed his eyes, daring me to challenge him some more. *Ha.* He obviously didn't know me well. I gave that look right back to him.

"You can interfere all you want out on the field, but in my free time I can do what I want and you can't stop me. You're not on the job anymore. Here, you're just my obnoxious neighbor." He could try and stop me, but I'd just go back later. It didn't matter that I was feeling exhausted already; I would do it to spite him.

"Actually a big part of my job is injury prevention, and since I'm trying to prevent you from unnecessarily injuring yourself, I'm still on the job. In fact, I should be getting overtime for this," he grumbled.

"Well you're not, so why don't you just leave me alone and mind your own business?" He finally released my arm and I thought I'd won, that he was giving up.

"Fine. Go back in there." I started to do exactly that. "But I'll tell Coach you've become a liability for the team. I won't release you for practice because you're determined to put yourself at risk which in turn could put other players at risk. You won't set foot out on that field all season." I sucked in a sharp breath and turned back around. He was serious. He couldn't do that. I mean he could, but . . . I was having trouble breathing. Everything was crashing down around me. Angry tears welled in my eyes and I fought to hold them back. I clenched my fists together, my nails digging into my skin.

"You can't do that."

"I don't want to do it, but you're not giving me a choice."

"Screw you," I yelled almost frantic. "You do have a choice. Just stay out of my life and stop pretending to care so much when you hardly know me. You don't know anything about me or what the last month has been like for me, but I have to play. You can't take that away from me too!"

"I do care, which is why if you want to play this year you need to listen to me. I know what this game means to you, and I'll work with you. Promise me you won't pull anything like this again. No pushing yourself outside of practice, and I'll clear you tomorrow on the condition that you are completely honest with yourself and me. You've been through a trauma that's as real as any physical injury. You can't over exert yourself." I had to play, even if that meant letting this bossy jackass tell me what to do. I just nodded. "You also have to communicate with me openly any time you're not feeling one hundred percent. Even if we have to modify your practices until you're feeling better, but I'll make sure that you're healthy and ready for the first match."

If he could guarantee me that, I'd do whatever he asked. "Deal."

He ran a hand through his tousled hair. "You should see a doctor as well. You can't ignore your body if it's telling you something is wrong. And you need to eat more."

"I already know what's wrong," I said bitterly. "I'm not going to a doctor. They'll tell me I'm depressed. Well duh, I'm depressed; the love of my life is dead. I don't want to be medicated. What I want, what will help me, is to play."

He nodded. He was more understanding than I expected him to be. "Okay. Then you'll play."

"Thank you."

I didn't realize then just how wrong we both were, how over my days playing for the team were.

Five

"When we least expect it, life sets us a challenge to test our courage and willingness to change; at such a moment, there is no point in pretending that nothing has happened or in saying that we are not yet ready. The challenge will not wait. Life does not look back."
— Paulo Coelho

I dribbled around Jess, but she stayed right on me. I kept moving toward the goal and Erica came at me from the left but I outmaneuvered her and got within range of the goal. Just as I was about to take the shot the goal blurred in front of my eyes. Everything around me became dizzy for a moment and I stumbled. Erica was there and reached out to steady me.

"You alright, Liv?" She kept her hand on my shoulder until she was reassured I wasn't going to eat grass. Jess and a few of the other girls gathered around us with concern on their faces.

"I just got a little dizzy. I think maybe I'm dehydrated."

Walsh, our assistant coach, who'd been working with our group, was walking over. "What's going on, Tate?"

The dizziness had faded and I was standing on my own. Erica and the others stepped back to let Coach Walsh through. "Just got a little light headed for a minute, Coach."

He looked at me closely and then sighed, "Okay. Why don't you take a ten minute break? Get some water and have a seat, then you can come back out here and we'll do some shooting drills." I nodded and walked off the field. I didn't want to. It took everything I had not to put up a fight, but I'd made a deal with Casey and he was standing off to the side watching me.

He beckoned me over, but I ignored him and continued walking toward my bag. Once he could no longer see my face I grinned slightly. Just because I agreed to do things his way didn't mean I wouldn't take a tiny bit of satisfaction in challenging him when I could. I grabbed my water bottle and plopped down on the ground.

Casey moved toward me with an annoyed expression. I had to fight to keep the grin from spreading. When he reached where I was sitting, he stood there, staring down at me for a minute. He was a tiny bit intimidating looming over me, which was probably his intention. He let out an exasperated breath and then took a seat next to me. "You really are a pain in the ass, you know that?"

This time I let him see my smile. "I've been told that a time or two."

"Somehow I doubt only a time or two." He shook his head and smiled back before his face took on a more serious expression. "So what was up out there?"

"I was feeling and playing alright until a few minutes ago. I went to take the shot but I got dizzy and couldn't. It only lasted for a second, but I could barely stand."

He looked away from me and stared at the ground for a minute, contemplating something. "You said you've also been nauseous lately, that's why you're not eating, and overly tired?" I could see his brain working, he was trying to put something together, but I wasn't connecting the dots that he was.

"Yeah, they're all symptoms of stress and serious depression. I'm not sure how long it will last, but I think the team will give me something else to focus on, and it should pass."

He didn't look like he agreed with me. "Olivia, those aren't just symptoms of depression." His eyes wouldn't meet mine. His knees were bent and his arms rested across them while he continued to stare at the ground between his feet. Finally he looked over at me, and I didn't understand the look I saw. "Is there any chance that . . . that you could be . . . pregnant?" His question startled me and my heart stopped for a second.

No. Absolutely not. There's no way . . . Except that wasn't entirely true.

33

"No," I whispered shaking my head. "I was on birth control. I can't be . . . No," I repeated, but I think in my heart I knew. I stood up and Casey followed me to my feet.

"If you're certain, one hundred percent, then I believe you, but you really need to be positive. If there's even the slightest chance that you are, you have to know for sure and I can't let you back out there until you do." His voice was gentle, but I was panicking. I grabbed my bag and split. This time he didn't holler after me.

I sat outside the pharmacy for twenty minutes trying to work up the courage to go in. I let out a shaky breath and forced myself out of the car. I had to know. That's what I kept telling myself while I worked my way through the aisles searching for what I needed. When I found them; there were at least five different ones to choose from. I didn't want to stand around reading labels so I just grabbed two of the brand I recognized from all of the commercials and hurried to checkout.

When I got back to the apartment, as badly as I wanted to know, I was too terrified to find out. I set the sack on the counter and then busied myself with every menial task I could find. I washed the few dishes sitting in my sink and then started a load of laundry, downing glass after glass of water. When I couldn't find any more household chores to tackle, I completed the FAFSA form and got that filed. Depending on what results I got today, it might be more important than ever.

After that was finished, I climbed in the shower. The hot water cascaded down my body, soothing and relaxing my achy muscles. My soapy hands traveled over my skin, scrubbing away the layer of sweat. They lingered for a moment on my belly, but I didn't give myself time to dwell on the possibility. There was no point in playing what if, and after I rinsed off and climbed out of the shower, I realized how silly it was for me to avoid taking the test. The truth, whatever it was, wouldn't change with more time. I couldn't hide from it. I either was, or I wasn't, and it was time to find out.

I was. At least that's what the first pink lines indicated, but I'd heard that you should never trust one so I ripped open the second box, but after a few minutes it only confirmed what the first one had told me and what I think I'd known the second Casey said it.

I'm pregnant.

I didn't know what to do. My heart was beating erratically, racing and skipping beats while my breaths were coming in shallow and rapid.

I'm pregnant.

That was the only thought my brain could form as my body moved on autopilot out of the bathroom. Without thinking about it I reached for my cell phone and pulled up Mel's number. I needed to call someone. I needed her to tell me what to do. I was two seconds away from collapsing and having a full scale meltdown. When she didn't answer, my feet carried me out of my apartment and I found myself knocking on the door of three-oh-seven. I don't know why I ended up there other than I was desperate, and scared and in shock, but he would know what to do. I hoped he was home, I didn't even know what time it was. I guessed that practice had been over for a while but I wasn't sure what hours he was at the fitness center. I was still clutching my cell in one hand and before I could check the clock on it, the door was pulled open and Casey stared back at me.

I couldn't speak, and I could only imagine what my face looked like. I still held the tiny pee stick with the two pink lines in my other hand. His eyes found it and then understanding spread over his features.

"Come inside." His voice was soft and reassuring. I just knew he would help me. I followed him inside and after he shut the door behind us, he led me over to the large, cushiony, black sofa in the middle of his living room. He had one of the larger apartments in the building, two bedrooms, like the one Ty and I had shared.

Ty. He'll never get to meet his son or daughter.

My baby will grow up without a dad.

I'm going to need a second bedroom.

How will I be able to afford a bigger place?

Oh God. I need Ty.

I need a job.

I can't do this.

I should have got the damn shot.

My thoughts all ran into each other, a blur of panic and desperation. Casey sat down beside me, but I barely registered it. All I could think about was the life inside of me, and how unready I was to deal with this. I didn't bother to ask myself how it could have happened. I already knew. Our anniversary had been just two weeks before Ty died. He'd planned an amazing night; flowers, a romantic dinner at a fancy restaurant, sneaking into the pool at the apartment after hours and we'd . . . well yeah. I was on birth control, the pill because I hated shots, but later that night I got an awful case of food poisoning from dinner. He'd been so sweet and stayed up with me, holding my hair when I threw up, bringing me ginger ale and crackers and then holding my hair when I threw that up too. It lasted almost two days, but I hadn't even thought about the effect all the throwing up would have on my birth control when he climbed into bed with me the night I was finally feeling better. And then he made me feel *a lot* better.

Casey shifted next to me and I remembered where I was. He touched my arm gently. At first the contact was startling but then it felt comforting to know I wasn't completely alone.

"It's going to be alright Olivia." He sounded so confident. I wished I could be so sure. He eased the hand that was grasping my phone open. I hadn't realized how tightly I'd been gripping it. He took it from me and set it on the coffee table. We both looked at the small object in my other hand. He slid a newspaper over in front of me and I placed it on that.

"Have you told anyone else yet?" I shook my head. "Do you want to tell me what's going on in that head of yours?" I shook my head again. He let out a deep breath and stood up. I heard him go into the kitchen and open a few cupboards and run water for a second, but I just sat there, unmoving, beginning to question the rationality of my showing up at his door.

Minutes passed, and I remained on his couch in silence while my thoughts and emotions collided in a perfect storm. Wave after wave of uncertainty and fear crashed over me, threatening to pull me under. I didn't think my life could take anymore upheaval, but it was out of my control. Just when I'd thought I was coming to terms with what my life would be, everything changed again.

"Here, drink this." Casey returned and handed me what looked like a cup of tea. I inhaled. Peppermint chamomile. It was hot, but soothing as I took the first sip.

"Thank you," I breathed. "I don't even know what I'm doing here, but thank you."

"Do you want to call Melodie or anyone?"

I shook my head. "I tried before, but she didn't answer, and now I'm not sure if I'm ready for her or anyone else to know anyway." I hadn't even said it out loud. Who would I tell first? Mel? My parents? Ellie? I didn't know what anyone's reaction would be; I was still working through my own.

"Tate–" Before he could finish his phone started playing an Ashes and Embers song I loved. Ty and I saw them when they came to Texas on their first tour last year, before they'd blown up and become one of the biggest names in music. Casey looked at me apologetically. "Sorry, just a second."

He pulled it from his pocket and answered. "Hey." I couldn't tell who he was talking to or what they were saying. "No, I'm still at home." It sounded like whoever it was expected him to be somewhere else. "No, look I'm really sorry babe but something came up. I can't make it tonight." I was screwing up his plans. He had more important things to do than make me tea and sit here with me when I should just call Mel. I stood to leave feeling like an idiot. "Wait, don't go." He reached out to stop me. "No, I wasn't talking to you, I'm sorry Annie, I've gotta go. I'll call you later." He hung up the phone and set it back on the table.

"I shouldn't have come over here. I'm sorry I barged in on your evening. I can go back to my place. I don't know why I came to you, this isn't your problem," I apologized.

"I don't want you to go. I'm glad you came over. You shouldn't be by yourself right now." I didn't want to be myself, but I could call Mel

37

and she would come and Casey could keep his plans with his girlfriend. I wasn't even aware that he had a girlfriend. As far as I knew, no one on the team was. Though, the rest of the girls had been trying to find out for a year.

"I'll call Mel," I told him.

"If that's what you want, then you should call her, but you came over here for a reason." I just didn't know what that reason was at the moment. "You can talk to me or you can just hang out here. If you're hungry I can make you something to eat, whatever you want." He looked at me, waiting for me to decide.

"I'm not sure what I want," I whispered honestly.

"I think you came over here because there was no risk in telling me. Sometimes it's safer to tell our secrets to people we barely know. I'm not your mom or your best friend. I won't freak out or ask you a million questions or expect anything from you. I already suspected you might be. You can trust me to listen or just sit here with you if that's what you need. We're on the same team and I just want to help you." I could see the sincerity in his eyes, he really meant it, but his words only served to remind me of the reality of my situation.

"Except we're not on the same team anymore, are we? I'm done. I won't be able to set foot on that field again." The truth stared back at me. I could see it in his eyes. He knew I was right.

"So you've decided what you're going to do?" There never really was a decision to make. I would never have an abortion, and as unready as I was to be a mom, I couldn't give away a part of Ty; something we made in an act of love. No, the only thing I was sure of in all of this was that I was keeping our baby.

"I'm going to be a mom." There, I said it. I took a deep breath as panic threatened to rise again.

You can do this Liv. You've got to. For Ty and for your baby.

I felt the frenzy ease, and calm assurance take its place. I could do this. I would do this. Because like I said, no matter how terrified I felt, there really was only one choice for me. In that moment another part of

38

me died, my dreams of playing soccer professionally died, but a new one came alive in me.

I'm going to be a mom.

I let it soak in.

Six

"All changes, even the most longed for, have their melancholy; for what we leave behind us is a part of ourselves; we must die to one life before we can enter another."
— Anatole France

"This doesn't have to be it for you. You could stay on the team in a coaching capacity, help with training." I'm not sure how much time had passed, with the two of us just sitting there in silence, but Casey was still next to me on his couch, leaning forward with his elbows resting on his knees and head cocked toward me. His features were soft as he tried to reassure me. "You're still a team captain and I know it's not how you imagined the season going, but the rest of the girls still need a leader and you were chosen for that position."

The team was everything to me, all I had left, or at least all I thought I had left, but something, or someone else, had to matter more. I couldn't put me first; it couldn't just be about what I wanted anymore.

"I don't think so. I had to move here because I couldn't afford my other apartment anymore. I've been stressing for weeks because I need to find a part time job, now," I sighed, "now a part time job probably won't cut it. It would have been hard enough to balance school, the team and just a few hours of work a week. I have to give something up, and the only thing that can go is the team." He nodded and something about the look in his eyes told me he really understood what it meant for me to let that go, to give up the one thing that up until a few hours ago was the most important to me. Everything changed the second I saw that positive result.

"I'm really sorry Olivia. I know this has to be hard for you. No matter what though, you're still a part of the team, and you can still come to me for anything. I'm not an expert on pregnancy, but I still want to help you any way I can, even if you just need someone to talk to."

"Why?" It didn't make sense to me that he was willing to go out of his way for me when we hardly knew each other and he no longer had any work obligation to my well being. He seemed a little taken aback by my question though. "I don't mean to sound unappreciative, it's just that you don't have to do any of this for me. You don't even know me." I thought I saw something like guilt or maybe remorse flash in his eyes, but then he looked away briefly and when he faced me again, it was gone.

"You're right that I don't have to help you, but I want to because I do know what it's like to have to give up a dream." I probably knew even less about Casey than he knew about me, but I knew that he was telling me the truth. I could see it on his face and hear it in his voice. He'd been where I was, obviously not in the same way, but something told me he was the only person I knew who really could understand. I didn't feel comfortable enough to ask him about his past, but I wasn't ready to go back to my own apartment yet.

"Thank you. It really means a lot to me. I don't know how I'll do this without him," I choked out the last part and wiped away the tear that escaped. I used to long for the day that I would have Ty's baby inside of me, I just never thought it would be like this.

"You will. I know that you're smart and strong." He briefly put his hand on my forearm and gave it a reassuring squeeze. "I have no doubt that you'll do great."

"I don't know the first thing about being pregnant or having a baby," I snorted. I had to be almost seven weeks along, and clearly I hadn't been taking care of myself, who knows if I'd already screwed up and hurt my baby.

God, please don't let me have failed my baby already.

"Okay, then let's find out." He hopped up and I looked at him confused.

"What do you mean?"

"You said you don't know about being pregnant so we can look it up." He stood and walked over to the island counter in his kitchen. A laptop was opened up. He pulled a stool out and sat down in front of the screen. He looked back at me. "Come on." He slid out another stool.

"You don't have to. I can go home and research myself. I've taken up enough of your night."

"I thought we already established that I'm not doing this because I have to. If you don't want to do this here with me I understand, but don't leave because you think you're inconveniencing me. You're not," he insisted. I reached forward and checked my phone. Mel still hadn't returned my call and it would be nice to have someone to do this with. Besides he was basically a medical professional. Sort of.

"Okay." I slid onto the stool next to him and he gave me a playful smile while he pulled up an internet search. Wow. There were a lot of sites out there with information for pregnant women. "Where do we start?"

"Ummm . . . how about this one?" He clicked and it brought up a website devoted to expecting mothers. There were links to pages on everything from nutrition to the actual birthing process. I wasn't ready to go there yet.

"There, first trimester. Let's start there." He clicked where I indicated. Ten minutes later I felt like my brain was overwhelmed with all the information; what I should and shouldn't eat, how much weight I should expect to gain, what exorcises and activities were safe and which weren't and all of the symptoms that were typical in the early stages of pregnancy.

I peeked at Casey's face. He looked like he was in pain and I had to stifle a giggle. I bet he was regretting offering his help now. He'd fidgeted a little when we went through the fitness and activity section and read about kegals, but when we got to the bottom of that page where it listed safe sexual practices during pregnancy, his face turned ten shades of red. He couldn't even look me in the eye while he tried to ask if I wanted to read through that information. I just reached forward and clicked on to the next page. I really didn't need that information. If it wasn't such a harsh reminder of who should have been sitting next to me looking all this up, I would have laughed at Casey's reaction.

He'd been silent ever since, letting me take over navigating through the pages while he sat there uncomfortably. It was probably a good thing I hadn't wanted to read up on the birthing process yet. I think he was pretty thoroughly embarrassed; I should probably put him out of his misery. I just wanted to look at one more heading titled *Fetal Development Week By Week*. It had growth charts, pictures, diagrams and videos. I clicked the six week mark.

Is that what my baby looks like?

My hand went to my belly and rested there. The picture showed the inside of a womb, the fetus resembled a kidney bean shaped blob. *Wow.* It said the heart was already beating at this point. My baby had a heartbeat. Yesterday I didn't even know I was carrying another life, and then, like it happened overnight, I'm finding out that there's another heart pounding away inside of me.

"Wow. It's so tiny," Casey finally spoke. It really was. An amazing, miraculous, tiny life and it was my job to take care of it, protect it and love it.

"I think that's enough for tonight." I could tell he tried to hide his relief, but it was obvious. "I'm sorry I put you through that," I chuckled. "At least you'll be prepared someday. You'll wow your girlfriend or wife with your pregnancy expertise." I was trying to lighten the mood, make things less awkward. It earned me a half-smile and an almost laugh that made me curious.

"Do you want to have kids?" Maybe it was slightly personal but after an hour of pouring over the intimate details of a pregnancy together, I didn't feel quite so awkward asking him.

"Yeah. When I find the right person, I do."

"Is Annie the right person?" That was definitely personal and so not my business, but I was curious about the guy who blushed like a schoolgirl at pregnancy sex, but hadn't bolted and left me to search the web on my own. Casey had always seemed a little mysterious; he was a part of the team but kept to himself. At times he had come off as arrogant and unfriendly, but the glimpses I'd seen of him in the last week led me to believe I may have been off in my presumptions.

"Er . . ." He raked his fingers through his hair and shifted on his seat. "I'm not sure. Maybe. We've been together for almost a year and she wants to talk about moving in together but I just don't know," he sighed. "Is it alright if I ask you something?"

"Sure," I replied hesitantly.

"How long were you and Tyler together?" I smiled at his question, even though it sent a sharp pang of loss through my heart.

"Our moms were high school friends and we grew up just down the street from each other, but we really couldn't stand each other when we were younger. He was only one year older, but he acted like that made him so much superior. I couldn't stand that he always thought he was better and smarter, and treated me like a silly little girl most of the time. At ten I realized I was in love with him, but he was a little slow on the pickup. He didn't figure it out until my freshman year of high school." I laughed thinking about when Ty finally asked me out, not that he really asked.

"Another boy asked me to homecoming; I didn't want to go with him but Ty had already asked someone else, a girl from his class. At school he barely gave me – a lowly freshman – the time of day. I didn't want to miss the dance, so I said yes to Jeff. That night I was so jealous of the girl Ty was with, that I let my date lead me out into an empty hallway. He was nice, but he was also a teenage boy. He tried to grope me and shove his tongue in my mouth. He wasn't being aggressive just overly enthusiastic, but Ty caught us and punched him in the face. While Jeff was in the bathroom cleaning up the blood from his nose, Ty told me that nobody was allowed to kiss me but him, and he finally gave me the kiss I'd been waiting forever for. We were together from that moment on. When he graduated he kept his job at a local garage in Abilene while he waited for me to finish high school, and then he packed up and followed me here and we got married after I completed my freshman year."

44

"That's really amazing, what you two had. I know you don't need me to tell you that though." I'd made it through the story without tears, but they weren't far off, they never were. It wouldn't take much to bring them to the surface so I forced a smile and just nodded. A few minutes of silence passed, not uncomfortably, before I spoke again.

"I remember one day after I realized I was in love with him, most of that day he'd been a real pain in my ass, teasin' me and just being a typical boy, but at the end of that day something just clicked in me and I knew he was the only boy I wanted to fight with for the rest of my life. When he went home, I looked my mama in the eye, dead serious and told her that I was gonna marry that boy and love him forever. I could tell she was amused and didn't take me seriously at ten years old. She just chuckled and told me that forever was a long time, before leaving me in kitchen to stare out the window, watching him walk down the street. I'd wanted to argue with her, tell her how wrong she was because I couldn't imagine that forever would ever be long enough with Ty, but now that he's gone, I finally get it, because forever without him . . ." I couldn't even finish because it was too hard to imagine, let alone speak out loud.

It was the first time I had been able to talk about Ty without breaking down in tears. The pain still felt as fresh as it had that first week, but now there was also the tiniest glimmer of hope and peace that came from knowing I had a part of him growing inside of me, proof of our love that would stay with me even though he was gone. Someday I would get to tell our child these stories, about the incredible man that he was. I think Casey sensed how close I was to the edge and he didn't push the subject any further or ask anymore about Ty.

"Are you hungry? I can make us something to eat," he offered. I glanced over at the clock on his computer, it was after six. I was hungry, and determined to make sure my baby was getting nutrients, but having dinner with Casey would just be too awkward, even though he really did put me at ease and his offer was merely a friendly one.

"Thanks, but I think I should probably just go. I have to call people eventually and after reading all that, I have a mental list about a hundred things long that I need to write down before I forget everything."

"That's probably best." He smiled and shook his head. "I don't know what I would have made you if you had accepted anyway. I think I have some chicken in the freezer and Oreos in the cupboard. I need to go grocery shopping." That was another thing I needed to add to my to-do list. "At least tell me you have something better than that waiting for you at your place?"

I cringed. "Frozen pizza and yogurt," I admitted abashedly. He chuckled and I sighed. "Yeah I need to go grocery shopping too."

"Then it's settled, go grab what you need and we'll go to the store. I'll drive and you can start working on that list." I tugged my bottom lip between my teeth and reluctantly considered going with him. "Don't think about it so hard. We both need to go to the store and might as well ride together, so just say 'okay Casey'."

"Okay Casey," I echoed sarcastically, and rolled my eyes. He smirked and grabbed his keys, then ushered me out the door. I popped into my apartment quickly to grab my purse and a notepad before following him out of the building. I realized I'd never really paid attention to what kind of car Casey drove, but when he led me to the old Mustang, I wondered how I'd ever missed it.

"That's a beautiful car," I told him. Being with Ty had given me an appreciation for vintage cars. The black Shelby GTO before me was definitely a classic.

"Thanks," he responded as we climbed in.

While he drove I started making my list: *eggs, nuts, fruits and veggies, chicken breasts, prenatal vitamins* . . . The longer my list got the more worried I became. Eating right wasn't going to be cheap. It was definitely going to cost more than the fifty dollars I'd allotted myself for groceries to last the rest of this month. My phone ringing interrupted my worried thoughts. Mel was finally returning my call.

"Hey," I answered, deciding that I wouldn't tell her over the phone.

"Hey. Sorry I didn't answer when you called. A few of us went to the lake after practice with some of the guys on the football team." Last

46

summer we were at the lake every chance we got. I hadn't been once this summer. I was glad she went though.

"It's alright. Did you guys have a good time?"

Her concern was evident.

"I'm fine, I just . . . there's something I need to tell you. Can we meet up in the morning before you go to practice?"

"Won't you be at practice too? Why can't you tell me there?"

"Can we please just meet tomorrow, and I'll tell you everything then?" I pleaded.

"No. I'm coming over now." I knew there would be no talking her out of it. She was almost as stubborn as I was once she made up her mind.

"You don't have to, it can wait until tomorrow," I tried to persuade her.

"Too bad I'm already on my way." I doubted she really was, but knew she would be soon.

"You can't right now. I'm at the grocery store," I told her as Casey pulled in to the parking lot. "Give me an hour."

Seven

"Sometimes God calms the storm, but sometimes God lets the storm rage and calms His child." —Leslie Gould

I started emptying bags and shoving groceries in the fridge and cupboards, ignoring the prying eyes staring at me from the stool where Mel was perched. I knew I had about two minutes, if I was lucky, before she started bombarding me with questions. She'd pulled up at the apartment complex about five seconds after Casey and I returned. Her face scrunched up in confusion when she watched me climb out of his car. I didn't know what she would grill me about first, but even without looking I could feel her eyes boring into me. Her curiosity had a palpable presence in the room and I didn't even have to wait two minutes.

"So you live in the same building as Hunt, and you two go grocery shopping together?" Her voice was hesitant, but it was obvious she was working up to something. I placed the last few items in the freezer before turning to face her. She didn't need me to answer her question. It was more of an observation anyway, since she'd clearly seen us pulling grocery sacks out of his car and then watched him enter the apartment down the hall after a brief and somewhat awkward goodbye, during which Mel shot daggers at him with her eyes. Now she was struggling to string together words and I knew she must be uncomfortable. She wasn't one to hold back her opinion, ever.

"Look, Liv, I know you've been through hell and you're still grieving, but I don't think you're making the best choices. This isn't healthy and I don't want you to regret it later once it's too late for you to take it back." It hurt just a little that she was jumping to conclusions about Casey, that she actually thought there could be anything going on, but I let her off the hook, because I knew she was trying to be a good friend.

"I'm pregnant, Mel," I said, wanting to just get it over with and put her Casey assumptions to rest. Of course I didn't expect her to jump to more wrong conclusions. Her eyebrows shot up and she jumped out of her seat, a look of rage taking over her pretty face. I didn't quite understand her reaction at first.

"That bastard," she muttered under her breath. "I'm gonna kill him. I thought he was just being concerned, a nice guy. Sonuva bitch. I didn't know he was gonna try to take advantage of you in your state. I'm fixin' to go over there right now and give him a piece of mind," she continued ranting all the way to the door before I finally figured out what set her off. She thought Casey was the father. She thought he and I were . . . I would have laughed, except that the idea of me with anyone else was more heartbreaking than funny.

"I'm more than six weeks along Mel. It's not Casey's," I said softly. She froze in her tracks, hand on the door knob. "Casey's just been a good neighbor and sort of a friend the last few days."

"Oh Liv," she whispered and turned to face me, her expression pained. Seeing it, I felt all the familiar sorrow rise up. My chest tightened and I looked down at the floor rather than see my agony mirrored in her eyes. Before I knew it, she was in front of me, yanking me into her arms and I was clinging to her and my last ounce of control, which was slipping.

She didn't say anything and I didn't need her to. She squeezed me tightly while I tried to blink away the moisture pooling in my eyes. I took a few deep breaths and then pulled away, wiping the few tears that escaped with the back of my hand. I walked over and sat down on the couch. She followed and sat down next to me.

"I'm so sorry Liv. I'm an idiot. I just thought . . . I mean, I shouldn't have assumed, but I just . . . lately at practice you two have seemed closer, and then grocery shopping. I'm sorry."

"It's okay. He was just trying to help, but don't worry, I doubt we'll be grocery shopping together again. It was hard to be there with him, doing something so ordinary that Ty and I did together. It was another reminder that I won't have him to fight with when I want to buy three packages of Oreos. He won't be there to try and convince me that his protein, granola crap is better. I never thought I would miss that, but I do. So much. I'd eat that cardboard stuff every day for the rest of my life if I could just hear his voice or see his smile even one more time," I swore, but it wouldn't do me any good. I'd already tried begging, pleading and bargaining with God.

"Every day it's the little things like that. I wake up wondering how I'll get through another day. How I'll survive living with this gaping hole inside me, and now that I'm gonna have our baby, I'm so scared. I need him. I need him so bad. I don't want to do this without him."

"I know babe, but you have to. You have to be strong for you and for Ty and most of all for your baby. You will do this, but you won't be alone. You've got me and your parents and Ellie and so many people who love you and even though Ty's not here, he's still with you." She gripped my hand in hers offering the comfort and reassurance I desperately needed.

"I wish I could believe that, but I don't feel him. I just feel empty," I confessed somberly.

"Come on babe, do you really think there's any way he would leave you alone? He loved you more than I've ever seen anyone love another person. You two had the kind of love that keeps Disney in business. It's the reason Taylor Swift writes songs and the reason I keep downloading those damn romance novels. Everyone wants that fairytale and you had it. That's not the kind of love that ever ends. He's watching over you. I know it because I know there's no power, not even death, which could stop that kind of love."

"You said it yourself Mel, I had it, but it's gone now, and even if he's watching over me, he's still gone and my baby will never know him."

"That's not true. Your baby will know Tyler because, gone or not, he's a part of you, and you'll share that with your baby. You will love your baby enough for the both of you, and then I will be there to love my little niece or nephew some more." She was right, my baby might not have a father but he or she would never want for love. I would make sure of that. My hand went to my stomach and I imagined the little heartbeat thudding away inside of there as my little one was stitched together and formed.

"You're right," I released a deep breath. "Now if only I could find a job, then I might actually believe I can do this," I told her.

"If you need money-"

I stopped her right there. "No, Mel."

"But I have it, more than I need and I'd happily help you out," she argued.

"I know you would, but I can't let you," I insisted. She rolled her eyes but didn't push.

"Fine, but you can't stop me from spoiling that baby all I want."

I smiled. I was lucky to have her and my baby was too. "You're going to be an amazing aunt."

"You're going to be an amazing mom."

I hope so. God please help me take care of my baby, I prayed. I knew I couldn't do this on my own strength.

"So, I know there's nothing going on with Casey, it was stupid of me to think there was, but did you know he lived here when you moved in? Have you guys been spending a lot of time together?"

"I ran into him in the stairwell when I was moving the last of my stuff I, and no, we haven't been spending a lot of time together. He's just checked up on me a few times, and he was actually the one who figured out I was pregnant at practice today," I explained.

"He did?"

"Yeah, he wasn't convinced my symptoms were from depression and asked if there was any way I could be pregnant. He suggested, well pretty much refused to let me play until I took a test to be sure. I sort of freaked out after I did. I called you and when you didn't answer, I ended up knocking on his door." I didn't know how to explain why I had, why I trusted him. Maybe it was the way he had refused to coddle me on the field and he told me the truth when I needed to hear it even if

51

I didn't want to. He was the only person in the last month to yell at me and tell me I was being reckless and get me to see reason.

It used to be Ty who did that. He loved my crazy, but he wasn't afraid to call me on it when I pushed it too far. Even when he was right, it usually only spurred me on and brought out my stubborn streak. I'd push and his patience never ceased to amaze me. He always tempered the fire in me. I hadn't felt that fire in a long time. I'd thought it had gone out until the other day outside when Casey challenged me and threatened to have me yanked off the field. I knew Casey wasn't Tyler; I didn't want him to be. It just felt good to be me again for a few minutes. To fight. To remember that I was a fighter.

"Then I guess it's a good thing for him. Who knows how long you would have gone on before figuring it out."

"Yeah, he's been surprisingly helpful, even tonight, helping me to deal after I found out. Although I'm pretty sure I freaked him out. I was a little bit crazy, but he let me in and listened to me. He even made me tea and helped me look up pregnancy information." Now that I thought about it, I really owed him, and not just for today.

"He's always seemed like good guy," she remarked and then grinned. "And he's hot as hell." Clearly Mel wasn't immune to all that was Casey Hunt. "I think most of the girls on the team would kill to be in your position, living just down the hall from him." She was probably right, but I wasn't one of those girls. Someone had died though, and Mel realized what she'd said.

"Shoot! I'm so sorry, that sounded really insensitive." Her face scrunched up with worry, like she was afraid of my reaction. I hated that she had to walk on eggshells around me. "I wasn't thinking. You know I have a problem with that." I did, and it was one of the things I loved about her. She was always unfiltered.

"It's okay. Really. I can't get upset over every little thing someone says. I know you didn't mean anything by it, so no need to apologize," I assured her.

"Okay, but seriously, you might want to keep it on the down low that you live in the same building as him. Once the team finds out, they'll start inviting themselves over all the time."

"He has a girlfriend," I pointed out.

"That's disappointing." I raised my eyebrows. "I meant for the rest of the girls, they'll be disappointed when they find out."

"Uh huh, sure," I teased. "Do I need to worry about you inviting yourself over all the time now?"

"Please bitch, I come over when I want regardless of the hottie down the hall." We both laughed. "Besides, you know I don't go after taken guys."

That was true. She could be too guy crazy for her own good sometimes, but she had boundaries. Unlike some of the other girls. I got along well with most of my teammates, but a few of them were pretty shameless and didn't care one way or the other if a guy they wanted was in a relationship. My freshman year, before Casey started working for the school, Jamie Parker, one of our defenders, actually had the nerve to flirt with Tyler after one of our games. At the next practice my foot slipped on the ball and it accidentally hit her in the face and busted her nose. She didn't flirt with Tyler again, but she still went after other girls' boyfriends.

She was one of the ones who'd had her eye on Casey from the beginning. No matter how much they flirted with him though, he always pretended not to notice. He got bonus points in my book for that. It pissed Jamie off to no end that he showed zero interest in her and that gave me immense pleasure.

"I can't believe you're not going to be out there on the field with me. I don't know what we're going to do without you. When will you tell coach?" Mel changed the subject back to my predicament.

"I'm still having a hard time accepting that I won't be able to play anymore. I don't want to give it up, but it stopped being all about me when I peed on that stick." *Oh no. The stick.* "Shoot."

"What?"

"I left my pee stick sitting on Hunt's coffee table," I cringed.

"Seriously?" she tried not to laugh.

"It's not funny. It's bad enough that I knocked on his door earlier and practically waved the thing his face. Should I go back over there and get it?" I couldn't believe I left it sitting there.

"Honestly, I think you should leave it for him to deal with." She was still trying to contain her amusement. She was failing.

"Stop it. It's just a pregnancy test. It's not like I left a tampon or a vibrator sitting there." Although I had to admit, it would probably make Casey feel just as awkward when he noticed it, if he hadn't already.

Mel hung out and helped me cook dinner and we chatted about random things, mostly the football player she had her eye on. She didn't bring up Ty or the baby again. That was one of the things I had come to appreciate the most about Mel over the last month, she was able to read me well and know when I'd had all I could take, when I was at my limit.

Today I had been pushed past my limits with so many conflicting emotions, grief, joy, hope, fear. It was all too much, and when I was finally alone in my apartment again, it was so overwhelming I felt like I was going to collapse.

"God, please give me strength. Give me strength to love this baby, to be a mother. I don't know how to face this. I don't know if my heart can handle it. I'm so scared of letting my baby down, of letting Ty down."

I'd never really considered my faith much before, and by that I meant I went to church as a girl, and Ty and I had tried to make it on the occasional Sunday when he wasn't working or I wasn't buried in homework, practices and games. To me faith was just a word, something I thought I had, but I'd never really been tested until now. Now I understood that having faith meant trusting God and still believing even when I'd lost all reason to. And I didn't know if I could.

Eight

"If God sends us on stony paths, He provides strong shoes."
— *Corrie Ten Boom*

My nose was in my phone, replying to a text from Mel when I heard the door behind me open. Casey was stepping out of his apartment dressed in shorts and a Red Raiders tee, his usual practice attire.

"Hey," he called when he saw me and I stopped in the hall to let him catch up. "How are you feeling today?"

"Better. Mel helped me to process some more. Don't know what I would have done if it weren't for the two of you being there yesterday, so thank you, especially since I know it had to be a little awkward for you." I remembered the pregnancy test. "And I'm sorry for, uh, leaving my pregnancy test sitting on your coffee table."

"Oh," he blushed, "yeah, don't' worry about it. I just, uh stuck it in the bathroom. I didn't know what to do with it, if uh, I should throw it away or if you wanted it, but I'm glad I could help yesterday, even though I don't really feel like I did anything."

"No, you really did," I felt myself blushing a little and I didn't know why I felt embarrassed. "And you can just toss it. I mean, I peed on it so it wasn't like I was planning to keep it. Sorry again, for leaving it and barging in on you yesterday with my craziness.

"It's okay. Really not a big deal at all," he tried to reassure me, but I was still embarrassed.

"Are you going to talk to coach today?"

"Yeah. I need to get it out of the way."

"You want a ride then?" he offered casually.

"Casey, I'm pregnant, not crippled. I can still drive for a while longer I think; besides I actually have to run a few other errands afterward, so I won't be staying long." It wasn't entirely true, but I didn't want to stay for the whole practice. There was no point; it wouldn't do me any good to watch something I couldn't be a part of anymore. Besides, I needed to seriously start my job search, like yesterday."

We both bypassed the elevator and headed for the stairwell.

"You have a problem with elevators too?" I asked him.

"Nah. I just take the stairs for the exercise," he said and held the stairwell door open for me. "Wait, are you afraid of elevators?" he grinned.

"Psh. No, of course not. I want the exercise too," I lied, but not very well. He chuckled and shook his head.

"You are afraid of elevators," he teased.

"Okay, yeah I am, but have you ever seen a horror movie in which someone didn't die in an elevator?" I retorted.

"Yeah, actually lots of them," he shot back playfully as we continued our way down three flights of stairs.

"Well whatever, when I was trapped in an elevator for almost an hour, all I could think about were the ones I'd seen where some poor sucker met an untimely death in one. I've avoided them at all costs since then." He laughed again.

"It's not funny," I glanced over my shoulder and glared at him. "It was a traumatic experience."

"I'm sure it was. I'm sorry I laughed." He didn't sound all that sorry considering he was still biting back laughter.

"I can tell." I narrowed my eyes and he only continued to smile at me, clearly enjoying himself. "So now that you know one of my biggest fears, it's only fair that you tell me one of yours," I insisted as we reached the bottom of the stairs.

He wore a serious expression and didn't respond at first. We kept moving until we pushed through the doors to the building and stepped out into the morning sun. I wasn't letting him off the hook though.

"Come on Hunt, what are you afraid of?" I taunted him.

"Zombies. I'm afraid of being attacked by zombies." He grinned and I rolled my eyes.

56

"That's a ridiculous answer, you can't be afraid of something that doesn't exist."

"Your fear of elevators is ridiculous," he shot back.

"Did you know that approximately thirty people die in elevator accidents each year, and something like twenty people are injured in elevator related accidents every day. So who's the ridiculous one now?" I countered smugly.

"Still you," he answered and walked over to his car. Before he got in he turned back. "You know how many people will die in a year if the zombie apocalypse does happen?" He didn't wait for me to respond. "A lot more than thirty." I shook my head as he got in his car. I walked over to my own and slid into the driver's seat.

I pulled out of the parking lot right behind him and my nerves sky rocketed. All playfulness and humor were gone. I wasn't looking forward to telling coach. I felt like I was letting him and my teammates down. I also wasn't sure what their reactions would be. I didn't want any more pity. I hoped they wouldn't be too disappointed, or judge me for getting pregnant. Would they look and me and think there was no way I was ready to be a single mom? I kind of wouldn't blame them when I was trying so hard not to think that way. Would any of them wonder if I'd jumped into bed with someone after Ty like Mel had?

Just the idea of anyone thinking that had my blood boiling, but if there's two things people in Texas take seriously, it's football – not the kind I prefer – and gossip. Don't matter if it's true, people like to talk and news travels faster than a prairie fire with a tail wind. I'd have to call Mama and Ellie right away before they heard it from someone else. There were enough kids from my high school here at the university that all it would take was one of them making a phone call or sending a text to someone back in Abilene. Mama would have an absolute conniption if the whole town knew before she did.

I also expected that she would use this announcement to try and convince me to move in with her and Dad again. Convincing them I could do this on my own would be harder than convincing myself. I knew the baby would be happy news for all of them though, especially

Ellie. She wasn't quiet about wanting grandbabies, and having this part of Ty would mean just as much to her as it did me. Maybe tomorrow I would just drive down there and go see her. Telling her in person would be best and then I could call Mama.

Once we reached the school, I pulled my car into the space next to Casey's and took a deep breath. He climbed out and stood there, obviously waiting for me. I couldn't put it off any longer. Coach needed to know so he could move someone into my position, although my guess was that he'd been preparing for that possibility since the first practice when I played so horribly.

I forced myself out of the car, and the two of us walked in silence over to the field. Most of my teammates, or former teammates now, were already warming up. Mel was out on the field and when she saw me walking up she shot me a reassuring smile. Coach Davis and Coach Walsh were both standing on the side discussing something, but they paused when I approached. I was glad that Casey stayed at my side, his presence was oddly comforting.

"Hey Tate, how are you feeling?" Walsh asked. He and Coach Davis both looked concerned.

"I'm okay." I dropped my gaze, afraid to say the next part. I hated letting people down, I hated that I had to walk away from the team, and I hated people feeling sorry for me, but there was no way around this.

"Not practicing today though?" I looked up and saw Coach Davis' brow wrinkled in confusion like he knew there was something else coming.

"No. I actually need to talk to you about that. I, er, won't be practicing anymore. I need to leave the team." There, it was final. Both of their faces registered surprise.

"Tate, I understand yer goin' through a real tough time, something nobody as young as you should ever have to experience. You have to do what's best for you, but we can hold a spot on the team. You can come to practices when you feel up to it, travel with the team, that way if you decide at some point that you want play again, you'll still be a part of this team."

His offer was generous and not one he would make for any other player, but I knew he didn't want to lose me. He also knew how much this dream meant to me and probably expected I would regret it down the road if I just walked away.

"Coach, this isn't because of . . ." My voice was shaky and weak. I sighed and tried to find the words. "I'm not leaving the team because Tyler's gone. I have to leave because I'm pregnant." Once again both of their faces looked shocked, then grim as they realized I would in no way be coming back to the team. Finally came the sympathy eyes.

"Tate, I'm so sorry for everything you've been through. No matter what, yer still a part of this team and are welcome to join us in any capacity that you want. Even if you can't be out on that field, the girls could really use you here, helping to coach and you can still travel with us, whatever you want." I appreciated that he was trying to find a way for me to stay a part of the team. I wished I could accept, but I couldn't.

"I would really like to, but things are kinda tight for me right now already. I really need to find a job before I have to worry about other expenses as well," I explained, trying not to make too big of a deal out of it. I didn't want to give anyone more reason to think I couldn't handle this.

"Well, I might be able to do somethin' about that; it wouldn't be a lot, but I'm permitted to bring on another assistant, and the school allows for student interns. It's only a part time gig and the pay wouldn't be great, but-"

"I'll do it." I didn't even stop to think about it, even if I should have given it more thought.

"Okay then. We'll just move ya around where we need ya, but Hunt here has been whinin' for an assistant since last season, so I'll probably stick ya with him."

"Umm, I'm not really qualified to be an athletic trainer." I'm pretty sure they had to have a master's and I had only just declared a major at the end of last semester because the school forced me to pick one.

"Darlin', if this Yankee boy could figure it out, it can't be all that hard." Davis smirked at Casey. "Besides, you've been an athlete yer whole life; I'd say yer pretty familiar with sports medicine. He can train ya and tell you anythin' else ya need to know."

"Okay." It was a job, and I didn't have to completely give up the team. I'd do whatever Coach asked. "Thank you so much, Coach."

"No problem sweetheart. Now, I'll need ya to fill out some paperwork and there's a code of conduct manual and some other stuff you need to read to make it official."

"Oh, I have somewhere I need to be, can I do it tomorrow?" I asked, thinking it would be better to make the trip to Abilene today, so that I could hopefully start working tomorrow. "There are still a few people I need to tell."

"If you need to go, I can get the paperwork and bring it to you tonight," Casey offered and Coach gave him an odd look. "Tate just moved into my apartment building," he explained.

"That would be great. I need to drive down to Abilene, but I'll be back tonight and I can be here for practice in the morning."

I was probably the most excited I'd been since learning I was pregnant. The news had been shadowed by the worry of how I would support myself and my little one. Now, I not only had a way to start doing that, but it would keep me close to my team and the sport I loved. I could finally let go of some of the stress and just be thankful for the little miracle inside of me. More than ever, I just wanted to go see Ellie and tell her.

Coach agreed and I turned to head back to my car, but stopped and faced the three of them again. "I would really appreciate it if I could be the one to tell the rest of the team. I don't want to hide it, but I'm just not ready for the whole world to know yet."

"Of course." Coach Davis and Coach Walsh both nodded and I thanked them again and flashed Casey a small smile before leaving.

Nine

I pulled up to Ellie's just after two. She ran an in home day care, and when I knocked on the door I could hear several small voices chattering in the background. Beth answered with a polite smile that grew bigger when she saw it was me. She wrapped her arms around my waist and pulled me inside. I squeezed her back and let her tug me farther into the house.

"Mama, Livvie is here." My chest tightened for a brief moment hearing her use Ty's nickname for me. Then Ellie stepped into sight with a big grin and the warmth in her eyes made me forget all about it. She stood in front of me, taking in my appearance.

Her face scrunched up. "Child, yer thin as a rake. If ya get any skinnier, you'll be able to shade yourself under the clothesline," she admonished me. "Git' your scrawny butt in the kitchen n' lemme fix you somethin' to eat."

I tried telling her she didn't need to fuss over me, but she wouldn't hear it.

"Beth can you go check on those Turner boys and make sure they aren't picking on the girls again, and you," she turned back to me, "I don't want to hear 'nuther word until you've had somethin' to eat." She sat me down at the kitchen table and went about fixing me a plate. She set a tall glass of sweet tea in front of me while she slathered a piece of cornbread in butter. She pulled a dish of some casserole from the fridge and started to serve it up, but I stopped her.

"Really the cornbread is fine. I stopped for a smoothie on the way down here and I don't think my stomach could handle much else." She eyed me skeptically and muttered something about how a smoothie wasn't a meal, but she covered the casserole and returned it to the fridge before setting the cornbread in front of me. Ellie made the best cornbread in all of Texas, and everyone knows that Texans make the best cornbread in the world, and I was practically drooling over it when I brought the first bite to my mouth.

"Mmmm," I groaned in delight. I swallowed and then quickly devoured the rest of it. "So good. Thank you."

"Any time sweetheart. I'll wrap the rest up and send it home with you." I knew better than to argue. There would be no stopping her from sending me with the cornbread and whatever else she wrapped up, especially not once she found out about the baby.

She pulled out the chair next to me and slid into it. Her eyes were sad and serious as she looked at me intently. "Now honey, I need you to be honest with me, how're ya really doin? You don't look well. I'm worried 'bout ya, up there all by yourself. Yer not pushin' yourself too hard on that team, are ya?" She sounded so much like my mother.

"That's actually why I came to see you. I'm not on the team anymore. Not playing anyway, and as for being skinny, that's not going to be a problem much longer. I'll be getting real fat over the next seven or eight months." I watched her face, waiting for understanding to sink in. Her confusion only lasted a second, and then her eyes got huge and she gasped.

"Baby girl, are you tellin' me yer pregnant?" I nodded and she sucked in another deep breath and covered her mouth with one hand. Her eyes watered and she struggled to speak. "Yer having Ty's baby?" she choked out. When I nodded again the tears streamed down her cheeks and a smile split her face. She stood and tugged me up into her arms. She was so excited, and then we were both crying. Beth came into the room, six small children in tow, breaking up the moment.

"Mama, they're ready for . . ." She took in the two of us crying and hugging and didn't quite know how to react. "Their snack," she finished. Ellie finally released me and wiped her eyes.

"There's fruit already sliced in the fridge and everyone gets a cookie," Ellie exclaimed.

"Mama, is everything okay?" Beth's eyes bounced back and forth between the two of us.

"Everything is fine. Let's get the kids their snack and then Olivia has some news." Beth still looked a little unsure. "It's good news sweetheart." With that reassurance, she started getting the kids seated around two smaller children's tables.

After they had been served their snack and juice, Ellie led the two of us to the far end of the kitchen so we could share the news with Beth. I met Beth's uneasy stare and smiled at the teenager, who although she looked nothing like her big brother, reminded me so much of him. He'd absolutely adored his sister and I did too.

"Beth," I said softly. "I really hope you enjoy being around kids, because you're gonna be an aunt." Her eyes dropped to my belly then shot back up to my face.

"Really?"

"Yes. I think I'm about seven weeks along," I informed them and then watched some of the light leave their eyes. They could do the math, they knew it had happened just before the accident, and it was another reminder of how long we'd been without him. Beth stepped forward and pulled me into another hug. Ellie joined and I was sandwiched between the two of them. When we pulled apart, they both had tears in their eyes but smiles on their faces. I blinked, trying to clear the wetness from my own eyes. For a change they weren't sad tears, not entirely.

I almost didn't recognize the strange, happy feeling bubbling up inside of me. It wasn't absolute; it couldn't be with Ty missing, but it gave me hope to know that I could still feel happiness, that it wasn't gone forever. It was like Ty had known he was leaving me and that I would need a reason to keep going, to keep breathing, and he gave me one. Gave us all one.

I stayed with Ellie and Beth until the sun was dropping in the sky. Ellie was full of advice and even had several tips for helping me to deal with the nausea that had been plaguing me. She couldn't help but reminisce about her pregnancies and baby Ty. I thought about what an amazing job Ellie had done raising him and Beth on her own.

I didn't know much about Ty's daddy. I hardly remembered him. I just remembered that he split when Ty was seven and it absolutely crushed him. I could still remember Mama bringing me with her to their house after it happened. Mama would sit with Ellie and Ty's Aunt Karen, and tell me to go play with Ty and Beth. Ty was real mean then, like a rabid dog. I hadn't understood at the time, but now I knew his heart had been broken. Even when we were older he didn't like to talk about his father much. I probably should have made him open up about it more. I knew he held so much inside.

I got it though; I knew how hard it was to talk about the painful stuff. I couldn't even imagine the betrayal of having a parent leave me like that, or if Ty had chosen to leave. No matter how it happened, by their choice or not, it always hurt to lose someone. I just couldn't afford to lock it up inside. I had to be able to talk about him, to tell our child about him. Ty would have loved our baby more than anything, and I would make sure he or she knew that, and I would do everything I could to be half as good a mom as Ellie was.

She'd picked up the pieces of her heartbreak and stayed strong for her kids. She started a business at home so she could provide for them and still be there to help with homework and dinner. My parents were great. Like any, they weren't perfect, but they gave me a good life and I was thankful for them and their strong marriage, but there was something about Ellie. I couldn't help but admire her more than anyone. Maybe it was because now I saw just how hard it was to lose the love of your life, to feel like your heart was ripped from your chest, and have to keep living, to keep going.

She did it with grace and class, never letting anger or bitterness get the best of her. I wondered how she managed, because I knew that anger and bitterness came so much easier. I could feel them on a daily basis, churning in my gut, waiting for me to give in to those emotions. A part of me wanted to be mad at the world, at God, at the lady behind the wheel, even Ty for going on those damn early morning runs. I wanted to be able to blame someone, but the truth was it was nobody's fault. It was just life.

"How did you do it?" I asked her when she walked me outside, carrying two foil wrapped plates loaded with cornbread, and enough other food to feed me for days.

"What baby?" We stopped at my car and I opened the passenger door to set the plates inside.

"How did you do it on your own?"

"I wasn't on my own. I had your parents and the kids' aunt and uncle, and the ladies from church; they were all there for me so much during that time. They helped me to see that just because one part of my life came to an end, didn't mean my life was over. I had two beautiful children who needed their mother to be strong, so I was strong, and when I wasn't I leaned on God for His strength. They needed me to take care of them so I took care of them and God took care of me. It wasn't a choice. I just did it because that's what they needed. It will be the same for you. When that baby is here, you won't have to ask what to do or how to do it, you'll just know and you'll do it because your baby will need you to. It won't be easy, but I have faith that you'll be just fine." I hoped she was right.

"You won't be on your own either. You've got lots of people who love you, and you know I'll be here whenever you need me."

"I know that. I'm just scared that I won't be any good at this without Ty. I'm afraid I won't be able to give our baby everything because I'm only half of me. He took the other half with him."

"That's not true baby girl. You will be an amazing mother. The baby will help heal your heart and I have no doubt that you will love your child with everything. It's not until we have children that we even realize just how much love we have to give."

I thanked her for everything then hugged her goodbye and pressed a kiss to her cheek. She squeezed my hand in hers before releasing it so I could climb into my car.

"Make sure you call yer Mama right away so I can start telling everyone I'm going to be a grandma." She grinned and I promised her I would call my parents as soon as I got home. Then I started up the car and pulled away from my second home.

On the way into town I hadn't paid much attention to the things around me because I was so anxious to see Ellie and share the news, but now everything about being back in Abilene sank in. I hadn't been home since the funeral and it was like a weight pressing down on me. Just about everywhere I looked as I drove through, there was a memory waiting.

I passed Rose Park and was taken back to when I was nine and Ty and his buddies dared me to jump off the top of the slide. I sprained my ankle and Ty practically carried me all the way home, apologizing over and over for daring me to do it. I think maybe even then I'd known I loved him. But the next day he and his friends went swimming and he refused to take me. Said he didn't want to have to babysit a cripple, and he went back to being the bane of my existence for another few years.

65

My chest tightened as I thought about taking a detour to the cemetery to visit him, but I kept driving instead. Ellie and Beth told me that they'd gone to his grave several times in the past few weeks, so maybe it was weird that I didn't want to. It wasn't because I was afraid that it would be too emotional. All it took was getting out of bed to make me emotional. I just didn't feel any connection to that place. I didn't feel anything for that slab of stone that rested above the wooden box that didn't even really hold my husband. He wasn't there, so to me it didn't make sense to seek him out there. Instead, I took a deep breath and told him what I was feeling right there in the car.

"I miss you so much Ty. If it's possible I think I miss you more every day instead of less, especially now. I'm going to have our baby without you and I'm scared to death. I don't know how I'll do it. I know you would've been real excited for the baby, even though we said we weren't ready yet. I still would have been scared, but you would've promised to take care of me and our child. You would've told me everything was gonna be okay, and I would have believed you. I really wish you were here to make me feel okay right now. Everyone else has been telling me that, but I feel like nothing is okay. I'm so lost without you, but I promise I'll try. I'll do this for you and our baby. Love you forever, Ty."

When I got home I called my parents and Mama's reaction was exactly what I had expected; she gushed and squealed for five minutes, and then went back to worrying about me. She did everything she could to convince me to move to Jefferson to be near them. She had a hard time accepting it when I told her I wouldn't, that more than ever I needed to finish school. I explained to her that I had a job and wanted to stay here.

Once she relented, she offered her own pregnancy wisdom until I was sure I would never remember all tips and remedies she and Ellie shared. Promising to call again tomorrow, I finally said goodnight.

Hanging up, I knew I needed to get my rest so I would be ready for my first day of working with the team, but I also needed the paperwork from Casey. I had hoped he would have dropped it off by now since I had been home for over an hour. It was almost ten and I wasn't sure what time he went to bed so I was reluctant to knock on his door, but I really wanted to get everything filled out tonight.

I decided I would just go over there and knock lightly, that way if he was in bed, hopefully I wouldn't wake him. I stepped into my slippers and threw a sweater on over the skimpy tank top I was wearing with my pajamas.

The thing about apartments is they usually have thin walls, but even if they don't, proximity to your neighbors means that if any shouting happens, everyone can usually hear. Man did I hear shouting as I made my way over to Casey's apartment. It was coming from his unit. It sounded like he had a very angry female inside.

I decided to go back to my own apartment and get the papers from him tomorrow, but I was stopped in my tracks only a few feet from his door when it was wrenched open and his angry female stepped out. She saw me and froze. Her expression became even angrier as she glared at me. I saw Casey in the doorway behind her; he gave me a grim smile, but before I could say anything, the girl, who I could only assume was Annie, spoke up.

"Is that her?" She was furious, and whoever 'her' was, I was glad it couldn't be me. I started to back away, but then Casey said something that shocked me.

"Yes, but if you'll just let me explain–" So the 'her' was me, but what did I do?

"I've got all the explanation I need." She stormed past me, spitting out "skank" under her breath on her way by. I stood there, not really sure what had just happened or why it involved me.

"You might as well come in so I can at least give you an explanation. She won't be coming back tonight," Casey sighed. I really wanted that explanation, and my papers, so I stepped inside and let him close the door behind me. He walked over to the sofa and picked up a small stack of papers from the coffee table.

"I assume you were coming to get these?" He held them out to me. I nodded and took them from him, not sure what to say. "I'm really sorry about that. Annie is completely overreacting and won't give me a chance to explain the situation."

"What happened?" I asked. He walked back over to the couch and plopped down, letting out a deep breath. I stayed where I was, a few feet away.

"She found the pregnancy test in the trash in the bathroom and now she thinks I cheated on her."

"Crap."

"That pretty much sums it up."

"I'm really sorry again that I left it. You shouldn't have had to deal with it."

"No, don't be. It's fine; it shouldn't have been a big deal, but she wouldn't listen for even five seconds so I could tell her the truth." I still felt bad. He'd been nothing but nice to me and it just completely screwed up his relationship.

"Geez, everyone sure seems to enjoy jumping to that conclusion," I told him, shaking my head.

"What do you mean?" He looked at me curiously.

"When I first told Mel, she thought you and me . . . Well I guess she saw us together and assumed." I looked away, somewhat embarrassed, not really sure why I shared that. He let out a sharp laugh and ran his hand through his hair.

"That's really messed up."

"Yeah," I agreed. "I'm really sorry I caused problems with your girlfriend. I'll stay away and if you want me to talk to her I will," I offered. It was the least I could do, if she would even listen to me, considering she thought I was a boyfriend stealing slut.

"No, it's okay. She'll calm down and I'll talk to her, but you don't need to worry about it or stay away. We're friends and neighbors, and now co-workers; if you need something don't be afraid to come over here."

Friends. Huh. I guess we sort of were. "Thanks Hunt," I said, smiling faintly.

"Anytime, Tate." He returned the smile and I let myself out, still feeling guilty about Annie. I was almost back to my own apartment when Casey pulled his door open again.

"Hey, do you want a ride to work tomorrow?"

"Oh, ummm . . . sure." It wouldn't hurt to save on the gas.

"Okay, see ya in the morning."

"Night."

Ten

"Hope is the thing with feathers that perches in the soul."
—Emily Dickinson

The day of my first doctor's appointment, I sat in my living room with bills spread across the coffee table, trying to work out a budget while I waited for Mel to pick me up. It was depressing when I saw just how quickly my paychecks were going to disappear. By the time I paid rent, my insurances, phone bill and cable bill, I was probably going to have to dip into my remaining savings to cover other expenses.

Getting a second job would be almost impossible once classes started. I had to find areas to cut. I guess I didn't really need cable. If I continued to get rides to work with Casey like I'd been doing, I would save on gas. I could probably walk to campus other times while the weather remained nice.

I was still looking for more ways to save when Mel showed up. She'd insisted on accompanying me to my first appointment and I was grateful; it wasn't something I wanted to do alone. I was nervous and wishing Ty was here, but I got through it with Mel by my side. The nurses and doctor were great, but it was just an uncomfortable experience that I wouldn't have wanted to endure alone. I had to answer a million questions and pee in a cup and be poked by a needle, and then because of my circumstances and how worried I was about the health of my baby, the doctor wanted to do a pelvic exam rather than wait a few weeks for when they would normally do the first ultrasound. I was glad and even though I hadn't enjoyed the invasive experience, it was worth it. I had the very first picture of my little jelly bean baby, even though at this point it looked like a mutant jelly bean that was sprouting tiny arms and legs.

I was eight weeks along and so far everything was normal. I was still experiencing some morning sickness, but the ginger tea Ellie recommended and drinking lots of water all day long seemed to be helping. The doctor told me I could expect the nausea to let up some in the next month, but if it didn't it was nothing to worry about. I hoped it would end, but I wasn't looking forward to the tradeoff of symptoms and changes.

The thought of my clothes no longer fitting me and having to replace my wardrobe stressed me out. I'd only gained two pounds, but I knew that would change soon. As it was, my bras were already snugger and I was convinced all of that two pounds had gone there. Ty would've loved it. I almost laughed thinking about how much. Almost.

"No bras." Ty stated seriously.

"What?"

"You heard me; if you're saying no shoes on the carpet then I want my rule to be no bras in the apartment."

"You can't make that your rule." I rolled my eyes, we'd only been living in our new apartment for a week and already I could see our cleaning deposit going down the drain with his work boots on the beige carpet.

"Yes I can."

"What if we have company?"

"Fine, I'll revise it; no bras, except when there's company."

"What if a man comes to the door and I have to answer it?"

"What the hell man is gonna be coming to the door?" I secretly loved it when he got all possessive.

"I don't know. A salesman or maybe one of the neighbors." He just harrumphed like it was entirely inconceivable that any man could possibly have a legitimate reason to come to our door.

"Fine then, no bras when we're both home, with no company. You can wear one when you're here by yourself in case you have to answer the door, but it better come off the minute I get home from work." He was so sexy when he got all bossy and demanding, but I couldn't help rile him up.

"And what if I don't follow your rule?"

His eyes took on a dangerous glint and I started to back away from him. "Then it will be my pleasure to enforce it."

I took off toward the bedroom but didn't make it two steps before his hands were around my waist, lifting me off the ground. I pretended to struggle, but really I was just squirming because his hand fumbling up my shirt tickled as he tried to get to my bra clasp.

"Mmmm," he moaned into my neck when he had it undone and his hands slid around to my front. His touch was warm and a little rough from working as a mechanic, but it felt so good and I melted into him, letting out a feminine sigh. "This is my new favorite rule," he whispered in my ear and then carried me off to our bedroom.

He enjoyed enforcing that rule every chance he got, and I could only imagine how much more he would have enjoyed it now that there was more to enjoy.

"Thanks for going with me," I told Mel when she pulled up to my apartment building to drop me off.

"I wanted to be there." She squeezed my hand. "I want to be here for you and my little niece or nephew any way I can."

"Hopefully at the next one we'll find out which it's gonna be." Everything had come up normal and my jelly bean appeared perfectly healthy. Unless any complications arose between now and then, I didn't have to go back until the sixteen week mark.

"I can't wait to plan the baby shower. It's going to be so much fun." I could only imagine what she would come up with. "Are you hoping for a boy or a girl?"

"I don't know, I guess it doesn't matter." Truth was, I hadn't let myself think about it much. It was painful; thinking about gender meant thinking about names and colors and all the things Ty should be here to decide on with me. As long as my jelly bean was just a jelly bean, I could put it all off for a few more weeks.

"Either way, he or she is gonna be the most beautiful baby."

"I hope so, because right now it kind of looks like an alien," I joked as I climbed out of the car. Mel just shook her head and laughed. "See you tomorrow." I closed the door behind me and she waited for me to get inside before heading out of the city to visit her parents.

As soon as I was inside my apartment, I had to call Ellie and my mom to let them know how the appointment went. They were anxious for every detail. Like Mel, they were also excited to find out the sex of the baby so they could start shopping. Every day that I talked to them they helped me make lists of things I would need, and which ones I would need ten or twenty of. It was daunting.

After my phone calls and a quick lunch, all I wanted to do was lie down on the couch and take a nap, but the doctor had recommended moving around after eating to help with the nausea. The Texas sun was shining outside, and I decided a walk would be good for me. My apartment wasn't far from Yellow House Canyon, and I loved walking that area around Mackenzie Park.

I changed into a pair of khaki shorts and a blue Houston Dash tank top, slathering on sun screen, because even though I was Texas born, I remained fairer skinned than most Texas natives. I grabbed a granola bar and an apple to take with me, tossing them in a small pack with my water bottle.

In the parking lot I spotted Casey kissing Annie goodbye before she climbed into her car. After the awkward confrontation last week, it hadn't taken them long to make up. I guess she had calmed down and finally listened. She didn't apologize to me of course, but it seemed she and Hunt were doing just fine. I was glad for him. When she pulled away, he turned around to head back inside but caught my gaze. I smiled and gave him a slight wave while making my way to my own car. Before I could climb in, Casey jogged over.

"Hey," I greeted.

"Hey, how did the appointment go?" He seemed genuinely interested. I was surprised he even remembered it was today, although I had mentioned it yesterday at work.

"Oh, it was fine. I mean I'm not exactly an expert on how they're supposed to go, but it wasn't terrible."

He chuckled softly. "That's a good thing." We both just stood there, quietly for a minute. I wasn't quite sure what else to say and he didn't seem to know either.

"I got a picture of the baby, do you want to see? Or, wait, is that weird? You probably don't want to see."

He just laughed lightly again. "Sure, I'd like to see."

I reached into my purse and pulled out the little ultrasound picture, handing it to him. He looked at it and I could tell by the way his brow scrunched up that he wasn't able to make it out any better than I had at first.

"That's the head," I told him, pointing out the same spot the doctor had showed me. "Those are the little arms and legs. I know they look more like tentacles right now, but the doctor assured me I don't have an alien growing inside me, and that it will get more baby-like soon," I joked, earning a grin from Casey.

"Yeah, I can see it now. Actually the baby already looks a lot like you," he teased and I smacked his arm. "No, but seriously, that's really cool, Tate." He handed the picture back to me. I smiled and looked down at my little jelly bean again.

"Yeah, I like seeing it. Having a picture, even one that's barely discernible, just makes it so much more real for me. It was definitely worth it."

"What was worth it?"

I realized I probably should have left off that last part. "You don't want to know how they take this picture." I scrunched up my face thinking back on the appointment again and how uncomfortable it was to have that wand/probe thingy inside of me.

"Don't they just run a sonogram over your stomach?"

"That's what they'll do at my next appointment, but right now they said it was too early to see much, so they had to, umm, go inside to see it." I wished I had just kept my mouth shut. I don't know why I even brought it up. I should probably just stop talking to Hunt altogether about my pregnancy; it always ended up getting awkward. It shouldn't have been, it was a natural part of pregnancy, but Casey's cheeks turned pink and he looked away running a hand over the back of his neck.

"I'm just gonna shut up now and leave. I'm sorry; this is all just new to me and I seem to have a problem with over sharing around you." I turned to get in my car.

"It's okay, really," he tried to reassure me, but his face was still flushed. "So where are you off to?" He nodded at my backpack.

"I'm going over to Mackenzie Park to walk around."

"By yourself?"

"Yeah." I didn't see why that mattered. I was perfectly capable of going on my own, and I didn't mind. Alone time was something I was getting used to. I had to, because when Mel wasn't around, I didn't have anyone else. I didn't want to come across as a friendless loner and tell him that though. I still texted some of my other friends and I saw the girls on the team almost every day, but doing stuff like we used to, hanging out, girls nights and all that was more than I felt up to anymore. It was hard to be the girl they all knew, it was easier not to have to pretend.

"Want some company?"

"It's fine, I really don't mind going by myself."

"I didn't ask because I think you mind going alone. I'm really just being rude and inviting myself along. It's a beautiful day and I've lived here for a year now, but haven't explored the area much. I've heard it's nice around there and I'd love to check it out if you don't mind me tagging along."

For some reason I didn't. I was looking forward to enjoying some peace, and being reminded that there were still beautiful things in this world; I thought he might be able to understand that and appreciate it. I don't know why, since I really didn't know him all that well.

"Sure, that would be okay."

"Okay, let me just run up and change and I'll drive."

"I don't mind driving," I told him.

"I'll drive," he insisted before disappearing inside. I didn't know if my driving frightened him or if he was just a control freak, but he always insisted on driving. I'd offered a few times in the mornings but he wouldn't let me. We always rode to campus in his car. I wouldn't complain though. It saved me gas money and I kind of loved his Mustang. Ty really would have loved it. In the last few months before he died, he'd actually been looking for either an old Shelby or Chevelle to rebuild. The day before our anniversary, I'd gone with him to look at a few, but none of them had been 'the one' for him.

It was ridiculous how picky he was about finding the right car. Said she had to speak to him whatever that meant. When I gave him a bad time about how selective he was being over a car, he told me I should feel special because he'd been even more selective with the girl he wanted to spend the rest of his life with. I'd completely melted and quit complaining about all the cars he wanted to look at. I just wished he'd been able to find his dream car.

"Hey, we good to go?" I didn't notice that Casey had come back down.

"Yeah, I'm good." I followed him over to his car. He set his own pack in the back and I climbed in the passenger seat.

"You sure you're feeling up to this? You looked a little out of it back there."

"Yeah, I was just thinking and got a little lost in my own head, but I'm fine."

"You've eaten right?"

I chuckled, "Yes Dr. Hunt, I've eaten. I've got water and snacks and I promise I'm feeling okay."

"Just making sure." He started the car and backed out. "Must have been some heavy thinking you were doing."

"I was actually thinking about your car."

"You were?"

"Sort of. Ty loved vintage cars, like really, really loved them. I think you guys would have gotten along well. You would have liked him," I added. They had met before; Ty made it to just about every game and team function, but they never made it past a basic introduction.

"I'm sure I would've," he said quietly, his features becoming thoughtful before he looked over at me. "He seemed like a really great guy. I guess he had to be to get you to fall in love with him." He smiled sweetly, but his eyes remained somber and returned to the road.

"He was the best."

The rest of the ride was quiet except for the music playing.

"This is a huge park," Casey commented as we walked through it.

"They have a lot here; baseball fields, disc golf, horse trails, paths to the canyon. There's even a small water park on the far side," I filled him in. "It's one of my favorite places in Lubbock."

"I can see why." I led him through the different areas of the park to show him some of what it had to offer before leading him to my favorite walking paths. It wasn't the most beautiful place I'd ever seen. Texas summers were hot and pretty dry, so not everything was luscious and green, but there were lots of wildflowers, and a stream that ran along the path in some parts. I don't know if the views were post card worthy, but they were breath taking in their own way, and it was always nice to get away from the bustle of the city without actually having to leave the city, and be reminded that there was always beauty around if you just looked for it.

"Are you ready for classes to start?" Casey asked when we stopped for a water break. We'd been walking comfortably, side by side, for a while. He was easy to be around and it seemed we were both content to enjoy our surroundings without feeling the need to keep a conversation going the whole time. I appreciated that, but I also found that finding things to talk about wasn't that difficult with him.

"I guess," I shrugged. The team had already played their first match and classes were starting up next week.

"You don't sound too sure."

"I just don't know what I'm doing. Every other junior has declared a major by now and is pursuing it with a goal in mind. I never gave it much thought because I was so sure it wouldn't matter once I got my chance with the Dash. I never considered what I would do if that wasn't an option anymore."

"Don't stress it; you'll figure it out, and who says your chance with the Dash is gone? You're still young. You've got plenty of playing years left and you're good enough. You could try out in another year or so."

"I don't think so."

"Why not?

"Since I was eight years old I wanted to be a professional soccer player. That's always been my dream. Yes, I wanted to get married and start a family, but I always saw the kids coming later. Well, it's not later and I'm going to have a baby. Not only that, but I'm going to be a single parent. I can't devote my life to soccer *and* being a good mom. Only one can have my all. The timing might not be what I wanted, but I do want this baby. He or she won't come second to anything, not even my dreams. So there's no point in going after it if I can't give it everything. It sucks. It hurts like hell to kiss it all goodbye, and I'm trying not to be bitter and angry but it's hard. So damn hard."

"I understand." His eyes convinced me that he did. I wondered what he had lost or had to sacrifice, but just because I was sharing didn't mean I felt right asking him to. The conversation stopped there, and we started moving again. A while later I paused long enough to pull the apple out of my bag.

76

"I've got a granola bar in here if you'd like it," I offered Casey, but he opened up his bag and pulled out his own protein bar and a Reese's. "Never mind. I see you've got the good stuff." We munched as we walked and when I finished the apple, I ate the granola bar too.

"Want half?" Casey held out the second peanut butter cup to me.

"If you insist," I grinned and snatched the chocolate and peanut butter goodness from him before he changed his mind. "Mmmm, I love Reese's," I groaned, savoring it.

"I can tell," Casey smirked.

"I can't help it. Chocolate and peanut butter, it just doesn't get better than that."

"I agree."

"Ty used to bribe me with them. He always kept a stash somewhere in the apartment. I could never find where he hid them, but he would pull one out when he was trying to get his way."

"Did it work?"

"Usually," I admitted, smiling. "I can remember so many times we'd argue about what movie or show to watch, or he'd want a back rub, and he'd have a Reese's ready to persuade me."

"It's cool that you can talk about him."

"I couldn't at first. I tried not to even think, because every thought was of him and what I'd lost. It was the worst pain I'd ever felt. It still is. I didn't think I would survive it. To be honest, I didn't want to," I confessed, feeling the well of tears. "Every memory is like a knife gutting me, but at the same time they sustain me. Knowing that I had him, that he was mine and I was loved, and that nothing, not even losing him can take that away from me, is all I'm hanging onto. And this baby." I rested a hand over my stomach, taking in a deep breath to push the tears back.

Casey approached me and I could tell he wasn't quite sure what to do, but he put his arms around me and hugged me tentatively. "I'm sorry for bringing it up. I can't even pretend to know what that feels like, but I think you're incredibly strong and brave." At first the hug was awkward, and we were both feeling it, but his words were so sincere and full of compassion that I gave in to it. I sunk into his arms and tried not to cry all over his shirt.

77

He held me a little tighter. His arms were comforting. They were strong and his chest was hard and lean. I fit against him perfectly with my head tucked under his chin. I found myself breathing in his scent. It was different than Ty's, yet also similar in that it was very male and wasn't overpowering. He smelled good, but not like he bathed in cologne. Except for the smell, I could have closed my eyes and let myself believe Ty was holding me, but he wasn't. It was Casey. I started to pull away and he let me go.

"It's okay," I told him. "You didn't do anything wrong. I'm sorry I got all weepy on you."

"Don't be sorry. You don't have to be so strong all the time. You can be whatever you want with me." He looked away, seeming shy all of the sudden.

"Thank you. You have no idea how much that means." Even with my parents, I felt like I had to put on a front so they wouldn't worry. Mel was the only other one who didn't care, who let me feel however I wanted. His eyes met mine again and he nodded in understanding. It was strange that in such a short time I felt like I could be more real and open with him than just about anyone besides Mel. We walked a ways further before deciding we should head back to the car.

"How are things with Annie?" I asked, feeling slightly bad that it seemed like we only ever talked about me and my problems. "Looked like you two are good again."

"Since we talked things have been fine."

"That's good."

"Yeah."

I didn't know what else to say about her and he didn't seem to want to elaborate. I felt weird for even bringing it up. He was very private about his relationship. In fact, he was pretty private with his personal life in general. He was getting a good look into mine, and I didn't know much about him except that he was a nice guy, good at his job and not from Texas. "Hey Hunt, where are you from?"

He smiled and shook his head. "Does it even really matter? To you guys aren't there just like Texans and then non-Texans? Do you even differentiate between the rest of us?" he joked and I grinned because it was almost true.

"Nah, you're right, we don't, but I'm just curious."

78

"I'm from Jasper, Indiana."

Huh. Indiana. I didn't know much about Indiana. "Is Jasper a big city?"

He laughed, "No, it's one of the smaller towns in Indiana. It's like a tenth of the size of Lubbock, and the population is only about fifteen thousand." That was pretty small. Abilene is small compared to Lubbock, but it's still bigger than that.

"What was it like growing up there?" Sometimes I wished I'd grown up in a small town. Movies and books always made it seem so charming. Then I would think about how fast gossip spread in Abilene, and change my mind. I couldn't imagine how much worse it would be in an even smaller town; to literally have everyone in your business. Or maybe nosiness was only a Texas thing, but I doubted that.

"It was nice, most of the time. I knew everyone in my high school, but sometimes having everyone know you wasn't such a good thing. There's definitely a lot more to do in a big city too. So I guess it's like everywhere else, there's good and bad. Except of course Texas," he added. "There's nothing bad about Texas," his sarcasm was amusing.

"Damn right ther ain't." I made sure to lay the drawl on real thick. He grinned and rolled his eyes. "So Indiana boy, was it the job that brought ya here to the greatest state in our fine country?"

"Sumptin' like dat, and I heard da girls down her are real perty." He did his best impression of a Texas accent and I couldn't help but laugh.

"Well you found yourself one, so it looks like it was a smart move for you."

"Technically, Annie is from Oklahoma, but she's lived in Texas since she was fifteen, so she's close enough to a Texas girl."

"Hmph," I snorted.

He shook his head and bit back a smirk. "Man you guys are a tough bunch. You really don't cut anyone slack, do ya?"

"Nope."

"I've noticed. I've also noticed you only have three beverages, coke, Bud Light and sweet tea.

"Hey now, watch yourself. I don't care for Bud, but you best not go sayin' nothin' about sweat tea, or we'll make you go back to Indiana." He laughed, it was rich and deep. He had a nice laugh.

We were almost back to the car and I finished off the last of my water. It was nearing five o'clock and the sun hadn't let up at all. I wiped the sweat from my face. I was looking forward to the air conditioning in his car.

Casey turned to me as we approached the car. "Something else, you guys have some weird sayings. A lot of crazy shit comes out of the mouths of Texans."

I gave him a raised brow. "Are you trying to pick a fight?"

He grinned and shook his head. "And everything leads to a fight. I'm surprised you guys don't still have duels in the streets at noon."

I glared at him. "We Texans are a civilized bunch."

"And you're the most stubborn people I've ever met," he teased some more walking around to the driver's side.

"Excuse me, but you're pretty stubborn yourself."

"I'm not saying I can't be stubborn at times, but stubbornness is the primary part of your make-up, like a natural state of being for you."

"Is not. I'm a very agreeable person." He barked out a laugh and I glared at him over the roof of the car. "What? I am," I insisted.

"You might be the most stubborn person I've ever met. Especially out on the field."

"Am. Not."

"How many yellow cards have you gotten for arguing with refs?" Okay he had a point, but it wasn't my fault they were blind and had fewer brains than a scarecrow. I started to shoot him another dirty look.

He threw his hands up in surrender. "Hey, I'm not saying it's a bad thing. It gets you into trouble sometimes, but your stubbornness is also part of what makes you such a good player and strong person. You refuse to quit and you push yourself. You're kind of a force to be reckoned with, Tate." He said before opening the door and climbing in. I pulled my own door open and slid in.

"Okay, you might be onto something there."

"You did hear the part where I said it can get you into trouble?" He started up the car and navigated out of the parking lot.

"Yeah, yeah. You and my mother. She likes to tell people that I'm the only hell she ever raised."

"I don't doubt that at all." His grin widened. "You've got wild child and trouble maker written all over you. I can only imagine what you were like as a kid and a teenager."

"I wasn't that bad, not really." He looked at me skeptically. "Okay, okay. I would, on occasion, get in a little bit of trouble, but nothing serious. Ty always made sure of that."

"He wasn't the Clyde to your Bonnie?"

I laughed this time. "No way, more like my Jiminy Cricket. Always protected me and kept me from doin anything too stupid. If anyone, Mel's my Clyde, or Thelma or whatever you want to call us."

"I can see that. You and Ross are definitely a pair."

"At least that's how things were anyway. I don't feel like that girl anymore," I told him.

"Of course you're not the same. How could you be after everything you've gone through and what you're still going through, but she's not completely gone either. I've seen glimpses of that spitfire and she's still in there." He seemed so sure. I wasn't so sure, but for once I didn't argue. I was quiet the rest of the ride. When we got back, I thanked Casey for going with me and said goodnight outside my door. I'd had a really good day hanging out with him even though conversation got heavier at times than I'd expected, but there were a few more things I could add to my list of things I knew about Casey Hunt. He was a small town boy from Jasper, Indiana. He was a good listener, and he could make me laugh. I'd laughed more today than I had in the last two months.

Eleven

"A true friend can see your tears under the rain."
— *Ali Alotaibi*

September flew by, and the team was off to a great start for the season. They'd won all six of their matches and Coach had high hopes for the rest. I continued to split time helping out during practices and working with Casey in the fitness center in between classes. I was getting a couple more hours each week than I had at first, but I was still struggling to stretch my paychecks.

I was in the second trimester of my pregnancy and I'd picked up another three pounds. I was hooking my bras on the last notch and living in athletic shorts and yoga pants because most of my jeans were just a little too snug to be comfortable anymore.

My pregnancy was out in the open, but aside from a few stares it wasn't a big scandal or anything. A few of the girls on the team were a little more distant, but it didn't bother me because we'd never been particularly close to begin with. I focused on school and taking care of myself, hanging out with Mel most evenings. She came over almost every day after practice, and we did homework or just hung out. She was relentless with the baby names, but I avoided it as much as I could. I still had a little time before my next appointment. Until I knew the gender, I didn't see the rush in choosing a name.

After that day at the park, I didn't see Casey much outside of work. I would occasionally pass him in the hall when we were coming and going, and we would always exchange friendly hellos and chat for a minute. A couple of times I almost invited him over for dinner to thank him for helping me out at work, and just to have the company, but I never did. Something stopped me; I think having him over for dinner would feel too date like, and I didn't want that.

Dating was something I wasn't ready to consider. At all. I couldn't imagine that changing in the foreseeable future either. A few guys had tried flirting with me in some of my classes, but I killed that right away.

I was pretty blunt in telling them that I was knocked up, and that seemed to do the trick. Some were observant enough to notice the ring and ask. I hated when they asked. I didn't know what to say. My heart and soul were still very much married, even if legally I wasn't anymore. I didn't have it in me to explain that, so I would just mumble "yes" and walk away or bury my head in my notes so they would get the hint.

It had happened today in my Psych class when the instructor had us pair up to discuss the lecture material. My partner, Liam, was a really nice guy. I'd talked to him a few other times in class. He hadn't been trying to flirt, just curious, but he could barely meet my eyes after I told him the truth, and just like that the rest of that class period was shot. The afternoon got better when I met up with Mel after classes and decided the best thing for it was an afternoon at the campus leisure pool since we had the day off from practice.

Mel was coming out of the bathroom at the same time I stepped out of my bedroom. I had a loose tank top and a pair shorts on over my pink and green bikini. Mel looked hot in her bright yellow bikini top and denim shorts, but she gave me a slight frown.

"Aww, you can't cover it up. Come on, I want to see the bump," she whined. I did have a bump; it was small, but it was visible and Mel was way too obsessed with it. "Pleeease."

"I need you to put sunscreen on my back." I ignored her, pulling the tank top off, much to her satisfaction. She grinned and immediately knelt in front of my tummy.

"Hey little jelly bean," we'd both taken to calling the baby that. "This is your Auntie Melodie. I love you so much already. I can't wait to meet you, but you gotta do some more growing first." I smiled down at her. As ridiculous as my best friend was, she was also really sweet and I didn't mind her talking to my jelly bean.

"Okay Auntie Mel, come on." I walked into the bathroom to get the sunscreen.

"Damn Liv, what are these marks?" She ran her fingers over my back, touching the tender spots where my bra straps had been digging in.

"Nothing. Can you just put the sunscreen on so we can go?" She took the bottle from my hand, but she wasn't dropping the subject.

"It's not nothing. Your bras are obviously too tight, you shouldn't be wearing them," she insisted, rubbing the cool lotion all over my skin.

"It's really not that bad. I'll get new ones soon." I put the bottle back in the cupboard and pulled the tank on again. Mel followed me out to the living room, where we both slipped our flip flops on, and grabbed beach towels.

"It's not fine Liv. You really can't wear the bras you have any more if they don't fit you right. It's not good for you."

"I know," I sighed, frustrated. "But I don't have a choice right now. I can't afford to go shopping for new things yet. I'll be okay for just another couple weeks and when I get my next check I should be able to get a few new ones," I explained, hoping she would understand and let it go.

"Oh hell no." She stopped me before I could pull the front door open. "Why didn't you say something before? When we're done at the pool we are going shopping, and I'm buying you new bras. If you try to argue with me I will leave you at home and go buy them myself."

"Mel that's really not-"

"I said no arguing."

"Really Mel I appreciate it, but I can't let you buy my stuff for me. I'll be able to get them soon, I promise."

"You need them now, and this isn't just for you, this is for my little niece or nephew. You stressing over money isn't good for you or the baby. This is something I can do to help. I know you won't let me give you money, but you are going to let me buy you some things." I knew her bossy heart was in the right place and as much as I hated to accept it, I did need it.

"Fine, but that's it. Just a couple bras," I gave in and she hugged me like I just told her we could go to Disneyland. I had to pry myself out of her arms. "Come on, let's go." I tugged her after me and pulled the door to my apartment open.

"Your boobs do look really great; you have to admit that. Is it normal for them to get so big? They're really full and perky. I think they've gotten bigger than mine." She reached out to touch one of my breasts and I smacked her hand away.

84

"Seriously, can we stop talking about my boobs?" She started laughing while I shut the door behind us and locked it. When I turned, I noticed she had stopped laughing and was frozen in place staring at something over my shoulder with a stupid grin on her face. I turned my head to look, right as she opened her mouth and spoke, "Oh hey, Casey."

Sure enough, he was standing outside his apartment, looking at the two of us. His red face told me he'd overheard us, and I wanted to kill Mel. She seemed to be amused with the situation.

"Hi," Casey replied uncomfortably and I could tell he wanted to be anywhere but right there, much like I did, but Mel was determined to drag out our embarrassment.

"What are you up to today?" she asked him.

"Oh I, er, I was just heading out to go see my girlfriend. What about you two? Going swimming?"

"Yep. It's such a great day for it, don't cha think?"

"Yeah, it's really nice out. Have fun."

"We will," I said, finally grabbing Mel's arm and dragging her toward the stairs. It was awkward because Casey followed behind us. I could tell Mel was trying not to giggle, but she was having a hard time holding it in.

"See ya later," Casey said once we were all outside. I waved, but didn't say anything, and yanked Mel over to her car, and we both climbed in. Once the doors were shut I reached over and smacked her, just as she burst out laughing.

"It's not funny, that was so embarrassing," I groaned, but she continued to laugh as she pulled her car out onto the road.

"It wasn't that bad."

"Yes it was. You were talking about my boobs in front of Casey. How is that not that bad? Did you see how red his face was?"

"You said you guys are friends now, so it's not that big of a deal. He's a guy, I guarantee he's looked at your boobs at some point anyway, and if you weren't hiding under baggy t-shirts lately, he would have noticed for himself."

"Stop it, he's not like that and we're just barely friends."

"Whatever, you're overreacting you prude."

"I hate you."

85

"No you don't. You love me." She smirked.

"Whatever."

First thing I did when we made it to the pool was shove her in. As soon as she set her towel and belongings down, she walked over to ledge of the pool to talk to someone that had waved when we walked by. Before she got the chance to say anything, I gave her a push and she hit the water with a decent splash. She popped up sputtering and laughing and it was my turn to smirk at her.

"Bitch." She grinned and I chuckled along with the people around her. I went and stripped out of my shirt and shorts, then walked back over and lowered myself into the pool where I had pushed her in. She was chatting with a small group of girls I didn't recognize.

"This is my best friend Olivia," she introduced me. "This is Sarah, and Jenny; they're in my journalism class," she pointed out the red head and the tall blonde, "and this is their friend Tricia." She indicated the one with skin like a caramel latte, who I guessed was part Latino. They all smiled big and friendly and I immediately felt at ease around them. They didn't stare or do any of that sizing up crap that a lot of girls do.

Mel and I spent most of our time at the pool hanging out with them. When a group of guys they seemed to know, came over to join us, it didn't take long for me to get uncomfortable with the way one of them was blatantly ogling my newly enlarged breasts. Mel noticed right away that I didn't like it and she quickly made an excuse for us to move to a different area of the pool to ditch them. What surprised me was that the other girls blew off the guys and followed us. I liked them even more after that.

After an hour at the pool, Mel and I both admitted to be starving. She wanted to grab dinner before we went shopping so we said goodbye and drove back to my apartment to change, and then Mel treated me to our favorite barbecue place. After we finished eating, Mel dragged me over to the South Plains Mall, and the first place we headed was Victoria's Secret. The sales girl was super sweet when she greeted us and Mel wasted no time in enlisting her help.

"My friend here is pregnant and her boobs are getting huge. She needs to be measured." Huge was a bit of an overstatement, but that was Mel. The sales girl just laughed and proceeded to take my measurements, then asked what I was looking for in a bra. Mel and I both answered at the same time, but our responses were very different.

"Something comfortable."

"Pretty and sexy."

I rolled my eyes at Mel and then looked back at the sales girl. "Comfort is definitely my priority," I informed her and she showed me several that she insisted were their most comfortable bras, and most of them were really cute too, so Mel didn't object to the ones I picked out to try on.

I ended up choosing three in light, pretty colors. Mel wouldn't let me get away with only three though. She insisted on grabbing up a hot pink one with a bit of lace and a black and purple one. We probably argued for ten minutes; me telling her that I didn't need that many, and her telling me to shut up and accept them. She won and I left with five new bras. I thanked her repeatedly, but she told me shut up then too. If Casey thought I was the most stubborn person he'd met, he really needed to spend more time around Mel and he would change his mind.

When we walked out of Victoria's Secret, Mel said there was another stop she wanted to make, so I followed her through the mall expecting that she would lead me to the MAC counter; she was always buying new makeup. But when she finally stopped in front of a store I looked up at the sign and then glared at her.

"I thought *you* wanted to look at something."

"I do." She grinned.

"This is a maternity store."

"I know, and I want to look at maternity clothes."

"Oh, you're pregnant too?" She only rolled her eyes, not finding me funny, and then tried to pull me inside the store. "You're not buying me anything else," I said adamantly as she continued to drag me inside.

"Look, you can either pick some things out, or I'll come back and pick out what I want you to have. Then I'll take them home and wash them so that you can't return them. You might as well get what you want, because this is happening."

I sighed, realizing that it would be pointless to fight her on it. "Fine."

We went in and looked around. I immediately went to the sale rack and found a couple cute tops and a pair of shorts. I showed my selection to Mel and she looked pleased.

"Now can we get out of here?" I asked, making my way to the counter. She grabbed my arm and stopped me.

"Nope. If you think I'm letting you get out of here with two shirts and one pair of shorts, you're not as smart as I thought you were." She pulled two dresses off the rack next to us and threw them over my arm, then moved over to the pants section and started grabbing several different sizes in jeans and leggings.

"Mel, I don't need all those." I tried to stop her, but she kept grabbing them.

"You will." She continued to pull things off the racks and shelves.

"Mel, stop, this is too much."

"No, it's not." She stopped grabbing stuff and turned to look at me. "It's not enough. It will never be enough. You've gone through hell, and are still going through hell every single day. I see it, even though you try to hide it and smile and put on a brave face. I know you're still dying inside and there's nothing I can do to make it better. I wish like hell I could. I wish I could trade places with Ty so that he could be here with you, but I can't. I can do this though. I can help make this part easier for you and take away some of your financial stress. It's not much, but it's all I can do, so please just let me do it for you." Tears were building behind her pretty hazel eyes and I felt them leaking from my own. I had no idea that's how she felt.

"Mel, it's more than enough. You've done so much for me. You don't even know how much you've helped me to make it through this, and I wouldn't wish for one second that he were here instead of you, so please don't say that. Don't ever say you want to trade places with him. God, I want him back, but never like that. I love you, and you can buy me whatever you want if it will make you feel better, but please don't do it out of guilt that Ty's gone and you're still here." I grabbed her and hugged her to me, squishing the clothes between us as we let our tears fall on each other's shoulders.

We left the mall loaded down with bags. I'd let Mel have her way and she bought me clothes for every stage of my pregnancy. I told her over and over that she didn't need to, but it seemed to make her happy and I really did love everything we picked out.

"Thank you, Mel. This really means a lot to me." I couldn't even express how grateful I was, but the look on her face when she smiled back at me, said she knew.

Twelve

"So how are classes going?" Casey asked on Monday afternoon as we were leaving practice.

"Good, I think I'm doing well anyway," I told him, but I didn't know what else to say; I still sort of felt like I was floating without a direction.

"I never did ask what you declared your major."

"I actually picked Exercise and Sports Sciences," I chuckled because it was the major I would need to become an athletic trainer. "So, working with you has actually helped me out already."

"Trying to take my job now?"

"No. I don't think I want your job."

"Where are you?" he asked as we got closer to the parking lot. I had an early class this morning so I didn't catch a ride with him.

"I walked."

"Want a ride home?" he offered.

"Sure." I followed him over to his car and we tossed our bags in the back. A few of the girls from the team were walking past us and gave me a funny look. Jamie was one of them and I wanted to groan. It wasn't like I'd been hiding that I occasionally caught rides with Casey, but we hadn't advertised it either. There was nothing to advertise, but Jamie wouldn't see it that way. I had no choice but to ignore her and the other girls, and climb in the car.

"So, you don't want to be an athletic trainer? Not liking it so far?" Casey asked as he started it up.

"It's not that I don't like it, and I know it would be a good job; I'm just not sure that it's what I really want to do. I have no idea what I really want to do." I was looking out the window as we drove through the parking lot. Jamie's eyes found mine when we drove past her. She, Cassie and Erica were all climbing into her convertible. The look she

90

gave me was anything but friendly. Casey didn't see it though and kept right on with our conversation.

"You wouldn't have to work with college teams; there are a lot of options for an athletic trainer out there. I mean, you're ideal to work with athletes, especially soccer players, because of your experience, but you can do a lot with that degree. I just think you should consider the options because you're really good at it."

I snorted; I didn't really think I'd been exceptional at it in any way.

"I'm serious. You understand the players and you're smart. You definitely wouldn't let any athlete try to walk all over you. You'd have no problem telling them what's up. That's important, because in case you haven't noticed, athletes tend to be a stubborn bunch who sometimes think they know better than you do." I just grinned and rolled my eyes.

"You're also kind and compassionate, which you need to be when you're working with the athletes who may never recover fully from injuries."

"Wow, uh thanks. I will definitely think about it." It actually meant a lot to have Casey think that highly of me. I'd been worried when coach stuck me with him that I'd get in his way because I didn't know what I was doing. It was nice to hear him say I was good at it. Maybe it was a good career option for me. I'd have to explore the possibilities.

"I'm only being honest." He flashed me a quick smile and then returned his eyes to the road. "So how is everything else, with the, er . . ."

"Pregnancy?"

"Yeah, sorry. I just don't know if you like talking about it, or if it's weird for me to ask." We were in uncomfortable territory again. It was time to take a page from Mel's book; the only way for it to not be awkward was if I didn't let it be.

"No, it's okay. It's not weird and I don't mind, and I promise I won't traumatize you with the bodily changes I'm undergoing."

He exhaled a low laugh and shook his head. "That was definitely a moment when I wished I could walk through walls so I could sink back into my apartment. I felt like such a creeper for having listened to you guys."

91

I chuckled at his confession. "It wasn't your fault. Mel has a big mouth and no tact. She says what's on her mind without worrying about who's listening. I was so embarrassed though, you weren't the only one wishing to disappear through the walls."

"You shouldn't feel embarrassed. It's natural during pregnancy for, er, that to happen and you should be able to talk to your friend about it." I looked at him and couldn't stop the smile that spread across my face, because while he was telling me not to be embarrassed, he was growing more and more embarrassed by the second. "And I'm just going to stop talking right now because I'm making it worse."

I laughed. "It's okay. I'm not as embarrassed anymore, and I'm kind of enjoying how flustered you're getting," I teased.

"Glad I could help," he muttered. "How did we even get to talking about this?"

"You asked how my pregnancy is going. The answer to that is pretty much all of me is getting bigger, but that's about all that's going on. I go back to the doc on October eighteenth and should be able to find out if it's a boy or girl."

"Are you excited to find out?"

I'd been asked a million times, and usually I said yes immediately because that's what everyone expected me to say, but with Casey I hesitated. "I guess I am."

"Have you picked out names yet?"

"No, I haven't even thought about it," I admitted.

"Really? I thought that was something girls did at like twelve."

I laughed again. "When I was twelve I wanted two sons and I planned to name them David and Beckham."

He grimaced. "Really? You were a Beckham groupie?"

"Hey, he wears Calvin Klein really well, but don't worry, I got over that stage and I just . . . I don't know . . . I guess I always expected that when it came time to pick baby names, Ty would decide with me, so I've been putting it off."

"Shit, I'm sorry. I shouldn't have brought it up."

"No, it's fine. You're not the first person who's asked me that. It was just the first time I've admitted out loud why I don't want to think about names yet."

We pulled up to our building and he shut off the car, and then looked over at me seriously. "Listen, Tate, I know you've got Melodie and your family, but if there's ever anything you need, or any way I can help you, please don't be afraid to ask. I'd like to help you out any way I can, even if it's just to be someone you can talk to and be honest with about the things you don't want to tell everyone else."

"Thanks, Hunt. You've already done a lot and I appreciate it."

"It's really no problem."

We grabbed our bags from the back and made our way inside and up to our floor.

"Hey," I stopped him at my door, "do you want to come over for dinner? I'm going to attempt to make my mother in law's cornbread and white chicken chili."

"Oh. Um . . ."

"It's okay if not. I just wanted to say thank you for everything and pay you back for when you made dinner for me, but it's not a big deal if you don't want to."

"No, no. I actually do. That sounds really good. I'll just grab a quick shower and then is it okay if I come over and help you make it?"

"Yeah, that would be great. Usually Mel comes over after practice to hang out and then we make dinner, but she had a date tonight so it will be nice to have the company."

"Okay, then I'll be over in about fifteen minutes." He disappeared inside his apartment and while I waited, I got all of the ingredients ready and started sautéing the chicken. While that cooked I looked around and made sure my apartment was tidy. I washed the few dishes sitting in the sink and stacked the books I had scattered on the counters and coffee table. I grabbed the items of clothing that were strewn about and tossed them in my bedroom before checking on the chicken. I was just flipping it over when he knocked. That was a fast fifteen minutes.

"Come in," I hollered. He walked in wearing a pair of snug fitting jeans that hung low on his hips, and a white fitted t-shirt that showed off his trim waist and lean muscles. It was rare that I saw him in anything other than shorts or warm-up pants, but it was a good look on him, made better by the way his mussed up locks framed his face as if he'd done a quick towel dry on it and then hurried over here, which was probably exactly what he'd done.

93

I didn't usually pay much attention to how Casey looked, or any guy for that matter anymore, yet I couldn't help but notice how attractive he was right then. I shifted my eyes back down to the chicken so hopefully he wouldn't notice I had just checked him out. I didn't want to make him feel uncomfortable or give him the impression that I invited him over for reasons other than what I told him. I really wanted to keep his friendship without things getting weird between us because for five seconds I woke back up to the fact that Casey was incredibly good looking.

"Started without me?" He approached the kitchen.

"Just the chicken. There's still plenty to do." I informed him and set him to chopping the onion and peppers and other vegetables. Fifteen minutes later, I added *good cook* to my growing mental list of things I knew about him. He was right at home in my kitchen, and in fact seemed more confident than I was preparing the meal and I was no slouch in the kitchen. He did most of the work, chopping, mixing and stirring like he'd made this meal a thousand times.

"So, who taught you how to cook?" I asked him, trying not to sound too impressed.

"My mom insisted all of her kids learn to cook before going off to college. She had me in the kitchen slicing and dicing when I would have much rather been outside shooting hoops or kicking a ball around."

"Well you're really handy with that knife. I mean you brought me dinner that other time and it was great, but watching you, I can see now that you've got mad skills in the kitchen." I guess I wasn't doing a very good job of not being impressed, but I couldn't help it. I didn't know too many guys who could cook like him. In fact, I didn't think I knew any. Learning to grill was a must, and just about every guy in Texas could do that, but it wasn't the same as knowing how to cook.

"Thanks. One of these days I need to remember to thank my mom because my mad skills have definitely come in handy with the ladies. They love a guy who can cook."

I laughed, but I couldn't deny it. "It's so true. I'm sure you've had plenty of them falling all over themselves. I tried to teach Ty to cook a few times but he always said he'd already gotten the girl so he didn't need to learn."

Casey chuckled. "Not all of us are so lucky. Amazing girls aren't easy to come by." He winked at me. Did he just call me amazing? A blush spread over my cheeks, but I didn't think he noticed as he carried on stirring the chili. "Those of us who didn't find one early in life have to try and win them with cooking skills, heroic feats and displays of supreme physical strength and athletic ability."

I laughed, "Is that how you won Annie over?"

"Something like that." He had an odd look on his face, like he was perplexed by something, and I wondered what he was thinking about.

"I bet she enjoys having you cook for her."

"It doesn't take much work to prepare salad," he commented dryly.

"Ah, she's one of those girls?" I asked and then realized how that sounded. "Not that there's anything wrong with being health conscious," I added so I wouldn't come across as judgmental. I just liked to eat. Especially lately.

"She does some modeling part time here and in Dallas occasionally, so she's really concerned with her body image. Sometimes I wish she wouldn't be. It would be nice to enjoy one meal where she wasn't mentally calculating the calorie, fat and carb intake of everything." He sounded a little frustrated, like it was a sore subject between the two of them. I wasn't at all surprised that she modeled. She was gorgeous with a tiny figure.

"I'm sure if she tasted your cooking she'd change her mind and say to hell with the calorie counting," I joked trying to lighten the mood.

"I'm not so sure about that. She's beautiful, and five pounds, or even ten, wouldn't change that, but she's convinced it would."

"That's unfortunate, but you can feel free to bring me food any time you get the urge to cook for someone; I promise it won't go to waste with this pregnant girl."

"I'll remember that," he chuckled softly and went back to the food prep, dumping everything in the large pot on the stove. He started adding various seasonings and bringing the wooden spoon to his lips periodically, tasting and then stirring in more. God, he could have his own cooking show and women everywhere would be hooked on that shit. Me though, I felt an ache swell in my chest watching him so at home in my kitchen. It was all wrong.

95

It should have been Ty, and by now the smoke detectors should have been going off because he was helpless in the kitchen. That didn't mean he didn't try. So many nights we ended up ordering pizza after his plans for a romantic dinner ended up blackened on the bottom of some pan. He would give me a big rueful grin and say, "Sorry babe," then promise to make it up to me after dinner. Which he always did.

Something wet ran down my cheeks and I realized the memories were causing my eyes to leak. Damn leaky eyes worse than a faucet.

"Here, come taste this and tell me–" Casey looked up and caught me wiping at my eyes. "Hey, you okay?" he asked softly, setting the spoon down.

"I'm fine, must just be a delayed reaction to the onions."

He wasn't fooled. "Talk to me, Tate. What's going on?"

"It's nothing, just . . . Ty was such a terrible cook," I made some kind of noise that was part laugh and part dying animal and Casey rounded the counter and pulled me into his chest.

"I'm so sorry. I shouldn't have – I should probably go." He released me and I wiped at my face some more, trying to dry my eyes and pull it together.

"No, you don't have to go," I told him.

"I don't want to make anything harder for you than it already is."

"You're not. You didn't do anything wrong. It just doesn't take much to start the water works. Changing out the roll on the toilet paper holder makes me cry because Ty would never do it. He would always set the new roll on top of the empty one and it drove me crazy. Believe it or not, it's worse when I'm by myself, so please stay."

Just then the timer for the cornbread went off and rather than pathetically beg Casey not to leave, I grabbed an oven mitt and went to pull it out, but he came over and bumped me out of the way with his hip and took the oven mitt from me.

"Sit," he ordered softly and I slid into a seat on the backside of the counter and watched him pull the dish from the oven and then finish preparing the chili. Once he was satisfied, he proceeded to grab dishes from my cupboards and dish us both up. He set a bowl in front of me and a glass of milk. "Don't even think about asking for sweet tea." He narrowed his eyes and I gave him my best innocent smile.

"I wasn't going to." That was a lie. Sweet tea went with everything.

96

He took a seat beside me and we both dug in. It was delicious, but I hadn't expected it to be anything else.

"So you said your mom wanted all of her kids to be able to cook, how many siblings do you have?"

"Three sisters," he answered.

"Wow, the only boy. Must've been rough for ya. They older or younger?"

"They certainly loved ganging up on me. Kelly and Marissa are both older, and Jessie is the baby." I could see the affection he had for them on his face and hear it in his voice. I was a little bit envious. Casey's phone buzzed. He looked down to check it, but ignored it and then fixed his attention back on me. "What about you?"

"Only child. My mom had a miscarriage early on and they thought they wouldn't be able to get pregnant after that. Then I came along a few years later. After that they kept trying, but were never able to get pregnant again. I think my parents are especially excited about being grandparents, because they always wanted more kids." I'd always wanted siblings as well, especially when I was younger. I think that's why I originally attached myself to Ty. I just wanted another kid to play with.

"Do you get to see your parents much?"

"Not really. I try to as often as I can, but when I graduated high school and moved up here from Abilene, which is a couple hours southeast, they moved out to Jefferson, way over, almost on the Louisiana border. They opened up a bed and breakfast there. They love it, but don't get much time away and it's a long trip, so it made it hard for us to see them except on the holidays. They'll be coming out next month for the baby shower though. What about you? Do you make it home to see your family often?"

"I usually go back to Indiana for all the holidays and a couple times in between, and I try to get out to California to visit Marissa as often as I can."

We continued to chat and ask questions while we ate and my momentary breakdown was forgotten. I learned that his parents were still happily married after almost thirty-five years. His dad was a cop and his mom was a teacher. Marissa lived in LA and was a lawyer, but his other two sisters were still in Indiana. Jessie was only a year behind

97

me in school and working on a teaching degree and Kelly was a stay at home mom.

We both cleaned our plates and Casey went back for more and then helped me put the little bit of leftovers away. He even stuck around to help me do dishes. His phone went off twice more and he still didn't answer. I didn't want to be nosy and ask who was calling even though I was curious.

"Thank you so much for dinner, but I've got to get going," he said as soon as the dishes were dried and put away. He looked down to check his phone again.

"No problem, but really I should be thanking you since you did most of the work. I hope I didn't keep you from anything."

"No, it's nothing. I'm staying with Annie tonight since I won't see her for a few days. She was probably just calling to find out when I'd be over." The team had a match in Phoenix on Wednesday, so we were leaving for Arizona in the morning. I was glad that I still got to travel with them.

"Yeah, I need to finish my homework and study so that I won't get behind while we're gone." I wasn't looking forward to the six chapters I needed to read, but we said goodnight and while he went to spend the night with the girl he loved, I curled up on the couch with a boring text book.

I really miss you Ty.

Thirteen

"If I listen closely, I can hear the rustle of angle wings
And I know that you're still with us."

Where are you Mel? I wondered, going back and forth between checking the time on my phone and looking out the window. She should have been here fifteen minutes ago to pick me up for my appointment. She wasn't answering her phone; it was going straight to voicemail. I would have just gone without her, but I really didn't want to be alone when I found out my baby's sex.

Five more minutes passed, and I was just about to try calling her again, when my phone rang.

Finally.

"Mel, where are you?"

"I'm so sorry. There was a bad wreck out here on the highway and I was stuck sitting for almost thirty minutes. I couldn't call you because my phone was dead; I think I left my charger at your place. Traffic was hardly moving so I turned around and went back to my parents' place. I'm going to head home the long way, but I won't make it in time. I'm so sorry."

"It's okay, don't worry about it. I'll be fine, but I gotta go or I'm gonna be late." I hung up and tried not to be upset. I could handle one appointment on my own. I survived Ty's birthday over the weekend so I could get through this. Or at least I should have been able to, but letting my mind go back to the weekend and how difficult Sunday had been didn't actually help.

Sunday had sucked. The entire week leading up to it had sucked. Instead of planning a surprise party, or hunting for the perfect gift, or cooking his favorite dinner and dessert, I'd driven down to Abilene on Saturday. I spent the night with Ellie and Beth since it was a rough day for all of us, and then came home Sunday evening to my quiet, empty apartment. He would have turned twenty-two and would have been so excited to find out the sex of our baby, but now it just felt like one more thing I didn't want to face.

I was tempted to call and reschedule my appointment, ready to climb back into bed and do some serious wallowing, but I didn't. I took a couple deep breaths and grabbed my purse. Life without Ty wasn't going to get any easier; I had to learn to deal and stop hiding from it. I pushed open the door to my apartment and came face to face with Casey in the hall, a stack of mail in his hand.

"Hey, Tate." He gave a smile and I forced myself to smile back as I locked up my apartment.

"Hey."

"Headed out?"

"Yeah, today's the big day," my voice came out a little shaky and higher than usual when my attempt to sound excited failed.

"Oh, that's right. You ready to find out?"

"Mmhmm," I jerked my head in a quick nod; I could feel my emotions slipping and his eyes turned sympathetic.

"Mel going with you?"

This time I shook my head side to side. "No. She uh, couldn't make it." I was embarrassed that I was on the verge of crying in front of him again. "I better get going so I'm not late."

I ignored the sad smile he gave me and hurried toward the stairwell. Halfway there, I made an impulsive decision and turned. "Hey Casey."

He was at his door, but he looked back. "Yeah?"

"Is there any way—" Someone inside his apartment pulled the door open and then Annie appeared.

"There you are baby. What took so long to grab the mail?"

"Just a sec babe," he told her, and turned to me again. Annie's eyes found me and narrowed. "What is it, Tate?" Casey's voice was so full of concern and I felt even more pathetic because I was being so silly.

"It's nothing." I hated the way my voice trembled. "You guys have a great afternoon, I need to go." I started to turn but he called out.

"Olivia, wait." Then he turned to Annie and spoke softly. I was unable to hear what he said, but I could see her scowl when he said it. Then he jogged over to where I was.

100

"It's obviously not nothing or you wouldn't have stopped me. Are you sure you're okay going by yourself." He could see through me so easily. I ducked my eyes, but gave my head a tiny shake.

"You want me to go?"

"I can't ask you to do that." My eyes flashed to Annie, who was still scowling at the two of us. "I'm just being overly emotional. I'll be fine."

"Olivia, stop getting down on yourself for being emotional. You're allowed to feel whatever you're feeling, and it's okay to not want to do this alone. And you didn't ask; I offered. So would you like for me to go with you?"

"Yes, but I don't think you should." Again I worried about how Annie would feel, but he ignored my concerns.

"Go wait down at my car while I talk to her and grab my keys. And don't worry about her, she'll be fine." He didn't give me a chance to argue, before he left me standing there. I went down to wait at his car like he said and it was only a couple minutes before the two of them came out. They sure weren't holding hands. Annie stormed to her car and he watched her go with a frustrated look.

"I really didn't mean to cause any problems," I told him when he came over and unlocked the car. "You don't have to go. I can do this on my own. I need to learn how at some point."

"But not today." His warm brown eyes met mine and he reached to pull the door open for me.

He got us to the Medical Pavilion with just minutes to spare. They were running on time and almost as soon as I signed in, I was called back. I was nervous and my heart rate kicked up. Casey must have noticed that I was struggling, because he grabbed my hand in his and followed me to the back. He let go when I had to step up on the scale and then go through all the checks.

When the nurse led us back to the exam room, he stood quietly just inside while she checked my blood pressure and asked me routine questions. Then she told me I could lay back and relax while we waited for the ultrasound tech. I doubted I would be able to relax.

"How're you doing?" Casey came to sit at my side once she left the room.

Instead of answering, I just reached for his hand again. He took mine and gave it a reassuring squeeze. "You got this."

We didn't have to wait long for the tech to come in and get the sonogram machine going. I was glad this one would be different than my first one. She had me lay back and then raised my shirt up so she could spread the goo over my rounded stomach. I'd expected it to be cold, but was surprised when it was actually slightly warm. She grabbed the Doppler and brought it to my stomach, her eyes on the screen. I hadn't even realized that I'd reached for Casey's hand again and was holding my breath while she searched for the heartbeat. When it filled the room, I let out my breath and he gave me another squeeze.

"Strong, steady heartbeat," the tech murmured and I smiled up at Casey, who smiled back. "Now let's see what we can find." She continued to move the Doppler over my stomach and my nerves went into overdrive. It was then that I could be truly honest with myself about why I was so scared to know. It wasn't just that it would mean I finally had to start thinking about names and make decisions without Ty. It was that I was about to find out if I had a mini Ty inside of me.

I knew that no matter what, I would see him in our baby, but if I had a son, would I see Ty even more every time I looked at him? Would it break my heart? Did I want that? I couldn't decide if I was more afraid that I was having a son, or that I wasn't. Yes, the thought of having a little boy who looked like his father was painful, but it also filled me with hope.

I stared at the screen, waiting for a clear image to appear. This time when I saw it I was able to make it out much better. I'd looked at enough ultrasound pictures online to know what I was searching for. After a minute my heart stopped. "Is that-?"

"Yes, I think it's safe to say you're having a boy. Congratulations." She captured the pictures while I sucked in a sharp breath and the tears immediately started falling. They were mostly tears of joy, but my heart still hurt so much. I squeezed my eyes shut.

We're having a boy Ty. A boy. He's going to be perfect, but I wish you were here so badly. I wish you would get to see your son being born, and watch him grow up, and teach him how to throw a football, but I promise to tell him all about you. I'll make sure he knows what a good man his father was, and I hope he turns out just like you.

When I finally pried my eyes open, both the nurse and Casey were looking at me with concern. I tried to apologize for losing it, but I couldn't form words for fear of turning hysterical.

"Can you give us a minute?" Casey asked. She nodded and then swiftly discarded her gloves and left the room, but not before handing Casey the cloth to clean my stomach. As soon as she was gone, he stood and wrapped one arm around my shoulder, tugging me into his side while he gently wiped up the gel. I grabbed his shirt and turned my face to bury it against him.

"It's okay. I'm here and we can sit here however long you need." He just held me and let me cry. At some point he tossed aside the cloth and took a seat on the edge of my exam bed and wrapped his other arm around me, stroking a hand up and down my back.

"I'm so, so sorry Olivia. You're not alone though; he's here with you. He'll always be with you. In your heart and in your son. You'll be okay, I promise, and you're going to be such a great mom to that little boy. He's the luckiest baby in the whole world to have you." I cried more at his sweet words before I was able to pull myself together. I took a few deep breaths and then I pulled away, tugging my shirt down when I realized my stomach was still exposed.

"Bet you're regretting coming with me now," I tried to laugh. "I'm such a mess," I sniffed. I was too embarrassed to meet his eyes, but he didn't let me hide. He tipped my chin up with his forefinger. There was so much kindness and compassion on his face that it almost broke me again.

"You don't ever have to be ashamed in front of me. If you want to cry for another hour, I'll tell the nurses to stay the hell away until you're done; whatever you need." His expression told me he was dead serious, that he would do that for me.

"You don't need to do that. I'm just having a weak moment."

"There's nothing weak about you. You're the strongest person I've ever met." He cupped my face between his hands, using thumbs to wipe away the tears that spilled from my eyes and I blinked furiously to try and stop anymore from spilling. His hands lingered there just a moment before he dropped them and walked over to the desk and brought me a tissue.

We got through the rest of my appointment without anymore tears. When it was all done I had another picture to show off, and an appointment scheduled for four weeks away. Baby and I were healthy. My little boy was growing strong.

We didn't talk much on the drive; I think he sensed that I needed the quiet. There was a lot going on inside of me and I felt like pregnancy hormones multiplied everything by ten. When we were back at the apartment complex, he paused outside my door, looking like he wanted to say something, but then decided against it.

"I guess I'll see you later, Tate." It wasn't until he started walking toward his own apartment, that I grabbed him and hugged him.

"Thank you so much. I couldn't have handled that on my own."

He wound his arms around me tightly. "Any time. I mean that too." He took a step back and gently turned my chin with his fingers so that I was looking at his door. "I'm right there. You can come to me any time. Even if I'm not home, I want you to know that I'm here if you need me. You've got my number. Don't be afraid to use it."

I promised him that I wouldn't, and then I crawled into my apartment and curled up in my bed and fired off a single text message.

It's a boy.

Twenty minutes later I heard my apartment door open and then Mel walked into the room and climbed up beside me. She took my hand in hers and laid her head next to mine. "He's going to be beautiful, like both of his parents." Her words wrung the last few tears out of me, and after they had fallen I turned to face Mel.

"I hope he has Tyler's eyes. And his smile. I miss his eyes and his smile," I whispered.

"I hope he has his mama's heart, because she has the most amazing heart," she whispered back. I was wrong; I had a couple tears left.

We lay there quietly for a while. I thought a lot about my son and Tyler, and all the traits he could pass on to our baby, all the ones I hoped they'd share, and all the things I wanted to teach him. I'd learn to throw a football if I had to, and I would buy him model cars just I like I did Ty. I wanted to find as many ways as I could for my son to be close to his dad. Then I had a thought that actually made me giggle. I slapped a hand over my mouth surprised by the sound of my own laughter. Mel looked at me puzzled, and I giggled again. I couldn't help it. "I hope he can dance better than Ty."

Mel's expression cracked and then she too was giggling, which only made me laugh harder until were both gasping, trying to suppress our laughter. Ty had a lot of talents, but dancing was not one of them. Not even close.

"Don't worry, I'll teach the little man to dance," she assured me. She leaned her face down next to my belly. "I promise Jelly Bean, I won't let you embarrass yourself like your daddy used to." I grinned at her and she smiled back, but then her face fell. "I'm really sorry I wasn't there with you. I know how badly you didn't want to go alone."

"I didn't go alone."

"What do you mean?"

"Casey went with me."

"Casey went?" I picked up on a hint of disapproval.

"Yes," I said defensively. I didn't like that she was going to make more out of it than it was. "It was just as hard as I knew it would be, and having him there helped. He handled my breakdown really well. I'm not sure I would have made it through without someone there."

"Then I'm glad you had someone. It just seems like he's around a lot when you need someone. I know he's a good guy, but I also know things can get blurred at times in emotional situations. You're really vulnerable right now, and it wouldn't be good for either one of you if something happened."

I sat up and scowled at her. "Are you serious right now, Mel? You really think that's what's going on, that I could do that?"

"Well, no, but-"

"There's nothing going on, so just don't even go there. Yes, Casey has been here for me. He lives two doors down and I'm thankful for that, thankful for him, because he is a really good guy, but the thought of being *with* another guy, in any way, makes me sick to my stomach. This isn't some break up I'm going to rebound from and then regret it later." It was one thing to get the funny looks and subtle prying from the other girls on the team, especially Jamie. What they thought didn't bother me, but Mel was supposed to know me better than that and it hurt that she didn't.

105

"I'm sorry, Liv. I didn't mean . . . I don't know what I was thinking, or maybe I wasn't thinking. I just worry about you and I can't stand the thought of anything, or anyone else, hurting you more."

"I know I've done a lot of impulsive and reckless things Mel, but not that." I felt dejected. "Casey's not like that either."

"I believe you, I do. I'm sorry. Like I said I just worry so much about you being vulnerable and I know sometimes guys can't help but want to play the white knight."

"Vulnerable or not, the last thing I'm thinking about is another guy. It hurts too much to even imagine the day when I could love or even like somebody else in that way. I don't know if I'll ever be ready for another relationship."

"I'm really sorry Liv. I am. I shouldn't have said anything." Her eyes pleaded for understanding, and a small part of me did understand where she was coming from, but it was overshadowed by the part of me that was mad at her for even making those presumptions.

"I know you are Mel, and I know it only came out of your concern for me, but I think I'd really just like to be alone right now. It's been a crappy couple days and I just don't have it in me to deal with anything else." She looked hurt by my dismissal, and I almost regretted it, but I didn't take it back.

"Please forgive me for being stupid. Don't be mad at me." I couldn't help it, I was mad.

"I know you meant well, but please just go for now." She nodded solemnly and stood up to leave, but before she was out of the room I called her name and she turned back to look at me. Even if I was upset I couldn't let her leave without making sure she knew that I loved her. There was nothing like living with the regret of knowing you missed your last chance to tell someone you loved them before it was too late. I wouldn't do that again.

"I love you," I said it just loud enough for her to hear, and the relief on her face sent a pang of guilt through me.

"I love you too. I'll see you tomorrow?" she asked hopefully.

"Yeah, I'll call you." I couldn't stay mad at her long for trying to look out for me, even if she was way off.

I laid there for quite a while, trying to let the things Mel said go. I didn't want to be mad at her, but hearing her give weight to the same rumors that had been going around the team bothered me more than I wanted to admit. For the most part I just ignored them, hoping that eventually they would see that there really wasn't anything going on, and move on, but it didn't seem to be working. And now Mel was having those thoughts.

I knew I'd never get to sleep if I let myself lay there and dwell on it any longer, so I did what I always did at night, the one thing that helped me to find a little bit of peace. I talked to Ty. About everything and anything, even Casey, but mostly our son. I talked until I felt my eyelids grow heavy and my words became yawns, and in the few minutes of quiet before I finally fell asleep I almost thought I heard him whispering back to me. It was more of a feeling than actual words, but it felt like he was telling me everything was going to be okay.

Fourteen

*"The most beautiful people we have known are those
who have known defeat, known suffering, known struggle,
known loss, and have found their way out of the depths . . .
Beautiful people do not just happen."*
— Elisabeth Kübler-Ross

"Mint green and yellow?" Mel asked, making notes on her tablet.

"Yes," I confirmed.

"But you don't want a theme?" This was the fourth time she had asked if I wanted a theme.

"Isn't baby the theme? Why do I have to pick something else?" Not for the first time, I heard a low chuckle coming from the seat in front of mine.

"Well, I guess you don't *have* to, but I mean there are just so many options. Like you could do baby jungle animals, or just pick one animal, like monkeys. Monkeys are cute. Or dinosaurs. Oooh, you could go with Disney babies. That's a classic, but I need something to work with for decorations and the cake, even if you just want baby footprints."

We'd been discussing ideas for my baby shower since we boarded the plane to Missouri an hour ago. I was almost ready to tell her to do whatever she wanted. I didn't realize there were so many decisions to make, but she wanted me to be involved in all of it. I think she just wanted me to be happy, but didn't realize I would have been happier letting her decide. We had to go over game ideas, the guest list, where we wanted to have it and if I wanted to register on any baby sites.

"I don't know." She gave me a frustrated look. "Okay, okay, I think I like the footprints idea."

She perked right up. "Perfect, that will be so cute. Ooh, we could have the cake frosted yellow with little green and blue footprints going up it and maybe baby blocks. No, not blocks, but a giant bow. Yeah, oh it could be like a present with ribbon going around it too, with a gift tag

108

that says something like 'welcome baby' or 'it's a boy' or if he has a name by then it could have his name on it. Is he going to have a name by then?"

Something else she'd been subtly pressuring me about. I'd actually tried. I even got on one of those baby name sites, but there were just so many and it felt overwhelming. None of them felt right yet, but the baby shower was still a little over three weeks away.

"Maybe."

She gave me another withering look. "I swear this baby is going to be born Jelly Bean."

I just shrugged, but then she grew serious.

"I know this isn't easy and I'm sorry if I'm making you crazy. Don't worry about the name. The right one will come to you when you're ready. We can always just put Jelly Bean on the cake." She smiled. "Ooh, we could put jelly beans out in little dishes all over the place," a-a-and crazy baby shower planner was back. "That would be so cute."

I just nodded in agreement.

"Now we just need to decide what kind of cake you want." She looked at me expectantly.

"Umm, the kind you eat." Once again the familiar chuckle sounded in front of us. Mel shot daggers at the back of his seat.

"Perhaps you have a recommendation, Hunt?" I had to bite back my own laughter. He turned around and leaned back over his seat, flashing a megawatt smile at her.

"Nope. You're doing an amazing job. I won't pretend to know anything about the complexities involved in selecting the flavor for a baby shower cake," he teased her playfully and then winked at me before facing forward and dropping back into his seat. "But I do like chocolate."

She rolled her eyes. "You're not even invited."

He laughed but she ignored it and turned back to me. "There are so many cake flavors out there nowadays. If you can think of it, someone can make it. At one of my mom's parties she had this champagne cake with a peach custard filling. It was amazing." She continued to rattle off flavor ideas that I'm sure would have been fitting for the most extravagant event, but they weren't really me.

109

"What about something simple, like white cake with chocolate filling and buttercream frosting?" She looked at me as if I had just asked if we could serve mud pies. "Hey, you can have the fancy ass cake at your baby shower. I want simple, something that everyone will like."

"Fine," she feigned irritation, but I knew that if I asked for mud pies, she would let me have mud pies. By the time our plane touched down in Kansas City we had every detail worked out for the party and Mel was excited to implement all of her wonderful ideas and throw me the greatest baby shower Texas had ever seen. In the mean time, the team had a Championship to try and win.

Which they almost did. After a couple of close wins over the next two days, they ended up losing to Oklahoma State in the final match. It was only the second game they'd lost all season, and even though we didn't take the championship, everyone wanted to go out to celebrate that night after the match. I decided to opt out since dancing and drinking didn't appeal to me in my current condition. I was beat and just wanted to curl up and maybe watch a movie.

"Are you sure you don't want to go out with us?" Mel asked as she, Amy and Becca finished applying their makeup in our hotel room.

"I'm sure. Getting all sweaty on the dance floor is really the last thing I want to do tonight, but I hope you girls have fun."

Fifteen minutes later they were all dolled up in tight dresses and high heels, not that Mel needed those extra five inches, and on their way out the door. I was comfy in a pair of cotton shorts and my Red Raiders hoodie. I flopped down on the bed with the television remote in hand and started searching for a movie.

I was trying to decide between Bruce Willis in one of the Die Hards and some new Liam Neeson movie, when my phone buzzed with a text message. I reached over and grabbed it from the nightstand. It was from Casey.

You going out with everyone else?

No, I stayed behind, I sent back. Thirty seconds later he replied.

Me too :)

Not in the partying mood?

No. I'd rather stay in and order room service and watch a movie tonight.

Woah don't get too wild ;)

What about you, miss excitement? What grand plans do you have for the evening?

I'm gonna watch a movie :)

Woah don't get too wild, he fed my line right back to me.

I'm pregnant. What's your excuse? Where's your team spirit?

I must have forgotten to pack it.

Before I could type out another message my phone rang.

"You should really remember to pack it next time," I answered.

He chuckled, "If bringing my team spirit means I have to go out with those girls, I think I'll leave it at home next time too."

"Don't lie, you're probably just disappointed you didn't get invited."

"Oh, to the contrary my friend, Jamie did invite me to go with them, but as the song goes, that girl is poison. Her intentions are written all over her face. I try to stay away from that one." I could almost hear him shudder and I tried not to laugh because it was so true. She had zero shame and lately had been coming on to Casey stronger than usual.

"That's probably a wise decision."

"Speaking of wise decisions, I've got a pizza coming and I'm planning on watching that new Liam Neeson movie if you're interested."

"You say pizza? Well sure, if you're going to twist my arm."

"That was easy. I really thought I was going to have to work a lot harder to get you out of your room."

"What can I say; you had me at pizza."

His low chuckle came through the phone, "You pregnant chicks are too easy. All it takes is the mention of food."

"You got me," I didn't argue. Neither did I mention that it was also his company. Hanging out with him seemed less pathetic than watching the movie by myself.

"Well I'm one floor up from you, room five-ten."

"See ya in a minute." When I hung up I tucked my phone into my pocket, flipped off the TV and stepped into my flip flops. I left one lamp on and turned out the rest of the lights and slipped out the door. I only had to stand outside Casey's room for a second after knocking before he pulled the door open and invited me in. We almost matched, with him in a pair of athletic shorts and his own team sweatshirt. Here we were in a big city on a Saturday night, and we both looked ready for bed.

Unlike me, Casey had a room to himself; all of the coaching staff did. I'm sure I could have asked for my own room, but I didn't mind rooming with Mel and Becca and Amy. His room was almost identical to ours. Same tan walls with modern art and sleek furnishings. The only difference was, instead of two double beds, he had one big king bed in the middle of his room and a small couch on the far side.

His computer was sitting open on the desk near the window as well as an Indiana University baseball cap, which I'd learned is where he went to school, but other than that I didn't see any of his personal belongings lying around. He was probably already packed up and ready for our flight home in the morning. "Isn't it frowned upon for staff to wear gear from another school?" I joked.

He just grinned. "You can take the boy out of Indiana . . ."

I pulled out the chair from the desk and flopped down. There was a knock at the door.

"Make yourself at home," he told me and moved to answer it. As soon as he pulled it open I could smell the pizza and my stomach growled. Casey grabbed the food and plates, and then slipped the kid a tip before closing the door.

He set everything down on the small coffee table and opened the pizza box, then walked over to the mini fridge. The pizza looked as amazing as it smelled. My stomach growled again and he turned and grinned at me. "You weren't kidding, you really are here for the pizza," he then pulled two bottles of water from the fridge and handed me one.

"Thanks," I said, taking it from him and then stealing a slice of the chicken and pineapple pizza that had my mouth watering. Casey put two slices on his own plate and then moved to sit on the foot of the bed.

"Come on." He gestured for me to join him, so I did. "How are you feeling tonight?"

"Fine, baby and me are both good," I answered him, and took a bite of the deliciously cheesy pizza.

"I don't mean the pregnancy. I mean how are you feeling about the match?" I wasn't quite sure what he was asking.

"Well, I'm proud of the team, but of course a little disappointed that they didn't get the championship."

"And thinking that if you had been out there things might have been different?"

"No."

He lowered his chin and cocked a skeptical eyebrow at me.

"Okay, maybe I did think it, but it's okay, really. I've accepted that my playing days are over." *Liar.* The truth was it was still so hard to watch from the sidelines, to not be a part of the action out on the field.

"Remember you're talking to me and you can be honest with me. I see your face every time the team takes the field. You stare at the ground with sad eyes, like your heart is breaking, and then by the second half you always look ready to tackle one of the girls for her jersey so you can get out there."

I stared back at him, surprised that he had seen through me so easily. I thought I'd kept my emotions in check. I tried to encourage the girls and cheer for my team while on the inside my heart was breaking. "Am I really that terrible at hiding it?"

"No, but I recognize it. Four years ago that was me, only I was a lot worse at hiding it. I was angry, kicking things and getting in everyone's faces."

"You used to play?" It was obvious that he was a natural athlete, but I'd had no idea he played for a team.

"I started for Indiana University until my senior year when I tore my ACL half way through the season."

"Ouch." At least giving up the game was my choice. I could still play at the same level if I wanted to after the baby, but with an injury like that he wouldn't have been the same player even after recovering.

"You're telling me. Before it happened I was about to be picked up by the Houston Dynamo. That's how I ended up in Texas. They'd already flown me down a few times to check out the team and the area. When Coach Davis contacted me after I graduated, and offered me the athletic trainer position, I jumped at it. It was a chance to stay a part of the sport, and I liked Texas, and I needed a fresh start."

"I had no idea." But it was a relief to know that someone really did understand exactly how I was feeling, as much as anyone could.

113

"It still sucks sometimes, when I flip on a game and think, 'man that could've been me.' Soccer was the only thing I saw in my future, and then it was gone, just like that." *Exactly.* "I had such a hard time accepting it and didn't know who I was without it."

That was exactly how I felt. I didn't know who I was without Ty and soccer. "I used to be so sure of myself. I just knew I was going to play professional soccer. My parents always encouraged me, and Tyler was my biggest supporter. Nobody ever told me I couldn't do it. I knew it would be hard, but I just never considered the possibility that it wouldn't happen. I didn't have a back-up plan. I never let myself want anything else, so now I don't know what I want. I feel lost," I confessed.

"I know."

"Is that why you've been so determined to help me?"

"It's one reason," he admitted. "I remember what it felt like for those first six months; they were the worst. I was drowning in my anger and couldn't look past it long enough to see that my life wasn't over. Even after I accepted it, I was still so mad. I blew my senior year, wasted it being angry and feeling sorry for myself, and not caring about anything but what I'd lost. I had to repeat that whole year." He fixed his eyes on mine. "I want you to realize that you're not just a damn good soccer player. There's more to you than that. You're fierce and almost unstoppable out there on that field because you're a fighter even off the field. This isn't the end for you. It's the beginning of something unexpected, but it can still be great. You might not believe that right now. I know I didn't when I was in your place, but now . . ." He looked away for a moment before bringing his eyes back to lock on mine. "Now, I can see that things worked out how they were meant to."

"You mean you wouldn't change it, go back if you could?"

"I don't know. I can't say that for sure, but I do know that I'm exactly where I'm meant to be." He was obviously talking about his life in Lubbock, his job and his relationship with Annie, but for a brief second, I almost thought he meant here in this room with me. I brushed that thought away immediately, not even sure where it came from.

I never did ask him what his other reasons were for wanting to help me. It didn't really matter, I was just thankful. It had been so hard trying to act like I was doing fine at every practice and game, not even able to talk to Mel because there was no way for her to understand. She didn't realize how much it killed me every time she put on her jersey and laced up her cleats and ran out on that field. Casey saw it even when I thought I was doing a good job of hiding it, because he understood it. He'd been through it and he'd come out of it alright, better than alright. His outlook was inspiring. Our situations weren't the same, but at one point in his life he'd thought he lost everything that mattered, and here he was, on the other side of it, living his life and enjoying life again. It was encouraging.

We finished off the pizza while the movie started, and when we were both done, he took care of our plates. Before sitting back down, he flipped off the lights and then turned on the lamp next to the bed. Instead of returning to his spot at the edge, he climbed all the way up to the head of the bed, and adjusted the pillows behind his back. He stretched his legs out in front of him, then grabbed one of the pillows on the opposite side of the bed and tossed it at my face.

"Might as well get comfy," he said, so I followed suit and scooted up the bed so that my position mirrored his. There was plenty of room between us and I felt comfortable enough with Casey that I could relax without it being weird.

We didn't talk much, except to comment here or there on the movie, but when it was over we both agreed that Liam Neeson was as bad ass as ever.

"So, you want to head back to your room or you up for another movie?" he asked as the credits rolled at the end of the film. Surprisingly, as exhausted as my body felt, I wasn't actually tired yet so I decided to stay.

"I'll watch another one." We scrolled through the options and decided on a newer cop comedy that neither of us had seen. It was funny, but part way through, my exhaustion caught up with me and I didn't even realize when my eyes drifted shut and I dozed off. Next thing I knew, I was waking up and the TV was off, but I could hear Casey talking to someone. I opened my eyes and he was standing across the room on his phone. He smiled at me briefly when he saw I was awake, and then continued his conversation.

"Yeah. Our plane will get in around one tomorrow . . . Yeah, that sounds good . . . I miss you too, but I'll see you then . . ." He exhaled

115

deeply at whatever the person – most likely Annie – had said. "Come on, don't be like that." He lowered his voice, but I still couldn't help but overhear his side of the conversation.

"Don't. You know how I feel . . . I'm sorry. Don't be upset, it's not like that . . . Please can we just not do this tonight? I'll be home tomorrow and we can talk then . . . Goodnight." I felt extremely awkward having intruded on a private moment that I shouldn't have overheard.

He hung up his phone and ran a hand through his already mussed hair. I could tell he was frustrated or stressed and I just wanted to give him his privacy, so I stood up to go.

"I'm sorry I fell asleep. I'll get out of here now," I stretched and yawned deeply.

"It's okay, you don't have to apologize. Not for falling asleep or what you just heard. It's really fine."

I just nodded and walked over to the door. "Goodnight Hunt. Thanks for the pizza and letting me hang out, and just for understanding and sharing with me what you did."

"Night, Tate."

I made it all the way to my room before I realized that I'd left my phone and key card in Casey's room. I started back down the hall toward the stairwell, but the elevator dinged as I walked past. Thinking it might be Casey with my phone, I stopped and waited for it to open. Instead of Casey, a bunch of the girls from the team spilled out. Mel and Amy were among them. So was Jamie.

"Hey!" Mel exclaimed cheerfully, more than a little tipsy. "Where are you going?"

"Snack machine," I lied and it was believable considering she knew that it was usually at night that the cravings would hit.

Some of the other girls started shuffling toward their rooms, but then the second elevator dinged open and this time Casey did step out. My phone and key card were in his hand. He stopped short when he saw everyone.

Jamie sauntered over to him, "What are you doing on our floor?" she gave him a grin that said she was pleased to see him. His eyes flashed to mine briefly and then he made the same decision I had and lied, even though we had nothing to hide.

116

"Must have hit the wrong button. Have a good night ladies." He backtracked into the elevator and the doors shut behind him. Everyone dispersed to their rooms while Mel, Becca and Amy waited at our door for me to unlock it.

"Shoot, I think I left the key in the room," I told them.

"Well then I guess it's a good thing we got back when we did." Mel rifled through her clutch until she found hers and let us in. "You didn't get too wild while we were gone, did you?"

"Just watched a couple movies." I flopped down on the bed Mel and I were sharing. She went about stripping right in the middle of the room while Amy shut herself in the bathroom and Becca dug through her bags.

"How scandalous," the sarcasm rolled off Mel's lips and she threw her dress at me, the fabric smacked me in the face. I swiped it to the floor, thinking it probably wouldn't take long for the three of them to pass out once they climbed into bed. Then I could slip upstairs and retrieve my things from Casey. Mel threw herself down next to me in her t-shirt and underwear and rolled close. "You know what would be really scandalous?" she drunk whispered, which was still loud enough for Becca to hear. Mel was the only one who thought she was being quiet.

"What?" I humored her.

"If you spent the night hanging out in Casey's room," she narrowed her eyes on me and my expression froze. How the hell did she know? "It would certainly explain why he got off the elevator with your phone in his hand," she smirked and my eyes shot to Becca who was clearly listening, but ducked her head and pretended she hadn't been. I glared at Mel and she gave me an apologetic look.

I just sighed. I had to explain or it would look worse. "We were both around the hotel tonight so we watched a movie in his room and ate pizza. It's not a big deal, but you know how gossipy the girls can be," I made a point of emphasizing that last part. "Just didn't want anyone jumping to conclusions." I hoped that would be enough to keep Becca from feeding the rumors, and Amy if she was listening.

"I know there's nothing going on with you and Hunt and I'll smack a bitch that says otherwise." Mel snuggled in closer and I gave her a shove.

"Come on. Cuddle me," she whined, latching onto me like I was her body pillow. I gave her another hard shove and suppressed a laugh when she rolled off the bed. "Bitch," she moaned from the floor. She popped up a few minutes later as Amy was coming out of the bathroom and Becca traded places with her. "I just texted your phone and told Casey it was safe to bring it down."

Sure enough, a few minutes later he knocked at the door and returned my phone and room key. I only hoped in the morning that it wouldn't be team knowledge. Of course that hope was in vain. Becca was close with Cassie and Jamie.

The next morning, Jamie made it a point to come over and ask me about my night while we waited in the airport to board our flight home. Mel snapped at her and told her to back off, but it was clear what Jamie had been insinuating and the damage was done. There were a few snickers when she walked back over to her little group. Becca at least had the decency to appear guilty and avoided my gaze while a few of the others sent me dirty looks. I would have understood their hostility if it was because they thought I was hooking up with Casey while he had a girlfriend – now that they all knew about her – but most of them couldn't care less that he was in a relationship. Jamie and those girls were pissed because they wanted him and thought I had him. At this point, I doubted there was anything I could do to convince them otherwise, so I just kept my distance and hoped they didn't say anything in front of Casey or the other coaches. The last thing I wanted was to create drama and cause trouble for Casey.

Fifteen

"And I need you tonight
I'll fall asleep and it's alright
Close my eyes and I'll be by your side"
– On Top of the World

"Uhn," I groaned when I walked into Casey's office rubbing my sore arms. I plopped down in the chair opposite him and sighed at the relief of giving my legs a break. Thankfully the day was almost over, I just had to wait for Casey to finish up whatever he was working on and then we could go.

"What's wrong?" he looked up from his computer at me.

"I'm just really sore. I feel like every muscle in my body is aching right now."

"Did you push yourself too hard?" I could tell he was ready to lecture me again.

"No, I swear I didn't. I've been taking it easy, nothing to strenuous. Yesterday I upped the weights, but only by like five pounds, and I swam a few extra laps, but that's it."

"You still doing the warm ups and drinking plenty of water and stretching?"

"Yes. I don't understand why everything hurts today," I whined. He wheeled his chair out from his desk and around to where I was sitting. He reached out and took my left arm in his hand. He started massaging the muscles all the way up my forearm to my shoulders and neck. This time when I groaned it was in pleasure.

"That feels good," I told him. He continued to work the tension and ache out of my sore muscles down my other arm. I let out a little whimper of protest when he released my arm, but then he wheeled around to my front and grabbed one of my legs, pulling it up into his lap. I leaned my head back against the chair and closed my eyes when he started massaging my calf. He moved closer to me as he worked his way up my leg. His hands were just above my knee at the edge of my

119

athletic shorts when the sound of his office door opening startled me out of my relaxed state.

Casey's hands stilled as I opened my eyes and looked up to see the last person in the world that I wanted to see, standing there, shooting daggers at me with her eyes.

"Do you need something Jamie?" Casey asked her and she shifted her attention to him, flashing a dangerous smile.

"Coach asked me to bring this to you." She held up a stack of papers. "I didn't realize I would be interrupting."

"You weren't interrupting anything Jamie." He wheeled his chair back a few feet, releasing my leg.

"Sure didn't look that way to me," she mumbled. Casey stood up and reached for the papers she was holding. At first she seemed reluctant to release them, but he tugged them from her grip. Still, she stood there staring at him. Casey shifted uncomfortably.

"Was there anything else you needed?" he asked her.

"Well now that you mention it, I've been having some pains in my lower back; maybe I can schedule a personal massage too."

"I'll see you tomorrow at practice, Jamie," he said, clearly dismissing her. She shot me another glare before turning and walking out of the room.

"I think I'm going to have to break that girl's nose again," I grumbled under my breath. There was no way she would ever believe my relationship with Casey was innocent now.

"Again?" Casey raised his eyebrows and I had no choice but to tell him about our incident freshman year when I didn't like the way she looked at Ty. He enjoyed that and laughed.

"God, I wish I had seen it."

"You might just get to yet. She has it out for me I think."

"It's not you." He looked away, almost shamefully.

"Well yeah, I think it's pretty clear that it's you she has a thing for, but we've never gotten along."

"It's hard to get along with a troll," he joked, only it wasn't really a joke. "But don't worry about her. We haven't done anything to give her ammo. You're hardly the first athlete I've given a massage to. Everyone knows she just likes to stir up trouble."

I snorted. That was an understatement. I thought about letting him know that Becca had blabbed about us hanging out at the hotel last weekend, but decided if she hadn't said anything yet, she probably wouldn't bring it up. Casey pushed the door shut again and then slid back into his chair.

"Here, give me your other leg." He patted his knee.

"Are you sure? I mean, I'll be fine. It's okay really. I'm not actually that sore." Even if Jamie hadn't interrupted I didn't want to admit how intimate the moment had started to feel with his strong hands moving over my bare skin. It would be better if we both just went home and forgot all about it.

"Tate, just give me your damn leg and then we can go home." He made it sound like no big deal, and I guess to him it wasn't. After all, like he said, it wasn't uncommon for him to give an athlete a massage. I was reading too much into just like Jamie had, maybe because I'd only ever received massages from one other guy. But if Casey could be professional about it, so could I. I lifted my leg and placed it in his lap.

At first I stayed sitting up and tried not to pay attention to how good it felt, but after a couple minutes I found myself relaxing into the chair again. I couldn't help it. He knew what he was doing with those hands. They were warm and a little rough against my smooth skin, making it all the more obvious that they were a guy's hands.

I opened my eyes to see Casey staring intently at me as his hands reached my thigh again. My breath hitched and for a brief second, I almost thought something was passing between the two of us, but then he looked away and the moment was broken. Then I felt silly for even thinking it was a moment, and letting my mind wander that direction.

I missed the intimacy that came with having a lover. I missed having someone to touch and touch me back. I missed the feel of Ty's hands on my body as he made me feel pleasure like nothing else. I missed the feel of my soul connecting with his when we came together. It had been almost five months since I'd had that, and the desire to feel it again was just getting to me and making my pregnancy hormones go wonky. I felt my face flush in embarrassment at reacting to Casey's innocent touch in that way. He was focused intently on my leg, so I hoped he didn't notice. I was relieved when he finished and put distance between us again, even as something on the inside of me lamented the loss of his touch. Only I knew it wasn't really his touch I craved and I immediately felt guilty for thinking just for a second that anyone's touch could replace what I'd lost.

"Ready to go?" Casey asked after he'd gathered up his things and shut his computer down.

"Yup." I avoided looking him in the eye, afraid he'd see the indecent turn my thoughts had taken. I just couldn't help it, and it wasn't like I wanted to act on them. Ty and I had a very healthy sex life and now I was knocked up, emotional and hormonal, not to mention celibate for the foreseeable future. It wasn't the greatest combination. I took a deep breath and then exhaled a sigh before following Casey out of his office.

"Everything alright?" he asked as we made our way out of the fitness center.

"Trust me; you don't want to know what's going on in my head right now. It's a whole lot of crazy."

"Oh yeah? Crazy huh?" He grinned at me.

"Consider yourself warned if you and Annie ever decide to have kids. Pregnancy . . ." I shook my head. "Just, yeah, crazy is the only word for how I feel sometimes. Most of the time. Hell, almost all the time." I expected him to laugh or make some joke, but instead it looked like he was lost inside his own head and not even listening. A frown was etched across his face.

"Now it's my turn to ask you if you're alright; did I scare you with my craziness?" We'd reached the parking lot and he unlocked his car and slid inside. I walked over to the passenger's side and did the same, waiting for him to say something.

"It's nothing. I was just thinking." I knew it was definitely something, but I couldn't make him talk to me if he didn't want to. I had a feeling it had to do with my comment about him and Annie. I probably shouldn't have said that when I knew he didn't like talking about the two of them. I was also aware that there was still some tension in their relationship. From the few phone conversations I'd overheard since Kansas City, I could tell things weren't perfect between them, but I thought they were working through it.

I tried not to spend any more time contemplating their relationship since it wasn't my business, but I didn't like not knowing what was bothering Casey. Any time he noticed I was upset he did whatever he could to cheer me up, even if it was as simple as bringing a Reese's to work with him. Yet, as close as we'd become, he still kept so much of himself closed off to me. I wished there was a way I could let him know that he could talk to me, without seeming like I was prying. After a few minutes of semi-awkward silence in the car, I felt like I needed to say something.

"I'm sorry if I said something I shouldn't have. You know, about you guys having kids."

He sighed but kept his eyes forward on the road. "It's fine you didn't say anything wrong. It's just sometimes I . . ."

"What?"

"Never mind. I don't know what I'm saying," he trailed off.

"You know you can talk to me right? I'm a good listener."

"I appreciate that Tate, but I really can't."

"Because of Annie?"

"It's not that I don't want to talk to you, it just wouldn't be right."

I felt like a complete idiot, of course he shouldn't talk to me about her. Their relationship needed to stay between them. I don't know what I was thinking, except that I was too nosy for my own good sometimes. Discussing his and Annie's relationship with me would be crossing a line and a violation of Annie's trust. I knew Casey was a good guy but my respect for him went up a notch.

"You're a good guy, Hunt."

"I don't know about that," he muttered.

Why didn't he think he was a good guy? I was an expert on good guys. I'd had the best guy, so I knew what they looked like, and Casey was definitely one of the good ones. We were both quiet the rest of the drive. He seemed to be lost in his thoughts and from the troubled expression he still wore, they were clearly weighing on him. I didn't know what to say, so I didn't say anything until we were in the hall outside my apartment.

"Night, Hunt. See ya tomorrow."

"Night."

I climbed into bed and my mind went back to how I'd felt earlier with Casey's hands on me. I closed my eyes and let myself imagine that it had been Ty working out my sore muscles after an especially hard practice. Only in my fantasy Ty's hands didn't stop below the hem of my shorts. His hands kept going and I came apart under his touch. My body heated up and I squirmed beneath the covers. I had to throw them off because I was too warm. I felt like my skin was on fire and I was so turned on I didn't know how I'd ever find relief from the pressure building inside me. I pulled a pillow over my face to muffle the frustrated scream I let out. I tossed and turned for a while before I ever fell asleep, and when I did, what I dreamed about was just as torturous.

Ty came up behind me and wrapped his arms around my waist. I let myself lean into his embrace and rest my head against his hard chest. "I ran you a bath. Let me take care of you for the night."

"Uhn," I groaned blissfully. "Have I told you how much I love you, husband?" He just chuckled, placed a soft kiss behind my ear and led me to the bathroom. I could feel the steam coming off the bathtub and I couldn't wait to slide under the hot water. I pulled my sweaty practice shirt over my head, followed by my sports bra, and this time I wasn't the one that let out a groan of satisfaction. Ty was standing behind me. I looked over my shoulder and winked at him before slowly sliding my shorts and panties down. I watched his eyes trace over the curve of my spine down to my backside. He closed his eyes and let out a deep breath.

"You better get in that tub before I drag you out of here and spoil my attempt to do something nice for you." He kept his eyes closed tightly, and I could tell from the tension in his muscles that he was restraining himself.

"Oh, I think you'd make it real nice for me," I teased.

He chuckled soft and low. "Get in the water, Livvie. I've got to go check on dinner."

I tried to hide my grimace.

"I saw that," he threw over his shoulder as he exited the bathroom.

When he came back, I was covered by the layer of bubbles on top of the water. I was leaning against the back of the tub and my eyes were shut, but I heard him walk over to the side of the tub and sit on the ledge.

"Sit up," his command was soft, but his voice was firm. I opened my eyes and did as he'd said. The tops of my breasts rose above the water and when my chest heaved with each breath I took, more of me was revealed to him. I could see the desire pooling in his eyes.

He sat on the corner of the tub and began massaging my neck. I closed my eyes again and sighed. After a few minutes it wasn't enough though.

"You know, you could massage a lot more of me if you were in here with me." In that moment the large bathtub was my favorite feature in the whole apartment. He stood and stripped out of his clothes. I watched him intently, running my eyes over every delicious inch of him. I scooted forward so that he could slide in behind me and then leaned back against his solid chest. His hands moved around my waist and started massaging my front. As one hand moved higher while the other snaked lower I felt him harden against my lower back.

Ten minutes later the bathroom floor was covered in water and I lay sated against his chest. Tyler stood with me wrapped around his waist and stepped out of the tub. He didn't bother to grab a towel as he carried me to our bedroom.

"What about dinner?" I giggled.

"I'd rather just skip to dessert." He tossed me down on the bed and then lowered himself over me.

If I thought I was worked up before falling asleep, my body was positively humming when I woke frustrated and needing relief. What I wouldn't give to have Ty in bed with me now to relive that moment again and again.

"Ty you suck for leaving me in this condition. I'm not supposed to have to go through this. You weren't supposed to leave me. You shouldn't have gone running that morning. You should have stayed in bed with me. You should have stayed. You promised you'd always be here and now you're not," I cried angrily. It was easier to let myself be angry than to give into the soul crushing sorrow. It was the first time I'd really let myself be mad at him. I knew he didn't choose to leave me, that he had no control over it, but I just needed to let myself be mad.

125

Sixteen

"Make-up can only make you look pretty on the outside but it doesn't help if you're ugly on the inside. Unless you eat the make-up."
—Audrey Hepburn

I adjusted the neckline of my black halter dress one last time, making sure everything was where it was supposed to be, before I walked into the banquet hall. It was elegantly decorated in our school colors. The tables were covered in black tablecloths with beautiful red rose centerpieces and red cloth napkins at every place setting.

Looking around the room, and seeing how good everyone looked, all dressed up for our end of season banquet, caused me to self-consciously glance down at myself. The soft, lightweight material of my dress was fitted around my breasts and flowed down in an empire waist, over my belly, which was getting a little rounder every day, and stopped just above my knees. Mel had helped me pick it out for tonight. I really liked it and had left the apartment feeling good in it, so I don't know why I was suddenly self-conscious. I guess I was still learning to be comfortable in my constantly changing body. Fat was a word I tried not to entertain. I'd always thought pregnant women were beautiful, but now that I was experiencing it myself, it was difficult to feel beautiful.

"You look really nice," a familiar deep voice spoke softly in my ear. I spun around and looked up into the warm brown eyes of the tall figure before me.

"Thank you. You don't look too bad yourself, Hunt," I said, running my eyes over him. The bold red tie he wore stood out against the fitted dark grey dress shirt tucked into a pair of black dress pants. His hair was styled in that strategically messy way that he managed to pull off and still appear flawless. I had to look away to hide my blush once I realized my eyes had been lingering a little too long, and a little too appreciatively. My hand flitted to my own hair in a nervous gesture and I ran my fingers through the curls that fell loosely over my shoulders.

"Thanks," his tone was light and playful.

When I brought my eyes back to his face he was grinning at me, obviously aware that I had been admiring him, but rather than let it fluster me, I decided to ignore it. He had to know he was an attractive guy, and I'd have to be blind not to notice. It didn't mean anything, so there was no point in trying to hide it.

"Where's Annie?" I asked, taking a quick look around the room, but not seeing her. I was surprised that she wasn't at his side. Since our awkward conversation that night in his car, any troubles they'd been having had disappeared. Just a few days ago, I accidently walked in on a heated make out session between them in his office. The sight of her straddling his lap, and his hands roaming over the skin underneath her shirt, sent a bolt of desire right through me. I'd stood there frozen for a moment while Casey looked up at me embarrassed and Annie sent me death glares.

After making a hasty exit, I'd realized the image of the two of them together bothered me more than I cared to admit. I didn't like her, but I wondered if I'd dislike her so much if she wasn't dating Casey. I just didn't think she was right for him. I had a hard time telling myself it didn't matter what I thought. It just seemed that the last few weeks that their relationship had been going so well, Casey was more distant with me. It was probably better so there were no more confusing feelings messing with me, but I missed spending time with him.

"She went to the ladies' room. You want to sit with us?" He indicated a nearby table where I saw a few purses and jackets already claiming chairs. I didn't want to be rude, but I was pretty sure he was only asking to be polite because we both knew Annie would probably stab me with her salad fork if she found me at their table when she got back.

"I think Mel is saving a seat for me. I should probably find her."

"Okay, well enjoy the evening and I'll talk to you later," he excused himself back to his table, and I looked around for Mel. I spotted her over by the drink table with, Mark, her date for the evening and flavor of the month. Amy and Coach Walsh were with them. I started to head that way, but before I made it, Jamie stepped in front of me with a fake smile plastered on her face. She was wearing an almost inappropriately short red dress that hugged her slim body and accentuated every curve. Her blonde hair was pulled into some fancy side twist and I hated how good she looked. She wasn't just pretty, she was seriously gorgeous, and it drove me nuts because it did not match her insides at all. On the inside that girl was all troll.

She hardly even pretended to be civil anymore when it was just the two of us, and she had several of the girls on her side. I tried to brush it off and not let it get to me, but the truth was it really hurt to see the looks some of them would give me, or overhear them whispering about me. They were my teammates, or at least they used to be. Casey was a wedge that Jamie had successfully driven between me and the girls I used to consider friends.

"Wow, you've gotten pretty bold, *Tate*," she said my name like it was an insult. "Throwing yourself at him when his girlfriend is here. I wonder how she'd feel about that. I got the chance to chat with her earlier, and I didn't get the impression that she's your biggest fan. What a shock. I mean, I figured y'all must be so close since you and Casey spend so much time together, but now I'm wondering if Annie knows just how tight you are with her boyfriend."

I took a deep breath to keep myself from doing what I really wanted, which was hit her in that perfectly made up face. "So you think convincing her that there's something going on with me and Casey will do what exactly? Break them up so you can have at him? Yeah, I'm sure that will warm him up to you real nicely. Or are you just trying to get closer to her in hopes that it will get you closer to him? Either way, good luck with that." I ignored the death glare she gave me and brushed past her only to stop short when she spoke again.

"Just tell me, were you hooking up with him before your husband died, or did you bury him before you hopped beds? Is that baby your carrying even Tyler's, or are you just afraid of people finding out what a whore you really are?"

I turned around slowly, clenching my fists at my side. "You don't know what the hell you're talking about, so back the hell off before you really piss me off."

"Whatever, just own up to being a slut instead of pretending to be the poor little widow to get everyone to feel sorry for you and we wouldn't have an issue. You and me aren't all that different; I'm just sick of the perfect little, grieving wife act you've been putting on," she sneered.

"Don't think for a second that you know anything about me. I'm nothing like you, Jamie." I left her standing there rather than wring her neck for what she'd said.

"What did the shrew say now?" Mel asked when I came to stand next to her. She was shooting daggers with her eyes over my shoulder, and when I turned to look, Jamie was still standing there glaring at me.

"Just stirring up more shit," I said loud enough for only her to hear.

"Bitch," she muttered under breath. I just nodded. Then my phone buzzed inside of my clutch. I pulled it out and read the message.

Everything okay with Jamie?

It was Casey and he must have seen that little confrontation.

I looked over to where he was sitting, and he was looking back at me with a concerned expression. I still didn't see Annie with him. It only took a second to figure out why. Jamie had hi-jacked her now and appeared to be cozying up to her. Just what I needed; those two becoming bff's. I sighed and started typing out a response.

I need to talk to you for a minute.

If Jamie was going to try to manipulate Annie now, I needed to tell Casey.

Out in the hall.

I read his message and looked back up to see him walk over to where Annie was standing with Jamie. He whispered something in her ear and then kissed her on the cheek before walking out of the room.

"I'll be right back," I told Mel. She gave me a questioning look. "I'll explain when I get back." I stepped out into the long hallway and looked left, then right. He was leaning against the wall about fifteen feet away.

"What's up?" he asked when I walked over and joined him.

"I need to tell you something," I said reluctantly.

Casey picked up on my hesitation and immediately straightened. He took a step closer to me so that we were only inches apart and put his hands on my upper arms.

"Whatever it is, you can talk to me." I wasn't so sure anymore, considering how little we'd been talking lately, but I still knew I had to

129

give him the heads up, so I looked down at the floor to avoid seeing his reaction when I told him.

"I think Jamie is telling Annie that we've been hooking up."

He released my arms and seemed to relax. "Because she walked in on me massaging your leg? Let her say whatever she wants. It was completely innocent. We know it and she knows it and I'll make sure Annie knows it."

"It's not just that."

"Look, whatever else she wants to say, I'm not worried and you shouldn't be either."

"She knows about us hanging out in Kansas City in your hotel room."

"What?" he frowned.

"Becca told everyone after Mel's big mouth spilled it, and then it looked like we were trying to hide it. It didn't help that the rumors started before then."

"Why didn't you tell me?" He was biting back frustration.

"I thought it was better to ignore her, that if you confronted her, or tried to deny anything, it would only spur her on. I didn't realize she would take it this far." I dropped my eyes to my feet because I knew if he was frustrated that I hadn't told him about that, he wasn't gonna like the next part either. "She also thinks that it started before Ty died. I'm not sure, but she might even be telling people that my baby isn't his."

"What the fuck, she's saying it's mine?" he growled.

"I think so."

He let out a frustrated curse. I'd never seen this side of him before. He was always so laid back, but not right now. Right now he looked ready to tear someone apart. "How long has this been going on, Tate?"

"A while, I don't know."

"Dammit, you should have talked to me about this when it first started."

"I thought I could handle it," I said softly.

"When are you going to realize you don't have to take on everything by yourself?" he snapped, and I was startled that he seemed to be upset with me. "This involved me. You should have come to me and then maybe I could have done something about Jamie before it got to this."

130

"I'm sorry. I've tried telling her, I've tried telling all of them, that we're just friends, but it doesn't make a difference. Jealousy makes girls do ugly shit."

"Jealousy," he snorted incredulously. "So you're plan was to just sit back and take it until Jamie decided to ruin my relationship?" He had every right to be mad, and I should have given him the heads up sooner, but I was tired of apologizing and feeling bad. My own frustration spiked.

"I'm sorry I didn't want to tell you that my former teammates think I'm a cheating, home-wrecking slut, but I didn't expect Jamie or any of them to go this far. Now you know and you can do whatever you'd like, about it." I shoved past him, but stopped halfway to the exit and turned back to say one more thing. "I guess it's a good thing the season is over. We should probably keep our distance after tonight and nobody will have a reason to say anything else."

His chest heaved and he let out a heavy breath. Some of his anger melted away and he dropped his head to rake a hand through it, before looking back up at me and holding my gaze. "Maybe you're right and that's for the best." I couldn't tell if he really meant it, or if like me he was just trying to do the right thing for both of us.

Maybe they were all right and our friendship wasn't normal. I didn't want to admit it, but I'd just lost my husband and he had a girlfriend. What should people think of how close we were? Most days it was one of the only things that felt right anymore, but maybe it was an unhealthy attachment for me. Hell if I knew what normal or healthy was. I was just trying to hold myself together, and Casey helped, but if no one understood it, maybe there was a reason why.

I tugged my lip between my teeth and shifted uncomfortably, "So, I guess I'll see you around. If Mel asks, you can just tell her I wasn't feeling well and headed home." I was on the verge of tears and didn't even know why except that it felt like I was losing someone else, but I couldn't ask him to put his relationship with Annie at risk anymore. He'd done enough and it wasn't fair to him. He didn't owe me anything, and for all I knew he could get in trouble with the school if the rumors got around to the wrong people. I wasn't sure if it mattered that I wasn't technically a player anymore, I was sort of his intern and still a student. I'm sure it would be frowned on even though they wouldn't be able to prove anything, because there was nothing. It could still make things really difficult for him. It was already making things difficult for him.

He gave me a terse nod and then brushed past me to head back into the ballroom before the tears that I was fighting back could start falling. Jamie got what she wanted after all. I took off for the parking lot as the first tear trickled down my cheek.

I'm not sure if I'd ever really hated anyone before, not even her when she flirted with Tyler, because I knew she could never get to him. Now she had successfully taken away one of the very few people that was helping me survive this hell I was in, and I hated her for that. I was already out of the building and in my car when my phone rang. I almost didn't answer, I didn't know what to tell her, but if I ignored her, she would probably come after me.

"Hey Mel, I'm not feeling good, nauseous and all, so I'm–"

"What the hell happened in the hall? You disappeared for five minutes and then Casey just marched in here and dragged both Jamie and Annie out of the room?"

I cleared my throat and tried to keep my voice from shaking. "I'll talk to you about it tomorrow."

"Wait–"

I disconnected the call and backed my car out of the parking lot, wiping my eyes with the back of my hand. Why couldn't Jamie just be a human being for once and understand? And why did giving Casey up feel like this? I'd let him in even when I'd been shutting everyone else out. He'd gotten to me with how much he seemed to care, like it was his personal mission. He'd helped ease my grief and fear when even Mel couldn't, but still it didn't make sense for me to be losing it like this.

Damn pregnancy hormones. I wasn't in control of anything, not even my own body.

Once I was inside my apartment, I flung myself down on the couch and hugged a throw pillow to my chest, burying my face in it. All of my anger and frustration pressed down on me, and the only way I could release it was to scream into the pillow. It was overwhelming and I didn't know how to make it stop. I jerked myself up and threw the pillow across the room, wishing I could throw something at Jamie's face, and Casey's face. I didn't even know why I wanted to hit him, but I was too mad to care about being rational. Someone knocked on the door. I got up, ready to tell Mel that I wanted to be left alone tonight. I wasn't prepared to see Casey standing on the other side.

"What are you doing here?" I asked him, inwardly cringing at how much of a mess I must look. I was sure my make up was running all over my face.

"You were wrong." He scowled at me. My shoulders slumped as everything I had been feeling moments ago, drained out of me. I leaned my head against the doorframe.

"Can you be mad at me tomorrow and tell me what else I've done wrong then? I'd really just like to go to bed now." I didn't want to deal with anything anymore. Not him or Jamie or any of them. It was all too hard, and I only needed to worry about me and Jelly Bean.

"You think I'm mad at you?" His frown deepened and he obviously wasn't going to leave.

"After tonight, I would understand if you are. I'm sorry I didn't give you a heads up sooner. I just enjoyed hanging out with you and I know that was selfish, but I hate being by myself, because all I do is miss Tyler and soccer, and worry about how I'm going to screw up being a parent. I'll stay away though, I never meant to mess things up for you."

"Woah, woah. Slow down. I came over here to tell you to hell with staying away from each other. I thought about it, and that's stupid and fuck what everyone else thinks. You didn't mess anything up and you don't need to stay away from me. I should have said that earlier. I'm sorry I got so upset when you told me what was going on. I was pissed off, but not at you. I was mad that Jamie was taking her issues with me out on you, and that I hadn't known it was going on, and I was mad at myself for a lot of reasons, but none of them were your fault and only an asshole would stop being your friend when you need one."

"You're not an asshole."

He blew out a deep breath and scrubbed a hand over his face. "Actually I am. If I wasn't, there's a good chance none of this would be happening right now."

"What do you mean? I don't think you asked for Jamie to be such a bitch."

"Or maybe I did," he curled his hand around the back of his neck. "Can I come in and we can talk about it?" I hesitated for a moment and then pulled the door open wider. He walked over to the couch and sat down. I closed the door behind him and then took a seat on the arm of the couch.

"It is my fault Jamie has it out for you," he started in. "If I had known sooner that she was going this far, I would have put a stop to it." I still didn't quite understand why he thought it was his fault. She was a little swimfan over him, but he didn't ask for that.

"That doesn't make what she's doing your fault."

"It does, because a couple weeks before my first day with the team, I went out with some guys I met when I first moved here. We ended up at one of the bars not far from campus. I got a little drunk and made out with a random chick. We didn't hook up, but almost. I barely remembered it or her the next morning, which I know is a dick move, but new town, new job, new friends . . . it happened. But she certainly remembered me the first day of practice."

"It was Jamie?" I tried not to cringe, but couldn't help it.

"Unfortunately yes. I guess the bar wasn't too strict on IDs." I didn't find that surprising. Students around here knew which places carded and which ones were a little more lax, and I knew several girls on the team who were under twenty-one that had fake IDs. Shoot, I would be lying if I said I had never gone out as a freshman or sophomore.

"I apologized and told her it was a mistake that I wasn't interested in repeating. I knew she still had a little crush, but I really thought she'd let go of the idea of anything happening between us again."

"Must've been some kiss if she can't get over it." I was a little stunned that he had made out with Jamie, and it was the first thing that popped into my head.

He gave me a weak smile. "Wasn't one of my finer moments."

"She might disagree," I smirked.

"You're not funny."

I thought I was. "So, what happened after I left?"

"I made sure Jamie and Annie know that you haven't done anything wrong. That we haven't done anything wrong."

134

"Are you sure we haven't?" I still couldn't shake the doubt. "I mean, I know we haven't done anything, but I think it matters what people see." I wondered if people would be able to accept that we were just friends if he didn't look like he belonged on the cover of a magazine, advertising underwear. I wished I could make them understand that it didn't matter. My eyes worked just fine, but my heart didn't. I'd already given it away and it was meant to be forever. My forever came crashing down around me, but I couldn't just pick up those pieces and move on so easily. They didn't get that, because they didn't get the kind of love Tyler and I shared. Nobody could unless they'd had it and felt it for themselves.

"They only matter if you let them. I say fuck 'em." He shrugged nonchalantly.

"But you agreed with me earlier that we shouldn't spend time together anymore."

"Honestly, I don't give a damn what anyone else thinks or says about me. I care about how it affects you. So whatever you want, I'll do."

"I'd like to still be friends, but not if it's going to cost you your relationship or create trouble with your job."

"Don't worry about me," he brushed off my concerns. "I'm not interested in public opinion if it means I can't be there for the people who need me to be. I'd rather be the friend you believe I am, and have other people think the worst of me, than be an asshole to you, just so they don't."

"Are you and Annie going to be okay?"

"Yeah, we're okay," was all he said. "And you and me, we're okay too." He reached over and touched my arm reassuringly.

Something inside me swelled with relief. Casey was important to me. Whether it was or wasn't unhealthy for me to lean on him, I didn't care. He'd been a friend to me when it wasn't easy for him or conventional. He was there for me without hesitation or consideration for what it might cost him. You don't find that in people every day, and when you do, you hang on to that friend and you try to be that friend for them.

Seventeen

"Sometimes you will never know the value of a moment until it becomes a memory." — Dr. Seuss

"So, we're still going with 'Jelly Bean?' " Mel confirmed one last time before making the call to the cake shop. All week she'd been trying to subtly ask me if I had a name yet. The shower was tomorrow and I still didn't have one.

"Jelly Bean is fine," I mumbled, staring off at the view of her parents' property from the balcony where we sat. We were having the shower at their place. It was just a little ways outside the city, and big enough to accommodate the guest list, which was much larger than I would have preferred. An entire soccer team larger.

"Okay, what's wrong? You don't sound excited at all."

I wasn't. The banquet was only three days ago and I hadn't seen any of the girls since, but they'd all been invited long before then. Mel thought inviting everyone would help with some of the tension Jamie and Cassie had created. I hadn't been so sure, and now I really wasn't. Casey confronted Jamie and Annie, but I don't know if it did any good or what the rest of the team thought. If they didn't show, then I guess I would know where they stood. Not caring about their opinions was just harder than I thought it would be. Most of them had been my teammates for two years. I lost the sport I loved; I just never expected to lose almost all of the friends that had come with it.

"I just wish it was going to be a smaller group. You, your parents, mine, and Ellie and Beth. I don't need a big shower."

"It won't be that bad. Not as many of the girls as you think even agree with Jamie. Some of them just aren't sure what to believe because of how things have changed." I knew she meant how I had changed, but she wouldn't say that. "Most of them just don't know how to be around you anymore, but we'll have fun tomorrow. You'll see."

"Did I really push everyone away that much?"

"No, gosh. I'm not saying you did it, or that it's your fault. It just happened. You went through something horrible and your life was completely changed. They just can't relate to that, and sometimes people would rather avoid tragedy than face it because they don't know what to do. It's hard to be around someone in pain and not know how to help. Nobody likes feeling useless, so it was easier for them to let you pull away. Give them a chance and I think you'll be surprised at how many friends you still have."

I knew she had a point. They weren't the only ones who didn't know how to be anymore. I felt like such a different person, I didn't know if I could be the friend and teammate I was before.

"Okay," I sighed.

"Okay you'll try to be positive and have a good time tomorrow?"

"Yes."

I was still reluctant, and a little afraid that none of them would show, but like she often is, Mel was right. All but a few of the girls came the next day and we all had a really good time. My parents had flown in to Abilene and driven up with Ellie and Beth and my Aunt Jenny and Cousin Liz, so we had a full house. Mel had us jumping from one activity to the next, trying to guess baby food flavors and stealing safety pins any time someone said the word "baby." She kept things moving along and I didn't even have time to feel overwhelmed or sad like I did with most things baby related. We were all laughing as I watched them stuffing balloons in their shirts to make baby bellies and play pregnancy charades. Mel started trying to pop everyone else's balloons with her safety pin, and then it quickly turned into a dangerous game of balloon pop instead, with everyone chasing each other. My mom released her balloons and jumped out of the way. So did my aunt, but Ellie and Mel's mom were right in there with the rest of them, jabbing and dodging. Leave it to Mel and the girls to turn a baby shower into a violent, competitive sport.

Daddy had disappeared with Mel's dad at the beginning, saying it was a little too girly for them. They were probably off talking football. Daddy had a little bit of a man crush on Mr. Ross. He was a diehard Cowboys fan, and Mel's dad had been one of his favorite players back in the day. I would dare them to find a football game that had as much action as I was seeing while watching Mel try to tackle Sarah for her last balloon. Mr. Ross would've been proud.

"Okay, okay everyone," Mama tried to get their attention, but she didn't know my rowdy teammates well.

It wasn't until the last balloon was popped that they quit and party planner Mel took back over. "It's time for cake and gifts!"

Mrs. Ross went to the kitchen and came back with the cake. Mel had refused to let me peek at it until then, but it was as adorable as she promised. It looked like a delicious, edible present, decorated in baby footprints. Everyone gathered around the table to look at it.

"Does that say Jelly Bean?" Hailey asked, peering at the fondant gift tag.

"Yes it does, and that will be the little guy's name if Liv doesn't come up with a different one." Of course that started a discussion on baby name preferences. Everyone shared their favorite names while Mama cut and served the cake.

"As long as you don't name my grandson Angus," she winked at me, dragging a laugh from my lips. Ellie chuckled too. She was the only other one here who knew about Angus. Beth was probably too little at the time to remember him.

"I haven't thought about Angus in years," I smiled. Angus was the stuffed puppy I took everywhere as a kid, so much so that most of his fur had worn off and he'd had more plastic surgery to keep him together than all the Jacksons combined. Angus's untimely and unfortunate demise when I was nine had crushed me. At least until the next day . . . and just like that I was nine years old again . . .

"What are you doing dork?" Ugh, I looked up from where I was sitting under the oak tree in my front yard to see Ty, Chuck and Tommy cutting through the grass toward me. They must have been headed to the park down the street. Ty's friends were such jerks. Especially Chuck. He was the one who called me a dork.

"None of your business," I told them, pulling Angus into my lap. They liked to tease me for still playing with stuffed animals, but I didn't care. I'd been taking Angus on all of my adventures since I was five.

"Do you have any real friends, loser, or is your only friend that stuffed dog?" Chuck laughed.

138

"You're the loser," I shot back at him and stuck my tongue out.

"Whatever, you're just a stupid girl." He kicked at the ground, sending bits of grass and dirt at me.

"I'd be mean too if I got beat with the ugly stick as much as you did," I retorted. Ty and even Tommy snickered. Chuck's face turned beet red with anger. He bent down and snatched Angus from me before I could stop him.

"Hey, give him back!" I stood angrily to my feet. Chuck just laughed and held him away from me.

"Hey Tommy, catch." He threw Angus to Tommy and I chased after Tommy, but he threw him back to Chuck before I could catch him.

"Give him back!" I cried again and Chuck just laughed some more. "It's just a stupid stuffed animal you big baby." He held Angus over my head and even though Chuck was just a year older than me like Ty, he was a real big boy, almost as big as most of the sixth graders. I glared and continued to reach for him all the while fighting back my tears of frustration and anger until Ty, who'd just been watching, finally walked over.

"Give her back the dog, Chuck."

"No." He started swinging Angus around by one of his legs. Ty, who was almost as tall, just not quite as bulky, grabbed hold of Angus and tried to pull him from Chuck's hands.

"Quit being a jerk and just give the dog back," Ty grunted as he tugged.

"Why should I?" Chuck refused to let go and they continued to tug-of-war with my dog until all the sudden Chuck stumbled backwards still holding onto Angus' rear end, but his head was in Ty's hands and his stuffing had spilled out on the ground.

My eyes went wide and my lip trembled. Ty looked down at the head in his hands and then at me with big, apologetic eyes.

"It was just a stupid, old stuffed animal anyway." Chucked tossed the other half of Angus down, and then walked away. Tommy followed after him, but Ty got down on the ground and tried to retrieve all the bits of stuffing that had scattered. Once he had all of Angus gathered up, he walked over and held him out to me.

"I'm real sorry, Livvie. Chuck can be a jerk sometimes."

139

I snatched Angus' bits from him and ran inside to Mama, but she'd just looked at the torn animal and all his stuffing that was riddled with clumps of dirt and tiny twigs from the ground and told me she didn't think she could fix Angus this time. I ran to my room and cried, and she must have disposed of his poor little stuffed body because I never saw it again.

The next day Tyler showed up on our doorstep holding a worn teddy bear in his hands. "Here," he'd held him out to me. "I know he's not as special as Angus was to you, but this was my favorite teddy bear. My mom and dad gave him to me when Beth was born because I was so disappointed I wasn't getting a little brother. I named him Lukas. That's what I wanted my little brother's name to be, but you can call him whatever. I just want you to have him."

And that right there was the moment my little nine year old heart fell in love with Tyler Tate. I'd treasured that teddy bear until our dog Bilbo decided to make a chew toy out of Lukas and I forgot about him entirely . . . or at least I thought I had.

"Lukas," I muttered, my mind returning to the present. Everyone turned their heads to look at me. "His name is Lukas Tyler Tate." I didn't tell them how I came up with it or why I'd decided on it. I just smiled, knowing that Tyler had helped pick the name for our son after all. I linked my fingers and rested my hands over my belly. *Baby Lukas.* I smiled.

"I love it," Ellie said, and the twinkle in her bright eyes told me she knew exactly where the name came from. Everyone else gushed over it as well while they devoured the cake. I'd barely licked my fork clean of the last bite before Mel started thrusting gifts at me.

I'd never seen so much adorable baby stuff in all my life, and every time I opened something it was followed by a chorus of "Awww's" until I had a mountain of stuff.

Once I made it through all the packages, the party started winding down. Slowly, people said their goodbyes and the group shrunk until it was just me and Mel and our families starting the clean up. They helped me carry everything out to my car. We had a tough time getting it all to fit, but we managed. Then it was time to say goodbye to my family. My parents weren't able to take more time away from the inn, not with Thanksgiving next week. The holidays were a really busy time for them. I hugged and kissed everyone goodbye, and when I got to Daddy I felt him slip something into my hand. I peeked down and saw a few rolled up bills.

"No Daddy, I can't–"

"It's not much. I wish your mother and I could do more, but you're taking it baby girl."

I squeezed my father tightly. "Thank you Daddy. It's more than enough."

I hadn't realized how much I missed my parents until I was watching them leave. Mama had of course tried to talk me into going back with them again. My response was the same as it had been every other time, but it was hard to say goodbye. I wouldn't see them again until Christmas. I couldn't afford to go to Jefferson for Thanksgiving this year. I was going to spend it with Ellie and Beth. I hadn't told my parents money was an issue; I said I didn't want Ellie and Beth alone on their first Thanksgiving without Ty, which was actually true. They didn't have any other family close since Ellie's sister Karen had moved to Galveston, so I really did want to be there with them, and I knew Ty would want me to be with them.

It wouldn't be an easy day for any of us. Family and holiday traditions meant a lot to Ty, and every year he was always the thing I was most thankful for. Now I had someone else to be thankful for, but even baby Lukas couldn't take away that hurt and longing completely.

This holiday season was going to be a really tough time.

Eighteen

*"A mother's joy begins when new life is stirring inside...
when a tiny heartbeat is heard for the very first time
and a playful kick reminds her that she is never alone."*
—Anonymous

"You seriously won't take the elevator?" Mel whined as we made our second trip up the three flights to my apartment.

"You're welcome to if you want," I told her. I didn't care if it took us ten trips to get all of the baby gifts inside; I wasn't getting in that elevator. "Just think of it as your workout for the day since practices are over."

"Ugh," she groaned. "We haven't even got half the stuff up there yet."

"Toughen up, Auntie Mel."

She was still groaning when we pushed through the door and dropped the load off in my apartment.

"I wonder if Casey is home." Her eyes shot to his door. "He would probably help us."

"Don't even think about it. Come on." I grabbed her arm and pulled her after me.

"But there's soooo much stuff," she dragged out, being overdramatic. I rolled my eyes at her and tugged her along, but her complaining must have been loud enough to draw Casey out. Before we made it to the stairs again, I heard a door open. We turned around he was standing in the doorway of his apartment.

"I thought I heard you two out here."

"Oooh yay, Casey. Just in time," Mel said excitedly.

"Just in time for what?" He looked at her skeptically.

"To help us carry in all the loot from Liv's baby shower."

His face relaxed and he smiled. "Sure, no problem."

With Casey's help, we only had to make two more trips. He carried all the large stuff for us and I remembered how nice it was to have a guy around for the heavy lifting. Just another little thing I missed. We got everything up to my apartment and stacked in a pile in my living room. Afterward, Mel and Casey both headed out, and it was just me and Lukas. I sat on the couch rubbing a hand over my stomach. "Hey baby, it's Mommy. The doctor said you would be able to hear my voice by now," I said softly. My last check up was two days ago. I was almost half way now, and the doctor encouraged me to talk to him often.

"You're going to be the best dressed baby. You got a lot of cool stuff today, kiddo. Everyone is really excited to meet you, especially your grandmas and your Auntie Mel and Auntie Beth. I can't wait to meet you too. I love you so much Lukas. Your daddy would've loved you so much too. I know he'll be loving you from Heaven. If he were here, he would be hiding all the cute little soccer clothes you got. He'd make sure you were his little football guy. He'd wrap you up in that little Cowboys jersey from Mr. Ross, first chance he got, and that's the only thing you'd ever wear." I chuckled quietly just as someone knocked on the door.

Casey was standing there in the hallway with an extremely large, odd shaped and crudely wrapped gift sitting next to him on the ground and one small one in his hand.

"Even though the shower was a girl thing, I still wanted to get you something and this is from Coach Davis and Coach Walsh." He held out the little package.

"Wow, thank you. You guys didn't need to do anything though," I said, but took the package from him. I took a step back and pulled the door open wider so he could get that hulking thing inside. I'll admit I was really, really curious. He carefully and somewhat awkwardly carried it over to the couch and set it down on the floor. I took a seat and he sat next to me.

I opened the little one first, pulling out a mini Red Raiders jersey and sweatshirt. They were so adorable, and I couldn't believe they'd' had them specially made for me with my number and last name on the back.

"This is so cool," I gushed.

He grinned back at me. "I hope you like this one too."

143

I started tearing into the paper. When it was all on the ground, and the object inside was revealed, I gasped. "Oh my goodness, Hunt, this is amazing."

It was the most beautiful crib I had ever seen. I could tell it had been hand crafted from all natural wood, with a finish that highlighted the knots and grain of the different types of wood. It didn't sit real high off the ground. The frame was made from pieces of lighter and medium woods and the corners were joined together by thick branches of a darker wood that had been cut the right size for legs, and had a smooth finish as well. They curved up and outward, reaching just a little higher than the rest of the frame, except for one corner where the branch was a bit taller and curved inward, over the head of the crib, and from it dangled little wood carved stars and a moon like a mobile.

"You really like it?" he asked nervously.

"I love it. It's the most amazing crib I've ever seen. Where did you get it?"

"I had my brother in law make it for you. He owns his own business and makes this kind of stuff." *Wow.* He had it made for me.

"Thank you so much. Your brother in law is incredibly talented; please tell him I said that." I couldn't stop looking at it. "How did know I didn't already get a crib?"

"I told Mel a while back that I was having it made, and she said she would let your family know so they wouldn't get you one."

"Has she seen it?"

"Nope, I wanted you to be the first one. I wanted to make sure you liked it."

"Well I do, so much. Ty would have loved it too. I just can't get over how beautiful it is. You can't tell Mel how much I love it though, because she hates being outdone."

"I'm glad you like it. And don't worry, my lips are sealed."

"I just want to sit here and stare at it."

He chuckled. "So how was the baby shower?"

"It was really good, a lot better than I thought it would be," I admitted.

"Were you expecting it to go terribly?"

"I was just nervous since Mel invited the whole team, but everyone who showed up was really cool. A lot of them apologized before they left for the way things happened with all the Jamie stuff. I apologized too, so I think most of us are good now."

"Why did you apologize?" His brow pulled into a frown.

"For pulling away from everyone. I realized I stopped being a friend to them too, so I can't really blame them for what they thought."

"You shouldn't apologize. You're not responsible for anything that happened, even if you did pull away. As your friends they should have been the ones to reach out and be there for you, not jump to conclusions." Part of me agreed with him and wanted to hold it all against them, but I knew that wasn't right. I can't say that I would have been the perfect friend if the situation were reversed.

"I'm just glad to have it behind me now, and it's nice to know that not everyone feels the way Jamie does."

He made a disgusted noise when I said her name, but didn't say anything. I took a deep breath and then relaxed my body into the couch and leaned my head back into the cushion. Casey matched my position and we both sat there quietly. My eyes drifted shut and I would have fallen asleep right there if a sudden and unexpected movement hadn't startled me.

"Ooh," I squealed sitting up.

"What is it?" Casey's eyes were wide with concern, but instead of telling him I just grabbed his hand and placed it over my stomach.

"Do you feel that?"

He didn't move or say anything, he just stared confused at his hand on my belly, and then the baby kicked again and his head shot up.

"Holy shit," he exclaimed with a wide grin. "That's . . . wow . . . really . . . is it okay to say weird? Because it does feel kind of weird, but also really cool."

I chuckled.

"Does he move around a lot?"

"That's the first time I've felt him." I set my hand on my stomach, right next to where Casey was still holding his. We felt him move two more times before he settled down and the movement stopped. We both pulled our hands back at the same time. My eyes were watering and when Casey looked up again, his brow creased and his mouth turned down.

"What's wrong?" he asked softly. Having Casey's hand on my stomach and hearing how excited he got made me think of how much Ty would have enjoyed feeling our baby move inside of me.

"I'm sorry, I'm just emotional. It was such an incredible feeling. I wish Ty was here to feel it too."

"I'm really sorry. I shouldn't have . . . you probably want me to go." He started to stand up, but I reached for his arm to stop him.

"No, you don't have to. I'm glad someone was here to share this with. I'm not upset because it was you or that you're here, I'm just sad that he wasn't, if that makes sense at all," I tried to explain.

"Yeah, it does." He sat back down. "Jelly Bean has a strong kick. He'll be a good soccer player."

"What do you think, Lukas?" I returned my hand to my stomach. "You going to play soccer like Mommy, or football like Daddy?"

"Lukas, huh? Finally got the little guy a name?"

"Yeah, I decided today. Lukas Tyler Tate."

"Lukas is a good name. I like it."

"Me too. And Ty would have liked it. He actually picked it." I related the story of poor Angus and how I decided on the name Lukas. Afterward, Casey helped me move the crib behind the couch so that it would be out of the way, once I'd taken a picture of it to send to everyone. Then we stacked all the boxes back there and piled the clothes and blankets in it so that I actually had a living room again. The one thing my apartment definitely didn't have a lot of was space.

"I don't know how I'm going to be able to afford a bigger place and I just don't see it working here with a baby," I admitted to him. There was no avoiding the truth; seeing all of this stuff made the reality of it sink it. This place just wasn't big enough for me and baby to be comfortable. I could make it work if I had to, but it definitely wouldn't be ideal. My bedroom barely fit my bed and dresser and belongings.

"Things are still tight?" Casey asked.

"Yeah, the financial aid never came through." Too many students who needed help and not enough money to go around; I was left out of luck.

"That sucks. I wish I could help you."

"I know I'll figure something out. Besides you've already done more than enough for me." I looked down at the crib again. That alone would save me a lot of money. I made him promise me that he would pass along my gratitude to his brother-in-law and I thanked him again for the beautiful gift. When he was gone, I sent the picture to Mel.

Damn, that's even better than my gift.

I laughed. I knew her so well. We texted for a few minutes and I told her that I'd finally felt the baby move and I had to talk her out of rushing over here so she could spend the whole night with her hand glued to my belly waiting for it to happen again. I promised to spend the day with her tomorrow so that she would be around if I felt it.

"Goodnight baby boy," I whispered when I climbed into bed. Then I closed my eyes and let my heart go to Ty. "Thank you for Lukas," I breathed, grateful for the child inside of me and the name that he now had. "I love you forever."

The loneliness wasn't so bad that night and I slept better than I had in some time.

Nineteen

"Be brave. Take risks. Nothing can substitute experience."
— *Paulo Coelho*

Oh my God.
Oh my God.
Oh my God.
What did I do?
What the heck was I thinking?

This had to be the worst, most impulsive decision I had ever made, and it was too late to take it back. Maybe I should have sold the TV and Ty's Xbox instead. That would have helped a little, long enough for me to figure something else out. Anything other than what I did.

There was no way this would work. I'd lost my mind. I didn't know the first thing about how to do this, or where to even start. Sure I had all Ty's books, but I didn't actually know what the hell I was doing. I'm not even sure if I could blame the pregnancy hormones for this decision. When I read that email, I acted without even thinking. It was just so perfect, exactly what he would have wanted and the price was practically a steal, even in the condition it was in.

Maybe I could just list it and get the money back – probably even more than I paid – and find something else, but my chest tightened when I considered that. This was Ty's dream, and being so close to it made me feel close to him again. He would have jumped up and down in excitement like a little kid and given it some ridiculous name like Roxy or Fiona, and talked to her like she was a person.

Nope. There was no way I could sell the car that was now sitting in my parking spot, where my much newer Honda used to be parked. I'd sold it a few days after Thanksgiving, so I would have the money for a bigger place when it was time. Mel and Casey had been giving me rides for over a week while I tried to find something a little more used. This was not what I'd had in mind, but when I opened the email from someone Ty had run across during his car search, I jumped on it.

I couldn't believe it when I read Bill's message. An elderly lady who lived down the road from him had lost her husband ten years ago and wanted to get rid of his old car that was collecting dust in her shed. The pictures showed that the body was an ocean blue that, even faded, was a beautiful color. There were a few dents and dings and a little bit of rust, but for the most part it didn't look too bad. The interior was in even better condition. The email said it didn't run, but Bill mentioned the things he thought needed to be done to it. I didn't speak mechanic, but none of it sounded too complicated, so without thinking it through, I called the number he gave.

Ha. What the heck did I even know?

The lady had no idea what she was sitting on though. She only wanted five hundred bucks for the '69 Chevelle. Even though it needed work to run, it was worth more than that. I didn't know a lot, but I knew that much. Twenty minutes later the deal was done. I'd told her I didn't even need to see it first, I just wanted it.

I'd tried to talk her into taking a little bit more money since I had been planning on spending quite a bit more of what I got from the Honda to get a running car, but when she heard my story about Ty, she refused to accept more. She said it wasn't even really about the money, and she was glad the car was going to someone it would mean something to, because her husband had loved it as much as Ty would have.

We were both almost crying over the phone as we talked about the men we'd loved with our whole hearts. That was two days ago, and then about an hour ago, her neighbor, Bill, towed it for her and dropped it off to me, and now it was done. I almost laughed because I didn't even know how to change the oil in a vehicle, let alone how much work this car would require. Even if I was right, and it wasn't a lot of work, I was still in way over my head. I hadn't told Mel or my parents or anyone what I was doing because I had been afraid they would talk some sense into me. I probably should have let them. Too late now.

I guess the place to start would be calling the shop where Ty had worked, and seeing if Mick or one of the guys could come take a look at it, then go from there. I sighed and ran a hand through my hair.

Good job, Liv, what have you gotten yourself into now?

"Hey, what's this?" I almost jumped out of my skin I was so startled by Casey's voice. Lost in my own head and staring at the car, I hadn't noticed him pull up and walk over to me.

"This is Roxy. I think, I don't know, maybe Stella or Kitten."

Casey stared at me puzzled, then looked at the car and then back at me. "And who does she belong to?"

"Er, me . . ."

He nodded, not even fazed by my answer. "Mmhmm, and where did she come from?"

"A sweet old lady named Dorothy."

"I see. Does she run?"

"She's an eighty year old woman so I doubt it."

"Funny. I meant, does *Kitten* run?" he asked, humoring me.

"Not exactly."

"What's wrong with her?"

"I'm not sure, I mean, I have a list of what Bill thinks is wrong, but I don't really know what any of it means."

"I'm not even going to ask who Bill is, but I can tell you really thought this one through, Tate," he chuckled softly.

"Yeah, not so much," I admitted somewhat abashedly.

He just shook his head. "I think you better fill me in on exactly how this happened." So I recounted the whole story, how Bill said he had met Ty last April and Ty had given him my email so he could get in touch with us if he came across anything like what Ty was looking for, and then I told him about Dorothy and her husband Ed, and I ended with my plans to call the shop.

"I'm probably going to regret saying this, but I happen to know a little bit about old cars, and depending on what your mechanic says, I'll help you get it running."

My eyes got huge and I'm pretty sure my whole face lit up. I launched myself at him, almost tackling him to the ground, but he caught me. I pulled back to look at his face, "Really?"

He chuckled and nodded. "Sure, it looks like it could be fun."

I squealed and hugged him again. "Thank you, thank you, thank you. I had no idea what I was going to do. I was afraid I was going to have to sell it if I couldn't figure out how to fix it up on my own. I know what Ty used to make, and there's no way I could afford to pay someone that to do it for me, but I swear I'll cook for you, or clean your apartment or whatever you want. I'll be your slave if you'll really help me."

He laughed, "Well before you sign away your freedom, we should probably wait until the mechanic gives us the run down on it. I could probably figure out what's wrong with her, but it'd be better to have someone else who knows a little bit more take a look to be sure."

"Oh, yeah. Of course, I'll call right now." I pulled out my phone and brought up the number for the shop. Mick was the one to answer.

"Hey Mick, this is Olivia."

"Hey Liv, how are you doing?" I could hear the sadness in his voice. He had been Ty's closest friend once we moved up here. They were like brothers. I felt bad that I hadn't stayed in touch with him as much as I should have since he and the guys helped me move.

"I'm alright, but I actually have a favor to ask of you Mick."

"Anything for you. Whad'ya need?"

"Welllll . . . I sort of did something crazy."

He chuckled. "Why'm I not surprised to hear those words comin' outta your mouth. What'd ya do this time?"

"I bought a car, and I was sort of hoping you would come look at it and tell me what I need to do to make it run?"

He didn't even ask what kind of car or anything about it. "I get off in two hours and I'll be over."

"Thank you so much."

"No problem sweetheart. See ya in a bit."

I hung up and shot Casey a hesitant smile. "He's gonna come over in a little while when he gets off work."

He blew out a deep breath and slid a hand over his hair, staring at the car for a moment. "Okay then, let's go get something to eat while we wait."

Casey and I went up to his place where he cooked us a couple of burgers, and I threw together a salad with veggies from both our fridges. We ate out on the small balcony off his living room and he told me about how he and his dad had restored his car. It was something they worked on after his injury. It gave him something to focus on besides being angry all the time.

151

"So, I have to know," I said to him after he finished. "Did you name your car?" The cheeky grin told me all I needed to know. "Come on, what's her name?"

"Evelyn is her name, but my baby likes it when I call her Evie."

I laughed and shook my head. Guys. "Does Annie know about you two?" I teased.

"Oh yeah, she knows." I was realizing I really enjoyed playful Casey. I smiled a lot more when I was around him, especially when he was being a complete dork.

I rolled my eyes at him and snorted. "So the love of your life is a car."

"For now." He shrugged.

Huh. Not for the first time I wondered about his and Annie's relationship. I just couldn't imagine Casey being a bad boyfriend, but it seemed weird to me that he would be in a relationship with someone for a year and not be more serious about her. Or maybe I was way off. I couldn't help my curiosity though.

"You can tell me if I'm being nosy, but how did you and Annie meet?"

"A friend introduced us. One of the guys I met when I first moved here was dating her friend. I guess we just hit if off after that. So what time did your friend say he was coming over?" I knew an intentional subject change when I heard one.

"Should be pretty soon. Do you wanna go down and wait for him? You can look at the car if you want, and tell me what you think."

"Sure."

Casey and I were both sitting inside the car when I heard the rumble of a motorcycle pulling into the parking lot. I used to hear that sound every day. I'd missed it, but it just wasn't the same now because I knew it wouldn't be Ty climbing off the bike. It was good to see Mick though. He and James, Ty's other good work buddy, had told me to stop by the shop any time to see them, but I couldn't bring myself to go there yet. I used to visit Ty at work as often as I could, taking cookies and treats for all of the guys.

I hopped out of the passenger seat and greeted Mick with a hug when he pulled off his helmet. His eyes were glued to my stomach when we pulled apart. I hadn't even told him yet and I felt like such a jerk, especially when he looked between me and Casey, who was climbing out of the driver's seat. I could see the question that he didn't want to ask on his face.

"I guess now would be a good time to mention that you're going to be an uncle." I hoped that would reassure him of who the father was without having to acknowledge that he'd even questioned it. I couldn't really blame him for it either. I hadn't talked to him in months and then he shows up and I'm huge and sitting here with another guy.

His face broke out in a wide grin and I was confident that any doubt he'd had was gone. He pulled me in close for another hug and pressed a kiss on top of my head.

"Uncle Mick, I think I might like that. Man, I can't wait to tell the rest of the guys." Ty had considered all of them like family. I really should have told them sooner. His eyes flitted back to Casey and I introduced the two of them, making sure that he understood Casey was a just a neighbor and friend.

"So this the crazy thing you did Liv?" Mick asked, walking over to the Chevelle.

"Yep." I watched him walk around the car, taking everything in. He let out a low whistle.

"She sure is a beauty, would've given that man of yours a hard on." I choked out a laugh, but didn't deny it, mostly because it was true. I tugged my lip between my teeth nervously when he popped the hood and stuck his head underneath. I was terrified that he was going to tell me it would cost ten thousand dollars to fix or some outrageous amount that I could never afford.

I waited patiently up on the sidewalk while he slid into the driver's seat and twisted the key in the ignition, listening to the sounds it made, and then walked back to check something else under the hood. He poked around under there for a good twenty minutes before slamming it down and turning to face me.

He started to tell me what he'd found. He may as well have been speaking Chinese for all I understood it, but Casey seemed to know what he was saying and nodded along, even asked a couple of questions. When he was done, I just looked at Mick.

"Straight up, I don't understand any of what you just said. Ty never did manage to teach me to speak grease monkey. Can you just put me

153

out of my misery and give me a rough dollar amount for what it will cost me to fix it?"

"Well, really there's not too much wrong with her. The problem with these old cars though, is that they need to be taken apart and all the parts cleaned thoroughly to be sure. The labor time will kill you on that more than the parts. I'd love to say I could do it for you, but we're backed up as it is with restorations and the custom bike orders so it would be a while before I could get her into the shop. If you take it to someone else, they'll probably charge you close to six or seven grand, maybe more with a new paint job."

"Apart from the paint job, I'll be doing it, so we just need an estimate for parts," Casey informed him, earning a slight frown from Mick.

"You know what you're doin?" I could tell Mick was skeptical.

"My dad was a bit of a gear head and loved tinkering around on muscle cars. I started hanging around him in the garage helping when I was a kid. We rebuilt that one a few years back." He gestured to his beloved Evie. Mick's face perked up and the two started talking cars and parts again, afterward Mick seemed to accept that Casey was qualified enough to handle it, but I still didn't have the answer I needed.

"Soooo . . ."

"I should be able to get you most of the parts you need from the shop for under a grand. I'll have to look around for a bumper and front fender, but it shouldn't be too hard to find them. Should put you somewhere around twelve hundred."

Twelve hundred. I could do Twelve hundred. I wanted to scream and clap my hands, but I refrained and looked at Casey. "We can really do this?" I asked, still having a hard time believing that it could all work out this easily.

"Yeah, we can." He sounded confident. This time I did squeal a little.

Mick promised to help as much as he could with tracking down parts and providing Casey with any advice he needed once he got going. He said he would stop by when he could, to see how we were doing, and by 'we' I meant Casey because I think we all knew at this point that I really wouldn't be much help.

154

It did make me wish I had let Ty teach me more about cars. I just never thought he wouldn't be around to take care of me. I never thought I'd need to rely on anyone else, especially not myself, for this kind of thing.

After I said goodnight to both of them and was tucked away in my apartment, it took me a minute to realize that the giddy feeling inside of me was happiness. It wasn't complete, but it felt good.

"You and me are going to be alright baby boy." For the first time, I actually believed it.

Twenty

"Damn it!" I cried out as I tried, unsuccessfully, to force the ring back over my swollen finger. It had been a little tight last night before bed so I'd slipped it off, but now it wouldn't go back on. My eyes watered with frustration as I made one last attempt to slide it onto my fat finger.

I'd known this was coming, that at some point I would have to take my wedding ring off, but I wasn't ready. It felt too permanent, like I was accepting that I didn't have a husband. That I wasn't married anymore. It was the symbol of what we'd had, and taking it off felt like letting go of that. The world wouldn't know that I'd loved someone enough to bind myself to him for the rest of our lives. I had though; the rest of his life just hadn't been long enough.

I swore again and dropped the ring on the counter. There was no way it was going back on. I cried out and slammed my hand down on the counter, which hurt more than I'd been expecting it to. When I jerked my hand back, I knocked over the glass that was sitting there. It crashed to the floor and shattered. I slumped to the floor, clutching my hand and Ty's ring that hung from the chain around my neck.

The front door swung open, but I didn't bother to get up. I didn't care who it was. Really, there were only two people who would just walk into my apartment, so the chances were good that it was either Mel or Casey.

"Olivia!" Casey called out. My spot on the floor was blocked by the counter, but I still didn't get up.

"Over here," I mumbled, wiping at my cheeks with my fingers.

He stepped into the kitchen area and looked down at me worriedly. "Are you okay? I heard something crash."

"A glass broke," I said flatly.

He looked around the counter and floor, seeing the glass shards. His brow wrinkled and he looked back at me, clearly confused. "Was it a special glass?"

"No, just a regular glass."

He stared at me for a minute and then sighed, "You're not upset about a glass, are you?"

I shook my head.

"Want to give me a hint?"

"My fingers are fat."

"You dropped the glass because your fingers are fat?" I almost felt bad for the guy. He was trying.

"I didn't drop it. I knocked it over when I hit the counter."

"And you hit the counter because your fingers are fat?" He was struggling to make sense of it.

I nodded this time.

"Can we skip to the part where you tell me what's actually wrong so I can try fix it, because I don't really see this being about fat fingers either."

From my spot on the floor, I pointed to the counter where I'd left my wedding ring sitting. His eyes searched for a minute before landing on it and then they flashed back to my now bare left hand.

"It doesn't fit," I whispered. I wasn't sure what I was expecting him to say; maybe I thought he'd look at me with sad eyes and tell me it would be okay. I did not expect him to stand over me with a look of determination and tell me to get my ass up, but that's exactly what he did and I looked up at him incredulously. "What?"

"You heard me. Get up," he said firmly.

"No thanks. I think I'll just sit here a while," I mumbled.

"Olivia, you can either pick yourself up, dry those eyes and slide your ring onto the chain around your neck, or I can pick you up and drag you out of here, but sitting on that floor, feeling sorry for yourself is not an option." He stuck his hand out, waiting for me to take it, and I could see that he wasn't going to wait long before he hauled me up off the floor himself.

"Why can't you just let me be miserable?" I asked, letting him pull me up.

"Quit being stubborn and come on." He started dragging me out the front door, despite my protests.

"Seriously Casey, I'd rather be alone right now. I don't want to go anywhere."

"Too damn bad." He stopped and turned on me. "Look, that damn ring isn't what made you married and taking it off doesn't mean you were any less married. It's a ring. What you had, is bigger than a silly stone." His eyes softened and then he used the sleeve of his sweatshirt to dab at the moisture under my eyes. "I know it hurts and I get why you're sad, but you don't need a ring on your finger to remember that he loved you more than anything in this entire world and he wouldn't want you to be sad anymore. You're carrying a baby inside of you. His baby. That's fucking amazing. Be proud of your body, not mad at it."

Damn Casey Hunt.

He was right and who cared if the world couldn't see the ring on my finger and know what I had. I knew, and nothing could take that away from me. I used my own sleeve to wipe up the rest of the tears and then I drew in a few steadying breaths. "So where are we going?"

It was still early in the day and I was in my sweatpants and slippers. My hair was thrown up in a messy bun and I hadn't even been in the shower yet. My day was supposed to consist of nothing but studying for finals next week.

"We've got work to do," was the only response I got from him.

"What do you mean work?" Instead of answering me, he tugged me after him until we were standing outside, in front of where the Chevelle was parked yesterday, but was not today, which meant he'd had it towed to where he was going to be working on it. A buddy of his had offered to let him do the repairs in his garage since he had the tools and the space. Casey had just been waiting for Mick to get him the parts he needed to get started. If he'd had the car towed over there it meant the parts came in and he was ready to get going on it.

"Nuh uh, don't you mean *you* have work to do?" I started to turn around and head back inside but he darted around me to block my way.

"Oh no you don't, Tate. You're going to help me. Kitten needs some lovin' and you need a distraction." Casey had decided that first day that Kitten was the car's name now. I'd tried to take it back, but he wouldn't let me. He said it was too late, she liked her name. I tried to tell him *she* was a car, and didn't have feelings to care one way or the other if I called it Kitten, Bertha or Herbert the Pervert.

Casey's face had looked stricken when I said that. He tried to make me apologize; said that Kitten was sensitive and I'd hurt her feelings. I had to walk away. I couldn't argue with a crazy person. So I just accepted that her name was Kitten now.

"I don't even know what to do. I'm only going to get in the way." I gave him the most pathetic look I could muster, in hopes that he would be persuaded to let me out of this, but he saw right through it.

"You're going to learn. I picked up some of the parts from Mick this morning and got the car over to Trent's, so let's go."

I groaned, but let him lead me over to his car. When we slid in, I started to tell him that I needed to study, but as soon as he started the car up he cranked the volume on the stereo.

"Sorry, can't hear you," he yelled over the top of it and then started singing along with Led Zeppelin.

"You're an ass," I shouted.

"Sorry, still can't hear you," he grinned and continued on singing.

I ignored him because everything else only encouraged him. I didn't speak until we were standing outside Trent's house and Casey was introducing the two of us. Trent looked roughly the same age as Casey, with a similar lean build and a confident smile. His sandy blonde hair was cut short and barely visible under his baseball cap. A few days worth of scruff covered his handsome face.

"It's nice to meet you. Thank you so much for letting us use your garage."

He flashed me a mega watt smile that would have made any other female weak in the knees. "My pleasure, darlin'." The Texas boy charm was laid on real heavy.

"Can we get started already?" Casey interrupted, eliciting a chuckle from Trent, who shook his head and led us into his garage, where Kitten was already waiting. Trent asked about how I acquired her while he and Casey rounded up the tools.

"You planning on painting her when you're done fixin' up her insides?"

"She's going to paint her pink," Casey responded and Trent grimaced.

159

"Shut up, I am not painting her pink. I probably won't be painting her at all, at least not for a while. A decent paint job runs pretty pricey. I'll just be happy if we can get her running without me going broke."

They popped her hood and shifted into that foreign car speak. I just leaned against one of the work benches and watched the two of them. Occasionally Trent would ask me a question or toss a flirty comment my way. I could tell he was harmless though, but Casey kept shooting him dirty looks. At one point Trent leaned in while they had their heads under the hood and said something that caused Casey to give him a shove. Trent stepped back, chuckling and Casey tossed a grease rag at him. "Quit being a jackass and get the jack so we can get this thing up," Casey told him. I wasn't sure what to make of it, but I was amused with the two of them. They reminded me a lot of how Ty and Mick were together. I could see the four of them having been good friends in another life. It was easy to imagine them all in the garage, working on Kitten and bs-ing over a couple of beers.

"Olivia, grab that wrench over there and you can come help me undo these bolts," he called to me. I looked on the tool bench and saw several different sized wrenches. I looked back at him with my most annoyed expression.

"Problem?" he smirked.

"I'm guessing it matters what size."

"Size always matters," Trent piped up and I didn't have to look to see him grinning. Casey told me which wrench to grab and then he showed me how to undo the bolts holding the hood on. A few minutes later they were lifting the hood and pulling it away from the car. Then I sat back and watched them jack the car up so we could yank the motor out.

Once they had it raised up and the jack stands were in place, Casey called me back over and showed me how to drain the oil. Once that was done he set me to work unbolting the engine from the mounts. After that, I got out of the way again and they hoisted it out.

Trent had a job to get to after he'd helped Casey remove the engine, and he left Casey and me alone to work on the car. I lost track of time until my stomach and back made it painfully obvious that a few hours had passed. At first I'd been anxious to soak up every detail and learn all I could. I wanted to understand what it was about working on a car

160

that got Ty's blood pumping. He'd told me a thousand times how he felt when he was under the hood of a car. How good it felt to search out the problem and fix it like solving a puzzle. How much he enjoyed taking something that was broken or run down and restoring it to life, but I hadn't really gotten it until now. It was hard work, but that would make it all that much sweeter when she was done. I was excited to be putting myself into Kitten the same way Ty would have. I just didn't think I could take anymore today, but Casey was intent on what he was doing and didn't look anywhere near ready to call it quits for the day. I recognized that focused determination on his face. It was the same look Ty would wear.

I went back to the parts I was cleaning and ignored the growl of my stomach and ache in my back. I was pretty sure we'd replaced every gasket, plug and filter in the entire car. There were so many it was almost overwhelming, and even though he'd tried to explain what everything did, my non-mechanical brain couldn't keep it all straight. I just wanted a sandwich and a nap, but Casey was replacing some wires. I really couldn't tell you what they did, and I was past the point of caring anymore, but he was going out of his way to help me out. I didn't want to start complaining now, so I kept on scrubbing parts with my dirty rag and let him work.

Fifteen minutes – that felt more like fifty – passed and I wiped sweat from my forehead with the back of my arm. I was literally ready to throw in the towel, or throw it at Casey's head, when his phone rang. He stopped what he was doing and wiped his hands on his pants before answering. I continued with my task while listening to his side of the conversation.

"Hey . . . No, I told you babe, I was hanging out at Trent's today . . . I'm not sure how much longer . . . shit, is it really that late already? I'll be done here soon." It figured that he didn't even realize how long he'd been going at it. So much like Ty. He could lose an entire day under the hood of a car, which we'd just done.

"I didn't think you'd be interested, we're fixing up an old car . . ." I heard him telling her. "I'll call you when I'm leaving . . . Okay, talk to you in a while." When he hung up, he looked at me.

"Why didn't you tell me how late it was getting? Shit, you must be starving. I'm sorry I completely lost track of time. I just forgot how much fun this is." God, he really did sound just like Ty. How many times had he come home late for dinner and given me that same excuse? I'd always just smile and kiss him, because I loved everything about him, even the way he seemed to forget about the rest of the world when he was doing what he loved.

"It's okay. Ty was the same way, and I never had the heart to make him quit before he was ready either."

He gave me a gentle smile. "Come on Tate, we're done for today. Let's get you home." He had to help me up off the floor, and I groaned when I stood to my feet. My back was killing me, I was hot and hungry, and I had to pee like crazy.

"You really could have said something a while ago. I would have been fine to stop at any time."

"I know, you were just in the zone and I didn't want to complain when you don't even have to be helping me."

"In the zone?" he smiled.

"Yeah, that's what I called it when Ty would get lost under the hood. I don't know how many times I had to call down to the shop after hours to tell him to get his butt home, and he wouldn't have even realized how late it was. Today you just reminded me so much of him."

He wrapped an arm around my shoulder and set his chin on top of my head. "I should have been paying attention to you. This had to be hard on you and I wasn't even thinking about that. Not to mention that you needed to eat a while ago and you should be at home resting by now. I'm really sorry. If working on her is going to be too hard on you, you don't have to come back. Trent and I can finish her up."

"No, I want to help. I really did enjoy today. It has just been a long day and I swear this pregnancy makes me weepy even at the good memories. I feel like I have zero control over my emotions. They're all over the place and it only gets crazier the bigger I get, but it's not your fault."

"It's okay, I don't mind crazy you, but let's get you home."

We started picking up tools and parts to put them away for the night.

"You did awesome today, Tate," he told me once we were shutting and locking up the garage.

162

"Thanks. I'm not sure if I'll remember any of it tomorrow though. I just hope that I was actually helpful. I feel like I slowed you down more than anything."

"You did good work today; you should be proud of it. Not to many more days like this and we should have her running. Mick ordered most of the parts we need to finish her, and my dad tracked down the fender and bumper, both in better shape than the ones on there, at a place he goes to for all of his restoration projects. I'll bring them back with me after Christmas break."

Wednesday, Casey was off to Indiana for three weeks and Thursday I was leaving town as well. Mel's parents were letting me borrow one of their vehicles to drive down to Abilene so Ellie could give me a ride to the airport. My parents had booked a flight for me, so I could spend Christmas with them at the inn. Then the day after Christmas, it was back to Abilene to stay with Ellie and Beth until it was time for classes to start again.

Trent was willing to let Kitten take up space in his garage until then. I just hoped we would really be able to get her running as soon as the break was over. I wanted to be able to slide behind the wheel before I was too big to even fit behind the wheel. That wouldn't be long.

Casey took me home, even stopping to buy me a burger on the way, and we said goodnight. Once I was back in my apartment I stared at the ring sitting in the same place I left it, but I didn't let myself get worked up about it. I scooped it, fingering it in my hand for a moment before stringing it on the chain next to Ty's. I brought them both up and pressed the rings to my lips before letting them fall back to hang over my heart.

"Today started out pretty rough, Ty," I started to talk to him as I settled onto the couch to get in a little studying before the day was over. "But it's turning out alright. I really get now why you loved working on cars so much. I don't know if I'd go so far as to say it was fun for me, but it makes sense now why it was for you. I wish I'd gotten to have a day like today with you. I always thought we'd have more time. I'm sorry that I never went to work with you any of the times you offered. You'd love Kitten though, and I think you'd really like Casey too. He's been so great. If it weren't for him I probably would have spent the day crying and depressed. Instead, he had me taking apart thingamajigs and cleaning all sorts of whatsits." I knew Ty would be laughing in Heaven. I never could remember what parts were called, even on the occasions he tried to show me. The only one that stuck with me was dipstick. "I promise once we get her running, I'll take her back home and take her out on Old Anson Road and really see what she can do." The only trouble Ty ever got into when we were younger was behind the wheel of a car out on Old Anson Road.

I picked up my study material from the coffee table and started reviewing it until my eyes could hardly focus on the pages. I closed the book and crawled into bed and said my goodnights to Lukas and Ty, which had become a nightly routine. I would always regret never taking Ty up on one of his offers to teach me even the most basic car maintenance, but while I laid there reflecting on the day, I realized that maybe it was better that I didn't have any memories of working on a car with Ty. I was able to feel close to him and experience something he'd loved without it being tainted by another time. It wasn't just Ty's dream anymore that I was building; it was for me and Lukas too. I was actually looking forward to going back over to Trent's the next evening.

Twenty-One

"Did you ever know, my love, how much
you took away with you when you left?"
    — C.S. Lewis

"There. That'll do it," Casey declared. I'd just successfully put in a brand new alternator, with careful instruction from Casey, who oversaw the whole process. I knew he probably could've done it in half the time it took me, but I was still feeling proud.

"You did awesome, Tate." Casey held up his hand for a celebratory five. I smacked it, grinning, and then Lukas chose that minute to start doing aerobics, or at least that's how it felt. Definitely his father's child, getting excited about an old car even from the womb.

"We'll turn you into a gear head in no time," Trent chimed in. I doubted that, but maybe I'd at least come out of this knowing how to change my own oil.

The three of us continued to work, joking and ribbing each other while we tinkered. They were both really patient with me, taking the time to explain each step and show me how all the different parts worked together. Even though I was having a good time and enjoying the work, I didn't have the heart to tell them that after we got Kitten running, I never wanted to touch another wrench or ratchet again so this would all be wasted knowledge if any of it actually managed to stick.

I was trying to reattach a hose where Casey had showed me, but it was difficult to see and I was struggling to get it on. In trying to force it into place rather than ask for help, my hand slipped and I cut my finger along a sharp edge. I let out a little hiss of pain and yanked my hand back, dropping the small hose inside the car.

"Shit, you okay?" Casey grabbed my hand to inspect the damage, immediately grabbing for a clean towel to stop the bleeding. It was only a small cut, but it was deep. "You got it good," he grimaced.

"Let me take a look." Trent, who was an EMT, grabbed my hand, and after pulling away the towel declared. "It's nasty, but doesn't look like it needs any stitches." I was thankful for that, and maybe even a little thankful when I got to sit back and relax while they carried on working through the afternoon right up until evening set in.

"Uh, oh, I know that face," Casey commented after a while, bringing me out of my thoughts. "I think it must be quitting time."

"What face?" I wasn't making a face.

"Your hungry face," he smirked knowingly. "You get this dreamy look that I only see when you start thinking about food," he teased. It was true that I'd been thinking about dinner, but I didn't know he could tell.

"That's what that look is?" Trent's brow arched. "I could have sworn she was fantasizing about me." He winked.

Casey laughed. "If we don't feed her soon, you'll get to see her angry face, and then you might want to make sure to keep any wrenches out of her reach or you're liable to get hit over the head with one."

"Shut up, I do not get angry or mean." I scowled at him.

"See, it's already setting in."

I rolled my eyes, but didn't object when they started cleaning up for the night and talking about calling for some pizzas. After getting all the tools tucked away and washing up, Trent ordered the food and we kicked back inside his house. They tried turning on ESPN to catch the second half of a ball game, but by the time the pizza arrived, I talked them into putting on a movie. I was a little surprised Casey had even agreed to stick around for pizza, so I hadn't expected him to agree to a movie. The other nights we'd spent working on Kitten, we always left as soon as we wrapped up, usually so he could get to whatever plans he had with Annie, but tonight he didn't seem to be in any hurry.

We ate pizza and sat through the terrible b-rated horror film the guys had talked me into. When it was over, none of us were really sure about what we'd just watched.

"That was . . ." Casey seemed at a loss for words.

"Yeah," I agreed, wishing I could un-watch it. "Even Lukas was disturbed, I think. He's been squirming all night."

"I mean, I did not see that coming when that guy-"

"Don't remind me," I cut Casey off as Lukas kicked again. I hoped he wasn't traumatized in the womb.

"I'll admit, that was pretty twisted," Trent spoke up. He was the one who had suggested the movie. "So want to watch another one?" He grabbed up the controller for his X-Box and started scrolling through Netflix.

"Sure, why not," I sighed. This was the last time we'd all hang out until after Christmas since Casey was headed to Indiana tomorrow and I would be leaving town soon as well.

"Might as well, but first I need a beer. You want anything?" Casey looked at me.

"Just something to settle Lukas down. He's really active tonight." I set my hand over my stomach.

"A beer might knock him out," Casey joked and then got up and headed for the kitchen.

"Grab me one too, man," Trent called after him.

When Casey returned we settled back in with another slasher film. This one proved to be less disturbing, but twice as terrifying. Fifteen minutes in and I was hiding my face in a pillow and scooting closer to Casey.

"Scared, Tate?" he whispered.

"Nope, it's not me," I lied. "I don't think Lukas likes scary movies."

"Sure, blame little man you big scaredy cat." He leaned down closer to my stomach. "You're not scared are you? You're Mama's just a wuss."

Lukas kicked again and I frowned, grabbing Casey's hand and setting it over my stomach. "Seriously, feel this though. It's like he's doing karate in there."

"Do you think something's wrong?"

"I don't think so," I hadn't really considered it though. "He's not usually this active, but I think I would feel it if something was wrong."

We settled back into the movie and Lukas seemed to take a break from the aerobics, at least until the movie ended. By that time I'd already figured out who the killer was and dozed off for the last fifteen minutes.

"Hey, Tate," Casey gently shook me awake. I sat up, blinking the sleepiness from my eyes and trying to suppress a yawn. "I should probably get you home so you can get to bed, and I have an early morning." Lukas seemed to come awake at the same time I did, and I just hoped he would let me get some sleep tonight.

We said goodnight to Trent and walked out to Casey's car. We'd been driving for a few minutes with the stereo off, when Casey broke the quiet, asking me if I was excited to spend Christmas in Jefferson. I'd been leaning my head against the window, but when Lukas started moving again, I sat up and looked over at Casey.

"I think it's you."

"Huh?" he cast me a puzzled look before returning his eyes to the road.

"Keep talking," I told him.

"I'm confused. What exactly do you want me to say and why do I need to talk?" It didn't matter because I was pretty sure he'd just confirmed what I'd wanted to know.

"Your voice. He likes your voice."

He turned his head toward me again. "Yeah?" I could see the barest hint of a smile.

"Yeah. I think so; either that or he thinks you're as annoying as I do." I grinned "The doctor said he would start to be able to recognize and respond to different voices. He moves whenever you talk. I just didn't notice until now, but it's not surprising. He hears your voice a lot, and . . ." I trailed off. Lukas was responding to Casey's voice the way he would have Ty's voice if he was here.

"Tate?" I heard Casey, but I was too lost inside my own head. Is this how it would have been with Ty? Would Lukas have got excited every time his daddy came home from work? I could imagine Ty walking in the door, kissing me on the cheek and then kneeling down in front of me to kiss my stomach and talk to his son. I could imagine him singing country and rock 'n' roll to him in the car. I would pretend it drove me crazy, but secretly I would love it.

It was a nice fantasy, but Lukas wouldn't ever actually get to hear the sound of his father's voice. I closed my eyes and tried to hear it in my own mind. My chest tightened when I realized I could barely remember the sound of Ty's voice. It'd been six months since I last heard it. I never thought I would forget the sound of the voice that cheered me on at every game, that whispered sexy things in my ear

168

when we made love, and told me he loved me every single day. How could I lose that?

"Olivia, are you okay?"

"Yeah, I'm sorry, I was just . . ." I didn't know what to say. I didn't want to make Casey feel bad.

"Thinking about Tyler?"

"Yeah. It's just that in moments like these I realize what they're both missing."

"Are you upset that he knows my voice?" Casey asked hesitantly.

"No . . . I – I don't know. I'm not mad at you. This is just hard and somehow I feel like I've let Ty down, because I can barely remember the sound of his voice? What else am I going to forget? What else am I going to lose next? How will our son ever be able to know his father if I can't remember what he was like?"

Casey pulled the car into the parking lot outside our building and shut the engine off. "I don't think you need to worry about that," he said softly.

"How can you say that? You don't know that. It's only been six months," I cried. "I'm already forgetting things!"

"No you're not. You haven't forgotten his voice. Maybe you can't hear it in your head right now, but your heart still knows it. And you still know him. Maybe you won't be able to remember every detail all the time, but you'll never forget who he was. I'd be willing to make a bet with you that in ten years I could ask you what his favorite song was, or his favorite color, or what his most annoying habit was, or his favorite place to touch you, the exact shade of his eye color or the way he laughed and you'd be able to close your eyes and remember it all clear as day."

"How can you be so sure I won't lose him?"

"How could you think you ever would?"

I didn't have an answer for him except that I was afraid.

We walked upstairs to our apartments and said goodnight. I wished him a safe flight to Indiana before shutting myself inside my apartment, wondering if I wasn't a little bit mad at Casey. Or not mad at him, but a tiny bit bitter. I also had to ask myself if part of my fear was that I was trying to replace Ty with Casey.

I immediately brushed that thought away. It was ridiculous and not even possible. I was just overreacting, but I couldn't help thinking about how significant a role Casey was playing in my life, how many of the holes he'd begun to fill in it. Lately I'd been spending even more time with him than I had Mel. A lot of that had to do with the fact that she didn't know the first thing about fixing up a car, but it still made me question what I was doing with Casey and why the next three weeks seemed like they were going to drag by.

"Shit," I cried out in frustration. "Ty I don't know what the hell I'm doing. I'm not trying to replace you. No one can take your place. Casey is just my friend, but I feel like I need him. Things don't seem so hard or scary when he's around. I don't know what that means," I admitted out loud. "I love you Ty. I wish I could hear you say it back to me."

I walked to my bedroom and set my purse down on my dresser. My phone slid out of one of the pocket and I picked up. I stared at it for a moment before pulling up the video that I'd been too chicken to watch for the past six months. I needed it now, though. It started, and I smiled when I saw his face smiling back at me.

"Come on babe. For me?" I heard myself plead with him.

"No way." He grinned and shook his head.

There he was. That was the voice I'd been missing.

"There's no way I'm doing it," his deep voice protested.

"Pleeeeease," I begged so sweetly, knowing he wouldn't be able to resist, and he didn't. He let out a deep groan.

"Fine, but only because I can't say no to you."

His face moved closer to the camera and I knew he was pressing a kiss to my forehead before he leapt up on stage and took the mic from the guy standing up there. The sound of everyone in the bar cheering came through loud. I'd had just enough to drink that night to make me stand up and start whistling and hollering for him.

"This one's for my girl. Love you Livvie." He winked at me.

My tears came harder when he started singing Lonestar's *Amazed* to me. I had to stop the video before he finished.

That had been on my twentieth birthday, only months before his death. A group of us had gone out to our favorite bar. Mel and I and a few others had to sneak in, but we didn't get drunk, we never did. We knew better with scholarships and our positions on the team on the line.

We just liked to go out and dance and sing a little karaoke. That night was one of the few times Ty ever got up on the stage.

He was no rockstar, but he had a decent voice and his country boy charm made up for the rest. The crowd had cheered him on and enjoyed his performance. To me it hadn't just been good, it had been perfect; the most amazing thing I'd ever heard. He'd been perfect. Still was. I couldn't ever imagine anything sounding as sweet to me. It was ridiculous to think I ever could have forgotten that.

Twenty-Two

"The only way to make sense out of change is to plunge into it, move with it, and join the dance."
— Alan W. Watts

"Did you have a good time with your parents?" Ellie was waiting for me outside of security when my flight back from Jefferson landed the evening after Christmas.

"Yeah, it was really good," I told her as we made our way to the baggage carousels. "Things at the inn were crazy of course, they were completely booked up for the holiday and you know how Mom loves her holiday activities. Every day she had something different planned for the guests: ornament making, decorating the huge tree they put up in the foyer, building gingerbread houses, baking Christmas cookies and even bow making."

"That sounds like your mother," Ellie chuckled. Christmas time was my favorite time of the year, but I swear my mother missed her calling in life to be one of Santa's elves. She was like an eight year old hopped up on too much sugar all month long. She's one of those people who start listening to Christmas music the second Halloween is over, and by the day after Thanksgiving, she has every hall in the inn decked and made sure my dad has hung all the lights outside.

Things had always been like that growing up, but instead of the inn, it was our house. She would invite every kid in the neighborhood over for her holiday activities. Ty's mom dragged him and Beth to every one. Ty and I always found a way to make it a competition and fight over who made the best whatever my mom had us making. Eventually we outgrew our childish competitions and the holiday traditions were something else to be shared together, and eventually we made our own.

This year I didn't put a tree up in my apartment and had opted out of helping decorate the one at the inn. That was Ty's favorite thing to do together. We'd make hot cocoa with peppermint schnapps, turn on country Christmas and then argue about ornament placement until usually I ended up throwing tinsel at him, but by the time he put the angel on top we'd both agree that the tree was absolutely perfect. I just couldn't bring myself to do it without him yet. Maybe next year on Lukas' first Christmas I would be ready for that, but not yet.

I tried to be festive and participate in everything else my mother planned, but none of it was easy. Waking up yesterday morning and having Christmas without him was the hardest part of all.

When we got to Ellie's, I once again found myself settling into Ty's old room. This time I was able to look at the little pieces of him that remained and smile. The pain was still there, pressing in on me, but it wasn't the fresh, agonizing, feels like your insides are being shredded kind of pain that it had been last time I was in here.

I grabbed a photo of the two of us off his night stand. We were both so young, and his mischievous grin reminded me of what happened right after that picture had been snapped. It was taken after my soccer team won our first championship when I was twelve. Ellie and Beth and Ty had come out to watch and our parents made us take a picture afterward. I had a huge grin on my face, still running off the excitement of scoring the final goal. I didn't see the look in Ty's eye until it was too late and he'd dumped the full bottle of Gatorade over my head.

Beth stepped inside the room at that moment and caught me staring at the photo. She gave me a sad smile and came to sit on the bed next to me. "I hope someday that I have someone who loves me half as much as my brother loved you."

I smiled and wrapped my arm around her shoulder, hugging her to my side and leaning my head against hers. "You will," I whispered. "And Ty loved you so much too."

She leaned closer into me and wrapped her arms around my middle as much as she could, holding onto me a moment before she pulled away. I watched her push the pain back as I had done so many times. She cleared her throat, but her voice still came out a little shaky when she spoke.

"You've got visitors. Mama's got 'em in the kitchen and is probably feedin' 'em leftovers by now."

I was surprised to hear that anyone was here for me. I followed after her and found three familiar faces sitting around the kitchen table, smiling at me around bites of leftover turkey, ham and pecan pie as their eyes went from my face to my stomach. They all knew, but I guess it was probably different to see my ever growing belly in person. Before I even had time to greet my old friends, Ellie was pushing me down into a seat next to them and placing a full plate in front of me.

"I didn't know you guys were coming." I hadn't seen Missy, Tommy or Drew since the funeral. Once upon a time, the three of them had been our closest friends. Tommy had come a long way since his days of helping Chuck torment me. Chuck moved away when the boys were in fifth grade and I wasn't sad to see him go, but Ty and Tommy had remained good friends. All of us had drifted since high school though. Back then I would have considered Missy my best friend next to Ty, and I would always consider her a good friend, but it was nothing like my relationship with Mel. The three of them were still pretty tight though, and Missy and Tommy were even dating now.

They'd all moved to Dallas after graduating the same year as Ty. They had even tried to convince him to go with them, but he'd stayed for me. They hadn't really understood our relationship then. Not very many people expected high school romances to last.

"We stopped by to see Ellie when we all got to town last week and she said you would be getting into town today," Drew said in between shoveling bites of pie into his mouth. Drew had the build of a linebacker and if Ellie didn't watch him he'd have the rest of that pie finished off in a matter of minutes.

Ellie and Beth left us in the kitchen to catch up while we ate. They filled me in on their lives, but when it came time for me to share, I found myself holding back. There was a time when I would have told them every little detail, but that was a different lifetime ago even though it had only been a few years.

"So what are you guys up to tonight? Seeing anyone else from high school?" I asked.

"Actually we came by to steal you. Chris Miller is having a party tonight since a bunch of people from our class are in town," Missy informed me excitedly, even though in high school we all thought Chris was the biggest tool and never would have showed up at one of his notorious keggers. Seeing Chris and a bunch of people we used to go to school with was the last thing I wanted to do, but I gave in to their pleading, threw on a large hoodie that would hopefully save me from having to answer too much about my pregnancy, and let Ellie know I was going out.

An hour later I was sitting on a sofa in Chris Miller's living room, next to some kid whose name I was having a hard time remembering even though he'd been in my class. He was a part of the stoner crowd back then, and it didn't seem like much had changed. He'd plopped down next to me about thirty minutes ago and hadn't spoken a word in all that time. He would just occasionally glance at me. Several times I'd thought about getting up, but there wasn't really anywhere to escape to.

Missy and Tommy were standing nearby, red cups in hand, talking to Chris and some of his buddies I recognized. Drew had been sitting with me, doing a decent job of keeping me company until a girl he'd dated on and off in high school had showed up and stolen him away to do some catching up. From the look on her face I could only assume it was the type of catching up that would involve very little talking and even less clothing.

Being here was like hopping in a time machine and traveling back three years. The scene looked the same. For some reason it really bothered me. Maybe it was that so much had changed for me. My entire world had been ripped wide open and these people got to go on seemingly unaffected, without a care in the world.

"Hey there, beautiful." A guy I was confident had played football with Ty lowered himself into the empty spot between me and the guy whose name was still escaping me. "What's a pretty girl like you doing sittin here by yourself?"

"My friends are right over there," I said, not bothering to make eye contact. I didn't want to encourage him.

"Then what are you doing over here? You should be enjoying the party with everyone."

"I needed to sit down," I replied, finally looking at him and hoping he would pick up on my disinterest in this conversation. Instead his eyes seemed to light up and a wicked grin spread over his face.

"Had a little too much to drink did ya? If you're not feeling well, there are empty beds upstairs. I can take you up there so you can lie down, away from the party until you're feeling better." It seemed Ty's baggy sweatshirt was doing its job too well.

"No thanks," I snorted and heard a chuckle from the other side of this idiot. It seemed I wasn't the only one to see through this his offer.

"Then how about if we just go find somewhere quieter to sit and talk?"

I was about to tell him off for hitting on a pregnant chick, but stoner guy saved me from having to. "Back off Eric, she's not interested."

"Stay out of this Dixon." Josh Dixon; that was stoner guy's name.

"I'm warning you right now Eric, walk away or I'll make you walk away." I was surprised by the how threatening Josh sounded, but if I recalled, he used to get into some trouble for fighting back in high school.

"Whatever man." Eric scowled and sulked off across the room. I turned to face Josh who was regarding me carefully.

"Thanks," I said hesitantly. His face relaxed and he gave me a half smile.

"No problem, Olivia." My face must've registered my surprise because he chuckled. "What? Didn't think I knew who you were? I bet you don't remember me."

"I do. It took me a while," I admitted. "But I do remember you. I am a little surprised that you remember me. I don't think we had a single class together in school and we didn't exactly run in the same crowds." I could count the number of times we'd ever spoken to each other on one hand. He chuckled again.

"No we didn't. Olivia Adams wouldn't have been caught dead at a party like this one." He teased lightheartedly. "I'm actually surprised that you've graced us lowlife degenerates with your presence this evening." He grinned broadly, making it clear that he was only kidding.

"I'm not even sure what I'm doing here," I sighed. "My friends wanted to come and somehow I let them talk me into it." I looked over at Missy and Tommy laughing and drinking, having a good time. When I looked back over at Josh, I saw that his gaze had followed mine, and was taking in the same scene.

"I remember you all being close back then." He faced me again. "Is it just like old times?" I got the sense that he already knew it wasn't.

"To be honest, I'm wondering if we were ever as close as I thought we were. Maybe it's just been too long. People change, I suppose."

"Or maybe you've just been through real shit and they haven't moved past high school, still trying to live in the past."

"Maybe," I said quietly, and he didn't say anything for a long time. "Sometimes it's easier to try and hang on to the past."

"But you can't, can you? Eventually you have to let go and move on, or risk never moving on."

This is not how I saw my night going; having a deep, philosophical conversation with the biggest stoner from high school. I had to wonder if maybe I had misjudged him, because he seemed to get it better than the people who had claimed to be my friends for years.

"Yeah," I muttered, but before I had time to give it much more thought, Missy appeared in front of us, not bothering to hide the disgusted look she shot Josh.

"Hey, why don't you come over with us?" She nodded her head toward Tommy and that group.

"Actually, I think I'm going to head back to Ellie's."

"No, don't go. We've hardly gotten to talk or spend any time together." Josh laughed under his breath and Missy glared at him and then looked back at me. "Pleeease don't go Livvie," she drunkenly whined and it grated on my nerves – maybe more than it should have – that she used Ty's nickname for me.

"I'm sorry, but I'm tired and I really need to get some rest."

"Aww," she pouted. "Baby is a party pooper. Must suck not being able to have any fun." It took everything I had not to punch her in the face for that comment. I knew she was drunk and probably didn't mean to be so insensitive, but I couldn't believe she'd said it.

"I imagine what sucks is having inconsiderate assholes for friends," Josh muttered under his breath, but we both heard him. My eyebrows shot up and Missy looked ready to claw his eyes out. I stood and drew her attention back to me.

"Look, I appreciate you guys inviting me, and it was good to see ya'll, but this isn't my idea of a good time anymore. I'll be in town for another week, and you can call me if you want to grab lunch or something." After tonight, and seeing how different we both were, I wouldn't hold my breath for her call. On some level she had to know there wasn't much left of our friendship. It was better if we both just got on with our lives and appreciated the good times that we'd had when life had been simpler.

"Oh, okay, er yeah. I'm not sure where Drew is, but you can find a ride right?" she asked and when I told her I would, she returned to Tommy's side and whispered something in his ear. He turned around and gave me a slight wave and I returned it, but didn't bother to walk over there and say goodbye, and a second later his attention was back on Missy.

I pulled out my phone to call Beth to come get me, but Josh interrupted me before I hit send.

"Come on, I'll drive you."

I narrowed my eyes on him. "Are you safe to drive?"

He rolled his eyes and smirked a little. "Yes, I haven't had anything to drink or smoke all night, so come on."

I followed him out to his pick-up and climbed in the passenger side. When he started it up the radio blared some heavy metal music and he quickly reached to turn it down, but I think it was already too late for my poor eardrums.

"Sorry." He grinned sheepishly and then backed us out of Chris' driveway. I gave him Ellie's address and we were almost to her house before either one of us spoke again.

"I just want to say that I'm really sorry Olivia. I know we weren't friends, but you were always really nice, even if you thought I was a complete loser." He winked, letting me know he was only giving me a bad time. "And Tyler was a good guy."

"Thanks," I said as he pulled up outside Ellie's. "For everything tonight. I'm sorry for ever thinking you were just a loser pothead."

"No, it's okay. I am." He smiled. "But on occasion I have my moments. I just don't want people to expect it from me, so keep it to yourself." I laughed softly and said goodnight. He waited until I was inside before pulling away.

Twenty-Three

*"Everything grows rounder and wider and weirder,
and I sit here in the middle of it all and wonder
who in the world you will turn out to be."*
Carrie Fisher

The next day I woke up a little before noon to three unread text messages on my phone. One was from Casey, the second was from Mel and the other was from an unknown number. Casey and I hadn't talked much since the day he left for Indiana. He'd texted to wish me a Merry Christmas and I had done the same. I opened his message first, but he was only confirming what day I would be back in town, probably so he could let Trent know when we could finish Kitten up.

"I'll be back on the third."

I was pretty sure that was the same day he'd said his flight would get in. I stared at the screen waiting for a reply, but when one didn't come, I decided to check the other messages.

Mel wanted to know how the party had gone, so I filled her in on the events of the night before. She didn't think I would be missing out on anything either by moving on and leaving past friendships in the past. I in turn asked her how Paris with her parents was, and of course she was having a great time and had met some hot French guy named Julien. She sent me a picture and I had to laugh. He was very attractive, like male model attractive, definitely Mel's type, and would be the perfect winter break fling for her, but I hoped someday she would stop playing games and find someone to really give a chance. I knew why she was the way she was, why she had trust issues. She'd been used one too many times. I just wished she would see that not every guy would treat her that way. She deserved more than these meaningless hook-ups.

She was just getting ready to go out for the evening there, so I told her to have a good night and be safe. Casey still hadn't sent a reply so I

179

opened up the third message and was surprised when I saw who it was from.

Hey this is Josh. I had to play six degrees of Olivia Tate to get your number. My girlfriend, you might remember her, Caitlyn Thomas, is dragging me to some show at the contemp arts center at 1. It should be really lame and boring, but afterward they're playing all the die hard movies downtown. A few friends are meeting us there. Cait would probably like to have another chick to look at the artsy crap with if you wanna go with us to the show. If not you can just meet us at the theatre if you want to spend your day watching Bruce Willis kick some ass.

I found myself replying that I would love to go with them, before I even had a chance to think about it and talk myself out of being social. I hurried out of bed and rushed to dress. On my way out the door to meet Josh and Cait at the arts center I sent another quick text to Casey just because I did miss talking to him. I wasn't going to over analyze it anymore. He was just a friend and it was okay to miss him.

Hope you're having a good time with your family. Did you get the parts for Kitten? I can't wait to get home and finish her up.

This time a reply came immediately.

I got the parts. We'll have her up and running in no time. What are you up to today? You're back in Abilene now right?

I didn't text back right away since I was pushing it for time to get to the arts center, but once I was there I responded to him and we kept up a conversation throughout the rest of the day. The show at the arts center was a little on the boring side, but I snapped pictures of the funny art and sent them to Casey and he would respond with what he thought it looked like. Cait was an art major and even she thought some of the pieces were pretty weird, but I had a good time wandering through the exhibits with her and Josh. When we were done, Josh compared the exhibit to a bad experience he had with shrooms. We were all definitely ready for some Bruce Willis when we left there.

When we got to the theater is wasn't very packed, and our group made up most of the audience once the rest of their friends showed up. Some of them I remembered from high school and some I'd never met, but they were all really nice and cool. We laughed and yelled out every "Yippee ki-yay motherfucker."

The movie marathon ran the rest of the day and night, and we made several trips between movies to the concessions for food, drinks and candy. I continued to text Casey between movies as well, and even though I was having a really good time with everyone, I sort of wished he was there. He was enjoying time with him family and buddies back home, but he admitted that he was a little bit jealous that he was missing out on our all day Die Hard fest.

It was well after midnight by the time I got back to Ellie's. I felt completely exhausted even though I'd only sat in a theater all day. I crashed into bed and said goodnight to my guys.

"Love you Lukas. Love you Ty, I hope you can watch Die Hard in Heaven." They were some of his favorite movies.

As tired as I was, I didn't fall asleep right away. I hadn't texted Casey since the last movie started, but I found myself grabbing my phone and sending him a message, despite how late it was.

Are you awake?

Yeah. Did you make it home okay after the movie?

Yep, I just got home and now I'm tucked into bed safe and sound. Why are you still up?

Some crazy girl texted me and woke me up.

Crap, sorry. Go back to bed.

I'm just kidding Tate. I'm watching tv with Jessie.

Jerk :) What are you guys watching?

A few minutes went by.

Some movie.

What movie?

Again I waited several minutes before a message came through.

That vampire movie.

Haha, don't act like you don't know what it's called.

Shut up, my sister picked it.

Sure she did. Don't lie. You love it. I saw the books on your shelf at home.

Funny. I think that's actually your bookshelf.

Don't judge me.

We talked for a little while longer before sleep finally caught up with me, and I couldn't keep my eyes open any longer.

I hung out with Josh, Cait and their group two more times that week before I went back to Lubbock. I hadn't heard from Missy, Tommy or Drew again, and I didn't even feel a little bit bad about it. Before this visit, I'd been feeling guilty about not keeping in touch with them more since the funeral, but now I was able to let go of that guilt. I was thankful for what they had meant to Ty and me, for the friendship that we'd had, but I really felt like now I could go home and move past that.

"Call me after your appointment tomorrow," Ellie made me promise as I loaded up Mr. Ross' Jeep. "And take this." She thrust a big brown paper sack into my hands. I knew when I opened it I would find it full of food and snacks. I set it on the passenger seat and hugged and thanked her.

A sullen Beth was standing on the sidewalk waiting to say goodbye. I walked over to her. "I promise I'll be back to visit as soon as I can, and once the baby's here you guys will come see us. I was thinking that it should be really close to your spring break, so maybe you could stay with me for a week."

Her head shot up and her eyes met mine hopefully. "Really, you'd let me stay with you?"

"Of course. I'd love to have you there, and I think it would be really good for you to spend some time in the area, especially since your mom told me you applied to the university." I could tell she was surprised I knew. Ellie had just told me last night, but I wondered why Beth hadn't told me herself.

"Mom told ya?"

"Why didn't you tell me? That's really exciting news."

She chewed her lip nervously. "It just didn't seem all that important with everything you've got going on, and I was afraid you would think I picked that school for the wrong reasons. I didn't want you to think I was just trying to follow you."

"It is important. No matter what, I don't want you to think you can't tell me something like that. We're sisters, and nothing will change that. I'm always going to be here for you and I'm so proud of you. Tyler would've been too." She sniffed and nodded her head.

"I'll see you soon," I promised, and gave her one last hug before climbing into the Jeep. They both stood there, side by side and waved as I drove off.

As much as I would miss them, and my parents, I was looking forward to going back. Mel was home from Paris and anxious for me to return. I couldn't wait to hear more about her trip, even the very sexy Julien she had talked about in just about every one of her texts.

I was also excited to finish working on Kitten. Casey said we only had about one day's worth of work left. She might not be the most beautiful car until I could afford the paint job, and all the cosmetic beautification a car like that deserved, but she would run and she was mine.

Half way into the drive, my phone rang. I looked down and saw Casey's picture ID on the screen. I was just coming up on an exit and it would be the perfect time for a bathroom and lunch break.

"Hey," I answered. "I'm just pulling over so give me a second." I turned onto the exit ramp. Once I was parked outside of gas station I grabbed my phone again. "You still there?"

"I'm here."

"What's up?" I unbuckled and shut off the vehicle. I started gathering up the empty water bottles and fruit bar wrappers on the passenger seat.

"I was just checking to see what time you think you'll get in."

"I'm about an hour and a half away. Are you already back?"

"Yeah. I'll see ya when you get home. Drive safe."

"Okay, see ya in a little while."

We hung up and I ran inside the service station to use the restroom and buy a Reese's to go with my lunch. I sat in the Jeep and ate the turkey sandwich Ellie had packed, and then washed it down with the rich chocolate and peanut butter.

Back on the road I cranked up the volume on my stereo and started singing along with *Ashes and Embers'* new single. The rest of the drive passed pleasantly, except for how frequently I had to stop for bathroom breaks.

"We're back baby boy," I rubbed my stomach when we finally pulled up outside the apartment building. "Home sweet, home." Or at least as close to it as I could get without Ty.

Twenty-Four

"That it will never come again is what makes life so sweet."
—Emily Dickinson

I wasn't in my apartment two minutes before Casey was at the door.

"Welcome back," he grinned when I opened it. I wasn't sure if we should hug or not, but I decided to go for it. He squeezed me tightly and held on a little longer than usual. I got the feeling he'd missed me. I didn't mind though. I'd missed him too.

"So do you feel up to going over to Trent's?" There was almost a childlike excitement and hopefulness in his voice.

"Aww. Did you miss Kitten, Hunt? Won't Evie be jealous?" I heard his low laugh. I'd missed that too.

"Maybe, so what do you say? Are you ready to finish her up?"

"Casey, I just walked in the door. I haven't even finished unpacking my car or let Mel know I'm back. Besides, didn't you just get back? Don't you need to go see Annie?"

He brushed me off. "Oh come on, I thought you wanted to get her running as soon as possible. There's plenty of day left to get some work done. Maybe even have her running by tomorrow."

That got me. I was anxious to get behind her wheel. "Okay. At least let me change, and while I do that, you can go down to the Jeep and grab the rest of my bags." I tossed the keys at him.

He brought everything up while I changed into my designated mechanicing pants and a worn shirt of Ty's.

"You ready?" he asked when I walked back out into the living room. He really was eager to get over there and wasted no time in ushering me out the door, and leading me to the Mustang. When I saw the Jeep sitting next to it I remembered to text Mel to let her know I was back.

Yay! I'm coming over right now.

I'm actually going to work on the car. Casey is anxious to get it finished. I think he missed Kitten

184

Ya I'm sure it's the car he missed ;)
Don't go there Mel.
Fine. Txt me when you're home skank.
I will hooker.

After texting Mel, I took the time to let my mom and Ellie know I'd made it home safely as well. I was typing out a response back to my mom when we pulled up outside Trent's.

"Come on" Casey said taking my phone from me, and hopping out of the car.

"Hey!" I unbuckled and followed after him. He was halfway up the drive, and as amusing as his excitement was, I was a little bit annoyed that he couldn't even give me five damn seconds to text my mother. The front door opened up and Trent came out wearing his typical baseball cap and faded jeans, but he was missing a shirt, and "Dear Lord, have mercy" was all I wanted to say.

I made it my new mission to get my phone back and try and discreetly snap a picture to send to Mel. He was just her flavor of delicious, and from the little bit of time I'd spent with him, I got the feeling he might be a guy who could actually handle her intensity and level of crazy.

I didn't have to wait long for the chance either, I snatched my phone out of Casey's hand while he and Trent were talking, and I pretended to be texting again. Neither one of them was paying me enough attention to know differently. As soon as I sent the picture I'd snapped, I got an almost instant reply.

Who the hell is that? I'd like to lick sweat from those abs!!
That's Trent.
Can I come over and work on cars too, or maybe just do him on the hood of one?!!
What about Julien, your sexy Frenchman?
Forget Julien. I want to take a bite out of that hunk of delicious man meat! Can he be my Christmas present?

I slid my phone into my pocket and tried to hide my smile. I'd see what I could do. Trent was a sweet guy, but I didn't get the impression he took crap from anyone, and I didn't think Mel would be able to chew him up like she did most of her boy toys. She needed a good guy who could hold his own with her, and I thought Trent might just be one to give her a run for her money.

"Hey, did we come here to work on the car, or so you two could rekindle your bromance?"

They both turned amused expressions on me.

"Aww, Olivia, did you miss me?" Trent walked over and caught me in an affectionate headlock and mussed his hand over my hair playfully.

"Yes I did, but can we get in there so I can see my precious?"

"Okay, Casey, come on. The lady wants to see her car." The two of them exchanged a knowing look and I wondered what was up, because something definitely was. The three of us walked over to the garage and I expected Trent to open it, but he just stood there, looking at Casey, who suddenly seemed nervous. He looked back at me before reaching over and punching in the code for the garage door opener, then his eyes returned to me and he didn't look away.

As soon as the door was half way up I realized why he was watching me so intently. He wanted to see my reaction. My hand shot up and covered my mouth as I gasped. I stood there, literally speechless.

"What do you think?" he asked me apprehensively.

"She's perfect," I whispered in awe, and she was. Kitten's once faded and rusted Marina Blue paint was now bright and shiny. Every part of her had been buffed and waxed and polished, and looked brand new. The paint wasn't the only new thing either, she now had a hood with a scoop and on it was a big red bow.

"Merry Christmas, Tate." Casey was practically beaming, relieved by my reaction. I don't know what he could have been afraid of. How could I not love it? Yeah, I wanted to smack him because he shouldn't have done it, but it was really amazing.

"Thank you. I mean it's way too much, and I can't believe you did this, and I'm torn between hitting you and hugging you, but thank you!"

"Hug, you should definitely go with the hug."

I hugged them both, but held onto Casey just a little bit tighter and longer, and tried not to think about how good it felt to be in his arms. I was just overly emotional about everything these days.

186

"Ready to take her for a spin?" Casey grinned at me.

"What? She's ready to drive?" The paint job was one thing, but I thought he'd known how much I wanted to help with the rest. I tried to hide my disappointment that they'd finished her without me. I didn't want him to think I was ungrateful, so I dropped my eyes to the floor in hopes that he wouldn't see what I was thinking, but he caught my chin and tipped my head back up. He was grinning down at me.

"I didn't do any of it without you."

"Huh?" I was confused.

"She was ready before you even left. We finished her that last day, but I didn't want you to know until I had time to surprise you with this. Really all Trent and I had to do was remount the engine and put on the new hood, then attach the bumper and fender." This time I did hit him.

"Seriously? She was done the whole time?"

"Owe." He rubbed the spot on his arm where I punched him and Trent chuckled. "You have a funny way of saying thank you."

"I just can't believe you did all this," I huffed still a little shocked that he'd had this all planned out.

"Are you mad?"

"No I'm not mad. It's amazing. I just – when did you even have time to have all this done?"

"I arranged everything with Trent and Mick before I left, but then I had to come back early to take care of something else, so it worked out even better and I was able to get her ready for you." He looked away for a minute, but I could tell something was on his mind. He ran his hand through his hair to the back of his neck, and I wondered what he wasn't telling me, but he didn't give me a chance to ask. "So what do you say, ready to get behind that wheel and see how she handles?"

He dangled the keys in front of me. I didn't even hesitate to grab them from him and march over to the driver's side. I took another second to admire her before I climbed in, but then I leaned my head back out.

"You two coming or what?"

"Hell yes!" Trent hollered and tried to beat Casey to the passenger seat, but he ended up in the back. I put the key in the ignition, but at the last second Casey hopped back out and I wondered what he was doing. Until I saw him tear the bow off the hood.

187

"Start her up," he grinned excitedly once he was back in the seat next to me. I did, and Kitten purred. She purred and hummed like a fierce jungle cat. It was a beautiful sound and I wasn't the only one who thought so. I knew without a doubt that Lukas was his father's son. I couldn't hold back my laughter.

"What?" Casey looked puzzled.

"Lukas takes after his daddy. He started squirming as soon as I started her up."

"Atta boy." Casey grinned at the same time Trent said, "Smart kid."

The smile remained on my face the entire time I was behind the wheel.

"Hey do you guys want to come over for dinner tonight?" I asked when I put Kitten in park outside Trent's house. "I'd really like to thank both of you for helping me out."

"I never say no to a free meal from a pretty lady." Trent smiled and I thought *Merry Christmas Mel.* Casey was looking at me closely and frowning so I wiped the pleased expression off my face and looked at him expectantly.

"Um, yeah sure. That sounds fine."

"Great, and I hope you don't mind if my friend Melodie joins us," I said looking at Trent in the rearview. Out of the corner of my eye I could see Casey grinning and shaking his head. He must've caught on to what I was planning. Good, somebody should probably warn Trent anyway. They both climbed out, but Casey leaned his head back inside.

"I know what you're up to." I gave him my best *'who me?'* look. "Don't even try to deny it. Run along and we'll see you in a little while." As soon as he was out of sight in Trent's house I reached for my phone.

Get over to my place now. Trent's coming for dinner with Casey.
On my way!!!!!!!! Need me to grab anything from the store?
Can you grab salad fixings?
No problem.

I hoped Mel would give it a real chance if the two of them did hit it off. I was afraid that if Mel didn't deal with the issues that kept her from letting any guy in, one day it would be too late, and she would miss out on something amazing and regret it. I don't know why, but I really thought Trent could be that something amazing for her.

188

Mel wasn't far behind me when I got home. I was just putting the steaks in the marinade when she burst through the door in typical Mel fashion. "You have to tell me all about him and why you were hiding him from me."

I rolled my eyes at her. "Just start washing veggies."

She walked around the counter and set the grocery bag down. I shouldn't have been surprised to see her in a short skirt and tight shirt. It didn't matter that there'd been rainstorms on and off all day, Mel wasn't going to let a little thing like the weather get in her way. "You look like a prostitute."

"You look like a hobo," she countered as she pulled open my refrigerator and went to work washing and chopping the vegetables for salad. We worked side by side in silence until I turned to place the container of steaks in the fridge to soak in the marinade and felt something small hit the back of my head just before a baby carrot hit the ground and rolled to the base of the fridge. I turned to look at her with raised eyebrows.

"Really? Are we in fifth grade now?"

"Come on, you gotta give me something," she groaned. "Last name, occupation, secret fantasies, anything."

I laughed. "Sullivan. Paramedic and how the hell should I know?"

"Oooh. Paramedic; I can work with that."

I let out an exasperated sigh. I loved her to death, but sometimes I just wanted to smack her. "You know what else I can tell you about him?" I didn't wait for her to answer. "He's a genuinely nice guy. He's sweet and funny and has a pretty good bullshit radar. He's not the type of guy to just use a girl or let you use him for a week or two at your whim, so if that's what you've got in mind, you might as well just forget it."

"We'll see." This was definitely one of those times when I wanted to smack her.

"Someday Mel, you're gonna have to trust someone enough to let them see the real you. You can't keep this act up forever."

She didn't respond, just continued to chop and build the salad. I didn't push anymore. I knew I'd made my point and could only hope that she'd really heard me. I left her to finish prepping the food and hopped in the shower.

The baked potatoes were close to done and I was just getting ready to throw the steaks in to broil when the guys showed up. Casey strolled right in followed by Trent.

"Hey. Come on in and have a seat wherever. I'm just getting ready to throw the steaks in." I turned the oven to broil and started to transfer the steaks to the broiler pan.

"Hey, why don't we take those over to my place and we can throw them on the barbecue," Casey suggested. I didn't have a barbecue or a balcony to use it on like he did.

"Sure, that would be great." I switched the oven back to bake and looked over to see Mel eyeing Trent. "You two can get to know one another while we grill these, and keep an eye on the potatoes."

Mel wore the smile I recognized as her 'target acquired, preparing to launch' smile.

"Sure, that's fine." Trent might not have been so agreeable if he knew that look as well as I did. Nothing good ever followed it. I just hoped he didn't fall for it like most of the male population did. I followed Casey over to his apartment and out onto the balcony. He fired up the small barbecue and started laying out the steaks.

"I didn't know you hated Trent."

"What are you talking about? I like Trent."

"Then why exactly are you trying to feed him alive to Mel?" He smirked.

"Ha. Ha. Funny. I was under the impression that he could handle her."

"You know this is going to make things awkward if it backfires?"

"I'm choosing to believe that it won't."

"She's not going to be able to wrap him around her little finger. He'll see right through that shit."

"That's what I'm counting on."

"I warned him about her."

"Good. I was hoping you would."

"Okay then." I could tell he didn't know what to think about it, but he definitely didn't sound hopeful for the two of them. "So, you never told me why you had to come back early."

"Just something I needed to take care of." I was curious, but he wasn't saying anymore. He just flipped the steaks.

190

"By the way, I have something for you. It's not much though. I have it in my apartment. It seems kind of lame though now, after everything you did for me."

"Don't even worry about it. You didn't have to get me anything." Technically I didn't get it, I already had it, but I hoped that he would like it still.

When the steaks were done, we tossed them on a plate and carried them back to my apartment. I stopped with my hand on the doorknob when I heard Trent's voice. It was too low for me to make out. Casey was close on my heels or I would have cracked the door to try and listen. Instead, I pulled it open and stepped inside like I was oblivious to any conversation taking place.

When I saw Mel's face, I wished I had eavesdropped. Whatever Trent had said to her made an impact. I saw something like respect or admiration flash in her eyes. If I didn't know her so well I would have missed it, because she quickly covered it up with indifference. Hmmmm. This was interesting.

"The salad is ready and I think the potatoes are done too." She turned her back on all of us and started grabbing dishes from the cupboards. I glanced over at Trent, but he was looking away from me as well and seemed tense. Very interesting.

He exchanged a look with Casey, who tried hard to hide a smirk. Whatever, I would get it out of him later if I couldn't get it from Mel. A little bit of tension lingered between the two as we sat down to eat and I was starting to think Casey was right and this was a bad idea. Then he asked Mel about Paris and she started going on about her trip like nothing had happened, and for the rest of the evening she was charming, bubbly Mel, except I noticed that she avoided looking directly at Trent.

The guys had to take off not long after we finished eating. Trent was on shift tomorrow so he had an early morning. Casey stuck around and helped with the clean up and then cleared out too.

"You can bring my present over whenever. I'll just be sitting in my apartment, anxiously awaiting it," he informed me before leaving me with Mel.

"Spill," I demanded almost in the same second that the door shut behind Casey

"Spill what?" she feigned ignorance, but she wasn't fooling me.

"What happened with Trent while Casey and I were out of the apartment?"

"Nothing." She busied herself putting away the clean dishes,

"Don't even try that. You were looking at him like you were about to strip him down and ravish him right there on my couch when we left you two. Then you ignored him all night, so don't tell me that nothing happened. What did he say that pissed you off?"

"You want to talk about looks? Tell me what's up with you and Casey, because the way he's been looking at you lately–"

"Damn it Mel. Why do you do this? You're not supposed to shut me out, but if you don't want to talk, fine. Just don't bring me and Casey into this, because you know damn well there's nothing between us. He doesn't look at me in any way except as a friend."

"As soon as you come out of this denial you're in over Casey, I'll tell you what Trent said. Until then I think I should just head home. I don't want to argue with you." She grabbed her purse and keys and brushed past me, stopping only to kiss her fingers and press them to my belly. "Love you little man." Then she looked back up at me. "I'll talk to you tomorrow."

I didn't even know what to say as she walked out of my apartment. This wasn't like her at all. Trent really got to her and I wanted to know how.

I walked into my bedroom and grabbed the small, wrapped box from my nightstand and went to knock on Casey's door. When he answered I held the present out, but then yanked it back when he reached for it. "You want the present you tell me what was up with Trent and Mel. Have you talked to him?"

This wasn't just about satisfying my curiosity, although I was dying to know, this was also about protecting my best friend. If I had misjudged Trent and he had been cruel to her, I would make that boy sorry.

He pulled the door open wider and moved out of the doorway so I could pass. "Look, I don't know what went on with them, or what he said to her. It's between them, but if I had to guess, I'd say she probably came onto him strong and he shot her down."

Rejection would certainly piss her off; it wasn't something she was used to, but I still didn't think it was quite as simple as that.

"Can I have my present now?"

"Here," I handed it to him, "but before you get all excited, it really isn't much." I watched him peel back the paper to reveal the shoe box I'd put it in. When he opened the lid, his expression was unreadable and I got nervous.

"Is this . . . ?" I'd told Casey about Ty's model car collection when he commented on the ones I had sitting around the apartment. This one I'd had tucked away in a box in my closet. I thought Casey might like it since it was an exact replica of Evie, but I realized now that maybe it was a bad idea.

"Yeah, it is, but if it's weird and you don't want it that's fine." I still couldn't read him and I started to rethink giving him something that belonged to my dead husband. He probably thought it was really weird. "I know you didn't really know Ty," Casey looked away but the flash of emotion I'd seen in his eyes seemed odd. He'd looked almost nervous and he clearly didn't want me to catch it. "I'm sorry, this was a dumb idea. You don't have to keep it." I started to take it back from him, but he pulled it away from me.

"Olivia, I don't think you understand. It's not dumb at all. I'm just surprised you would give it to me."

"I just thought you might appreciate it, and it should be appreciated and displayed, not in a box in my closet. I actually helped him paint that one when we were seventeen."

"It's great, really. Thank you." He walked over to his entertainment center and moved a stack of video games to a lower shelf and then placed the car in the empty spot. He walked back over to where I was standing. "Seriously, thank you. It means a lot that you want me to have it." I looked up into those dark brown eyes, he was smiling down at me with so much affection that in that moment. I felt a blush spread over my cheeks and an unfamiliar, but pleasant, fluttering started in my stomach.

What was that about?

I was almost afraid of the answer, so I chose to ignore it.

Twenty-Five

"Hardships often prepare ordinary people
for an extraordinary destiny." — C.S. Lewis

"So how are your classes going this term?" Casey and I were walking out of the fitness center together after work.

"So far, pretty good, but we'll see." We were only two weeks into the new quarter.

"You don't sound too sure."

"Classes really are fine. I just don't know if I'm on the right track or if I'm wasting my time."

"Still not sure about the whole athletic training gig?"

"No, I guess not." As much as I appreciated the opportunity and all the encouragement Casey had given me, I couldn't see myself doing it long term.

"What are you doing tomorrow afternoon?"

"Uhh . . ." Tomorrow was Thursday and I didn't have anything planned after my classes let out. "Nothing."

"I want to show you something. It'll probably take about two hours, but I think you'll like it. I actually don't know why I didn't think of taking you sooner."

"What is it?"

"You'll see," he grinned.

"Okay, do I need to bring anything with me?" I was fishing for clues.

"Just dress comfortably." That didn't help at all, but he wouldn't tell me anything else. The next day when he knocked on my door, I was ready in a pair of yoga pants and trainers and looking forward to wherever we were going. He remained tight lipped, but that didn't stop me from harassing him on the drive.

"Are we there yet?" I asked him for the fifth time since we'd climbed into the car on our way to wherever. He was doing his best not to acknowledge my childish attempts at annoying him. I could tell he was cracking though. The corners of his mouth turned up in a barely noticeable smile.

"What about now? Are we there yet?" I asked again a few blocks later.

"Seriously? No we're not there yet," he exclaimed.

My face split into a satisfied grin.

"Dammit, you're impossible." He shook his head in amusement.

That only made my smile grow. "Thank you."

"It wasn't a compliment." His tone was all gruff and irritated but it didn't match his eyes. He was amused even if he didn't want to admit it. Ty was always the same way, preferring just to indulge me when I got feisty. He didn't even try to act frustrated with me and I would lose interest in pushing his buttons. Casey, however, reacted nicely when I pushed at his.

"Soo . . ." I started a minute later. "Are we–"

"I swear if you finish that, I will make you walk home."

"You wouldn't make a pregnant woman walk," I called his bluff.

"You're right, but I would blast Metallica the entire way home, and I might feel inclined to take the long route." It was his turn to smirk. I hated Metallica, and he knew it. I kept my mouth shut until we were pulling into a parking lot of a large building. He looked at me still smiling. "What? Not going to say it?" I narrowed my eyes. "Okay then I will. Yes. We're here."

"And where exactly is here?"

"You'll see. Come on." I followed him out of the car and around to the front of the building where I read the sign on the door. *Pediatric Physical Therapy.* I looked at Casey questioningly. This is not what I was expecting. "I volunteer here on Thursdays."

"What exactly is this place? I mean, obviously they work with kids."

"They work to rehabilitate kids who've suffered from injury, disease or disorders that affect their motor skills." He pulled the door open for me and then followed me inside. "To make it fun for the kids, a lot of their programs revolve around sports." He waved at the two girls sitting at the front desk. They looked to be in their late twenties, maybe early thirties, both attractive, and they gave Casey appreciative smiles as he ushered me through a door that led to a short hallway with several more doors widely spaced. There was a man, roughly forty, with kind eyes, pushing a little girl in a wheel chair toward us. She gave me a shy smile and then turned to look at Casey. An adorable blush spread over her freckled cheeks when he flashed his megawatt smile.

"Hey Jessica." He winked at her and she ducked her head bashfully.

"Hey, Casey." The man pushing her smiled. "The kids are excited to see you, who's this you've got with you?"

"This is Olivia. She's a friend who works with me at the college. I thought she might like to see what you guys do here."

"That's great. We can always use more volunteers around here. Go ahead and head on into the gym. Laura's in there today with the usual group." He flashed me another friendly smile and then continued pushing the little girl toward the door we just came through.

"Come on. He led me to the second door on the left and pushed through. The large room we stepped into didn't look like any gym I'd ever set foot in before. It was amazing.

One wall was lined with basketball hoops of different heights, and two little boys were attempting to shoot baskets with another middle-aged man. On the far end there was a miniature golf course set up and a girl about ten was being guided through it by a young woman. On the left side was a big rock climbing wall being used by three kids who appeared to be about twelve or thirteen. Everywhere I looked, there were kids engaged in different activities. There was a kind of bowling lane set up, t-ball stands in a small, netted batting cage and small goals along another wall.

"Wow. This place is incredible," I breathed in awe.

"I know. Right? This is my favorite room. They have a more traditional fitness center, as well, with bikes and weights and other equipment, but they try to split the time between there and in here so that it doesn't all feel like therapy but is fun for the kids as well. There's a pool too, and a trampoline room that's pretty sweet. They fit the programs to the needs and interests of each individual child. They work with kids all the way up to seventeen, but in here we work mostly with six to twelve year olds. They have a toddler room and another one for teens too."

One little boy, about eight, spotted Casey. He was working with another woman trying to kick a soccer ball into the nets, but he quickly lost interest and came toward us excitedly. He moved with a slight limp.

"Casey, you're here," he exclaimed, drawing the attention of the other kids and adults in the room.

"Hey buddy. Wow look at you go, you're getting pretty fast on that leg. You make any goals today?"

"Yeah. I got one. I might even get to go on the trampolines soon. Laura said so." They high fived and then did some super secret bro handshake.

"That's great man, but it looks like you better get back over there before she comes after you," Casey teased and the little guy's eyes got wide and he turned around and started to hurry back, but then looked over his shoulder at Casey.

"Can you and your friend work with me today?" His eyes darted to mine and then back to Casey's.

"Well let's go talk to Laura and see where she wants us today." He started after the little boy and I followed behind him. "Jace, this is my friend Olivia. Olivia this is one of my very best buddies Jace," he introduced us and I could see the pride light up Jace's face when Casey said he was his best buddy.

"It's very nice to meet you Jace. Do you like soccer?" He looked down at the floor and then up at me, his cheeks tinged with pink.

"I love it. I wanna be as good as Casey one day," he admitted somewhat nervously.

"Oh, I saw you when we first walked in here; I think you'll be better than him in no time."

His whole face lit up, and just like that it seemed I had made a new best friend. "You really think so?" His eyes shone with so much hope.

"I do, I might even be able to show you a few tricks that would help you out."

"Really? You play soccer too?" I nodded and his eyes went to my belly and then he looked back up at me skeptically. "Are you good?" I didn't even have the chance to answer because Casey did it for me.

"She's the best, little man, so I'd take her up on that offer if I were you."

197

Jace grinned and grabbed my hand and started dragging me off toward the woman I assumed was Laura. "Laura, this is Casey's friend Olivia. She's gonna help me play soccer today."

"Is that so?" She smiled at me and stuck her hand out. "I'm Laura Chambers and I'm the assistant director around here. Happy to have you with us today. Casey's been coming for almost a year now and the kids absolutely adore him."

"I can tell, and I'm happy to be here today. This is an amazing place."

"Thanks, we think so too." She turned back to Jace. "Hey, how about you work with Casey for a little bit while I show Olivia around, and tell her about what we do." His face fell a little. "Don't worry, I promise I'll bring her back to you."

His smile returned. "Okay. Come on Casey." He grabbed his hand and the two of them went over to the line of soccer balls.

"So, tell me a little bit about yourself," Laura said.

"Oh, ummm . . ." I didn't know quite what to say.

"How about this, tell me why you're here." Again I was caught off guard. She wasn't being rude or abrupt; I just wasn't expecting to have to talk about myself.

"Well, uh Casey brought me. He didn't tell me where we were going so I didn't know what we'd be doing today."

"I see. Well there must be a reason he brought you here."

"I think that maybe he thought this would help me."

"How so?"

"Well I'm studying sports medicine and working with Casey, but recently I've realized that I'm not sure if that's the right fit for me and I've talked to Casey about it."

"Ah, well then, let's see if this might be a better fit. Come on, I'll show you around our facility."

Half an hour later I had seen every inch of the place, and I was still in awe of everything they did. The whole place and the people who worked and volunteered were amazing. Their devotion to these kids and the compassion they had for them blew me away.

While touring the building, and getting to know Laura and the work they do, I got the chance to meet a sweet little girl named Amanda who was recovering from leukemia and had been bed ridden for months without much hope, but after a miraculous recovery the people here were helping her to not only regain strength in her muscles, but in her spirit as well. They gave her confidence and encouragement, and from her bright smile and positive attitude I never would have guessed that she was dying just a couple months ago.

When Laura led me back into the gym, I had no idea how I would ever thank Casey for bringing me here, and from the smile on his face when he saw my expression, he knew how I was feeling. I mouthed "thank you" to him and he simply nodded and then returned his attention to Jace.

"Hey Jace, I brought your new buddy back," Laura told him. He looked up and smile at me so big.

"You ready to learn how to kick Casey's butt?" I asked him and he nodded enthusiastically.

"Okay, then I'll leave you two and see how Levi and Adam are doing in the batting cages," Casey said and Laura joined him, leaving me with Jace. On our tour, Laura told me that Jace's stepfather had been physically abusing him while his mother worked and always passed it off as him being an accident prone child. He broke Jace's leg in several places and some of the ligaments had been torn. She didn't tell me how it had happened, and I didn't really want to know.

His mom finally figured out what had been going on and got out of that situation, but in the mean time Jace had to have surgery to repair his leg at a time when he was growing and developing. He spent months laid up in a cast and because of the seriousness of his injury and how young he was, he had lost some of his control over his leg and muscles, as well as the strength in his leg. The purpose of the soccer exercise was to help him regain some of that control. He struggled to be able to strike the ball with the correct part of his foot, and had zero aim because his leg almost flailed when he swung it out. Part of it was the injury, and part of it was just lack of coordination.

He was a determined kid though. We spent the remainder of the time at those nets. I recognized the fire in him and knew someday he might make a fine player, but right now he was getting frustrated that most of his shots went wide. We changed it up and passed the ball back and forth and then I tried to teach him to juggle it. He clapped and cheered as he watched me pass the ball between my feet, knees, shoulders and head. He had fun just trying to juggle it between his knees and then he was ready to try shooting goals again. I adjusted his stance and helped him swing his leg in slow motion to practice hitting the ball with the right part of his foot, and after a while he started making as many shots as he missed. When Casey and Laura came back he wanted to show off for them and beamed when all three of his shots went in the goal. I wanted to jump up and down in excitement for him.

"Way to go man. She'll have you ready for the pros in no time." Casey high fived him and Laura smiled at me.

"So what do you think?" she asked me while the boys celebrated.

"I think I'd like to come back next week if that's alright?"

"I think that would be great. I'll go get you the paperwork I'll need you to fill out and we'll have to run a background check, but I think you'll fit in perfectly around here."

I hadn't felt this excited about something in a long time. I'd needed to come here and meet Jace. I truly believed that I had something to offer these kids. I felt a sense of purpose that I had been lacking, rise up in me.

"Thank you again," I told Casey on our way back through the reception area. Once again the two receptionists admired him with hungry eyes and flirty grins. Something possessive in me reared up and I put my hand on his arm as we walked out. As soon as we were outside I pulled it away, not even sure why I had done it, except that I didn't like the way they looked at him.

"I'm glad you enjoyed it."

"I loved it."

"Yeah?" He smiled.

"I think I'm going to talk to my professors tomorrow." I knew what I wanted to do with my life, and Casey had helped me figure it out. I owed him more than I would ever be able to repay. I wondered if he would ever stop surprising me. Somehow I didn't think so. There was so much to him that I never would have guessed.

Twenty-Six

*"There's no vocabulary for love within a family,
love that's lived in but not looked at, love within the light
of which all else is seen, the love within which all other
love finds speech. This love is silent."*
—T.S. Eliot

"Wake up, Tate."

"Uhn," I groaned and tossed a pillow at the individual trying to disturb my beauty rest, but two seconds later it flew back at me and landed on my head.

"Come on, Tate. I need a favor."

"Go away. It's too early to get up."

"It's ten." I could hear the amusement in his voice.

That's too early for a pregnant girl on a Sunday."

"Please," he begged.

I exhaled a deep sigh and sat up, pushing my blanket aside and throwing my legs over the side of the bed. Casey's eyes widened and I remembered that last night I'd gotten too warm in bed and stripped out of my pajama bottoms, so I wasn't wearing anything except one of Ty's t-shirts and my panties. I looked down and saw that the shirt was riding up over my hips and my hot pink boy shorts were bared to him. He quickly looked away, but not before I saw the look of male appreciation on his face. I pulled the blanket back over my lap and felt a heated flush spread over my body.

"I'm so sorry. I knocked but you didn't hear me. I should've called, or . . . shit, I'm really sorry, Tate." I could tell he was just as embarrassed as I was, if not more so.

"It's okay, granted when I gave you a key it wasn't so you could interrupt my beauty sleep, but this isn't your fault. I wasn't thinking. I got warm last night, and, yeah . . . so what exactly is this favor? And you can turn back around. I'm covered."

"I need you to come to brunch with me," he said nervously.

"Why do you need me to go to brunch with you?"

"Because my parents just flew in for a surprise visit and they want to meet you."

"What?"

"My parents are in town, and Jessie is with them. They all really want to meet you."

"Why the heck do they want to meet me?"

"They just do. Please. For me?"

Nuh uh. Not happening.

I started shaking my head, but then he fixed me with those big brown eyes, batted his lashes and pouted his bottom lip, and all I could think was that I wanted to pull that lip between my teeth and nibble on it.

Oh shit. Where did that thought come from?

I didn't remember having one of *those* kinds of dreams last night where I woke up feeling frisky like this and aching for Ty. But I hadn't thought that about Ty. I'd thought it about Casey. Being caught in my underwear and then that lip of his took me from zero to really freaking turned on in about two-point-five seconds. I had to tell myself that thoughts like those about Casey were not okay. I needed to tell these damn hormones to settle the hell down, and then I had to get out of meeting Casey's family.

"Can't you just tell them I'm not feeling well or something?" It wouldn't actually be too far from the truth. Something about Casey just looked too darn good this morning. I couldn't help but notice the way his jeans were just snug enough to show off his strong thighs and tight butt, and the way his t-shirt hugged the contours of his muscles. His hair fell over his brow, still wet from a shower and I had to fight back the urge to run my hands through it. I wanted to grip it tight and pull on it, pull his face to mine and – *Whoa girl. Settle down and knock that shit off right now.*

See, something was definitely wrong with me. I felt my cheeks turn an even darker shade of pink than they already were, and I had to look away out of fear that Casey would be able to read my naughty thoughts on my face.

"Come on, Tate. I'm not asking for a kidney. I just want you to have a meal with my family. Besides, if I tell them you're sick, my mom will show up on your doorstep with soup, and she'll push her way right in here and then you'll wish you had just come to brunch."

"Why aren't you taking Annie?" I grumbled. "I'm sure they'd much rather spend time with your girlfriend than the neighbor girl you've taken pity on." I had no idea how much he'd even told them about me.

"Shut up, you're more than some neighbor, and I would take Annie, but she's not my girlfriend anymore."

What! She wasn't his girlfriend anymore? When the heck did that happen? For weeks I'd been asking him how she was and he always answered fine.

"To be honest though," he continued. "I'm not sure that they were ever big fans of hers."

"Hold up and go back to the part where she's not your girlfriend anymore."

"We broke up."

"Yeah, I caught that, but when and why?"And more importantly, why hadn't he told me? You're supposed to tell your friends that stuff.

"Over Christmas break. That was what I needed to come back to take care of. The time apart and spending time with my family helped me to realize a few things, and one of them was that Annie and I weren't working anymore so it wasn't fair to her or me to try and force it."

That was over a month ago! "Why did you let me keep asking about her?"

"I don't know; I just didn't want to talk about it. It wasn't important."

I looked at him like he was crazy. Since when is the ending of a long term relationship not important? They'd been together over a year and he didn't even seem the slightest bit affected.

"Listen, can we just forget about the Annie thing? Will you come or not?"

I sighed, even though I was upset that he hadn't told me about their breakup, it seemed really important to him that I go to brunch with him. "Fine. I'll go." I glared at him to make sure he knew just how not pleased I was with him at the moment.

"Give me all the dirty looks you want as long as you get up and tame that bird nest on your head, and come with me."

I cringed and my hand went to my hair. He was right, it was a mess, but still I could've hit him for commenting on it. "I think me and my bird nest are just going to stay right here," I said stubbornly.

He only smiled back at me. "Then I'll throw you over my shoulder and carry you out of here looking just like that."

I narrowed my eyes. "You can't," I said smugly, gesturing at my round belly.

"It was a figure of speech. I may not be able to literally throw you over my shoulder, but that stomach won't stop me from getting you out of this apartment. I can sure as hell still carry you."

"You wouldn't."

"I would, and you've got ten seconds before I do." We engaged in a staring contest. *Ten. Nine. Eight. He won't. Seven. Six. Five. He might. Four. Three. Two. Oh crap he totally will.* I could see it in his eyes and I quickly hopped up off the bed, blanket still wrapped around me this time, and shoved him out of the room so I could get dressed.

"Smart choice, Tate," I heard him say as the door closed behind him. I tugged on a pair of black leggings, a long sleeved tunic dress and a pair of brown riding style boots that zipped just below the knee. I grabbed a scarf and my purse, and then darted into the bathroom to fix my hair. I quickly brushed it out and then braided it over my shoulder and hurriedly put on some deodorant.

Casey was waiting, arms folded across his chest, resting on the back of my couch, looking especially smug. "You look nice." He gave me a cheeky grin.

"Does your mother know what a pain in the ass you are?"

"Yes. She does."

I rolled my eyes, but followed him out of the apartment and to his car. Even though I wanted to ask him more about Annie on the way to the restaurant, I didn't. When we got there, his family was already waiting. It was a Tex-Mex place that I'd eaten at before, and when we stepped inside and I smelled the food, my hunger kicked in. All I could think was breakfast tacos. Eggs, potatoes, beans, salsa . . . my mouth was already watering.

When we walked in, the hostess stepped forward to seat us, but Casey pointed out his parents and sister and grabbed my hand to lead me over to the table. For some reason, as we got closer to the table, my heart rate kicked up and I slipped my sweaty hand out of Casey's and wiped it on my dress.

"Relax, it's just my family. They're a little odd, but harmless," he whispered just before he steered me toward their table in the corner. A pair of sweet eyes looked up at us from the face of a beautiful woman, who I knew had to be in her fifties, but didn't look older than forty. She smiled, and I knew that smile. I saw it almost daily. However, she had pale blonde hair, graying at the roots, and hazel eyes, unlike Casey's dark ones. When I looked at the man sitting next to her, I knew where Casey got them from.

He was an older but almost identical version of Casey. His dark hair was heavily streaked with grey, and there were laugh lines etched in his face, but there was no question that he was Casey's father. Across from them sat Jessie, light haired and petite like her mother, but her big personality made up for whatever she lacked in height. She was the first to jump up and attach herself to her brother like a koala, and after she hugged him, she launched herself at me, and the next thing I knew, the bubbly blonde was squealing and squeezing me. I thought Lukas might pop out right there in the restaurant.

"It's so good to meet you Olivia. I've heard so much about you. I feel like we're friends already."

"Jess, how about we wait to attack the poor girl until after we've treated her to a meal?" their mother admonished playfully.

Jess pulled back and bit her lip nervously. "Sorry. I'm just really excited to meet you. Casey has told us so much about you." I raised an eyebrow at him and he just shrugged.

"But he didn't tell us you were so gorgeous, honey. Wow, you're a pretty thing," Mrs. Hunt stood, and I blushed at her comment.

"Thank you." It was a lie, sweet, but a lie. I was carrying an extra twenty pounds and hadn't even bothered with makeup, and I don't care what people say, pregnant women don't glow. We sweat and bloat, and it's not all that pretty, but I smiled and stuck my hand out anyway. Instead of taking it, she pulled me in for a hug, thankfully less aggressively than her daughter.

"You can call me Carol, and this is my husband John." He stood as well and stuck out his hand; I shook it.

"It's so nice to meet y'all," I said. Casey pulled out the chair next to his sister for me and he took the one on my other side. Once we were all seated, everyone busied themselves with menus and small talk. Casey asked Jessie how classes were going, and when her mother mentioned a boy that she'd been seeing, he started grilling her.

It was fun watching the way they all interacted. It was obvious how much they loved each other. It was written on their faces, and in the way they spoke to each other; the affection and amusement of the parents toward their children, and Casey's fierce protectiveness of his little sister.

It didn't take me long at all to let go of the nerves and relax around them. There was something so warm and encouraging about them. It hadn't made sense to me why I'd felt so comfortable around Casey in the beginning, why I so readily trusted him, but I had the same feeling around his sister and parents. It was something in their nature that just put you at ease.

I could imagine what it must be like when his entire family got together. I could picture them all laughing together. I could imagine Casey playing with his niece and nephews, or throwing back a beer with his dad and brothers-in-law while his mom and sisters baked cookies or pies over a glass of wine. It left me with a tiny pang of longing.

I had a great childhood and I never lacked for love from my parents, but I was a little bit envious of what Casey had. Neither of my parents came from big families, so I didn't have a lot of cousins or a lot of family period. Ty and I had wanted to make our own big family. In the deepest parts of my heart I still wanted it – this – what these people shared.

For that hour we sat in the restaurant, I almost felt like I was a part of them. I was included in their conversations and anytime they started talking about something, or telling a story that I wasn't familiar with, they made sure to explain it to me, and they asked me a lot of questions about myself. The crazy part, or at least it seemed that way to me, was that they all appeared genuinely interested in what I had to say, they weren't just being polite or friendly. That was rare these days and I think I fell a little bit more in love with them.

They asked a lot of Texas questions. It seems they thought Casey had been exaggerating us down here, but Texans don't require any exaggerating. They weren't pushy or intrusive, but they asked about Tyler too, and surprisingly it wasn't so hard to talk about him. Jessie sighed and got a dreamy look when I told them about the two of us growing up together.

"That's so sweet. It's like a movie romance," she commented. I just smiled. The truth was, it had been better than any movie, because it had been real. My real. Carol and John understood that. I didn't know their story, but I didn't need to in order to see the love they shared.

Watching the little touches and looks Casey's parents exchanged – ones that could only be shared between people who had loved each other for a lifetime – was harder than answering their questions about Ty. My parents loved each other deeply, but they didn't display it as outwardly as Casey's did. Making it that long and still cherishing the other person after that many years was something so rare and special. Seeing that, what Ty and I might have been at forty or fifty, was hard to bear, because I still wanted it. The kind of love that could withstand whatever the years brought.

I'd had it once, for a flash of time, maybe I could have it again.

No. Don't think that. Tyler was your once in a lifetime.

It wasn't the first time I had thought about falling in love again, but I was swamped with guilt, because it was the first time that a part of me actually wanted to. It felt like the deepest betrayal, especially with Tyler's baby inside of me, but it was so hard not to hope for something beautiful and amazing again when it was staring me in the face from across the table.

I knew that in their eighties, or even nineties, they would still be two of the most beautiful people I'd ever seen because of the way they loved each other and their family. Casey's kindness and generosity no longer bewildered me. It made perfect sense now, because I could see it in all of them. They were all kind of wonderful. He was kind of wonderful.

Twenty-Seven

"The soul should always stand ajar, ready to
welcome the ecstatic experience."
— Emily Dickinson

"Are you sure this is a good idea. You look like you're going to pop?" Mel sat on my bed and watched me pack my bag. It was so early I was having a hard time thinking of what I might be forgetting. I knew I should have finished packing last night, but Mel had stayed with me so that she would be here this morning to see me off if she couldn't talk me out of going. Incidentally we spent the whole night binging on junk food and watching movies, so now I was rushing.

"I'm not due for almost another month. I had my appointment yesterday and the doctor assured me that everything should be fine."

"So you're really abandoning me for spring break?"

"Come on, like you said I'm almost ready to pop. It's not like I would be a lot of fun anyway, and I'll be back Monday night and we'll still have a full week before classes start back up." Really I wasn't going to miss much of the actual break with her. Only two of my classes had finals this term, and I'd talked both of my instructors into letting me take them a couple days early so that my break could start sooner and I would be back here with plenty of time to move into the new apartment that had come available recently.

"That's still six days away, what am I supposed to do?" she whined melodramatically in typical Mel fashion.

"Why don't you give Trent a call and the two of you can hang out?" I smirked, earning myself a dirty look. She still refused to talk about whatever was said between the two of them that night. We'd all hung out as a group a few times since then and things were always tense between them, but there was something else burning just under the surface. If I had to put a name to it, I would say attraction – intense attraction – that neither one wanted to acknowledge.

My jab worked in quieting her down while I finished packing. When I heard the door to my apartment open, I was looking around my room for any last minute item I might need on this trip.

"You ready to go?" Casey called out.

"No. She changed her mind. She's not going," Mel hollered back. I tossed a flip flop that hadn't made it into the suitcase at her.

I zipped my bag and Casey appeared in the doorway.

"Need any help?" he asked.

"I don't think so. It's just this one bag."

He eyed it skeptically. "You sure you got everything you need? The weather will be colder in Indiana."

"Ha," Mel snorted. "It might look small, but you didn't see her cramming that thing full. She's got enough in there to last two weeks."

I rolled my eyes and started to grab my bag, but Casey reached forward and took it.

"Damn. I think she's right. This thing weighs a ton," he grunted

"Do I need to carry it myself?"

"No, no. I got it, but if I throw out my back, you may have to carry me," he teased and carried the bag out of the room.

"Come on Mel, quit moping. It's just a few days, and then next week we'll spend plenty of time together when you help me move."

"You're really gonna make me spend my spring break helping you move?" she complained, but I knew she was only giving me a bad time. In truth, I didn't even need to ask, she would be there regardless. She just wouldn't be Mel if she didn't gripe about it.

"Seriously, I'm only moving down one floor." One of the larger apartments in the building had opened up and would be ready next week, giving me just enough time to get settled before Lukas came. I was fortunate that it had come available. I'd been looking at other complexes for weeks, dreading moving to a new building. I had become attached to this place in the months that I'd been here. Mel thought it had more to do with an attachment I had to one particular tenant, than the building itself. The nervous excitement I felt thinking about the roadtrip ahead of me, and all the time I would be spending with him made me think that maybe she was more right that I wanted to admit.

209

Lately, it had gotten harder for me not to notice things like how dazzling his smile was, or how much I loved the sound of his laugh and the way his hair made me want to run my fingers through it. More and more I would find excuses to knock on his door, and every time he showed up at mine, my mood lifted. I wasn't quite prepared to deal with what all that meant, because as good as it felt, I could never escape the immense guilt and sorrow that followed.

"Don't mean to rush you," Casey popped his head back in the room. "But if we don't get on the road soon, we won't get to Jasper until three in the morning." I glanced at the clock on my night stand. It was only six, but we had a long drive ahead of us.

Mel and I followed Casey outside and I hugged her and promised to text her from the road and update her on our progress so she would know we were safe, and then Casey and I loaded up. We had roughly sixteen hours worth of driving ahead of us, more if we stopped often, which given my condition was probably going to be necessary. I tried to get comfy for the long trip, still finding it a little crazy that I was even going along with it.

Three days after I'd met Casey's parents and sister, I was hanging out at his place watching TV, and his phone rang. After answering it, he handed it to me. It was his sister Marissa calling to invite me to the surprise, thirty-fifth anniversary party they were throwing for their parents.

I was a little shocked to receive the invite, but she insisted it would mean a lot to her parents. Apparently they had gone back to Indiana and told the rest of the family how much they had enjoyed meeting me. Instantly I felt honored, but was still unsure about accepting the invite. It seemed like such an intimate family affair, but ultimately Marissa wouldn't take no for an answer. So here I was sitting in the passenger seat, next to Casey, on the way to meet the rest of his family.

I told myself I was doing this for his parents, and to satisfy my curiosity about where Casey grew up and to see a part of the country I had never been to, but that was because the other reason, the one that had more to do with a roadtrip and spending six days with my favorite neighbor, scared me too much.

"What are you thinking about?" Casey's question startled me out of my head.

"Oh, nothing important."

"You sure? You looked pretty deep in thought over there."

"Just wondering if I'll get to see any pictures of you with your braces and frosted hair."

"No," he declared. "Absolutely not. I can't believe they even brought that up. Like everyone didn't go through an awkward, embarrassing phase at one point in their life or another."

I chuckled and tried to see it in my head, but I just couldn't picture Casey looking awkward. I couldn't picture him as anything but the gorgeous guy before me with aviator shades on and sexy hair styled to look like he'd just gone all night with a couple of porn stars. I swallowed thickly and looked away. I don't know when exactly it happened, that I started devouring him with my eyes every time I looked at him, but it had become a problem in the last couple months.

It was like since that morning when he saw me in my underwear, someone had flipped a switch and suddenly my awareness of him had completely shifted. Nothing had changed between us, and he was still just Casey, so I knew it was me that was changing, and I didn't like it. I wasn't ready to have these kinds of thoughts and feelings for anyone, but I was helpless to stop them, and that scared and frustrated me, because I didn't know how it was possible to feel so many conflicting things.

"I'm telling you up front, there will be no looking at embarrassing photos from my childhood, and if you attempt to extract any more embarrassing stories from any of my family members, I won't be held responsible for my actions."

"Oh yeah? What are you going to do about it?" I taunted him. He turned his head toward me, and even through the shades, the intensity of his gaze burned. I couldn't look away, and it felt like we stayed locked on each other for minutes, but I knew it couldn't have been longer than a few seconds before he returned his eyes to the road. I looked down into my lap and felt the flush spread up my neck and over my cheeks.

"Trust me Tate, you don't want to find out." His voice was low and intimidating, and . . . *seductive*.

What the heck is happening to me?

My heart was skipping beats all over the place and my mouth felt dry. I had no witty retort or sassy comment. I had nothing. I was falling to pieces because of a look and a few words. I pulled my e-reader out of my purse and decided to hide from this reality where I was suddenly very attracted to Casey, by escaping into another reality. One with hot gargoyles and an even hotter bad boy demon.

Casey had planned our trip along the old route 66, so there were a lot of cool landmarks that we saw along the way. He turned on the classic rock and I felt like I was in an episode of Supernatural. I'm pretty sure every town we passed through had been featured in an episode. In Oklahoma we pulled over to take a picture of the two of us with a giant round barn in the background. A little later we stopped at a café that had been open since 1939, and had lunch. They cooked everything on the same grill they had been using for seventy some years, they called her Betsy and she did the job. The food was great and the people at the cafe were friendly and interesting. They prided themselves on the history of the place.

Once we were back on the road, I slept off and on for the next few hours, so I didn't see much until we were driving through Missouri and trying to find a place to eat dinner. I let Casey decide so he took us to a favorite grill of his that he said he stopped at just about every time he made the trip. After eating there I understood why.

By the time we'd finished eating it was dark out so we didn't stop for anymore tourist attractions. We were both tired of being in the car and wanted to get to Indiana as quickly as possible. I knew I'd get to see this side of the route in the daylight on the return trip, so we stopped only when it was absolutely necessary because I had to pee, unfortunately that was still pretty frequently.

At two in the morning the car finally pulled up to his parents' home. It was hard to see much in the dark, and I was half asleep, but it looked like a beautiful house with a great big yard.

"Well this is home sweet home," Casey announced as he turned the engine off.

"It's a really nice house," I told him looking out at it in the dark.

"Tomorrow I'll show you around, but tonight let's just get in and get you to bed."

"That sounds wonderful," I yawned. I wanted nothing more than to crawl into bed and sleep until noon. I'd slept a lot of the drive, but sleeping in a car wasn't restful sleep. Casey had to be ready to drop as well.

"Okay. So I'm sure my parents are asleep and they're expecting me, but not you. The apartment over the garage is mine so usually if I get in late, I just go straight up there without going through the house. You can either stay in there for tonight, there's an extra bed, or I can take you in the house to one of the guest bedrooms. Either way is fine with me, but if we go in through the house, the chances are good that the dog will wake up my parents, which is not big deal, they won't mind, but they will keep you up another half hour talking and trying to fix you something to eat."

"Just get me to a bed, yours is fine." *Crap.* That so did not come out the way I meant it to. "I mean, not your bed like with you, but the bed in your apartment. The extra one, separate from you," I flushed as I stumbled over my words and Casey only chuckled.

"I know what you meant. Come on." He grabbed both our bags from the back and led me up the driveway and into the garage through a side door and up a set of stairs. He fumbled with his keys trying to find the right one, but once he got the door unlocked it opened up into a cozy apartment. I didn't take much time to look around though. I zeroed in on the big, comfy looking bed on the far side of the room. It was the only bed I saw.

"I thought you said there were two beds?" I frowned.

"The couch is a futon. I'll sleep on that. You can take the bed." I started to argue, I didn't want to take his bed, but he wouldn't listen to a word of it. He shoved me into the bathroom with my bag to change, and when I came out he had already made his bed on the futon. He went into the bathroom and closed the door behind him.

I sighed when I climbed up on the queen sized mattress, which was one of those fancy memory foam ones, and felt like I was lying on a cloud. I burrowed into the blankets and snuggled one of the big, cushy pillows to my body. I never wanted to leave this bed. It was incredible.

Holy crap.

So was the view. The bathroom door opened and Casey stepped out in a pair of boxer briefs and nothing else. Even though it was dark, except for the little bit of light from the bathroom casting a soft glow around him, I could still make out every hard line and plane of his solid chest. He was all lean muscle and cut abs, and damn I needed to look away, but I couldn't. All of his shirts needed to be burned. That was a sight the female population should not be deprived of. Ever. Nope, I don't think I was going to be moving into a guest bedroom after all.

I just hoped he couldn't see me well enough to know that I was ogling him, because man was I ogling him. His skin looked so enticing and smooth, except for a fine sprinkling of hair on his chest and the trail that led from his belly button down into no man's land.

"The bed okay? Are you warm enough?" he asked.

"The bed is perfect." *You're perfect.* I couldn't believe I just thought that.

"Okay. Good." He turned and flipped off the light in the bathroom and by the time my eyes readjusted to the dark he was already tucked away in bed, which was probably good or I would have stared at him all night.

"Good night, Tate."

"Night, Hunt." I tried to clear that image from my mind, but there was no way I would be forgetting the sight of half naked Casey anytime soon. It wasn't long before I heard his breathing even out, and then I followed him into dreamland and slept sounder than I had in a long time.

Twenty-Eight

"Dwell in possibility."   *Emily Dickinson*

Casey was already up and in the main house when I woke the next morning. After using the bathroom, one look in the mirror above the bathroom sink told me I was in desperate need of a shower. My hair was a disaster and I felt sweaty and gross from the long day of traveling.

The heat of the spray cascading down my body washed all the grime away, and the tension in my muscles eased under the warmth. I felt infinitely better when I was dry and dressed again. I didn't see a clock anywhere in the room so I grabbed my phone to check the time and saw I had a text from Casey.

Hope you slept well. Come down to the house when you wake up. You can let yourself in.

I assumed I was meant to go in the front door and it was unlocked when I got to it. Casey had told me to let myself in, but I was unsure about just walking into someone else's house. I stood there for a minute debating whether or not I should knock, but decided to go ahead and go inside. I stood hesitantly in the foyer and looked around. The entryway opened up into a short hallway. On the right side was a set of stairs and to the left led into the living room and the rest of the house. I could hear the soft sound of voices coming from that direction, so I followed them through the living room and dining room to the kitchen.

Casey was the first to look up from his spot at the breakfast counter and see me standing in the doorway. He stopped what he was saying and flashed me a bright grin. His mother turned to see what he was looking at and almost dropped her cup of coffee when her eyes fell on me.

"Oh my goodness, Olivia!" She set her cup on the marble countertop and rushed over to pull me into a motherly embrace. "What a fantastic surprise. John get in here, you'll never believe who's here," she called out and a few seconds later Casey's dad appeared behind me.

"Ah, Olivia. So nice to have you here." He too hugged me affectionately.

"Come sit down, I'll fix you some breakfast." Carol ushered me over to the stool next to Casey. He was still grinning at his parents' reaction.

"Thank you." I took a seat and she went about setting a plate of warm blueberry pancakes and bacon in front of me with a glass of orange juice.

"Mmmm," I said biting in to the pancakes. They were delicious. I wasn't a morning person, so usually, before classes, I was a fruit and yogurt or muffin kind of girl; anything I could grab in a hurry on my way out the door. I loved breakfast though, so anytime I got to eat a real, hot, home cooked breakfast I savored it.

Carol chatted excitedly about the things they wanted to show me while I was here, insisting that Casey take me on a tour of the town. She ticked off a list of places and things she thought I would enjoy seeing.

"You should take her on the train ride tonight," she suggested to Casey.

"That's a good idea, but tonight won't work, we've already got plans," he stated nonchalantly, like it shouldn't be news to me, but it was.

"We do?" I asked confused. He nodded and reached his hand toward my plate. I tried to swat it away but he snatched the last bite of bacon and popped it in his mouth before I could stop him.

"I can't tell you what they are though, it's a surprise." He winked and hopped off the stool and then tugged me along after him. He kissed the top of his mom's head as we passed by on the way out of the kitchen.

"Thank you so much for breakfast," I said just before we disappeared around the corner. "Where are we going?"

"Right now, downtown to walk around. There's a farmers' market going on. The surprise is later." We spent the rest of the morning exploring the farmers' marker and then most of the afternoon walking around the town. He showed me all the major landmarks: city hall, the library, an old mill and his high school. He bought me lunch at a little pizza joint and then took me to the Riverwalk plaza, which was my

216

favorite of all the places he showed me. It had a beautiful walking path along the river.

Even though it was a little chilly out we stopped for ice cream on our way back to where he'd parked Evie. Casey was licking up some of the ice cream that was melting down the side of his cone and I just couldn't resist pushing it up into his face. I giggled as he looked at me shocked, chocolate fudge ice cream smeared all over his cheek.

"I can't believe you just did that." His stunned look quickly transformed into a dangerous one. His mouth turned up at the corners, and the smile that spread over his face worried me. I immediately stopped laughing.

"Whatever you're thinking about doing, you better not," I warned him, but it was futile. In a flash he was on me, smearing my own ice cream all over my face. It was in my eyelashes and up my nose.

"Okay, okay stop," I laughed, trying to escape the onslaught of mint chocolate chip. Casey was laughing hard too when he finally let me go. Ice cream dripped from my chin and I tried my best to give him an angry glare, but I felt too ridiculous, and I totally deserved it.

Thankfully we'd grabbed extra napkins from the ice cream parlor and he helped me to wipe up the mess, and then cleaned off his own face, but I still felt disgustingly sticky.

"Thank you for today. It was a pretty great right up until you turned me into a human ice cream cone," I told him once we were back in the car.

"The day isn't over yet, hopefully it will just get better." He still wouldn't share his secret plans.

It was just after three when we got back to his parents' place and he informed me I had an hour and a half to get ready for whatever it was. He said it didn't matter what I wore, so after taking another shower and scrubbing the stickiness from my face and hair, I pulled on a pair of dark grey leggings and a plum colored top with a long black sweater over it.

I curled my hair in soft waves that fell down my back, and after applying minimal makeup, finished the look with my favorite scarf and black suede ankle boots. I took one last peek in the mirror and was satisfied that even though I looked like a blimp, I was a semi-cute blimp. I tried to hide the silly smile that was plastered on my face, but I was feeling too exhilarated and nervous.

This felt so date-like, and I definitely had first date butterflies, even thought that wasn't what this was. At least I didn't think so. Did I want it to be a date? I didn't know, and I decided not to think too hard about it.

Casey was waiting in the kitchen, looking good in a pair of faded blue jeans that hugged his backside snuggly, and a long sleeve black button up with the sleeves rolled to his elbows. He was leaning over the counter, giving me an even better view of just how well those jeans were working for him, talking to his mom in hushed tones. I couldn't make out the words, but Carol's eyes flashed to me, she smiled and then looked at him pointedly. He turned to see me standing in the doorway and shot me a devastating grin. I had to look away, lest I turn into a blushing schoolgirl.

"Ready?"

"Yep," I replied lamely.

"You look really nice, Olivia." It was rare that Casey used my first name, and as much as I had grown used to him using my last name, I kind of liked hearing 'Olivia' on his lips. It was more feminine and intimate. I don't know why that mattered, but again I tried not to overanalyze.

"Thanks. You look good too." I was annoyed at the sudden shyness I heard in my own voice. This was Casey Hunt. Just Casey; and here I was turning into a fool. I wanted to look anywhere, but into his dark eyes, which I knew regarded me closely. Instead I looked over at his mom, but she had a knowing smile on her face that I found disconcerting.

"You kids have a good time and I'll see ya in the morning." That was the only clue I got about our plans for the night. We'd be out late if Carol didn't expect to see us again tonight.

I became more and more confused the farther Casey's car took us away from Jasper, but unlike the last time he'd had a surprise for me, I was too nervous to grill or pester him for information. We were both quiet for most of the drive and I wondered if he was nervous as well.

As we drove into Indianapolis, I noticed Casey seemed to get more and more nervous, fidgeting and tapping out beats on the steering

218

wheel and glancing uneasily at me several times. If this really had been a first date with someone I didn't know as well, this is the point where I would have started texting everyone in my phone where I was so that when I turned up missing they would know where to start looking. But it was Casey, and I knew this was his nervous excited behavior that came out when he wasn't sure how I was going to react to something.

I figured it out as soon as I saw the marquee on a building and noticed Casey slowing down to turn into the parking lot across the street. I snapped my head to look over at him, disbelieving.

"Are you serious?" I asked excitedly.

"I know your birthday is still a couple weeks away, but when I heard they were going to be here the same time we were, I wanted to surprise you. I hope you like it." Like wasn't a strong enough word; they were my favorite band.

"This is amazing Casey. Thank you, so much!"

He smiled in relief. "I know you saw them with Tyler and I wasn't sure if bringing you was a bad idea. I didn't want to upset you."

Oh.

I hadn't even thought of that, I hadn't thought of Ty at all, and part of me felt guilty and sad about that, but mostly I was thankful for it. I was unsure of a lot of things lately, especially about how I felt, but I knew that Ty would want me happy. He would want me to enjoy this and make another happy memory.

"That was a really good night, but this is going to be a good night too," I reassured him. "How did you get tickets last minute though? They sell out quickly."

"I have a friend who works for the event center and he hooked me up."

He must've been a very good friend, because he didn't just hook Casey up, he got us front row seats, almost dead center in front of the stage. I was close enough that I would probably be able to reach out and touch Kyden McCabe when he took the stage with the rest of the guys from Ashes and Embers.

The place was already packed, every seat occupied, the females were brimming with anticipation and lust for the guys that would be coming out on the stage before the night was over. I still couldn't believe we were front row.

219

"I need to hit the bathroom before it starts, you okay here?" Casey's breath was warm on my cheek as he leaned in close so that I could hear over the buzz of the crowd. Instead of trying to talk over them, I smiled and nodded. For once, I didn't need to pee. My eyes followed his steps as he moved up the aisle and disappeared into the mass of bodies. I took the opportunity to take in my surroundings. Mostly, my eyes met girls in too little clothing. The two girls to the right of me were maybe the only others ones who got the memo that it was below sixty degrees outside.

The girl in the seat directly beside mine was turned away talking to her friend. I wasn't trying to stare or eavesdrop on them, but I was admiring her hair. It was different shades of pink, purple and blue all wrapped up in an intricate braid, a rainbow of color. Her friend must've noticed my stare, because suddenly the girl with the colorful hair was turning to look at me. At first I was embarrassed, but her soft smile reassured me. There was something oddly familiar about her, like I'd seen her somewhere before, but I couldn't place her, which was odd considering how striking she was, even without the unique hair.

"Hi, my name is Jaxyn."

That's when I placed her. I'd seen her in several magazines.

Holy crap, that's Jaxyn McCabe. Girlfriend – no fiancé – of Kyden McCabe, the guy most of these barely dressed girls were lusting after. Yup, there was that gorgeous rock on her finger.

"Wow. H-hi. My name is Olivia. It's real nice to meet ya."

"It's nice to meet you too Olivia, this is my friend Sadie." Her red haired friend smiled.

"So Olivia, that doesn't sound like an Indiana accent, where are you from?"

"Texas, I'm here visiting with a friend."

"That cute guy who was sitting with you a minute ago?" I blushed and she grinned.

"Uh, yeah, that's my friend Casey. He's from here, so I'm visiting with him." I'd seen both of their eyes go to my stomach, not in a judgmental way, just curious.

"So, is this your first time at a show?" Jaxyn asked.

"No. My husband took me to see them when they came to Texas on their first tour, last year."

220

"Oh, you're married?" she seemed surprised.

"Yeah, er well no," I tried to explain. This wasn't something I made a habit of sharing with perfect strangers, but I found myself opening up anyway. "I was, but he died eight months ago."

"Oh, I'm so sorry." She took my hand in her own and squeezed it. There was so much understanding in both of their eyes; I got the feeling that they weren't strangers to loss of their own, especially Sadie. There was a look in her eye that I recognized from the mirror.

Casey returned and I introduced him to Jaxyn and Sadie. When they turned around I had to whisper in his ear who Jaxyn was. He wasn't fazed by my revelation of Jaxyn's somewhat celebrity status. We continued to chat with them right up until the opening band came on stage, and after that there was nothing but the music. Bob Marley once said that the thing about music is that when it hits you, there's no pain. It's true. Music has always been a release, an outlet for me. You can just get lost in it. The music washed over me and that's all I felt in the moment.

Sometimes a song can reach right inside you and expose everything you're keeping locked up in there, like the song was written just for you. It rips you apart and it's heartbreaking, but it's also healing and comforting knowing that someone else out there gets it. They're able to put words to what you're going through like they tore them right out of your chest, and it's beautiful in a way that even though it tears you up inside, it also pieces you back together. Then sometimes it's just an escape. It's just fun and freeing and makes you feel good, but either way, music is a balm for the soul.

By the time Ashes and Embers came on stage the energy rippling through the room was at an insane level. People were screaming and going nuts, especially the ladies. I looked over at Jaxyn to see how she felt about the girls screaming for her man, but she didn't seem bothered by it in the least, and it didn't take long to figure out why. The guys on stage were eating up the attention and adoration and giving it right back to the audience, putting on the show of their lives, but when Kyden's eyes would find Jaxyn's it was obvious she didn't have a damn thing to worry about. He performed for the fans but it was apparent to anyone who could make out his expression that he breathed for her. Thousands of adoring fans and she was the only one he really saw, and she wore the wide grin of someone who knew it.

The concert was amazing, even better than the first since this time it was their show, they weren't opening for anyone else. When it was time to file out of our seats, Jaxyn's hand reached out and grabbed my arm. She leaned over and whispered in my ear, "It's never too late for a happily ever after. Don't be afraid of it."

Her eyes flitted to Casey briefly and I flushed, but nodded in understanding. She gave me a quick hug and the next thing I knew tattooed arms were hauling her up on the stage. The bass player, Ace, reached a hand down and helped pull Sadie up as well while big security guys kept anyone else from being able to climb up. I waved goodbye to the two girls and followed Casey out of the madhouse.

By the time we escaped the parking lot, and were actually on the road back to Jasper, I thanked Casey one more time for the incredible night and then leaned my head against the window, using his sweatshirt as a pillow. I drifted off to sleep inhaling his clean, masculine scent and wondering if Jaxyn was right, if maybe my happily ever after wasn't really over.

Twenty-Nine

"Courage is being scared to death and saddling up anyway."
—John Wayne

The anniversary party went off perfectly on Saturday. Casey and I took Carol and John out to lunch, and they were so surprised when we got back to find a house full of guests. I finally got to meet Casey's older sisters. Marissa had flown in from California with her husband, and Kelly was there with her husband and three kids.

Their personalities were all so different; Marissa definitely gave off the California girl vibe, and she was very opinionated and spoke her mind, but she wasn't quite as bubbly as Jessie. Kelly, the oldest, was much more laid back and soft spoken, but the one thing they all had in common was that they were incredibly nice and welcoming. There were no handshakes when we were introduced, just hugs. They all treated me like we had been friends for years instead of just minutes. I even got the chance to thank Kelly's husband, Jason, in person for the amazing crib.

All evening long, there were kids, from toddlers to teenagers running through the house and yard. He had a lot of cousins, a lot of family period, and it was amazing to witness them all together, but better than that, they didn't make me feel like an outsider. I even got to meet two of Casey's best friends from high school who had grown up close to his family and made it to the party.

Max and Nick painted a picture of a very different Casey than the one I knew. It seemed in high school he was a bit of a troublemaker and heartbreaker. The three of them went to college together as well where they continued to raise hell. I heard about bar fights and all nighters and a string of girls in and out of their dorm rooms. I had a hard time reconciling that guy with the one I'd gotten to know.

The next morning Casey talked me into taking his dad's little boat out fishing on Lake Patoka with him. I didn't have a fishing license, but I sat in the boat and read while Casey trolled for fish. "So, is this how you would woo all the girls back in high school? Take 'em out on the boat and impress 'em with your fishin skills."

He looked over at me and shook his head, reeling in and recasting his line. "I'm gonna kill Max and Nick for bringing that shit up. You're never gonna let it go are you?"

"Come on, who knew you were such a player back in the day? I mean you alluded to a few drunken escapades when you told me about Jamie, but I didn't realize you were a regular backseat Casanova, stealing virtue and breaking hearts."

"Yeah, well that was a long time ago. I'm not interested in breaking anymore hearts." He slowly reeled in again.

"Did you break Annie's?" I don't know why I asked other than he'd still refused to ever talk about her with me.

He kept his eyes fixed out on the water, and after a minute I realized he still wasn't going to talk about her. I let it go and returned my attention to my book.

"Ooh," I cried out a few minutes later.

Casey looked over at me. "What is it?"

"Noth– ooh." *Shit, that doesn't feel good.* "Nothing. It's nothing." I didn't know if I was trying to reassure him or myself.

"Didn't seem like nothing."

"Just a contraction."

His eyebrows shot up and I swear he almost dropped his pole in the lake. "Shit."

"Calm down, it's not a big deal. I've had them before. They're Braxton-Hicks and the doctor said it's normal to have them later in the pregnancy, so you can relax and get rid of that panicked look on your face."

"If you're sure?" He still looked concerned.

"Yes, I am. I had a few last night and off and on this morning. They won't last; they just hurt like a bitch."

He seemed to relax, and I went back to reading. At least until a while later when I sucked in a sharp breath because of another painful contraction.

"Okay, that's it, we're going back," he insisted.

"It's fine. It's perfectly normal." I'd read all about Braxton-Hicks and Ellie and my mom had both warned me so I wouldn't be caught off guard.

"I know that going into labor is perfectly normal, but I'm not letting in happen in this shitty little boat."

"Relax, I'm not going into labor. The baby isn't coming for a few more weeks. Contractions can be caused by exhaustion, sitting in one position too long, even hunger. I'm sure that's what it is. My body probably thinks it's going to starve because you're not catching enough fish."

He ignored my joke and started putting away his pole and gear. "Either way, we should head back. We've been out here all morning and we both need some lunch."

I didn't argue with him since I was hungry and I wouldn't mind being able to get up and walk around. After getting the boat out of the water and back on the trailer on the back of his dad's truck, he took us to a little restaurant not far from the lake.

It was our last day and he'd wanted to bring me out here since it was one of his favorite places. His mom and sisters had invited me on their shopping trip this morning, but a day of hanging out on the water and doing some hiking appealed to me more. And I couldn't lie to myself, after the concert and Jaxyn's words, I'd been thinking more and more about the way Casey made me feel. I thought more time alone with him would help me figure out if it was more than friendship or not. So far it hadn't helped. I already knew I liked being around him, and he was funny and attractive and occasionally gave me the flutters in my tummy, but that could just be the small person that was moving around in there, or possibly indigestion.

It was almost impossible for me to separate my friendly feelings from those that could be something more. I hadn't had a crush, or dealt with guy problems since I was fifteen and Ty kissed me at homecoming. I didn't know how to do this shit anymore, especially not with pregnancy hormones running rampant in my body making me freaking crazy.

I stared at him across the table, digging into his burger and fries, but that only made me realize how much more difficult it was to think anything through with a clear head when faced with his penetrating eyes and devilishly handsome face. It was easy to think about kissing him when staring at those lips, but I didn't know if it was actually what I wanted.

Casey chuckled and for a moment I wondered if he knew what I had been thinking, but of course that was impossible.

"What's so funny?"

"If you go into labor early, Lukas won't be a Texan; he'll be an Indiana boy."

"That's not true. He'd still be a Texas boy," I argued adamantly, glaring at him.

"Hey, you're the one who said if you ain't born in Texas, you ain't a Texan."

"I didn't say that, and even if I did, this situation would be different."

"Whatever you say." He took another huge bite of his burger.

"Besides, it doesn't matter. I'm not going into labor early."

An hour later we were hiking through one of the trails near the lake and I reached out to grab Casey's arm. "I think I'm going into labor," I breathed out through gritted teeth. The contractions hadn't let up, and even though they were still about thirty minutes apart, I knew what it meant that they hadn't stopped.

"Shit, are you serious?"

"Yeah. I am. The contractions are still coming, and they're long and painful."

"Shit, shit, shit. Why didn't you say so sooner?" Once again he was on the verge of panicking.

"Calm down, I'm not going to have the baby out here in the woods. My water hasn't broken. We've got plenty of time, but we should definitely head back." Trying to keep him calm actually helped me to stay calm even though I was a little bit terrified.

"Do you want me to call my mom, or yours? Just tell me what you want me to do."

"No, it's fine. Stop worrying and just get us back. That's all I need you to do." As far apart as my contractions were, I was confident it would be hours before my water broke. I knew calling my parents wouldn't change anything; they couldn't come, but they would worry. I'd let them know when I went to the hospital.

He got us back to his place in less than thirty minutes, despite his insistence that we rush straight to the hospital. I explained to him that labor can take hours and I didn't want to spend the entire day at hospital when Lukas might not even come until tonight, or even possibly tomorrow morning. I convinced him I would rather lay down at his house until it was closer to time. He helped me up the stairs to his little apartment and laid me down in the bed, flipping on the TV and refusing to leave my side. I dozed on and off and then woke a little while later cursing everyone and every website that told me contractions during the first pregnancy usually progressed slowly. That is not at all how it was happening.

"Uh, Casey, you probably should have called your mom." My last ones hadn't even been ten minutes apart.

He looked at me with wide eyes. "Are you serious?"

"Yep, sorry. I didn't think it would happen this fast. Everyone said it would happen slowly, but now my contractions aren't even ten minutes apart. I'm not sure but I don't think it usually goes that quickly. We might still have a plenty of time though, so go ahead and call them." They might be able to make it back from Indianapolis in time. He called and they immediately got in the car and headed back. His mom suggested that he go ahead and get me to the hospital, but we barely made it out to the driveway before it felt like I peed myself. I didn't even need to say anything, because when Casey looked over at me my expression must have said it all.

"Shit." He was saying that word a lot today.

Thankfully the hospital in Jasper wasn't far from his house, and he was helping me inside within ten minutes. They got me into a room and started asking a million questions about my pregnancy history, the doctor that had been treating me back in Texas, how far along I was, when the contractions had started, how quickly they'd progressed, if I'd had any complications so far, and then they asked if I wanted an epidural.

I'd had several conversations with Ellie and my mom and my doctor back home, and I'd decided I wanted to try natural birth, but as bad as the contractions were hurting, I was beginning to doubt that choice.

"I . . . er . . . I don't know." I looked over at Casey who was sitting in the corner of the room, looking pale and scared to death. I didn't know why I was looking to him, but I was. I was more than a little scared myself. I thought I'd have my mom and Ellie both with me. Mama was supposed to fly into Lubbock the week ahead of time and stay with me, and then we were going to call Ellie the minute I went into labor so that hopefully she could make it before the baby came. I was on my own now, except for Casey. We'd called everyone to let them know what was happening, but nobody could get here in time.

"Okay, you can have a little bit more time to think about it. We'll be back into check on you in a bit. Press this button if the contractions start coming two minutes apart, but that shouldn't happen for another couple hours." As of right now, they'd been coming regularly at five minute intervals, and according to the nurse I was about seven centimeters dilated so I had a ways to go.

"How are you doing?" Casey came over and sat down next to me once it was just the two of us in the room. I took a deep breath as another contraction hit, and at that moment I wanted to tell him that I was pretty sure I was dying, but I didn't want to freak him out any more. After almost a full minute of clenching my teeth through the pain I exhaled a deep breath.

"If Ty was here right now I would punch him in the nuts for knocking me up."

"That bad? Why don't you get the epidural?"

"I've heard it can make labor last longer. I just want this done." When the next contraction hit though, I was ready to holler for the nurse to get back in here and give me the damn thing. Unfortunately, by the time the nurse did come back it was too late for that. Everything started happening so fast. The contractions were only a minute apart and they were telling me I was at ten centimeters and it was almost time.

I tried to be strong, I really did, but I was alone. Casey's mom and sisters were still an hour out, and I could see the terror in his eyes that he was trying to hide, which is why I told him to go when they got ready to wheel me to delivery. He started to protest, and offered to stay with me, but I insisted I would be fine and he should go wait for his mom. I prayed he wouldn't look back and see the tears in my eyes as he walked out of the room.

Ty, I need you baby. I'm so damn scared. It hurts so much. I don't think I can do this.

Please God get me through this, please let my baby be healthy.

When I sent my prayers up, I didn't realize how much I would be depending on God to get my baby through this okay. I was more worried about how I was going to get through it okay, but that all changed when it was time to start pushing and I saw the doctor's eyes go wide with panic and the looks he gave the two nurse in the room. They didn't say a word, but they were communicating so much with their eyes and I knew something was wrong.

"What is it?" I cried out in pain, between sharp breaths.

In the calmest voice the doctor could manage he let me know that my baby was not, in fact, okay. "I need you to breathe and not tense up Olivia, we need to deliver your baby as quickly as possible. The umbilical cord has slipped through your cervix ahead of the baby. We call this an umbilical cord prolapse. The cord is being compressed, which decreases and can even cut off blood and oxygen flow to the baby completely. Normally we do a cesarean in situations like these, but in your case it happened so close to delivery that we're not going to do that, but we need to get your baby out now, so when I tell you to push you have to push. Can you do that Olivia?"

I was so scared I couldn't even speak. I just nodded, but then I was able to get out two words. I looked right at one of the nurses and cried, "Get Casey." I thought I could do this alone, but that was before. She understood my plea and rushed from the room. She came back only moments later with him in tow. At that point there was no hiding my tears or pretending to be strong.

He rushed to my side and grabbed my hand and did everything he could to comfort me, telling me it was going to be okay, but all I registered was the pain and all I heard were my own screams, but when that doctor said push, I pushed, and I tried to remember my breathing. I probably crushed Casey's hand but he didn't try to let go once.

Please God, please don't take Lukas, please let him be okay. I won't survive losing him too. Please God let my baby be okay.

It felt like hours of screaming and pushing and being terrified that I was going to have a dead baby, before I got any relief. After I pushed that last time and then I saw the nurse smiling at me and holding my son I just started sobbing, and when I heard his first cry, I thanked God over and over. He was so beautiful and perfect when she put him in my arms. I didn't want to give him back up to her, afraid that if I let him go something could go wrong, but they assured me he was healthy and I would get him back soon.

My entire body sagged in relief and from exhaustion. I was too overwhelmed to even know what I was feeling except grateful that my baby was alive and healthy. I was an absolute wreck, and even Casey looked wrought, but he never left my side. He grabbed my hand again and leaned down to wrap his other arm around me. He pressed a kiss on top of my hair and then rested his forehead against mine.

"You were so amazing, so strong. I can't believe how fucking incredible you were. I–" he let out a heavy breath and then pulled away. "You were just so amazing."

"Thank you for being here. You shouldn't have had to do this, but just thank you. I couldn't have done it without you." It was true, and in that moment I knew it wasn't just that I had wanted someone with me. I had wanted Casey. I had needed Casey, and with that I had the answer to my earlier questions. I had feelings for him that went beyond friendship. Now I had to figure out what to do about them.

That could wait though. Right now the only thing that mattered was my son, my beautiful son. Lukas Tyler Tate, born March twenty-first at six-twenty-seven p.m. weighing six pounds and two ounces. I felt whole again in a way I never thought I would. Lukas Tyler Tate. My son. My miracle. My everything.

Thirty

"A new baby is like the beginning of all things- wonder, hope, a dream of possibilities." ⸱ Eda J LeShan

Even though Lukas was born three weeks premature, he was strong and healthy. I was released the next afternoon and they kept him one more day to make sure that there were no lasting complications from the early birth and difficulties with the cord. On Wednesday, I got to take my beautiful boy back to Casey's parents'. We wouldn't be going home until the next day.

I was completely enamored with the little guy and all I wanted to do was hold him in my arms, but he seemed to have that effect on everyone. One look into his innocent blue eyes and he had us all wrapped around his tiny little fingers. Carol and John, Casey's sisters, even his niece and nephews fell in love with him and doted on him any chance they got.

I had been completely unprepared to have him here in Indiana so I had nothing. They quickly took care of that, supplying me with clothes, blankets, bottles, diapers and all the things I had in stacks at home. Kelly even brought me a car seat she still had from when her youngest was a baby. Any time I tried to thank them, or offered to pay them back for all they had done, they wouldn't hear it. They just said that's what family does for each other, and in that moment I wanted to cry because they considered me a part of their big, wonderful family.

My parents and Ellie and Beth were all anxious for us to get back to Lubbock. They would be waiting, and even though I was just as excited for them to meet Lukas, I was a little sad that I would be saying goodbye to these amazing people in the morning. They extended an invitation that we were welcome to return any time, with or without Casey.

Mel of course was pissed that she missed it and even more pissed that Casey got to meet Lukas before she did, but mostly she was ecstatic to finally get to be Auntie Mel and start lavishing my son with

231

love and attention. She'd even rounded up the team to get my stuff moved into the new apartment so it would be ready when we got home tomorrow night.

There was so much excitement and buzz surrounding the little guy, even some of the neighbors and random cousins I'd only briefly met at the party were dropping off gifts and wanting to get a peek at the precious little guy. I would expect no less back in Abilene with the people I'd known my whole life, that's just what close communities do, but these people were almost strangers to me, and yet not a one of them acted like it. It was pretty incredible.

That night I was content though, after so many visitors and having to share my little man, to just sit up in Casey's apartment, in the quiet, snuggling him. I couldn't remember the last time I'd felt such peace and happiness. Not since Ty had held me in his arms.

Casey plopped down next to me, and he too seemed at ease, just sitting there, basking in the new baby joy, watching him sleep. Casey had yet to hold him, seeming too nervous, but I'd noticed that wherever Lukas was, Casey naturally gravitated toward him. He was always close by, watching over him in the same way that I was, like he needed to be near him.

"Here, you take him." I held him out, but Casey made no move to take him from me.

"No, that's alright. You just hold him now that you've got him to yourself," he protested.

"You should hold him." I set Lukas in his arms and then sat back and watched. Casey couldn't take his eyes off Lukas, and the smile on his face completely melted my heart. He was in love with my son too, and the emotion that surged through me was staggering.

"He's so small, and . . ."

"Perfect," I finished for him.

"Yeah, perfect. That's the only word that fits." His voice was soft and almost reverent. Casey stayed that way for a good hour, just holding Lukas to his chest, while we watched an old movie. Usually after only a few minutes of Carol or John or one of Casey's sisters holding my son, I was antsy and anxious to get him back in my own arms, but I wasn't feeling that now at all. It felt okay to be sitting next to the two of them. My heart ached thinking of how much Tyler would

232

have loved to hold his son in that way, but I didn't let it tear me up inside.

Ty I wish you could be here. I'll always love you, and I promise Lukas will know all about his Daddy, but please forgive me for being glad Casey is here. I know you would want me to be happy, and I know you would want me and our son to be taken care of so I hope you understand. Casey will never take your place, but I think, maybe that he will be really good for Lukas and me. I love you baby, but I've got to figure out how to start letting you go.

I wasn't exactly sure how to do that. I still didn't know if my heart was ready to move on, but I knew that this was the first step toward that. Hanging on to Ty's ghost wasn't good for me or Lukas. Acceptance. I think I was finally there, and although not all of my guilt and grief was erased, I truly believed that Tyler wouldn't hold my happiness against me. He was so incredibly selfless, and I think that he might have even liked Casey if they'd ever had the chance to be friends.

I must have drifted to sleep during the movie, and some time later I woke to Lukas' soft cries and Casey's voice soothing him with words that were as familiar to me as my favorite song. I opened my eyes and saw Casey sitting on the bed, rocking Lukas with one arm, and holding the book open with the other while he read.

". . . and very slowly she rocked him back and forth, back and forth, back and forth. And while she held him, she sang–"

"I'll love you forever, I'll like you for always, as long as I'm living my baby you'll be," I finished for him as I made my way over to them. Casey's eyes met mine, but then he continued to read, picking up right where I left off. When he was finished with the story, Lukas was sound asleep again and Casey laid him down on the center of the bed and tucked his baby blanket snugly around him.

"I hope this is okay. He woke up, but you looked like you needed the sleep, so I changed him and then gave him a little bit of water in his bottle. I wasn't quite sure what to do with the milk." His face flushed red and I hide to bite back a chuckle. I'd pumped breast milk and had it in the fridge but it seemed that Casey wasn't comfortable handling, or even talking about breast milk.

"It's great, thank you." I'd fed him not long before he'd fallen asleep the first time, so he should be fine for another hour or two without milk anyway. I was just floored that Casey had changed his diaper and taken care of him so well while I slept. "I love that book. I think I made my mom read it to me every single night until I was too cool to have my mom read to me at bedtime. She bought me a copy of it and gave it to me at my baby shower for Lukas."

"Yeah, me too. It was my favorite as a kid. My mom read it to all of us kids, but I stole it and have had it up here on my shelf for years. My sister looked for it when she was pregnant with my first niece, but I never told her I had it. I just let her buy a new one."

"You really are a devious troublemaker."

"Was. I *was* a devious troublemaker," he corrected me.

"But you're changed and grown up now?" I raised my eyebrow doubtfully.

"Absolutely."

"So what changed? What made you decide to give up the women and bar fights?" I was mostly messing with him, but also sort of curious how he became this guy.

"It just got old. I really was a little shit in high school, got myself suspended a couple of times. Soccer season was the only time I stayed out of trouble, and it was no different when I got to college. After my injury was probably the worst. I actually ended up getting arrested after one incident and spent a couple nights in jail. My dad wanted to teach me a lesson and knock some sense into me."

"Did it work?"

"Not really. I was still pissed, but we started working on Evie and that helped, and then Coach Davis contacted me and I had something to focus on again, a reason to push myself. I was still an arrogant, hot tempered jackass, but after that night, and then the first day of practice with you guys, I realized I didn't like the guy I was and it wasn't going to get me what I wanted in life."

"Because of Jamie?"

"That and I just really didn't want to blow the opportunity I had. That first day I felt like I was meant to be a part of the team, like I really had a chance to be better than myself. People only change when they want to, and I found my reason to get my shit together and stop being such a punk." His eyes shifted downward, almost like he was embarrassed or uneasy.

"So, you stopped partying and fighting and breaking hearts, got yourself a nice respectable girlfriend and became this great guy? As much as I like this Casey, I think I might have liked to meet the other one. Although I don't think I would have been friends with that guy," I admitted, and Casey snorted like I'd just said something profoundly amusing.

"No, you wouldn't have. I don't miss him at all. I started volunteering not long after that, and doing everything I could to become the guy I wanted to be. I thought Annie was the type of girl I should be with, but that was a mistake. I never should have let it last as long as I did." It was the first time he had actually talked to me about their relationship. Maybe it meant he was finally ready to share what had happened with them.

"The only time you ever talked to me about the two of you was the day I showed up distraught with my pregnancy test in hand, you said you weren't sure if she was your one."

"I knew she wasn't the one, I just didn't want to admit that I was wasting my time. I didn't want to admit a lot of things." He took a deep breath and ran a hand through his hair. I think he regretted opening up to me. "Anyway, we should both get some rest while we can, long drive tomorrow."

Just like that the conversation was over and I knew I wouldn't be getting anything else out him tonight, but I still had questions. Like why did he stay with her so long if he knew she wasn't the one? Sometimes I felt like Casey knew me better than anyone and I thought I knew him pretty well, but I couldn't help but feel like there was still this part of himself that he didn't want me to see, or a secret or . . . I don't know but something. I couldn't even say what it was that made me think that, except that there had been too many times when he'd been on the verge of saying something to me and stopped himself, or the way he constantly steered conversations in a different direction if I got to close to certain subjects.

Maybe it was nothing, and I was reading too much into it.

In the morning I felt like a zombie trying to pack up the rest of our stuff and feeding Lukas before we hit the road. Thankfully the little guy was lulled to sleep by the car and slept soundly for most of the drive. Unfortunately not everything went smoothly. A couple hours into the drive I got the call from Mel that a pipe had broken in the bathroom of my new apartment and flooded it. My old apartment was already rented out and the new tenant would be moving in next week, so I officially had nowhere to live. There weren't any other available apartments in either building. In a college town, affordable places to live weren't easy to come by. The landlord was willing to give me a couple of extra days to figure something out, but my stuff needed to be out of the apartment by Sunday.

"What's going on?" Casey asked when I hung up with Mel. I filled him in on what had happened and instead of acknowledging the crappiness of my circumstance he just told me to call Mel back.

"Why?" I asked before hitting the call button.

"Tell her to call Trent, he's got a key to my place and they can move most of your stuff into there and the extra furniture can go to Trent's. He's got plenty of room."

"Wait, no, we can't move in with you."

"Why not?"

"Because, you don't know what you're offering. I've got a newborn baby. He's going to cry and smell. A lot. Plus we'd be completely invading your privacy and taking over your place."

"Is that all?" he asked.

"Well–"

"Tate, just call her back and tell her to do it. It's not like it's permanent. You need a place to go; I've got the extra room. You guys can stay until you figure something out, or until the repairs are done on the unit downstairs. I really don't care how long you stay. It's not like you weren't spending half your time at my place anyway."

"Are you sure?" It wasn't like I had a lot of other options. Sarah and Tricia had moved in with Mel at the beginning of the term so she didn't have room for two more, and I didn't know how long it would take to search for a new place.

"Make the call."

I did, and then it was done. Late that night when we pulled up to the building, everything inside was ready. My bed and Lukas' crib were both set up inside Casey's spare bedroom and we were able to crawl into bed as soon as we walked in the door. I saw stacks of boxes against the wall, but everything could wait until morning, or whenever I had the energy to deal with it.

Thirty-One

"May your choices reflect your hopes, not your fears."
— Nelson Mandela

How could he do this?

To me. To us. To Lukas.

I gripped the steering wheel tighter and willed myself not to start crying. I blinked back the moisture in my eyes that blurred the sign on the side of the freeway that said we still had over fifty miles to go before we'd reach Abilene.

Everything had been going great. Why couldn't he just leave things how they were?

I thought back over the last few weeks at Casey's. He'd been so much help with Lukas and we got along great, even though they always say that when you live with someone, you get to see a side of them you never have before. Usually it's not all roses and sunshine, but cohabitating with Casey was comfortable and easy. If anything, the more I saw of him, the more convinced I became that it was really time to start letting my heart move on so that I could open it up again to something else, someone else. It was going to be a process, but I was ready to take it on, day by day letting go of Ty a little more so that I could see if there was even enough of me left to give to someone else. I wanted to try. Casey made me want to try, but then he had to go and say those words.

The ones that terrified me and made me doubt everything. The ones I hadn't been ready to hear. The ones I might not ever be ready to hear again, and now I didn't know what to do. So I was running to Ellie. I just wished I could rewind this day and change what happened when I got home from class. Stop Casey from uttering those words that might have just ruined everything between us before I even got to find out what was really there.

Casey looked up at me from his spot on the couch when I walked in the door. Right away I stopped, because I could see on his face that something was wrong. My first thought was Lukas.

"Is Lukas alright? Where is he?"

"Lukas is fine," Casey assured me. "But he's with Mel. I asked her if she would take him because there's something I need to talk to you about." In that moment he looked like he'd rather tell me anything but what he had to say, and my next worry was that he was going to ask us to move back out. Maybe having us here was too much for him. The crying baby, the spit up and diapers, the baby stuff that had taken over his apartment. Damn, I knew it was selfish of me to accept his offer in the first place.

"Whatever you need to tell me it will be okay." I wanted him to know that I would understand. I would hate to go, especially since the apartment downstairs wasn't ready yet. The water damage was more extensive than the landlord realized and the insurance company was dragging out the process of getting it repaired, trying to put the fault somewhere else so they didn't have to cover it. Of course we would go if that's what Casey wanted. We could figure something out for another couple weeks.

"I wish that were true. I'm just not sure that it will be, but I have to say it. I can't keep it from you any longer. I want to be completely honest with you so you know where I stand."

I started to get the feeling that he wasn't about to ask me to move out. I swallowed dryly and moved to sit next to him on the couch as knots started to form in my stomach. "What do you need to tell me Casey?"

"I hope I'm not crazy in saying this, but lately it's felt like things are changing between us." It came out more like a question, like he was asking me if I felt it. I just didn't know how to tell him I did, or where it was going to lead. He exhaled a deep breath. "I'm not trying to put any pressure on you; I need you to know that before I say anything else. It's just that if I'm not crazy . . . if you . . . shit I don't even know how to get this out." He dropped his head and raked a hand through his hair, curling it around the back of his neck.

I felt bad watching him war with his nervousness and insecurity about whatever he was trying to tell me and I wanted to put him at ease a little. "Let's just say you're not crazy."

He looked over at me hopefully, but then his eyes dimmed again. "I still think I am, because what I'm about to tell you will probably ruin it all."

"Just tell me," I said softly. Only if I had known what he was going to say, I would have stopped him, because once it was said it was out there and there was no taking it back.

"Do you remember when you asked me a few weeks ago what made me change? Why I gave up the girls and partying. I told you I found what made me want to be a better guy?"

"Yes," I said hesitantly. "You told me it was finding your place on the team and feeling a part of something again."

"That's right, but that's not all of it. There was something else. Someone else." He paused for a minute and looked at me like he was afraid to continue. I didn't say anything, I was still trying to figure out where he was going with this, and I had a suspicion that I knew.

"I still remember the first practice," he went on. "I was pretty nervous and afraid of looking like I didn't know what the hell I was doing, because I felt like I didn't. Coach introduced me to a few of the players and some of them were watching me while they warmed up and flashing flirty grins. I felt like prey that had been tossed into a den of hungry lions from the way some of them were staring at me, but really I worried I wouldn't be able to stop myself from making stupid mistakes that would ruin everything. I was seconds away from telling Coach that hiring me had been a bad idea.

"Then probably the most gorgeous girl I'd ever seen came walking out onto the field, and I knew it was a bad idea. I was convinced I needed to quit right there, but she walked over to me, and gave me a sweet smile. Not like the looks the other girls had given me, and then she said, 'Don't worry you'll be fine. You've got this. I believe in you,'" he quoted my words from that day. "

I asked her if she really meant it and you know what she did? She laughed and said, 'Nope. I have no idea if you can handle it or not. You just looked like you could use a pep talk, and really what's the worst that could happen? You just gotta watch out for the blonde one, she

240

likes to eat pretty boys like you alive.' Then you winked at me and walked away. I decided right then to stay, to prove to myself I could do it. It was time to quit screwing around and take the opportunity I'd been given seriously. Of course I hadn't seen Jamie yet, or I might have run." He forced a laugh but I couldn't force myself to say anything. I didn't know what to think about his story.

"I watched you all that first practice. I couldn't help it. You owned the field and commanded people's attention. You were confident, but not arrogant. Even as one of the younger players on the team, you stepped up to help encourage the other girls, already acting like a leader. And you had no problem putting Jamie in her place all day long. Anyone who watched you could see that there was a fire in you that was contagious. You loved the sport and you reminded me why I loved it, and why I still wanted to be a part of it.

"You had my attention from then on. I never intended to act on anything I was feeling; I just couldn't help but be drawn to you. I didn't find out you were married until the first game when he came to watch. I swear after that I tried not to watch you or even think about you, and I sure as hell didn't mean to fall in love with you, but fuck, I couldn't help it." He went on, but I was stuck on what he'd just said. I don't even think I heard the rest."

"You were funny and such a smart ass, and had that temper of yours that got you in trouble with Coach and the refs, but only drove me crazy. It was part of what made you so fierce and full of life. I avoided you and did everything I could to make sure we didn't have to work together. Then I met Annie toward the end of the season, and I guess at first she reminded me of you. She was a passionate and fun person, but wasn't a party girl, which is what I was looking for. I thought she was the perfect girl to make me forget about you and for a while we were good. She turned out to be more like Jamie than you though. Still, I tried to make it work. I wanted it to work, but she was never the one for me. The last few months of our relationship we did nothing but argue, and I spent so much time trying to reassure her that she was the one I wanted to be with, but I think the reason she never believed me was because I didn't even believe me. It was you. Always you. Even when I knew it was wrong, it was still you."

"Casey," I choked out a hoarse whisper.

241

"I know, but you have to believe me when I say I never actually wanted to be sitting here. If I could make it so that Ty was here with you instead of me, I would, but I can't and since we are here, I can't hide how I feel anymore, how I've felt about you from the beginning. I love you. I am in love with you."

I closed my eyes, trying to shut it all out. "Don't."

"No, look at me. Olivia, look at me," he repeated when I wouldn't. I forced myself to meet his gaze. It was gentle, and full of understanding, but also sadness. "I don't need you to say it, or feel it, or even want it. I know you're not ready for that, I just needed you to know the truth."

I shook my head. "I wish you hadn't. I wish you never told me, because I don't want it. I don't want you to love me Casey. I can't love you."

"I know not right now–"

"No, maybe not ever." I stood. "This wasn't fair of you Casey."

"I'm sorry, but I just thought you were feeling some of what I've been feeling."

"I don't know what I'm feeling," I cried. "But I know that I'm still in love with my husband and I probably always will be, but now I can't look at you without hearing your words and it makes me feel bad," I admitted.

"That wasn't my intention. I just wanted you to know the truth before anything happened between us."

"Well now nothing can, because I won't be able to be around you without feeling like you expect more from me, more than I can give, more than I'll maybe ever be able to give, and that's not fair. I don't want to hurt you."

"You won't." He stood up and reached for my hand, but I pulled back. "I don't expect anything."

"But you want it. You want it and I don't think I can give it to you."

"Nothing has to change. I'm okay with the way things are between us."

"But you just changed everything, Casey."

He'd watched me pack a bag with some of mine and Lukas' things, looking crushed and so full of regret. I think we were both wishing we could rewind, but we couldn't. He didn't try to stop me from leaving, not that he could have. I went to Mel's and got Lukas. She tried to get me to talk to her, but I couldn't. Not yet. I didn't even know what to tell her.

Congrats, you were right. Casey did have feelings for me all along, and the worst part is I think I might be developing them for him, but now we'll never know because he had to go and tell me he's in love with me and ruin everything?

I don't think so.

I'd talk to Mel when I got back, after I talked to Ellie. She would understand. Mel would tell me I was being a crazy person and that if I had feelings for Casey then it shouldn't matter if he was in love with me. But feelings weren't the same as love and it did matter.

God, how had I not seen it all this time? He'd really been in love with me and I had no clue, but looking back it made sense why he wanted to be there for me, why he was so good to me, but that only made me feel worse.

Ellie was surprised to see me when I showed up at her door. Of course she wasted no time in letting me in and taking Lukas from me to fuss over him, but I could see that she was dying to ask me what we were doing. She had that concerned Mom look and didn't believe for one second that I'd just decided out of the blue to surprise her with a visit. She knew there was a reason I was there, but she waited until Beth got home from cheer practice and took Lukas before she pulled me into the kitchen and sat me down.

"Tell me what's going on, baby girl? Not that I'm not thrilled to see you and my grandson, but I know when something is troubling one of my babies, and girl I can see you got a heart full of trouble right now."

She knew all about Casey and had even met him when she and Beth came up to Lubbock to meet Lukas right after we got back from Indiana. She also knew Lukas and I were living with him temporarily, so I jumped right in and started telling her about how close Casey and I had gotten over the months, especially the last two. I was nervous and hesitant about telling her that I'd begun to think I was developing feelings for him, afraid of what she would think, but I had to get it all out, and then I told her everything Casey told me earlier that day and how it ended with me leaving.

243

Ellie just grabbed my hand in hers and spoke in a gentle voice, "Baby girl, none of that is news to me. I'm just glad one of you finally got the courage to say something. I saw the way that boy looked at you, and the way you were around him."

"How was I around him?"

"At peace. When you're both in the same room, you naturally gravitate to each other, seek each other out and I don't think either one of you even realizes it, or maybe that boy does, but has just been trying to give you time to come to terms with it."

"Well he didn't give me time. He had to go and mess it all up!"

"What did he mess up?"

"Everything. He's asking for something I can't give him and now I don't know how to be around him at all."

She clucked her tongue, "It doesn't sound to me like he asked for anything. In fact, it seems to me that he's trying to give you whatever you need, including time to accept how he feels."

"But that's just it, I can't accept it. I don't want him to be in love with me. I'm not ready to let anyone love me yet."

She frowned, "Well that's the thing about love, you don't get to decide who you feel it for or who feels it for you. There's no letting about it. He loves you and that's just the way it is. As for you not being ready, I call hogwash on that."

"But I'm not. It hasn't even been a year. How can I be expected to fall for someone else so soon? It's not right."

"Sweetie, instead of telling yourself it's too soon, you need to open those eyes and see that you're one of the lucky ones. You don't have to wait years to find love and happiness again, and you're not doing anything wrong letting yourself have it. It doesn't mean you loved my son any less. I believe God is trying to tell you, child, that you have grieved enough, just like I believe that if Ty were here right now and could talk to you, he would tell you that even one day of your tears was one day too many. It was never God's intention for us to know this kind of heartache, and I know that the only thing my son ever wanted was your happiness. And there is no timeline on when you're allowed to feel it again. If God sent you love again, you don't turn that away because you think that somehow you need to suffer longer before your heart can be ready for it. You just say thank you and you accept the miracle baby girl. To do any less than that would a damn shame."

"That's just it, I don't know if it is love."

"But do you really want to risk walking away if it could be?"

"I don't know."

"Well you better figure it out girly."

"He's just so different from Ty. I don't see how we could be right for each other. Sometimes I think he's the sweetest guy in the world, and the only one who really knows me anymore, but I wonder if he really does, or if he sees some other version of me. Ty knew all of me, the good and the bad. Right now I don't even know who I am anymore, so how could Casey possibly know? And he can be so damn stubborn. We argue and butt heads and he always thinks he's right."

Ellie just chuckled and shook her head. "I think that maybe he's perfect for you."

"*Ty* was perfect for me. He was my one."

"That may be true, but I don't believe for one second that God can't give second chances, even at love. And we both know that you wouldn't want another one like Ty, and there isn't another Ty out there. He calmed you and was the voice of reason that kept you grounded. The two of you balanced each other, but that's not what you need anymore. You've been forced to face some of the harsher realities of life, and it's changed you, but the girl you used to be is still there. She won't be the same, but now what you need is someone who re-ignites that fire in you. You need someone who pushes you and sparks that passion that made you such a fighter. I think you need to let Casey breathe the life back into you and remind you of who you are, because I do think he knows who that is, even if you doubt it or don't know yourself. And you can be secure enough in the love that you and Ty shared to know that nothing can take it away, not even loving someone else."

Lukas and I stayed the night with Ellie, but by the next morning I knew what I needed to do. I'd spent most of the night lying awake in Ty's old bed talking to him and thinking about what Ellie had said. We had breakfast with her and Beth, but then we said goodbye. Ellie gave me an encouraging smile and pulled me into her arms, whispering in my ear, "It will be okay baby girl. Don't let holding on to the past keep you from embracing your future, and remember that no matter what the future holds, it doesn't change the past. You can have both."

Her words were the last bit of reassurance I needed before I loaded Lukas into the car and drove us back to Lubbock. Evie was parked in his spot, so I knew he'd skipped work today the same way I had skipped my classes. I thought I'd have a little more time to prepare what I wanted to say to him, but it might be better if I didn't think about it. I spent enough of yesterday and even the past couple months thinking so hard on everything that maybe it was time to just act.

I hesitated for just a moment outside his door, torn between knocking and just going in. With Lukas cradled in one arm, I fumbled with my keys and let myself in. Casey wasn't anywhere to be seen, which meant he was probably in his bedroom. I shut the door and slid our bag off my shoulder to the floor, but before I could go any further, the door to the spare room, the one Lukas and I had been using, opened and a worn looking Casey stepped out.

He was in a pair of old sweatpants and no shirt, with a couple days of growth shadowing his jaw and hair that hadn't seen a shower or a comb yet today, and still he was so damn beautiful. He just stood rooted in place, watching me.

"Hey, I'm home," I said softly and then thought about how true that was. Home. A few weeks at Casey's and that's exactly what it felt like I was walking into when I stepped through the door. I hadn't felt that since home stopped being the place I shared with Ty, because home is never just a place. It's about the people who make it that place. Right now it was about me admitting that wherever Lukas and Casey were is where I wanted to be, where I would feel at home. Being afraid of that didn't change it. The love that remained in my heart for Ty didn't lessen my love for Casey. I'd been wrong to think that I couldn't love both, that my heart didn't have the capacity to love that much.

Ellie helped me to see that, and now I just needed to make Casey see it.

"I wasn't sure you'd come back." He scratched a hand over his head and then glanced back at the room he'd just exited.

"I never should have left."

"But you came back."

"Mmhmm, and if you give me just a second to put Lukas down, I'll tell you why." I crossed the apartment toward him and he stepped out of the way to allow me into the bedroom where I laid Lukas down in his crib. Casey was still standing in the hall when I came back out, shutting the door softly behind me.

"So why did you come back?" he asked.

I took a tentative step toward him, and with it my knees started to feel a little shaky and some kind of herd of mutant butterflies chose that moment to start moving around inside my stomach. His eyes regarded me carefully as I leaned up on my toes and reached my hand up to his face to slowly bring it down to mine until we were forehead to forehead, nose to nose. There was only the tiniest gap between our lips, where our breath joined, and then I closed it. At first he was still as I moved my shy lips against his soft, full ones. In the next second, his arms came around me, pulling me in closer like I was the lifeline he was clinging too, and he was kissing me back. Slowly at first, but then I slid my hands through his thick hair until I was gripping the back of his neck. He pressed against me harder, but I still felt him holding back.

I ran my tongue along his bottom lip and his mouth opened to me. I swept my tongue inside entangling it with his. The heat between us intensified as the kiss became more passionate. His hands slid under the hem of my shirt and his fingers dug into my flesh. I groaned against his lips and he sucked my bottom lip between his teeth, biting it playfully. My heart was beating out of control, and with my body pressed so tightly to his, I was sure he could feel it about to burst right from my chest.

His breathing was heavy when we finally broke the kiss and he rested his forehead against mine. "Did you really just kiss me or am I imagining all this?" His warm breath tickled my skin.

I answered him by pressing feather light kisses along his jaw and then the corner of his mouth. He squeezed his eyes shut and sighed deeply, his hands still holding me tightly.

"If this is a dream, I don't want to wake up," he whispered.

"It's not a dream, Hunt."

His eyes opened and I saw all of my need and want mirrored in his dark gaze. "Are you sure about this Tate? If we do this, I can't go back. It will change everything. So if this isn't what you want, if I'm not

247

what you really want, then we can forget all about this and go on like we have been."

"I don't think I could ever forget that kiss," I breathed.

"Oh Thank God," he sighed. "Because there's no way in hell I could."

"I was just afraid before, and I'm still a little bit scared. I know what this is for you, and I hope that someday it will be that for me too. Right now I just want to take it slow and give it a chance if that works for you?"

"That more than works for me. I don't want to rush anything with this Olivia. We can go as slow as you need to. I'm just gonna ask that if you're feeling like it's too much or you start having doubts, just talk to me. We can figure this out as we go as long as we talk to each other."

"I'm going to need to go real slow. I was fifteen the last time I did any of this and I never thought I would have to worry about dating again. I'm not over Ty. I don't think I'll ever be *over* him. I'll always love him, but I'm ready to move past that, to the next part of my life. I'm ready to be happy again, and you and Lukas make me happy. So I'm embracing that. I can't guarantee that I won't freak out on you at some point. I've been struggling with this for a while, whether or not it's right, whether or not I can let go of the past, if I can let someone else into my heart, and I still don't have all those answers, but it feels right. You feel right. So I promise to try, and I promise to be open with you."

"That's all I'm asking." I felt his smile against my lips and this time when our mouths came together, it felt like we'd been doing this for years. I melted into him and he didn't hesitate to take control. It was only Lukas' cries that had us breaking apart with wide grins.

"I got him," Casey whispered and disappeared, only to reappear holding my precious baby close to his chest a minute later.

It was good to be home.

Thirty-Two

*"For it was not into my ear you whispered, but into my heart.
It was not my lips you kissed, but my soul."*
Judy Garland

"Can you grab the diaper bag and the bottle I left on the counter?" I asked while I searched the couch cushions for Lukas' hat.

"Got it." Casey walked over with Lukas in one arm and the diaper bag slung over his shoulder. "What are you looking for?"

"His hat. I know I set it on the arm of the couch earlier, but it's not here." I pushed the cushions back in place and looked around the floor again.

"Are you sure you didn't set it somewhere else?"

"Yes I'm sure. I set it on the couch so I wouldn't forget it when we left." I looked all over the room. There were blankets, stuffed animals and toys scattered throughout, but no hat.

"Can't you just grab a different one? Doesn't he have like twenty?"

"But that one matched his outfit. I'd have to completely change him," I sighed, frustrated and Casey looked at me like I was nuts.

"Liv, come on." He set the diaper bag down and grabbed my hand. He led me down the hall to mine and Lukas' room. He dragged me over to the dresser and opened the top drawer that was full of socks and hats. He reached in and pulled out a solid blue one. He held it out to me and I stared at it reluctantly.

He raised an eyebrow. "What?"

"The other one had a lion on it that matched his onesie."

He gave me another *'you've lost your mind'* look and put the blue one on Lukas himself.

"I thought you were supposed to be less crazy now," he muttered under his breath as he brushed past me. I grabbed a pair of rolled up socks and chucked them at his head. He chuckled and cooed at Lukas as he walked out of the room. "Mommy's a little violent."

I followed after them, grabbed my purse off the coffee table and took one more look around the room to make sure I wasn't forgetting anything else. Mel invited us over and we were already running a few minutes late, but that was pretty common these days. We were half way out the door when I stopped.

"Oooh," I exclaimed and ran back inside to the bathroom. It was lying on the counter next to the sink. I dashed back out with a triumphant grin on my face. I pulled the solid blue cap off Lukas' head and replaced it. I tossed the other one back inside. Casey rolled his eyes at me but didn't say anything. He just shut and locked the door behind us.

"I forgot I was going to stick it in the diaper bag, but I left it in the bathroom when I went to grab a pack of wipes."

"Well thank goodness you found it. It would've been a real tragedy not to have the matching lion hat." Casey leaned forward and pressed a quick kiss to my lips before pulling away so that his face was just inches from mine. "What does it say about me that I find your craziness oddly attractive?"

"It's just one of my many charming qualities." I closed the space between us and touched my lips to his again, and then again, but when I started to pull back Casey followed me and deepened the kiss. His tongue flitted across my bottom lip, looking for entrance. I opened to him, and his tongue swept inside tangling with mine. In the two weeks that we'd been doing that now, he hadn't gotten any less amazing at it, and I still reacted the same every time. I would have been content to stand in the hallway enjoying his kisses for hours, but Lukas had other plans. I quickly broke the kiss when his tiny fingers tangled in my hair and gave a sharp tug.

"Ahh!" For a little guy he sure had a tight grip. I disentangled his fingers from my hair while Casey laughed at me.

"Atta boy. Get her. Don't let her eat my face."

"Excuse me, if anyone was trying to eat anyone's face, it was the other way around."

"Whatever you say babe, you were practically mauling me."

"I was not." I glared at him.

"Mm. You're kind of sexy when you're mad." He winked at me and then walked away.

"You're lucky you're holding my kid," I called out and followed after him, thinking that he was kind of sexy all the time . . .

God, I wished I could rewind to that exact moment. It was one of the first moments where I convinced myself I could really have it again. Happiness, love, a family. That night the three of us went to Mel's for what I thought was just dinner, but was really a surprise belated birthday party for me, since my birthday had come and gone just days after I brought Lukas home from Indiana. I hadn't been up for celebrating then, but that night as Mel's we celebrated my twenty-first with all of my favorite people.

At the end of the night I remember reflecting; I was only twenty-one and yet there were so many titles and labels I'd held in those twenty-one years. Student. Wife. Team Captain. Widow. Mother. Some of them I'd seen coming and planned for, but some of them I never would have foreseen at twenty-one, never would have wanted. Yet, sitting in Casey's arms at the end of the night after we'd returned home and tucked Lukas into his crib, I realized that I didn't have to hang onto those titles as if they were all I would ever be now. I was twenty-one. Life wasn't promised a day beyond this one, but I was still young and God willing, I still had a lot of years to lose and gain more titles and figure out who I was. Some of those titles, like mother, would stick with me forever and be a huge part of me, the same way that Ty was, but I chose in that moment to no longer let widow define me or what the rest of my life was going to look like.

In that moment, I leaned my head back against Casey's chest and tilted my head to look at him. I embraced a new title. Girlfriend and it felt right. It didn't feel like a betrayal. It didn't feel like a poor substitute for what I'd had. It didn't feel like a replacement. It was just new. It was the next step in my journey and I was glad to be taking it with Casey. He stilled his fingers which had been idly playing with the strands of my hair and tipped his chin down. The contented smile on his face morphed into something more. Something deeper and something hotter. His other arm tightened around my waist, holding me to him while he dropped his mouth to mine.

Warm, gentle lips sealed over mine, and the hand at my waist slid up and curled itself around my ribcage; the bite of his fingers into my flesh drew a deep groan from my mouth which he swallowed. Needing more, he slid down the couch and shifted us both to our sides so that we were facing each other. Every time our eyes met, I could see so much in the way he looked at me. I could get lost in those brown eyes. They were filled with awe and passion and love. That last one was still hard to let myself accept and it scared me a little, but instead of running from it I wanted to leap right off the edge of this cliff I was on and dive in. To see that look in one man's eye during my life was enough of a miracle, but to see it again in the eyes of another amazing man had to be some kind of fairy tale or dream. But it wasn't, and every time Casey turned his warm gaze on me, I could feel him slipping inside my chest and stitching the pieces of me back together.

He held his palm against my cheek and then slid it back; threading his fingers through my hair, bunching them there and dragging my mouth back to his. Lips parted and our tongues met. We fed each other our need and desire as the kiss became more than just a kiss. With his eyes he could put my broken pieces together, but with his lips he breathed life back into me. I tried my best to give him back everything I was feeling in that moment. I just wished it could've lasted.

We'd kissed until we were both breathless and our lips bruised, and even then oxygen seemed so inessential. He was what I needed to breathe, the thing sustaining me.

Replaying it now, knowing what was coming, it was like watching the Titanic. You feel suffocated throughout the whole movie because you know it's coming, and yet it's dragged out over hours. In our case it was dragged out over the next couple months; I could see the montage of it all in my head. Flashes of lips and racing heartbeats and fingers entwined. Smiles and laughter and stolen moments in between baby cries and diaper changes and work and classes. There were barbecues and picnics and date nights. Every day he was patient and gentle with me. Never demanding, except when his mouth was claiming mine. He never asked more of me than I wanted to give him and he reminded me of why they call it falling in love. Because it's effortless and out of your control. For me it felt like I would never stop falling.

It was nothing like how it was with me and Ty and yet it was exactly the same. Every day I fell harder and faster until I knew that I wasn't just falling anymore. I was past that. I was in love and sinking deeper with no hope of climbing back up or out. And then last night . . . Last night I knew I didn't want to climb out. I was all in and even though I was sure Casey could see it in my eyes and hear it in my voice and feel it in my touch, I wanted to really show him. I'd finished my last final and was more than ready to embrace the summer break and the next step of the life Casey and I were building with Lukas. I wanted a night with no baby interruptions to make him see that I no longer doubted that my heart could belong completely to two people without me having to love one of them less. Mel took Lukas for the night – this is the point in the story where looking back you can see the iceberg ahead, but Jack and Rose are too caught up in their perfect moment to realize it's all about to end.

That night was our perfect moment. The moment where I decided not to hold anything back. I could squeeze my eyes shut and see the expression on Casey's face when he walked into the apartment to my candlelit dinner. My heart had sprouted wings. I'd actually felt nervous, but he put me at ease when he crossed the room, set his hands on my hips and bent down to kiss me, mumbling against my lips that dinner smelled delicious.

His hands slid around to my backside momentarily before he groaned and pulled away from me. I almost said to heck with dinner right there, but I'd planned everything out. We sat down to the meal I'd prepared, but I couldn't help but want to fast forward. The wait was worth it when he set his fork down, leaned back in his chair and asked me what was for dessert. I got up, rounded the small dining table and lowered myself to straddle his lap. I swear the look in his eyes when I leaned down to whisper "me" in his ear would forever be tattooed on my eyelids. So much desire pooled in his gaze which was like rich, decadent dark chocolate. His hands dug into the flesh at my hips and I watched the Adam's apple bob in his throat as he swallowed, but he didn't make a move.

"Casey James Hunt," I smirked, "are we going to sit here all night or are you going to carry me to bed so we can enjoy our dessert?"

He didn't have to be asked twice, and before I could even wrap my legs around his waist, he was shoving open his bedroom door and laying me gently on the bed. "Are you sure about this? There's no pressure. I'm perfectly fine just holding you all night."

"I'm not," I told him softly. We'd spent a lot of nights just holding each other. Tonight I wanted more. I wanted everything he had to give and I was going to give him all of me in return. We'd been waiting for the right time, and maybe the right time wouldn't be until there was a ring on my finger and he was stripping me out of a white dress, but whether or not we ever made it there, I was done waiting. I was more scared of waiting than I was of jumping in. Tomorrow wasn't promised and if we never got tomorrow, I needed Casey to know how I felt tonight.

"Then I want to see you." He tugged that full bottom lip between his teeth and I felt obliged to give him what he wanted. I sat up and yanked my top over my head. A second later I thought maybe I should have taken my time, tried to be sexier or more seductive, but from the look Casey was giving me, I threw that thought out the window because it was so not necessary. He was staring at me like I was his greatest fantasy come to life. He was still biting that lip and I noticed his breathing had increased as well.

I kept my eyes locked on his as I slid the soft, knee-length, flowy skirt I'd chosen for tonight down my legs and kicked it to the floor. He released his lip and drew in a deep breath. Slowly I twisted my arms behind my back to free the clasp on my bra, but Casey's rough voice stilled my hands.

"Stop."

Three easy strides put him directly in front of me. He swept my hair back and then gripped it tightly in his hand, tipping my chin up. He crushed his lips to mine while his other hand went around my back and took care of the clasp and then tugged the straps down my arms and pulled it free. It joined my skirt and top on the floor. I bunched my hands in his shirt and dragged him down with me as he placed a hand to my chest and gently pressed me down to the mattress. He pulled my hand away from his shirt and placed them at my sides. His heated gaze burned my skin, leaving a flush that followed the same path as his eyes. He dropped his lips in an open mouthed kiss to my stomach, just above the lacy edge of my underwear and a pulse went out from that spot shocking every inch of my body to life. His fingers curled inside the waistband and slowly dragged them down my legs and off. He rose to his full height over me and my body wanted to squirm, but I held still as he drank me in.

His tongue darted out to wet his bottom lip and then he bit the damn thing again and a shudder rocked through me. "Your turn," I managed to breathe out, sitting up on my elbows.

He pulled his shirt over his head and his chest was exposed to my greedy eyes. My hands itched to touch him everywhere, to trace every ridge of defined muscle. *Easy girl*, I had to tell myself before I pounced on him. He stripped down until he was in nothing but his navy blue boxer briefs. He was so beautiful, in a completely masculine way; hard and lean, every inch of him sculpted perfection. God's skills put Michelangelo's to shame. I was pretty sure I might die if I didn't get to touch him and I told him so. He chuckled, soft and low, but lowered himself over me, his hands on either side of my head holding him up while his knees pressed into my thighs caging me in.

"You're the most beautiful thing I've ever seen," he murmured and then his lips found my pulse. I tipped my head back and he traced the tip of his tongue along my throat, sending sparks out as he went. He swept my hair out of the way and then kissed just below my ear, before pulling my earlobe between his teeth. I couldn't keep my hands still anymore. I threaded my fingers through his hair, tugging as he tugged on my ear. He kissed his way back down to my shoulder, grazing his teeth over the most sensitive spot on my shoulder. A tremor shot down my spine and my lips parted breathlessly. His teeth latched onto that spot and his tongue came out to taste me again, hot and wet against my tender flesh. He scraped his teeth over my skin as he pulled back, and then blew warm breath over the spot. I shivered when it felt cool on my skin, wet from his kiss.

I scraped my nails down his back and he let the weight of his lower body press into me right where I needed him. He lifted my head and pulled all my hair back, so the it was fanned out across the pillow, and then he continued his slow, tortuous assault on my senses; kissing, sucking, biting and blowing all along my neck and shoulder and across my collarbone. I dug one hand into his back and the other in his hair, dragging his mouth up to mine. He rocked his hips into me the same time he thrust his tongue inside my mouth and I wasn't sure how my body wasn't on fire. We warred for control over the kiss, pushing back and forth, giving and taking, consuming each other while he continued a steady rhythm with his hips. I couldn't get enough of him. My hands were all over the place – his back, his firm buttocks, his hair – trying to get my fill of him.

One of his callous roughened hands snaked up my stomach, over my ribcage and wrapped around my aching breast. I had to rip my mouth away from his and draw in a deep breath when he squeezed the tender flesh and rubbed the rough pad of his thumb over the sensitive peak. He skimmed his lips over my jaw to my ear and the low rumble of his voice hummed against my skin when he spoke. "I can't get enough of you. I'll never get enough of you."

"Take all of me," I breathed, completely lost to his mastery over my body.

"I will, baby, I will," he whispered. "But I'm not done exploring yet." His lips left a hot trail down to my other breast and my back arched off the bed when his mouth closed around me. I curled on hand around the back of his neck and raked the other hand down his spine none too gently. He hissed and his teeth grazed my tender flesh. I sucked in a sharp breath and wound my hand in his hair, pulling on the short locks. He didn't stop. He continued to suck and bite, while his other hand released my other breast and slid down my stomach to my hot center.

There was too much pleasure being created by his mouth and fingers; I couldn't focus. I tipped my head back, squeezed my eyes and just tried to breathe as he wrung even more pleasure from my willing body. I could feel everything in me coming undone, and I was so close to that edge, another second and he would have tipped me over, but he withdrew his hand and shoved himself up onto one arm. My eyes flew open and a whimper of protest barely escaped my lips when I saw him shoving his boxer briefs down.

My stomach quivered and I felt it all the way down to my toes. When he was fully bared, I reached to take him in my hand, but he caught my wrist and pinned it over my head. "Uh uh," he whispered. "I'm going to make you feel good."

"But I want to do the same for you."

"Believe me, Liv, this is going to feel good for me too." He kissed me hard and rough before he rolled away momentarily to retrieve a condom from his nightstand, and then he was back over me. He tore it open with his teeth and rolled it on before getting himself into position. He brought his hand to my cheek and held my gaze in his. He lowered his mouth to mine. "I love you, no matter what happens after tonight, remember that much," he whispered against my lips just before he kissed me and pushed inside.

Over and over he withdrew and thrust back in and it was all I could do to hang onto him and not shatter into a million pieces beneath him. We became a tangle of limbs and heavy breathing, clinging to each other as he drove us both to the brink over and over, only to retreat and prolong the pleasure to the point that I didn't know how much more I could take. My fingers dug into his backside and I lifted my hips to meet each thrust as he drove harder and faster and this time there was no stopping it, not that he tried. We both went over that edge and fell apart together. I think my heart actually stopped at one point and then he collapsed on top of me.

"I think you just killed me with your penis powers," I managed to breathe out once I'd actually sucked oxygen back into my lungs. We were still connected and his deep laughter rolled through me.

"You're not dead baby, and I am nowhere near done with you."

He was telling the truth. I fell asleep in his arms, only to be awakened needing him twice more throughout the night. The second time, there was no hurry, but all of the same desperation and need. We both took our time exploring and teasing each other before he entered me again and made slow, sweet love to me. The third time was just before dawn and I crawled on top of him. He was not at all unhappy to be woken to me on top of him, and wasted no time in tearing open a condom and driving up into me.

When the sun was finally peeking through the curtains, even the hungry rumble of my stomach wasn't enough to get me out of the bed. I wasn't sure that I even had the strength to try, but Casey climbed out from under the blankets, despite my attempts to drag him back under, and he cooked us breakfast which we ate in bed. We didn't shower and dress until it was time to go pick Lukas up from Auntie Mel.

I actually let myself believe we were going to be a family. I thought that nothing could ruin my new happiness. I was so damn wrong.

Thirty-Three

I didn't know who I hated more in the moment after Casey made his confession; him or Annie. Her stupid smirk kept flashing in my mind. This is what she wanted. She was getting it, and that killed me. She'd knocked on Casey's door this morning with the intention of destroying us. I didn't buy her excuse about leaving a favorite necklace, not for one second, and I knew without a doubt that it was no accident that she showed up while he was at work. She'd meant to catch me alone so she could speak the words that would tear apart my chest and rip open all the wounds that had been healed.

She was a heartless shrew and I wished I hadn't been too stunned to punch her in her perfect face, even more than that, I wished I would have slammed the door on her when I first answered it. Maybe then I would still be living in my happy delusion. Instead, the words she had uttered shattered that.

"I think it's great that you were able to forgive Casey for getting your husband killed. I'm so happy the two of you were able to get past that."

That woman's face had been anything but happy, right up until my mouth fell open and I asked her what she was talking about. Then she looked as if she couldn't have been more pleased, even while she pretended to be sorry.

"Oops, I just thought he would have finally told you. You know what; I think I just remembered, I left my necklace at my sister's when I was visiting her, sorry to bother you for nothing."

She'd turned and walked away and I closed the door on her feeling as if she'd just taken something from me. Something I wouldn't ever be able to get back. It made no sense, because Casey wasn't responsible for Tyler's accident. He wasn't behind the wheel of the car that hit him,

258

but Annie had to know that, so why would she come here and say he got Ty killed? She wouldn't, unless she actually thought it was something that could tear Casey and me apart, and the only way that would happen is if what she was saying was true. But it couldn't be. No matter how I looked at it, I couldn't understand. It was like one of those abstract brain teasers where you stare at a picture forever and there's nothing there, until someone flips it upside down and suddenly your brain sees what's there. I just needed someone to flip this picture upside down for me.

Lukas cried and I had to go to him, but not even holding my baby could shake off the worry that had hold of my insides. "Shh, it's going to be okay," I cooed, wishing I had someone to hold me and whisper the same words of comfort.

They would have been a lie though.

Lukas was asleep again when Casey came in. I looked up at him from my place on the couch as he tossed his keys down on the small stand just inside the door. His eyes found me and he smiled, and for a fraction of a second that smile convinced me that everything was going to be okay, because this was Casey. Then his smile vanished.

"What's wrong, Liv?"

"Why would Annie say you're responsible for Tyler's death?" I could barely force the words out, but the second they were out I wished I could take them back and un-see the look of horror and guilt that crossed Casey's face. "Oh God." I thought I might be sick.

"I can explain," he said carefully.

"Please do," I choked. I was having trouble breathing.

He cautiously approached and then took a seat on the opposite end of the couch. There were only a few feet between us, but it felt like this huge chasm had opened up and now separated me from the guy I loved and who claimed to love me. But how could that be true if he was keeping something like this from me, if he really had a part in Ty's death? Just thinking it felt wrong, like my body couldn't even handle it and was rejecting it. I worried I might really be sick right there.

"You have to know that I never wanted to keep this from you. I could just never find a way to tell you."

"Well you better find a way right now."

259

"I used to run every day. I liked to go real early in the morning, before the sun was up." Ty always ran early too, said he liked to race the sunrise. "The morning of Tyler's accident I was running near campus."

Oh God.

"I saw him that morning. He recognized me running by him. I would have kept on running past him, but he called my name. I almost didn't hear it over the sound of my music, but I stopped and turned and got his fist in my face before I knew what was happening."

I was startled and confused. That didn't sound like Ty at all. He would never just hit someone, and he would certainly never sucker punch them.

"When I asked him why the hell he hit me, he said it was for being in love with his wife." Casey cast his eyes down as I ingested his words, then he lifted them back to mine. "I guess he knew. I tried to deny it, asked him what the hell he was talking about, but he told that a man always knows when another man is in love with wife. Said I looked at you the same way he did and he wasn't real thrilled about that. I didn't even know what to say to him, but I tried to apologize. He wouldn't hear it though, said he couldn't blame me; that loving you was easy, but he made it very clear that just because he understood, didn't mean he liked it, and he didn't want to see me watching you like that anymore.

"We were standing there on the corner, having probably the most uncomfortable conversation of my life. I had my back to the street and was just about to promise him I would keep my eyes off of you, even though I had no idea how I would do that, but I never got to make that promise anyway. Suddenly Tyler's eyes filled with panic and he gave me a hard shove. I didn't know what was happening, but the next thing I knew, I was on my ass in the street and an SUV hopped the curb before Tyler could get out of the way. It felt like I watched it happen in slow motion, but it was over before I could blink."

My hand flew up to cover my mouth and hold back the anguish clawing its way up my throat. I shook my head in disbelief, refusing to accept what he was telling me.

"The car barreled right over him and continued to hit a tree. Tyler wasn't moving when I got to him, but he came to as I was calling nine-one-one."

O God. "He was still alive?" Nobody had told me that. The story I got was that an elderly woman had a heart attack behind the wheel. It wasn't her fault; it was truly a tragic accident. The lady pulled through, but Ty was gone, died instantly. I even knew that there had been a witness to the whole thing. I just hadn't known it was Casey. I never asked and no one ever told me. He never told me.

"He was. I asked him why the hell he did that, pushed me out of the way when he knew he wouldn't have time to get out of the way himself, and he told me he'd done it for you. Said he wanted to be the man you thought he was."

I let out an awful sob and tears that I'd been holding back fell from my eyes and rolled down my cheeks. The only relief that I'd had about that morning was that Ty hadn't suffered, but now I could picture him lying on the cement, broken but still breathing. I wondered what he felt in his last moments, if he'd been scared, if he was in a lot of pain.

"He asked me to promise to take care of you, and I didn't know what else to do, so I promised him I would. I tried to get him to hang on until the ambulance got there, but he kept telling me it was okay, that he knew you were going to be okay. By the time they showed up it was too late. He was gone. His injuries were so extensive that the paramedics assumed he had died instantly and I didn't correct them. I was in shock."

My chest felt tight, like it was being compressed and I was suffocating. Each breath that I drew in was painful. My hand clutched at my shirt over my chest, squeezing so tightly that I could feel my nails digging into my palm through the fabric, as if I could hold the pain in, keep it back, keep my chest from ripping open. How could Tyler have thought it was okay? It wasn't okay. It wasn't okay that he left me, but even with his last breath he'd loved me, taken care of me, made sure that I would be okay. Oh God, it was like losing him all over again. The image of him lying there was burned into my mind. I felt the hot tears run down my cheeks, but no more sobs left my throat. They were trapped inside. Casey reached out to me and tried to pull me in his arms, but I pushed him away.

261

"Don't," the cry was strangled in my throat. Casey sat back, looking on helplessly.

"I'm so sorry Olivia. I never meant to keep any of this from you. I went to his memorial service with the intention of telling you that I'd been there that he'd pushed me out of the way – I just planned to leave out the part where I was in love with you – but when I saw you at the reception, you were just so broken and lost. I didn't know how to tell you, so I left. Later, I wanted to; believe me, I hated not telling you the truth, but I knew all of it would only hurt you and I couldn't take causing you anymore pain, not when none of it would bring him back. Before I knew it, it felt like it was too late to tell you, like I'd missed my opportunity and you would only hate me. Especially once things started happening between us and you knew how I felt."

"Just stop," I struggled to form words through the pain that was making it impossible to breathe. "I need you to leave right now."

"I'm so, so sorry. Just tell me what to do to make it better, anything, just please don't ask me to leave you like this."

"Just go. You can't be here. I can't look at you right now," The dam was breaking, and my body was trembling; I knew it was all about to pour out and he couldn't be here when that happened.

"Please don't do this. Don't ask me to go, Olivia. I'll do anything but that. Let me help you get through this," he begged and I could see the moisture in his own eyes; his pain only added to mine, and something inside me snapped.

"Leave!" I yelled through the first sob. "I don't want you," my voice broke before I could add "here" and Casey's eyes reflected the agony my words caused him. I could barely see through my tears, but I watched him get up, begging me with his eyes to change my mind, but I wouldn't. I couldn't stand to be near him.

"I love you. I'm so, so sorry." I watched the tears fall from his eyes just before he turned his back to me and walked out the door. He glanced over his shoulder at me one more time, giving me the chance to tell him to stop, but I didn't, and then he was gone and I was alone. I buried my face in the pillow and screamed, no longer able to hold any of it back. Sob after sob ripped through me and muffled against the pillow. I held the pillow like it was my life raft, and the only thing keeping me from going under as wave after wave battered me and the truth ripped through me, shredding apart every happy moment over the last several months that I'd been believing and living a lie. One where Casey was the good guy, my anchor in the storm, the one who helped me pick up the pieces of my heart and made my world whole again. All the while he'd kept the truth from me that if it wasn't for him, my world would never have been ripped apart to begin with. He was the reason I lost so much. He was the reason Lukas lost so much.

Rationally I knew the accident was still that – an accident. The blame or fault didn't belong on anyone, least of all Casey, but it didn't change what was. Tyler was gone. Traded his life for Casey's and now I felt like I'd done the same.

I don't know how long I lay there, crying into my pillow, but the next thing I knew, Mel barged in, her own eyes streaked with black tears and she threw herself down on the couch with me. Her arms wrapped around me and I gave up my hold on the pillow, choosing to let her hold me together while I fell apart some more.

I could only assume Casey had called her, because she didn't say a word, she just cried with me, and then once the tears dried up, she just sat with me. I felt my insides going cold as everything drained from my body while we sat there in silence. Lukas woke from his nap and Mel got up and changed and fed him while I sat in that spot on the couch, letting the numbness take over. I picked up the pillow and clutched it in my lap and tried to shut everything off. I was afraid I might never be able to get off that couch if I didn't, but then Mel walked over and tugged the pillow away and set Lukas in my arms.

"You gotta let yourself feel it, Liv, for as long as it takes you to work it out or you'll never get through this."

I didn't want to look down at my baby, because I knew the moment I did, I wouldn't be able to shut anything off. I'd have to do what she said and feel it all. I didn't want to, but it was like Lukas knew and he fussed and reached his tiny fingers up toward my face and I couldn't help myself. I looked down into Ty's big blue eyes and tears filled mine again.

"It's okay to feel it," Mel whispered.

She stayed with us at Casey's through the weekend, helping me care for Lukas and taking care of me, making sure I did the basics like eat, sleep and shower. Casey stayed away like I asked. It was what I needed while I struggled to deal with this new reality, but that didn't stop me from missing him like crazy. That was the hardest part. What were you supposed to do when it felt as if the only person who could put you back together was the one who broke you?

Thirty-Four

"Courage, dear heart." — *C.S. Lewis*

"Come on, time to get up missy. You've got a mess to fix." Mel yanked the covers away from me.

"Go away," I groaned.

"No. I gave you the weekend, but now it's time for you to get past this so you can work things out with Casey."

I sat up and glared at her. "Like hell. How am I supposed to get past this? He lied to me for months; betrayed my trust. He's the reason Tyler is gone."

"Oh, bullshit." Mel dropped down beside me. "We both know that's not true."

"Yes, it is," I clipped.

"No, it's not," she argued. "And if you weren't hurting so bad right now, you would be able to see that."

"I wouldn't be hurting right now if it wasn't for him."

"He's not the one causing the hurt, Liv."

"Then who is?" I huffed.

"Nobody sweetie, that's why it's so hard. You want to hold somebody responsible for the way you're feeling, but the truth is, there's nobody to blame except the unfairness of life."

"Life didn't lie to me and keep secrets," I pointed out.

"No, you're right. He did that, but you tell me, when would have been a good time for him to tell you? Right after it happened when you were a zombie who could barely get out of bed? When practices started up and you were trying so hard to convince everyone that you were dealing? When you found out you were pregnant and suddenly had another life to worry about on top of your own? You tell me when the right time was for him to turn your world upside down again and cause you more unnecessary pain."

"So you think he was right to keep it from me?"

She sighed, "No, I don't. I think you deserved to know what really happened, but I also think Casey was in a really hard place being the one who had to tell you."

"That doesn't matter. He should have found a way. Instead he let me fall for him."

"No, you did that all on your own, because Casey deserves your love. Deep down you still know that. If you want to be mad at him and hate him and hold him responsible for what happened, then you better be just as angry with Ty."

My jaw tensed and I felt my face flush with anger. "How dare you," I ground out through clenched teeth. "Tyler died that morning."

"I know that. I also know everything that happened, Liv. Casey told me because he was worried about you after you kicked him out. And I can understand why you did. How hard it must have been to hear. I even get you being angry at first, but now it's time for you to let that go and stop holding Casey responsible for Ty's actions. Ty stopped him. Ty punched him, and Ty pushed him out of the way. Casey didn't make him do any of those things."

"So now it's Ty's fault."

"No," she said, exasperated. "It's no one's fault. Ty loved you somethin' fierce and he wanted to make sure Casey knew that, but not even he faulted Casey for loving you babe, so why are you? He didn't do a damn thing wrong, never even once planned to act on his feelings for you. I know you might not want to hear this next part, but you don't need me to tell you what kind of man Tyler was, so can you honestly tell me you're not proud of the decision he made? He probably had less than a second to think about it, and without hesitation he chose to put someone else's life – someone he didn't even like – before his. Ty made that choice, not Casey, so quit blaming Casey for it, and start accepting that you just married a hero darlin'. Then accept that you found another one who's only ever put you first and done what he thought was best for you, even at the expense of his own feelings and what he had to have known it might cost him when the truth did come out. All that guy wants is for you to be happy, so let him make you happy."

"I don't think I can."

She gave me a frustrated look and let out a sigh; she was just about to start lecturing me again, but I didn't give her the chance.

"I know you're right. I knew it all along, but it doesn't matter. Whether Casey's at fault or not, when I look at him all I'm ever going to see is Tyler, now." He'd loved me to his very last breath, and used it to make sure that I would be okay when he was gone. How does one ever get over that kind of love? How could anything ever compare to that?

"I don't believe that for a second. You love Casey and none of this should change that."

"But it does, Mel." She just couldn't understand.

"You're scared Liv. I get it. You loved Ty, more than anything in this world, and you never thought you could love anyone else that way again, but then you fell for Casey and I know you Liv; I think you've just been waiting for an excuse to run rather than give him you're heart. You lost once, and you're terrified of your heart getting broken again. I understand that, but the Olivia I know wouldn't let a little risk stop her, in fact she lived for it, thrived on it."

"This isn't about risk, Mel. It's not even about me. I'm not mad at Casey anymore, if I ever was. I think these last three days I've spent crying, I was crying for Casey as much as I was Ty, because I knew I'd lost him like I lost Ty."

"Why do you think you've lost him?"

"Because, when Casey looks at me, he looks at me like I'm his whole world; like I'm the only girl he's ever loved and will ever love. I know that look, because it is the same way Ty looked at me. I thought I could do that again. Love. And God help me, I do love Casey. But my love isn't whole. The hurt I caused Casey when I made him leave, I hated that more than anything he told me. I don't want to be responsible for his pain again, and I will be if I go back to him, because whether it's right or not, I can't just put what I know behind me. Not right now, or probably any time soon. The last thing I want is for Casey to look at me with that love in his eyes and see someone who's stuck on a night in the past. He doesn't need to be reminded of that night every time he looks at me anymore than I do. He feels enough guilt already, Mel. The best thing I can do for him – for the both of us – is let him go so he can find someone without all this painful history."

267

"I don't think it's fair of you to make that decision for the both of you. You should talk to him before you do something I think you'll regret."

"Mel," I started to say, because I knew I wouldn't change my mind and there was nothing she or Casey could do, but she stood from the bed and stopped me.

"No, I'm taking Lukas out to my parents since they've been dying to see him, and you should call Casey and let him come home."

Mel left the apartment with baby and diaper bag in hand, and then it was just me and the quiet, thinking back over the past several months, not for the first time. We'd been living in a bubble, one where I pretended that what we felt for each other was enough. It was easy then, to be sure of him, of us, when he was holding and kissing me and putting me back together, but now there were just too many missing pieces and he couldn't be the one to put them back. Hell, I didn't even know if I could. All I knew is that it would be unfair to expect anymore of Casey.

I couldn't bring myself to call him and hear his voice, so I texted him and told him he could come home tonight, and then while I waited, I started packing. I was in the bedroom, putting the last of Luka's things in a box when I heard him come in. I stepped out into the hall and my heart sank in my stomach when I saw how drawn and worn he looked, like the last few days had been even harder on him than they had on me. I doubted he had showered or shaved since he left, and if the hollow-eyes and dark circles were any indication, I didn't think he'd been sleeping well either. I was afraid I was about to make it worse.

"Hey," I muttered weakly.

"I'm surprised you're still here. I figured I'd be coming home to an empty apartment," he said dejectedly.

"I wanted to be here when you got back, to talk," I swallowed nervously, suddenly doubting my decision and ability to do this. Maybe it would have been better if I had just slipped away and out of his life, but I owed him more than that.

"But you're still leaving." Looking into his anguished eyes was a mistake that threatened the careful hold I had on my heart. It was about to crack wide open. "God, please stop looking at me like that."

"Like what?" Like causing him pain was killing me? Because it was.

"Like you feel sorry for me. Like you can't say what you need to because you're afraid of hurting me."

"I am afraid of hurting you," I cracked.

He finally moved from the spot he'd been rooted to just inside the living room and came to stand in front of me. He lifted his hand like he was going to touch me, but then pulled back. "You don't have to say it, Tate." Hearing him revert back to my last name, like we were just Tate and Hunt again and Casey and Olivia were, stung even though it was the truth. "I knew this was coming.

"I wish I could say something to make it easier for both of us." The first tear fell and this time he didn't hesitate to draw me into him, holding me tightly to his chest.

"It's okay. I know, I know." More tears started falling. Even when I was breaking up with him and crushing his heart, he was still trying to comfort me, make it easier for me. "I just wish I could do something, anything to make this better for you, including go back to that day and trade places with Tyler, but I can't. I wish to hell I could, but I can't."

I pulled away, wiping at my tears and shaking my head. "No. Don't say that. That's not what I want at all. God Casey, please don't think I wish it was you, because I don't. I know Ty didn't regret his choice, and as much as I wasn't ready to lose him, I don't regret it either. What he did for you - that was who he was and a big part of why I loved him so much. A different choice would have made him a different man. I know I was mad at you, but I need you to know, I don't blame you at all."

"Then I don't understand why you're leaving."

"Because you deserve better than the girl standing in front of you." He frowned and I knew he was going to argue, but I tenderly pressed my finger to his lips. "Just hear me out."

His frown deepened, but he gave a nod.

I drew in a breath to hopefully steady my trembling nerves and voice. "I'm not whole, Casey, which means I can't love you with everything I am like you deserve to be loved. I thought I could let you and Lukas make me whole and that it would be enough, but the last couple days have shown me that it's not enough. Do not for one second

269

think that means you're not enough. It's because of you that I've made it this far, but it was never on you to save me or make me better. That was way too much to ask and expect of you. I have to figure out how to heal the rest of the way on my own. I haven't been alone in six years. I need to know that I can even stand on my own, and that I can take care of myself. I need to be whole again by myself before I can let myself be whole again with somebody else."

He grabbed my hand and interlocked our fingers. "What do you want me to do? Tell me to wait and I will."

I squeezed his hand. "I can't do that. I can't be that selfish with you when you've been so completely selfless with me. I don't know how long I'd be asking you to wait, or if that day you'd be waiting for would even come."

"I don't care. Be selfish dammit. I want you to be selfish with me. I don't care how long; I'll wait if you tell me there's a chance."

"I don't want you to wait, Casey." Those words were the hardest, most painful ones I think I'd ever spoken, and they were maybe the biggest lie I'd ever told. But the truth wouldn't be fair to him.

"Please don't say that." A watery sheen covered his pain filled eyes, and I hated that I was the cause of his tears and pain. I wished I could tell him that I believed in us the way he did, that I knew there was a future for us someday down the road, but I couldn't, because I wasn't sure that I would ever be able to give him what he wanted.

I reached the hand he wasn't holding up to rest against the side of his face. "You loved me back to life Casey, but now I want you to go live your life free from all the pain and sadness and guilt I've caused you. We both need to find a fresh start to be able to move on from this place of hurt." I dropped my hand, and he turned his head away, but it wasn't enough to keep me from seeing the struggle on his face to hold back the same emotions I was fighting. I didn't want to drag this out for him any longer.

"I'm going to Mel's tonight. She's got Lukas, and I'm going to stay with her until I can get into a place. I think for both our sake's it would be better if we didn't do the 'we can still be friends' lie. We both know that would be impossible. I hope it won't always be that way, but for now I don't want to cause you pain every time you see me. I'll

270

probably send Mick and the guys over to get our stuff. This will never be enough for all you've done, but thank you Casey. For everything."

I saw the tears in his eyes that he tried furiously to hide, and in the end he let me walk out of the apartment. When the door closed behind me I let my own tears fall. He wanted to understand, and I think maybe a part of him did, that's why he didn't put up more of a fight, but it didn't change that I'd just ripped out the heart of the one person left who meant the most to me after my son.

Even going to my baby boy and holding him in my arms didn't make me feel better about what I'd just given up, but I had to find strength without leaning on Casey's. I'd jumped right from grieving widow to expecting mother and hadn't gotten a chance to figure out who just Olivia was anymore. I spent that summer trying to figure it out, and little by little I did, but not once did I stop missing Casey.

I missed his smile and his laugh. I missed holding his hand just because. I missed the sight of him holding Lukas. I missed being able to rest my head on his lap when the day was finally done and it was finally quiet for the night, and I missed his kisses goodnight and the anticipation of a kiss good morning. Most of all, I missed the hope I'd found for a future that I wouldn't have with him now.

I hoped he was moving on. I hoped he wasn't sitting around missing me. Both of those were lies, but I truly didn't want him to be hurting.

Mel's roommates moved out at the beginning of summer and once I started staying with her and my stuff was at her place, it never left, even though Lukas and I did. Only temporarily. There was no way I was going back to my job at the fitness center, but I needed to be taking advantage of the summer while I wasn't in classes. Ellie said she could use an extra hand over the summer since enrollment at the day care was higher once kids were out of school. Lukas and I moved into Ty's room and spent the summer with her and Beth. Being back in Abilene and that house was actually more healing than I thought it would be.

The two hardest days of my life came and went. The first was June twenty-first. It would have been our two-year anniversary. Mel came down and spent the day with us and it was a day of sharing stories and tears and the top of our wedding cake that we would have eaten together to celebrate the day. It had been sitting in Ellie's freezer.

Unable to throw it away, she pulled it out and we all grabbed forks and sat there around the table reliving that day together instead.

I cried a lot, and a part of me wished that it was Casey sitting there with me as I relived the best and worst moments of my life, but he wasn't, and he couldn't be. That night, when I finally convinced Mel that I would be alright on my own and she went back to Lubbock and Ellie, Beth and Lukas were all tucked away in bed, I sat on the floor of the living room looking through pictures from the box that I'd finally been brave enough to open up with a bottle of wine. My phone chimed with a text message.

You don't have to reply. In fact you probably shouldn't, but I know today must've been hard for you and you're probably feeling especially alone tonight. I just want you to know you're not.

I didn't reply, like he said. I'm not sure that I would've even known what to say. I was afraid the only thing I'd be able to type out would have been something like *I love you.* The tears fell fast and hard. I leaned back against the couch, clutching my chest and trying to quiet my sobs so they wouldn't wake anyone.

After a few more sips directly from the bottle, I climbed up onto the couch and fell asleep hoping that maybe I would just sleep through the next two weeks, because I knew the hard days weren't over. The hardest was yet to come.

On the one-year anniversary of his death, I couldn't believe a year had officially gone by. One year. Twelve months. Fifty two weeks. Way too many days. That's how long I'd been without him, how long Ellie had been without her son, and Beth without her brother. We were still living, waking up every day and going on with our lives. Some days were good and some were bad, but it was okay, even though it didn't always feel that way, because a year ago I never thought I'd have another good day. In some ways it felt like just yesterday I woke up to that awful phone call, and in other ways it felt like another lifetime ago.

I watched my precious boy, who looked more and more like his daddy every day, lying on the floor, giggling and alternately sucking on the head of a toy dinosaur and his own hands. He was such a happy baby. He loved to smile and giggle and talk, not that he could form any real words yet, but that didn't stop him from jabbering away.

272

"Tyler was always such a happy baby like Lukas. He was a good baby," Ellie said with tears still in her eyes, looking at her grandson. Beth scooped him up and tried to hide her own sadness, bouncing Lukas on her lap while he squealed and tugged on her hair.

That night I waited to see if I would get another text, but I didn't. Still I opened up his last one and read it. Ellie came down at midnight and caught me staring at my phone in the living room.

"You should call him," she startled me. I wasn't surprised she knew what I was thinking.

"I'm not sure that would be a good idea."

"What are you still unsure of? I can see that you miss him, I just don't understand why, when he's right there." Ellie nodded at my phone.

"I do miss him, some days like crazy, but I miss me more. Especially after being back here. Back home. Before, when you told me not to be afraid of loving again, I needed to hear that. I needed to hear that it was okay to let Ty go and let myself be happy. It was just too soon. I wanted to be ready, but I wasn't. Casey fell in love with the girl I used to be, and I know he also loves the one that I am now, but I don't know if I do. I don't know if it's the real me, or if I'm trying too hard because I'm afraid of who I really see when I look in the mirror. I don't know who I am outside of a mother and grieving widow. I'm working on figuring it out, and putting myself back together, instead of expecting him to put me back together. When I do, then I can let someone love me. And maybe when that day comes, it will be Casey. But it may not be. "

"I just hope when that day comes, you don't look in the mirror and see regret," Ellie sighed, and for a moment I thought that was all she was going to say. "But maybe you're right. Maybe I shouldn't have pushed you into him. I just saw how happy you were, and all I want is for you to be happy again, but you gotta listen to your heart and your head baby girl. If they're both telling you you're not ready, then it's good that you figured it out now and not later, but make sure it's not just your fear you're listening to. It's one thing to be careful with your heart, but another to be so afraid that you lock it up."

Thirty-Five

"I am not afraid of storms, for I am learning to sail my ship." — Louisa May Alcott

Ellie's words from that night stayed with me through the rest of the summer. Fear definitely had a big part in why I'd walked away from Casey and us, but then again I had reason to be afraid. It wasn't just my heart I had to be careful with. There were three hearts involved. Whatever decision I made had the potential to not only hurt me, but Casey and Lukas as well.

Every morning I focused on the day ahead and promised myself I would live each one without letting the past hold me back, or the future scare me. That future and someday I kept thinking about would be here soon enough, and when it got here, I didn't want to look back and realize I'd missed out on the time I had, worrying about what was ahead instead of what was right in front of me.

The more I started just living and stopped trying to figure out how, the more my life became what I wanted it to be. I found more of my confidence every day, not relying on anyone but myself. I also stopped looking for myself and trying to be some version of a girl who didn't exist anymore or one who might never, and when I did, I found I was free to just be. That's when I learned who I was, or I guess who I was becoming, and that it didn't matter as much as I thought it did, because we're all in a constant state of change and growth, being shaped and transformed by the things happening in our lives. Over that summer and choosing to embrace life and live each moment as it came, I discovered that most of us spend too much time trying to figure out who we're supposed to be and where we're supposed to be instead of just being content with who we are and where we are.

I still had rough days, but instead of telling myself I was weak, or thinking of them as bad days and setbacks, I just looked at them as part of my journey. My only real complaint was that Lukas continued to grow much too quickly. It seemed like one day I blinked and suddenly he was crawling all over the place.

As the end of summer rapidly approached, I started preparing us to get back to our lives in Lubbock, and as I did that, I spent more time thinking about the guy we left behind there, and wondering more and more if this summer away had been better for me than I ever could have expected. The new perspective and attitude it had given me allowed me to see that not only did I not have to completely figure out who I was before I could start living my life, but I didn't even have to figure it out before I could let others – and by others I was obviously thinking Casey – into my life. I realized that the "right time" and the perfect "someday" are overrated when you have right now. I'd done what I said I wanted to, which was stand on my own two feet and gain some clarity. With it, I could see that growing and moving through life was better when you had someone by your side, growing with you. That part of the journey is in who you share in it with. I think that right there is the whole point of life and that people waste a lot of time and money trying to make it more complicated, when it's actually pretty simple.

What makes up your life isn't the job you have, the money in your bank account, the car in your garage or the status you hold. What makes your life – and makes it worth living – are the people you do life with and the value you place on relationships versus all those other things.

I wanted to do life with Casey. Even if it was messy and hard and we had to figure it out as we went. I didn't want to wait for a day when I felt ready anymore, and I think that meant I was ready. So now there was nothing stopping me from asking him if he wanted to jump on this crazy ride with me.

Except for four states and over one thousand miles.

I just didn't know that until it was too late.

I was anxious to get back home and tell Casey everything I'd figured out over the summer, so I convinced Beth to leave two weeks early. She was going with us since she would be starting school as A Red Raider in just a few short weeks and Ellie couldn't get away from the daycare to help her get settled into the dorm. I think Beth was just as anxious for this next step in our lives as I was. I spent the first day back getting her moved onto campus, and then Lukas and I showed her around the area and took her out to dinner for her first night.

I was dying to see Casey, but I knew this was a big moment for Beth. I could wait one day. One day wouldn't make a difference anyway. The next morning, Mel returned from vacation in South America to get ready for her final season with the team. I was there to meet her at the airport and it was so good to see her. I'd kept her updated via email over the last month she'd been gone, but it wasn't the same thing as talking to her. She only had one question on her mind though on the car ride to her place – or I guess our place now that Lukas and I were going to be living with her.

"Have you talked to Casey yet?"

I bit back a small smile. "Not yet. I want to go see him today."

She couldn't hold back her tiny squeal of excitement. "I'm so happy for you. I know you needed time, but I kept hoping when you came home, it would be to get your man back!"

"Don't get too excited," I told her. "I asked him not wait. Two months changed a lot for me. Maybe it changed a lot for him."

"You're cute, darlin'." She gave me look like she may as well have said, *"bless your heart,"* or *"you're an idiot."* "I doubt very much that two months has changed anything for that boy."

How very wrong she was.

She kept Lukas with her so I could go see about a boy, and it was only by chance that when I knocked on his apartment door he was even there. He froze for a moment when he pulled the door open, obviously surprised to see me standing there. Then he brushed it off.

"You come to say goodbye?" he asked solemnly.

I think my heart stopped. "Goodbye?" I tried to ask casually, as if my heart wasn't hanging on his answer.

He looked away, curling a hand around his neck, and then back at me. "I thought Mel would have told you I accepted a job offer from the university back home."

"She's been in South America." *He's leaving.* My stomach dropped.

"Oh. Well if you weren't coming to say goodbye, what are you doing here?"

I wanted to shout, *I'm here for you, ya big dummy,* but that suddenly seemed like it might not be such a good idea. "I uh, just got back to town today and wanted to see how you were doing, and see how your summer was."

"Oh, well then you're lucky you caught me today," he pulled his door open wider for me to follow him inside and when I did, I was stepping inside an empty apartment except for a few boxes stacked inside the door. "I just came back to get the last of my things and turn in my keys. I've already got most of my stuff set up in my apartment there."

"Why are you moving and leaving the team?"

"Why would I stay?" For a second I thought I saw a look cross his face, like he was actually begging me to give him a reason, but when I looked deeper I saw nothing. There was so much distance between us. Distance that I put there. He looked at me expectantly, but I stood there speechless because I wasn't sure what to say.

"I got the offer a while back. I thought I would turn it down, but then . . ." but then I told him to move on with his life and not wait for me to get mine straightened out. He let out a heavy breath and his voice softened. "I just couldn't stay. You were right about not wanting reminders every day. The offer was really good, and when I called them back, they still hadn't filled the position."

I opened my mouth to say something, anything, but I couldn't form the words that would make him stay. All I could get out was, "Oh."

"When I came to Texas it was for a fresh start, an opportunity to figure out who I wanted to be, but I never intended to stay. The plan was always to go back home. At least at first." He ducked his head, raking his hand through his hair, and I knew what he was telling me. I changed his plans. I was the only reason he would've stayed, and then I took that reason away, so of course he was leaving now.

"Most of my friends and my family are all back in Indiana. And a job with more money, working with one of the best men's teams in country – my old team. That's my home and dream job. I just figured it was time I got to it."

"That's really great," I squeaked out. "I'm happy for you." In my head I saw myself apologizing, telling him everything I'd figured out in the past two months and telling him I was ready now to let him back in.

I even saw myself begging him to stay and give us a chance for a new start, promising to fight for us. But I didn't – beg or fight.

"Thanks, and I'm glad you came by. I hoped I'd get the chance to tell you before I left, that even though this didn't work out the way I hoped it would for us, I don't regret coming here and falling in love with you. I could never regret that."

I didn't even know what to say to that, and I was afraid if I tried to say anything it would come out all wrong and sound a lot like, *I love you.* And I couldn't do that to him. Not now. So we stood there, awkwardly until he cleared his throat. "Well I need to get the rest of this stuff loaded up. Trent is waiting down there with his truck."

"Oh. Is he going with you?"

"Yeah, he decided some change would be good for him too, we got a place together."

"Oh. Okay. Um, you guys drive safe."

Drive safe? That's all you're going to say? You're just going to let him walk away?

That's exactly what I did. He walked away and I let him go. I hadn't gotten enough time with Tyler and now I didn't have enough time to make things right with Casey.

Mel's face looked so excited when I walked in the door, until she saw mine.

"What happened? It didn't go well?"

I filled her in on Casey's big move, slipping in that Trent was leaving too, just to see her reaction to that news. Apart from surprise, she brushed it right aside, and wanted to talk about Casey. "Did you tell him how you feel? All that stuff you told me about your journey and still growing and wanting to do it all with him?"

"How could I after he told me he was moving?"

"Easy! You just tell him! Then maybe he wouldn't be moving. In none of that did I hear you say that he said he wasn't in love with you anymore, and if he was willing to turn down that job and stay for you before, he probably still would."

"I couldn't do it, Mel. I've already put him through the wringer. I told him not to wait, that he should move on with his life. He's doing that, so how can I now tell him I changed my mind and don't want him to move on? It just wasn't meant to work out."

She snorted, "I don't believe that for a second, and I think Casey would want to know the truth. You should let him decide if it's too late. It's his choice to make."

"He made it Mel. He's moving on. He told me that was his dream job, and I know he misses his family and wants to be close to them. He's already accepted the job. Asking him to stay would not only be incredibly selfish of me, but he doesn't even have a job here anymore. I think he's given up enough and done enough for me."

"I still think that's for him to decide."

"And I think that you need to focus on this season and making it your best one yet, and I need to focus on the school year ahead, because before we know it, we'll both be graduating and out of here for good. I won't let this make me fall apart, Mel. That's one of the other things I've figured out. I'm more than my relationship or lack-of. It hurts that I missed this shot with Casey, but it doesn't mean it's the end of me. It doesn't even mean it's the end of us for good. It's just the end of us for now. Whatever life brings, I'm ready for it. No holding back. If anything, missing this opportunity with Casey has showed me that you should never hold back, because life won't hold back or wait for you."

She gave a sad nod and pulled me in for a hug. "Okay then, let's kick ass this year."

"Let's," I whispered, clinging to her a moment longer before letting go and looking her in the eye. "We're gonna be okay, Mel." I don't know why I felt like I needed to say that out loud, but I did.

Her brow creased. "I know we are," she said, like maybe she thought I was losing it, and she needed to humor me.

"But we're not just gonna be okay. We're gonna be more than that. We're gonna be happy. And not just someday when we graduate or when we get the job we want or the boyfriend or husband we want. We can decide to be happy right now, where we're at with what we have. I've got you and Lukas and that's a lot."

She blinked and I could see moisture pooling in her eyes as the wall she'd been putting up for so long started to come down. "We do have a lot, don't we?"

"Yeah, we do. Promise me this year, no pretending to be happy. No putting on a brave face or an act. I know you, Mel, and so often you have a smile on your face and are making everyone else laugh while I know you're hurting and I'm tired of waiting for you to talk to me about it. Even if you're never ready to talk about it, you don't have to be scared to let me or anyone else see the real you."

She swallowed, and blinked back more tears. "I don't know what I'm doing with my life, Liv. I'm playing a sport I don't even love because it's expected of me. I've wasted the last three years partying and sleeping with guys I don't love or even really like. I'm majoring in a subject I'm not sure if I like, because it went along with the image I'd created. I don't know if it's what I want anymore though, or if I ever wanted it."

This girl in front of me, so unsure of everything, was a far cry from the one I met on dorm move in day, who joked that she would interview me one day when I went pro and she became a sports journalist. Back then, her confidence and self-assuredness had intimidated me. Since then, I'd gotten to know her and knew that some of it was a front, a mask she wore to protect herself, but I'd never seen her like this, doubting herself and everything.

"Who expects it of you Mel? Your parents?" I didn't know where all this was coming from.

She sighed. "Them, everyone. As long as I can remember people have been asking if I was going be a professional athlete like my dad. My first memories are of t-ball and youth soccer. I don't even know when it was first suggested, or who suggested, that I carry it into sports journalism if I didn't play soccer professionally. The idea just seemed to please my parents and I really didn't know what I wanted, so I went with it. Maybe I will like it, I just don't know, because it doesn't feel like anything I've ever done has been for me. I've based everything off what I thought other people wanted from me. I don't even feel like I can have a meaningful relationship because I don't see how anyone could ever just want me, for me, when I don't even know who the real me is, and I don't think I like the girl I've been."

"Oh Mel." I wrapped my arms around her shoulders again. "I know the real you. I always have and I love you. You're not your major, your career, or your father. You're the girl who babysat me the first night I ever got really, really, piss myself drunk, because I was too embarrassed to let Tyler see me like that. You barely even knew me then. We'd only been roommates and teammates for two days and you sat on that bathroom floor with me all night. You're the best friend I've ever had. You're kind and generous and compassionate. You want to do everything for everyone else, and sometimes you forget to take care of yourself.

"And you feel things so deeply and you love people unconditionally, and because of that it makes you vulnerable. I think you've closed off your heart because that scares you. I know you've been hurt, but I've always known that you're not the girl you pretend to be. I've always known you deserved more than what you let yourself believe you do. Whatever career you choose doesn't define who you are, and neither do your mistakes. None of that changes who you are, and you are an amazing person. I wouldn't let anyone less than that be my baby's godmother."

She rested her head on my shoulder and I just held her and brushed my hand over her hair. "Now tell me what brought this on all of the sudden and who made you feel those things, so I can kick their ass?"

"Trent," she whispered. "But before you go bringing your wrath down on him, you need to know that he didn't say anything that wasn't true, that I didn't need to hear."

"What do you mean? What did he do?"

"He didn't want me. They always want me, but he didn't. I basically threw myself at him, and he said he wasn't impressed with my act. He said he wanted to see something real, said he wanted to get under my skin and find out who I was beneath the shallow, self-entitled Princess."

I didn't know whether to be pissed at him for making her feel self-conscious, or glad that he saw through her and finally got through to her.

"I couldn't believe he said those things to me. Nobody had ever talked to me like that. Nobody else ever told me they wanted anything more from me than a little bit of fun and a few nights in the sack. Nobody has ever wanted to know me, and I didn't know how to handle that or handle him, so I got pissed. I was so mad at him, ya know, like who the hell did he think he was? Really, I just didn't want him to be right, but I couldn't stop thinking about what he said, I still can't, because I wouldn't even know how to show him something real. I don't

281

know what's real. I think I was most afraid that he was wrong, and I really am just some superficial, stuck up, super slut."

"Melodie Josefina Ross you are not superficial, stuck up or a slut, so don't ever think that. We don't need anyone else to validate us or determine our worth." She just nodded, but I wasn't convinced that she believed me.

"I'm serious, Mel. You have to stop living for everyone else. I think you need to have a talk with coach, and I think you need to consider walking away from the team. It's clearly not what you want, and the people who love you – your parents included – will understand that. This is going to be a year of change for both of us, but I think it's also going to be a year of exciting new possibilities. The rest of your life is ahead of you, it's time for you to figure out what you want to do with it. It's time we both did that."

In a way we were both trying to find ourselves, figure out who we were without letting the things that had happened to us or the bad choices we had made, define us. Just like I'd decided I wasn't going to let widow be my word, the one that would determine the rest of my life, Mel now had a few that she didn't want to determine the rest of hers.

"Yeah, maybe it is," she agreed softly.

Thirty-Six

"There are all kinds of love in this world but never the same love twice." — F Scott Fitzgerald

One year later . . .

For the first time in almost two years, I felt the need to go back to the place where I'd watched my worst nightmare unfold. Maybe it was crazy to make the trip when there was still so much to be done before tomorrow morning, but when I told Mel what I wanted, she understood and promised to take care of everything. I loaded myself into Kitten, running my finger along the chain that used to hang around my neck, which now hung on my rearview mirror. Taking the rings off had been difficult, but I needed to do it. It might seem like a small thing, but it was my way of really giving myself permission to move on and let go. It was freeing. I would always have them, just like I would always have Ty, but I wouldn't let myself be chained to my past. I would forever miss him, but I wouldn't let missing him make me miss out on the rest of my life. Ty wouldn't want that.

I drove the two and a half hours south, until I was pulling up to the cemetery gates. Even though I hadn't come to visit even once, I still knew right where he was buried, and when I found his headstone I planted myself on the ground in front of it. I don't know how long I sat there just staring at it.

Tyler Andrew Tate.
Oct. 17, 1990 – Jul. 6, 2012
Beloved Husband, Son, Brother and Friend.
Forever In Our Hearts.

Twenty-one years of life squeezed into a tiny dash between two dates, and wrapped up in ten words. He was so much more than that though. The people who passed by and barely glanced at his grave couldn't really know who he was from a few words engraved on a chunk of marble. People decades from now might wander through here looking at names and wondering about the people they belonged to. They would know that Tyler had left people behind, that he'd died too young, but they wouldn't know how he lived, what he really meant to those of us who were left behind. We would know though. We would know that he was the best husband a girl could ask for, the kind of husband who cherished and respected his wife, would do anything for her; rub her aching feet or sit outside in a rainstorm to watch her kick a ball across a field for ninety minutes plus some. We would know that he was the kind of son who still let his mother kiss his cheeks, and the kind of brother who threatened any boy who messed with his little sister. He was the kind of guy who would get out of bed at two in the morning to help a friend broke down on the side of the road. Those were the kinds of things those of us who really knew and loved Tyler, would say about him.

I thought about what I would want my headstone to say, and what the people I left behind would remember me for. I hoped that they would say I was a good mother and a good friend. I wanted to be remembered for the way I loved people, boldly and fiercely. I didn't want them to say that I was a good mother and a good friend but was too afraid to take chances with my heart. I didn't want them to say that I let a good man, one of the best men, go because I was too foolish to go after him. I wanted my little dash to be full – full of so much life and love. Not just the years that I'd had Tyler, but every year that fell between the two dates they would engrave for me. I wanted people who would read it after I was gone to know that yes, I had been loved, but more than that, that I had loved. *She loved and was loved;* those were the words I wanted to be mine.

"I hope I know what I'm doing Ty," I whispered when I was back in my car on the road. "I love you baby. I hope you're with me on this because I don't think I'm done needing you. You're still my strength, and the boy who taught me what real love is. I'm gonna need that to do this."

I returned home late; Lukas was in bed and Mel was sitting up in the kitchen sipping a cup of tea. Not that this place would be our home for much longer. Tomorrow morning everything changed. Mel and I had graduated and we were both setting out on a new adventure. Our destination: Bloomington, Indiana; Home of the Hoosiers.

"You ready for this?" she asked.

"I guess we'll find out."

The next morning, we loaded our cars with boxes and filled the big trailer her parents' were pulling for us. Beth and Ellie were there to say goodbye to me and Lukas. It was hard knowing they would be so far away, but they were both excited for me, and they could appreciate the romance of what I was doing. My parents were the hardest ones to tell. They both thought it was another of my reckless, impulsive decisions. Mama didn't understand at all and was especially upset. I couldn't convince her that even though I was taking a huge risk, it was actually one of the least impulsive decisions I'd ever made. It had taken a year for me to get here, and now that I was, there was no turning back. We set out for Indiana before the sun was fully risen in the Texas sky.

I'd lived in Texas my whole life, never wanted to live anywhere else. I loved my home state; I loved being so close to Ellie and Beth. I loved Casey more. I was no longer afraid to admit it, no longer doubted it and was no longer willing to move on without at least letting him know that. Whatever happened after today, as long as I made sure that he knew I'd loved him back utterly and completely, I could live with anything else. Even Casey loving someone else if that was the case.

That would suck like letting a voodoo priestess stab all her pins right in my heart, but I knew it would heal. Because no matter how broken a heart is, no matter how many ways it gets broken or ripped apart, those little fragments still find a way to keep on beating. Even when every heart beat hurts, even when you are sure that those broken little shards can't hold together any longer, they do. And so would I if I got to Indiana and found that Casey had moved on. Because loss hadn't made my heart weak. It made it stronger. It'd been annihilated and I'd survived. I was a fighter.

On the long drive through Oklahoma I thought about the last year and everything that had led me to now. It was a good year. A hard year. Mel and I took some hits, had some victories and some failures, but we made it through, and like I told her, this year had brought us new possibilities. Mel quit the team and changed her direction. She still graduated with her degree in journalism, but she'd shifted focus at the

285

end to teaching, and now she was going to be continuing her education toward becoming a teacher at Indiana University.

As for me, at the end of this trip I was hoping there would be a man waiting, one who still thought there was a chance for us. But even if there wasn't, there was still an adventure to be had for me in Indiana. One I was looking forward to whether Casey was in or out. In a way he was the one responsible for the chance I had. If he hadn't taken me to meet Laura and Jace and everyone at the physical therapy center, I might still be sitting back in Lubbock trying to work up the courage to go after Casey.

Once Casey left Texas, I'd continued to go back and volunteer every week and eventually they took me on as a paid intern. I had planned to accept the permanent position Laura told me I would be offered once I graduated, and she did offer it to me, but she also gave me another choice that day she called me into her office to discuss the position.

"I called you in here to discuss something that I think will be a good thing." Laura smiled reassuringly. "First off, I just want to say congratulations on your upcoming graduation, and I want you to know how proud of you all of us here are."

"Thank you." I was proud of myself too. I'd finished my senior year while raising my child and working part time here. I was officially done with all my classes and just had to sit back and wait. In two weeks, for the second time in my life, I would put on a cap and gown. I'd enter the stadium with my fellow graduates and when I left I would no longer be a student. Twenty-two years to get to this point; eighteen years of schooling from pre-school to now. There were lots of bumps in the road and detours along the way, but now I was here and I was ready for the next challenge.

"Now's the part where I offer you a full time position here, putting that degree you've worked so hard for to use. Not that you haven't been doing that for a year already, but now we can make it official, give you an office, assign you your own patients, and work you even harder, but we'll also pay ya a bit more." She grinned. "What d'ya say?"

"Yes! Of course yes. I love it here; you know this is what I want."

"I'd hoped you would feel that way. There's not much that has to be done to make it official, a little bit of paperwork to sign, and that's it, but before we do that, I just want to say something else and I want you to listen to me."

"Okay," I said hesitantly.

"I'm going to give you the paperwork to take with you, and then I want you to take the next two weeks off to think about it." I started to interrupt, to tell her that I didn't need to think about it, but she stopped me. *"Sweetie, there are some choices in life that become defining for us, they determine the course of the rest of our life, and I think this is one of those for you and you need to be absolutely sure this is right choice."*

I didn't understand exactly what she was saying. Of course this choice would determine a lot about the rest of my life, it wouldn't just be a job anymore, it would be a career; one that I would hopefully have for the rest of my life, because I loved doing this work.

"I can see in your eyes that you think I'm talking about becoming a pediatric physical therapist, but I'm not. You have so much passion and compassion for these kids, I have no doubt this is what you're meant to do, but I don't know if here is where you're meant to be doing it."

"Do you not think I'm right for here?"

"Sweetie, I don't think here is right for you." That didn't make any sense to me. I had no idea what she was trying to tell me. *"Olivia, I know that you, better than most, know what is truly important in this life, what needs to be cherished above all else. You're an amazing young woman, and we would be lucky to have you here. So if in two weeks you bring this paperwork back to me, and can tell me that this is truly the place and the job for you, we will throw a party to welcome you on board. But just in case it's not, if there's something out there that's more important to you than this job, somewhere else you would rather be, I want you to know that I put a phone call into a center in Bloomington, Indiana, and after all the praises I sang you, I know that they're hoping to get a phone call from you."*

I'd made that phone call. The very next day. One day was all it took for me to see that Laura was right and there was somewhere else I wanted to be and if I didn't go, it would haunt me for the rest of my life. I would always wonder if giving him up was the biggest mistake I'd ever made. I also knew there was a chance he wouldn't be happy to see me; that he'd tell me it was too late, or that he'd moved on. So for me the question had never been *what if I stay?* Or even, *what if I go?* It was, *is Casey worth the risk?* The answer was absolutely, yes. Loving Casey would be an adventure of a lifetime; one I didn't want to miss out on and hopefully one he wanted to go on with me.

It was a long, full day of driving, and coffee was definitely my friend. Thankfully the road lulled Lukas to sleep and he slept most of the drive. We made it as far as Springfield, Missouri before stopping for the night. It was a late night lying awake in the hotel bed. I couldn't decide if it was excitement or dread in my belly. I think it was a bit of both.

When morning made itself known, I had to rely on coffee again to get me going. We were all a little sluggish getting back on the road, but once the caffeine was pumping through our veins, we checked out and loaded back up. It was just under five hundred miles to Bloomington and the beautiful ranch house Mel and I found online. It was a three bedroom, set on six acres on the outskirts of Bloomington, and even though we hadn't seen it yet in person, I was in love with it just from the pictures.

When we were close we gave the owners a call, and the couple was waiting for us when we pulled up the long gravel drive. The two story house really was even more beautiful than it'd looked in the pictures. The light brown paint was a little faded and weathered, and the yard could use some work, but it really was a charming place. The front porch ran the length of the house and at one end hung an old porch swing. Trees surrounded the property, and there was a large garden to one side of the house. It obviously hadn't been tended to in a while, but I was looking forward to working in it. Looking at all the open space I also decided I wanted to get Lukas a puppy.

We all shook hands with Mike and his wife Judy. They handed over keys and took us through a tour of the inside, which I fell in love with just as much as the rest of the property. It was spacious, and had been given a fresh coat of paint more recently than the outside. The carpet and flooring didn't look as if it had seen much wear, making me think it'd been replaced in the last couple years. The appliances were modern and the kitchen was bigger than any kitchen I'd ever had. With every room we entered, I started to feel giddier.

It was the kind of home I'd always dreamed of having. The empty rooms made it easy to imagine all the possibilities and ways we could make this place home. The best part of the rental agreement was that the Campbell's wanted to sell it eventually, and were willing to put our rent toward it if in a year or so I decided I wanted to buy it.

As soon as the Campbell's turned the place over and left us to settle in, we started unpacking. With Mel's dad there, the four of us managed to haul everything, including the furniture inside. Lukas was no help. We had to set up his pack 'n' play just to keep him from running underfoot. I swear that boy skipped walking and went right to running. He hadn't been doing it very long, but once he started, he was gone. Not even two yet and my hands were more than full.

That night we all sat around our dining room table, eating the pizza we'd ordered and sharing our ideas for the place. Mel's mom wanted to take us shopping tomorrow, but I gave Mel a look and she grinned. She knew where I was headed tomorrow, and when she told Mrs. Ross they would be going without me, they all gave me a meaningful look.

The next morning Mel and her mom insisted they keep Lukas, and wished me luck as I left the house. Mr. Ross went out and helped me unload the last thing from the bed of his pickup truck.

Ty's bike. His baby. His princess. Any other woman might have been jealous that he loved her so much

It was a big, sleek, black machine that he'd put a lot of love into over the years, and until a few months ago had been shut up inside Mr. Ross' garage doing nothing more than collecting dust. Where Kitten, purred, this baby growled. And I'd learned to ride it. I'd enlisted Mick's help for that undertaking. He spent a lot of hours teaching me the ins and outs of Sascha. That was the name Ty gave her. Yes, another her. I asked Mick why I couldn't call it, like Gage, or Ryker, or Dean. Those were sexy names, but he looked at me like I'd lost my damn mind and took the keys from me until I promised not to give her a dude's name. I figured if I couldn't rename her what I wanted, I might as well leave her Sascha.

I could have sold her and made a pretty penny, but I couldn't do it, so learning to ride seemed like my only other option. I'd always enjoyed the feeling of being on the back of her with Ty, but had been too scared to let him teach me, but Mel and I had made a pact to start doing the things that scared us.

Sascha definitely scared the shit out of me the first time I had her between my legs on my own, and yes it was super awkward thinking of a her between my legs, but I'd come to accept it. And eventually I even managed to tame the beast inside of her. Once that happened, once I'd learned to trust my instincts, feel the bike, and as corny as it sounded when Mick said it, be one with the bike, I never looked back. Mick joked that he'd created an adrenaline junkie and didn't know if Ty would be proud or kick his ass.

Once Mr. Ross had her out of the truck and I pulled my helmet on and threw my leg over her. I brought her engine to life with a rumble and I had to admit he might have been right. Every single time her engine turned over, my heart rate kicked up and that feeling never got old. My energy level only built once I flipped the kickstand up, pulled the clutch and shifted her into gear. That was nothing compared to the feeling I got though once I released the clutch and throttled it. I couldn't help the little breathless squeal that left my lips every time she shot forward, and then we were moving and there was nothing but freedom and exhilaration.

I'd looked up the directions for where I was going, and after a few wrong turns I found it. Several figures dotted the field ahead of me. I tried to spot him amongst them, but I was too far away to make out if he was there. I pulled the bike up to the far side of the field edging the parking lot. The rumble of the engine caused heads to turn my direction. I felt several sets of eyes on me as I climbed off the bike and tugged off my helmet, shaking out my hair.

A few pairs of eyes lingered, some on me and some on the bike. I took the opportunity to search for Casey. I didn't see him among the players and coaching staff, but I hoped they might be able to tell me where to find him. It had been my grand idea to surprise him at work rather than contact Trent to ask where they lived. As I approached, more heads turned my way and there were a few low whistles. I found the head coach and briefly wondered if he'd been coaching was Casey was a player.

"Can I help you?"

"I was hoping you could tell me where I might find Casey Hunt," I used my best *I swear I'm a friend and not a psycho stalker* voice.

"I'm afraid he's not here. Can I ask who you are, and I can pass along that you came looking for him?"

I tried not to show my disappointment, but I'm not sure I did that great of a job. "No, that's okay. I'm an old friend. I was just hoping to surprise him, but I'll get in touch with him another way, thank you.

I didn't stick around, but one of the players ran over to me before I made it to my bike. "Hey, he called. "You came to see Hunt?"

I shielded my eyes from the sun when I turned, and nodded.

He made a face like he was about to deliver bad news and really didn't want to. "Uh, well I'm not sure why you're looking from him, but he's out of town for a few days. Won't be back until the end of the week. Went to visit his girl." That was the part he hadn't wanted to tell me. It seemed even this perfect stranger could read my feeling for Casey on my face.

"Oh."

"Yeah. I just figured you might want to know since I think they're pretty serious, but I better get back to practice before Coach chews my ass. Good luck to ya."

I think I was in a bit of a daze climbing back on the bike. I had to block everything out for the ride back home. My new home. The one that wouldn't include Casey. Because he had moved on. I sucked in a deep breath. *It's okay. You were prepared for this. You're hurtling forward on a massive death machine, now is not the time to be distracted.*

I decided I needed a few minutes to process and clear my head, so I pulled into a little café and took a seat at the counter, deciding that some coffee and pie were needed to help with the disappointment that was steadily growing.

It was a couple hours later that I walked in the front door and set my helmet on the small table in the entryway that hadn't been there when I left. The further inside I went, the more it looked like I'd stepped into a page featured in some country living magazine. All of our stuff was still here, but it was apparent Mr. Ross had yet to get a handle on Mrs. Ross' shopping problem. Mostly because the only time

291

she really got out of control was when she was shopping for her daughter, or my son, and Mr. Ross didn't seem to mind.

My eyes landed on new end tables and throw pillows and wall hangings that were new additions to our décor. It was absolutely beautiful, and everything fit with the country feel and style of the house. The furniture was all soft, warm colors and natural woods. It seemed furniture wasn't the only new addition to our house. A chorus of tiny barks preceded two fur balls flying down the stairs and dancing around my feet. They were closely followed by Mel and her parents. Lukas was tucked safely in the arms of Mrs. Ross, but looked like he'd rather be down on the floor, where the action was, crawling with the puppies.

"Surprise." Mel smiled uneasily. "We got Lukas a puppy like you wanted."

I frowned. "That is not a puppy. That is two puppies."

"They're brother and sister, we couldn't break them up."

I shook my head and knelt down, rubbing my hands over their soft fur and scratching behind their ears. "What are we going to do with you two? Can't very well return you," I sighed, and looked up at Mel. "Do they at least have names?"

She shook her head. "They're mom was a pregnant rescue. They were born at the shelter, lab-shepherd mix. Only eight weeks old, and they weren't given names. The staff at the shelter just called them trouble and mayhem."

I gave her a look like, *seriously?* "Great," I muttered under my breath. Mel just grinned innocently. I looked at the boy who was trying to jump up on me and lick my face off. "I don't know whether you were trouble or mayhem mister, but we're going to call you Loki," I decided. He definitely looked like a troublemaker. I ruffled my hand over the girl's head and she stopped attacking my shoelaces to look up at me. She had darker coloring than her brother, mostly black, and I could see cleverness in her eyes. "Nyx," I declared.

"Yay!" Mel clapped her hands and then she was dragging me up to my feet. "Now enough about this, how did it go with Casey?" she asked hopefully. We all moved to the sectional and Mrs. Ross set Lukas down on the floor, and instantly he was mauled by the ferocious fur balls, and his giggles and happy squeals filled the room. Mr. Ross lowered his giant form to the floor, playing with Lukas and the pups, leaving us to the girl talk.

"Was he shocked to see you?" Mel was bursting with excitement and curiosity.

"I'll bet he was," Mrs. Ross' grin matched her daughter's.

"I didn't see him," I informed them, and their grins faded into disappointed pouts.

"Oh. Guess we didn't think about him not being there. Well, when are you going to try again?" Mel asked eagerly.

"I'm not." I cast my eyes down.

"What! Why?"

I looked back at Mel. "Because. He's out of town visiting his girlfriend, his very serious girlfriend according to one of his players."

"Oh."

I put on my best optimistic face, and hoped my voice wouldn't betray me. "It's okay. I still don't regret coming. This was about more than just a guy. I knew this was not only a possibility, but likely. He's a great guy. It would have been more shocking if someone hadn't snatched him up."

"But I was so sure it was going to work out. It would have been just like a movie or a Nicholas Sparks book or something," Mel lamented.

"But it's not, Mel. It's real life, but that doesn't mean we can't make this next chapter great. Remember; only good things ahead. This doesn't change that." That had been our motto this past year. It didn't mean we thought life wasn't going to throw us anymore curveballs, just that we were going to choose to focus on the good and let the bad roll off us. This was just going to be one of those moments that was a little harder for me to shake off, but I had to, because whether I was ready for it or not, life was going to go on, and next Monday morning I had a job to be at.

* * *

3 Days Later . . .

The steady rocking of the porch swing had almost lulled me into a nap when wheels on gravel woke me. I looked up to see a familiar black beauty coming down the drive and my heart leapt in my chest. I sat up straighter in the swing and instantly regretted that I hadn't gone straight from the garden to the shower, but instead had only made it as far as this spot on the swing. Dirt covered pretty much every inch of me. The battle between me and the weeds hadn't been pretty, and I was sure my hair was in a state as well, but that couldn't be helped now.

Then Casey climbed from Evie. He was everything I remembered and just as gorgeous as ever. I could see the shadow of light stubble covering his jaw. His hair was a little shorter than the last time I'd seen him, but it was still styled in that way that looked like he just climbed out of bed and ran a hand through it, messy yet perfect, a contradiction that he pulled off flawlessly. He wore a blue and gray Colts t-shirt and a pair of black athletic shorts that would have been unimpressive on anyone else, but made me want to strip him down and – crap, I needed to pull it together, but with every step that brought him closer, my breaths became heavier, my throat dried up, my heart kicked into overdrive, and my hands grew clammy at my sides.

It felt like the rest of the world was out of focus and all I could see was him, and then he was standing three feet in front of me like I'd pictured so many times in my head when I'd imagined this moment, but the real thing was so much better. There was a warmth and depth in those chocolate pools staring back at me that my imagination could never replicate. Fantasy could never touch reality, and the reality in front of me took me breath away and sent need coursing through my veins.

"Hi," I croaked. His stare was so intense that I looked away and began fidgeting with my hands while I waited for a response, but one never came. When I looked back up at him he was just watching me, his face an emotionless mask. His usually expressive eyes gave away nothing, and that's when reality sank back in and my face began heating with embarrassment. How could I explain what I was suddenly doing living in Indiana? How had he even figured out where I lived? Had he heard about my visit to his team? Was he here to tell me he didn't' want me here trying to disrupt his life when he was happy with someone else?

294

His head did a full sweep of the front of the property from his spot on the steps and then slowly he dragged his eyes back to me. "You really live here?"

I swallowed dryly and nodded.

"Well, damn," he muttered softly and I couldn't tell if it was an angry damn, a puzzled damn, a frustrated damn or what the hell kind of damn it was.

"Look Casey," I started to explain myself before he thought I was too pathetic. "I didn't just come for you if that's what you think. I got a good job offer and Mel transferred, and–" I never got to finish my last and, because Casey's long legs took the last steps and then he was standing directly in front of me and I couldn't even remember what else I'd been going to tell him.

"That's too bad," his low whisper slid across my body, leaving my skin tingling. "I was sort of hoping you came just for me." He grazed his thumb along my jaw line. My lips parted just slightly to suck in a soft breath.

"But what about the girl you were out of town visiting?"

He dropped his hand and his lips spread into a soft smile that reached his eyes. "That's a funny story. You see, I got to her place to find that she and her roommate had moved, and when I found somebody that knew where they went, I found out they'd packed up and headed for Bloomington."

"What?"

"The *girl* I went to see, that was you, babe."

"I don't understand. Why were you going to see me?"

"To convince you to come home with me, so imagine my surprise when I found out you'd stolen my thunder and beat me to it, and while I was running around Lubbock and Abilene looking for you, you were here making your grand gesture, and I missed it."

I felt my face crumble and I pinched my lips between my teeth, unable to stop the moisture from pooling my eyes. "You really went back for me?"

He cradled my face between his hands and lowered his face so that we were almost nose to nose and forehead to forehead. "Yeah, I did. That was the plan all along, sweetheart. The only reason I ever left you was because I knew you needed time. I told myself I'd give you one year."

I laughed but it came out part sob, "I only needed two months."

He pulled his head back, but still held my face in his hands. "What?"

"Two months was all it took. The day you told me you had taken the job here, I was at your apartment to tell you I loved you. The only reason I let you go was because I thought it was what you needed and wanted."

"You silly girl," he let out a soft, pained chuckle and dropped his forehead to mine. "All I ever wanted and needed was you and Lukas."

My face crumbled and my heart split wide open and warm tears spilled out.

"Please don't cry baby. Please don't cry," he whispered and pressed a light kiss to my forehead, as he took me in his arms and held me tightly. I gripped the front of his shirt, afraid to let him go for fear that I would find this was all an illusion, and I'd lose him all over again. He made soothing noises and rubbed my back.

"I'm so sorry. I've just missed you so much and I thought it was too late, that you'd moved on. I thought I'd really lost you," my words were slightly muffled because I was still pressing my face into his chest.

His cheek rested on my head as he spoke softly, "I told you I would wait as long as I had to, and I meant it. I'm yours. I've only ever been yours. You could never lose me. This right here – having you in my arms – this is my home, and it's so good to be home again. I've thought about it about every single day since I left, and imagined this moment a million times over, but the images in my head always fell short, because there's nothing like the real thing."

I pulled away just enough to look up at him. "I know exactly what you mean."

"And now you're here, you're really here in my arms." He said it like he was still having trouble believing it. I know I was.

"I'm really here, and you're here, and we're . . . here. Together," I exhaled deeply.

"I'm just sorry I missed your big moment. I was headed to the airport to come home when I got the text messages from some of the guys on the team about the hot chick on a motorcycle that came looking for me. I think a few of them might even be in love."

I chuckled.

"And now I just can't stop picturing you in leather pants," he grinned.

I set my hand on his chest. "Well, if you're real nice to me, I might put them on for you." He bit his bottom lip and his eyes grew excited. "And after I take you for a ride, you can take them off of me and take me for a ride."

His expression was wiped from his face and then his eyes went wild with desire and he leaned in real close. "Baby, you know I can be real nice." His lips were almost to mine when the front door was pulled open.

"Liv, Lukas woke up from his–" She stepped out and stopped short when she saw us just a hairsbreadth from kissing on our front porch.

She shrieked excitedly and started jumping up and down, and then managed to calm down long enough to force real words from her mouth again. "Forget I said anything, carry on. I'll just be inside." Then she hurried back in the house before I could stop her.

Both our bodies shook gently with laughter. Then he touched his forehead to mine again. "As much as I want to continue where we left off," he pulled back to look into my eyes, "can I see him?"

I nodded and led Casey inside and up to Lukas' room, where he was standing against the rails of his crib. He'd outgrown the one Casey had made for him a few months ago and I'd been forced to get a bigger one, but I'd saved it. Loki and Nyx were curled up on their dog beds at the foot of the crib. We had to move them in here when they refused to sleep anywhere but with Lukas. It became clear right away that they'd claimed him as theirs, and wherever he was, the pups were. They were also doing a great job of living up to their names. They got up to attack Casey's feet while I scooped up Lukas who was holding his hands out to me.

"He's so big," Casey commented and I detected just a tinge of sadness, and I felt it too, because Casey shouldn't have missed out on the last year. "Before you know it, you'll be teaching him to ride that bike."

I groaned, "Don't even joke about that. He's growing so fast." It felt like just yesterday he'd figured out how to roll over, and now he was stumbling around on his own and usually talking up a storm. But right now all he could do was stare at Casey.

"Hey, little man. I know you don't remember me, but we're going to be good buddies," I smiled and Casey ruffled his hand over Lukas' curls. He ducked his head into my chest.

"Don't worry, he'll get used to you and then you won't be able to get him out of your lap."

Lukas squirmed in my arms and started mumbling "down." I placed him on the floor and right away he ran to his little rubber ball and then plopped down on his butt. This was his new favorite game. He would roll the ball and Loki or Nyx would push it back to him with their nose, and he would giggle and then do it again.

I was watching this happen when Casey grabbed my arm and gently tugged me to him. I stumbled and then steadied myself with my hands on his chest. His arms wrapped around my waist. Warm fingers applied gentle pressure to the underside of my jaw, lifting my chin. Our gazes met, and what I saw in his caused my heart to swell just as his lips descended on mine. It was a soft, sweet, gentle press of his lips. I curled my fingers into his shirt and pushed up on my toes. He lightly traced his tongue over my bottom lip before playfully nipping it with his teeth. I smiled against his mouth and pushed my own tongue past his lips and ran it along the edge of his teeth.

That was all the encouragement he needed to deepen the kiss. His tongue pushed mine back and swept inside my mouth taking control of the kiss. Just like he'd said, it was like being home again; right where I belonged. Our mouths anchored us together, his lips tasted mine, and his hands held me tightly to his body, but it was into my heart that I felt him reaching, his touch permeating all the way to my soul and I couldn't get enough of him. He groaned and separated our mouths, resting his forehead against mine. I could feel his warm breath feather across my lips when he sighed, and his nose touched mine. He placed one last chaste kiss on my lips before pulling away.

"I need to stop now. I think Lukas is a little too young to witness a porno in his nursery."

I laughed and slapped his chest.

He bent down and whispered in my ear, "Later," before grazing his lips over the skin under my ear and down my jaw to me neck. My head lolled back and I wanted to be like, *screw later,* but then a ball rolled into our feet and the dogs danced around them. I wrapped my arms around Casey's torso and rested my head against his chest. His arms were still tight around me and he set his chin on top of my head.

Peace. Contentment. That's what I felt. This was my new perfect, and I would never take it for granted.

God had provided me with more than I ever could have dreamed of. Again. I was blessed with not one, but two great loves in this life – two chances at a happily ever after. I would never understand why some lived and some died. His plans were bigger than me, but here, in this moment, and every moment after, I would forever be thankful for the love a young boy who taught me so much about life. I would be thankful for the love of the friends and family who carried me when I lost that boy. There weren't even words to express how grateful I was for the love that had been placed in my heart and saved me when I found out I was going to be a mother, or the love of the man who, with patience, kindness and selflessness, helped me to pick up the pieces and rebuild something that, even though it would never replace what I'd lost, could be equally beautiful. No matter what became of our future, he'd left his fingerprints on every piece of my heart.

I would forever be marked by Tyler Tate and Casey Hunt.

*"It is a risk to love. What if it doesn't work out?
Ah, but what if it does?" — Peter McWilliams*

Acknowledgments

"Never lose an opportunity for seeing anything that is beautiful;
For beauty is God's handwriting — a wayside sacrament.
Welcome it in every fair face, in every fair sky, in every fair flower,
And thank God for it as a cup of His blessing."

– Ralph Waldo Emerson

Thank you God: the healer of our broken hearts, the redeemer of our stories, the truest lover of our souls. Thank you that though the journey is not always easy, you always provide the way, and you are always there. If we look hard enough, we can find the beauty and the light in even the darkest moments. And thank you to all who read this story. It changed a lot from when I published it the first time back in 2014 to now. I hope you all enjoyed it and will leave your feedback on any of the review sites. Your support and encouragement keeps me doing this, story after story.